Cupid Country Collection

Cupid Country Books 1-3

Cathryn Hein

First published 2025

ISBN 9780648582076

Cupid Country Collection is a work of fiction. All names, people, places, businesses or events or incidences, are either a product of the author's imagination or are used fictitiously. Any similarities to actual people, living or dead, or actual places or events are entirely coincidental.

Cover art by GetCovers.com

Visit the author's website at cathrynhein.com

For Jim

CUPID
COUNTRY
BOOK ONE

Cupid
Country

CHANCE

CATHRYN HEIN

Cupid Country Chance

Instant chemistry abounds in this feel-good small-town romance.

Everyone in town is talking about rural dating app Cupid Country and while schoolteacher Amber Dunn is curious, she's careful of her sweet reputation. A fake dating name seems a good solution, until gorgeous farmer Tom Jones accepts a match.

Their attraction is instant. Tom is handsome, kind and funny, and clearly as hungry for Amber as she is for him. Protected by her fake name, Amber sets her inner seductress loose, and indulges in a night of passion so intense, it must mean more.

A happy future awaits, but when a simple mishap by Tom leaves Amber angry and heartbroken, it seems fate has other ideas.

Will Amber's fake name cost her the man she loves? Or will Cupid help these lovers find each other again?

Chapter One

Tom Jones on a dating app? Amber sniggered and took another sip of wine. Some men had no imagination at all.

She looked a little closer. Tom Jones didn't look like a sleazebag. Short brown hair. Clean-shaven. Direct, milk chocolate gaze with a hint of a twinkle. Plain blue work shirt made soft from use. So normal he was almost unique.

Amber hesitated and swiped past. Normal was few and far between on this dating app. Some entrepreneurial tech genius from Levenham had developed the app for country singles, and for a while Cupid Country had been great, filled with rural people genuinely searching for love. Then the fakes had slithered in, the scammers and catfishers. The marrieds. By Amber's guess, the ratio of fraudulent profiles to honest ones was now two to five.

Although her grumbling was a bit rich, when she was one of those fakes.

Men whizzed past. She eye-rolled at the blokes in bogus uniforms, the gym-junkie types pouting and flexing their muscles, the dudes in flannelette shirts trying to appear casually rural but with crafty glints in their eyes. Others who suspiciously looked too well-ironed to be unmarried. Or not still living at home with mum.

With a sigh, she set her phone down, turned up the volume on the telly and pulled her blanket closer. On the screen, a drool-worthy Chris Hemsworth offered Natalie Portman a cheeky superhero grin. Amber gawped as she always did when faced with such manly perfection. What she'd do for a piece of that.

She watched the movie to its end, snuggled under her plush blanket on the couch, half dreaming of her own superhero. She thought she'd had one, but David had proved more Loki than Thor. She'd booted him onto the rubbish tip of cheater boyfriends a few months ago, where she hoped he was composting stinkily with all the other rotters.

Since then, it'd been drought land. Which was fine with Amber, but she missed sex, and David, annoyingly, had been rather good at it.

She tuned into the main music channel. Three men in baggy trousers were prancing about with antlers on their heads and shaking their fists. She flicked to the country music channel. A male singer crooned about giving him a chance. Him, she would. Those jeans fitted a tidy pair of legs, and an impressive set of biceps filled the short sleeves of his shirt. Not Hemsworth standard, but they'd do.

Which had her mind drifting back to Tom Jones. He'd looked like he'd have fine biceps, too.

Amber reopened Cupid Country. The icon on her profile showed two new messages. Though they were likely rubbish, she couldn't help the frisson of excitement those two little envelopes generated. She tapped to open the first message. The frisson shuddered to a stop. A dick pic. Not even an impressive one at that. She opened the next. Yep, another dick pic. Really? Did men truly believe that a woman would take one look at a purpled penis and think, now there's a man I can't say no to?

Amber deleted both messages and blocked and reported the profiles, wondering why she bothered. They'd only reincarnate themselves. She flopped her head against the couch armrest and stared at the ceiling. Why was she even doing this?

Because she couldn't help feeling hopeful that maybe, just maybe, there might be someone out there who was decent and kind and good-humoured and intelligent, and didn't think his penis was the entire reason for his existence.

She snorted. What a dreamer she was.

Amber rolled her head. Country music star Morgan Evans was singing "Kiss Somebody". The clip showed a boy saying goodbye to a girl. As their farewell drew to a close, the want between them was palpable, but they were too shy to make a move. Awkwardly, they hugged, and the boy walked off. The further away he got, the more he realised he should have kissed her.

An opportunity lost.

Maybe that's what Tom Jones was, too.

Mentally berating herself for being a sucker for punishment, Amber hunted for Tom Jones. She found him as before, staring straight down his arm at the camera in what was clearly a selfie. A lush paddock stretched behind him along with a vast sky, framing him in green and blue.

She tweaked the screen to zoom in on his face. A hint of a self-deprecating smile tugged at one side of his mouth as if he thought himself a bit of an idiot. Probably from choosing Tom Jones as an alias. Not that Amber could talk. She was using Amy Smythe as hers.

She switched to his details. They were scant—age twenty-seven, just over six feet tall, fit, likes football, the occasional movie or dinner out. Lives in Levenham and districts. Honest.

Huh. That's what they all said.

She checked the time. Ten o'clock. No good came from playing with dating apps this late on a Friday night.

Except ...

Tom Jones looked so normal. His bio seemed genuine, too. The sort of bio a bloke who was as nervous about online dating as she was would write.

She blew out a breath. If her friend Niamh was with her now, she'd tell her to pull herself together. Easy for her to say, unlike Niamh's name which bore no resemblance to its spelling and was pronounced "Neve", the same as "Steve". Amber's straitlaced mathematician friend had the self-control of a cyborg. Amber was more like a gambolling puppy driven by impulse and inquisitiveness, even if it led her into danger.

She looked again at Tom Jones, then at the telly. The boy, a bunch of flowers in his outstretched hand, was leaping over a child who'd wandered into his rushed path. Powered by regret as he chased after his girl, desperate to reclaim his lost moment.

Ah, what the hell.

She hit the "hello" button and prepared to type a message.

Instead, the chat screen opened. Tom must have been sweating on his phone.

Hi.

Amber chewed her lip, then typed, *That was quick.*

Movie just finished and I was checking my phone.

Tom's evening sounded about as thrilling as hers.

Were you watching Thor too?

I was.

Huh. How about that.

Chris Hemsworth fan?

More Natalie P. For the acting, of course.

Amber smiled. *What are you watching now?* If he replied "Morgan Evans", there'd be no stopping her.

Football replay.

Ah, well. A girl couldn't have everything.

Who do you go for?

Carlton. You? Please don't say Collingwood.

She laughed. Carlton and Collingwood hated one another. *You're safe. St Kilda.*

Okay. I don't mind the Saints. Bad loss last week.

I know. But this week we're at home against the Gold Coast so should have a win.

Us too. We're playing the Bulldogs.

Amber tried to think of something to continue the conversation, but nothing came to mind. Seconds passed. Then more. The moment felt swollen with anticipation. She watched the screen and wondered if Tom was feeling the same. Or maybe he was working on his dick pic. The thought popped her buoyant mood.

Then new words appeared.

Are you still there, Amy?

Still here.

Do you want to swap to voice? I'm not much of a typist. Or is it tappist?

From what she'd seen, Tom was doing well. Far better than anyone else she'd chatted to. He could punctuate and spell. Then again, that could be his autocorrect.

Amber hadn't used Cupid Country's voice function before. She hadn't made it that far with any other prospects, and she was wary of giving too much away. But there was something about Tom that made it seem okay and if she didn't say yes, Amber had the feeling she'd end up like the boy in the music video, kicking himself for the chance he didn't take.

Sure.

'Hi.' Tom's voice was deep and warm.

Her own came back breathless. 'Hi.'

He lapsed into quiet. Amber sank her fingers into the plush fibres of her blanket as her anticipation swelled.

'Sorry,' he said. 'I'm new and not very good at this. Never know what to say.'

'Me either.'

'I've only been on Cupid Country a few weeks.'

'Same here.' Not quite the truth, but Amber didn't want Tom to think her desperate. And it gave them something else in common besides spending their Friday nights at home in Levenham. A pleasant enough place in the far south-east of South Australia, but not exactly a town teeming with nightlife.

'How are you finding it?'

'Hit and miss. The dick pics are annoying.'

'You get those?' Tom sounded genuinely outraged.

'Unfortunately. Seriously, what is it with men and dick pics?'

'No idea. Some blokes are morons.'

They retreated once more into quiet. Amber squeezed her eyes shut. Why-oh-why couldn't she think of something clever to say? She was never usually this tongue-tied.

'Amy?'

'I'm still here.'

'Maybe we should do a Q and A type thing. Like a speed date. See if we like what we hear.'

Amber already liked what she'd heard, but a sexy voice meant little, and a Q and A was a clever idea—easy and would keep the words flowing. 'Okay. Do you want to go first or should I?'

'Ladies first, of course. Or is that being patronising?'

Amber's heart gave a little squeeze. A man who worried about being patronising? That was new. 'You're fine. Okay, an easy one. Dogs or cats?'

He laughed, a husky, engaging sound. 'Too easy. Dogs. You?'

'Dogs. Do you have any?'

'Yep. Two. They're working dogs. You?'

'No pets, sadly.' Although in that moment she wished she did so they could share funny pet stories. Maybe hear that sexy chuckle again. 'Your turn.'

'Your avatar. Does it look like you?'

Amber winced. She'd forgotten about that. Like using her true name, Amber had felt uncomfortable uploading a proper photo and had used an app to transform her head-shot into a cartoon.

'It does. Although it's given me more freckles than I actually have.'

'I thought those were cute.'

She held the phone away from her ear and stared at the screen. Was this niceness real? Surely not. Except it sounded real.

'And yours?' she asked. 'Is that muscled man the genuine you?'

'Muscled?'

'I spotted flexed biceps beneath that shirt.'

'Yep, all me.' Rustles sounded like he was moving about. Or removing clothes. Amber closed her eyes and willed him not to spoil things. 'Not the best shot. I took it on the farm. Felt like a dill.'

'I liked it,' she said, when what she was really thinking was, *I like you.*

'Thanks.' More rustling. 'Hey, Amy?'

'Yes?'

He didn't answer for a few seconds. 'Nothing. It doesn't matter.'

She sat up and tugged the blanket onto her lap. 'What?'

'I was going to ask if you wanted to meet. Then I figured that sounded too pushy.'

'It is a touch.'

He sighed. 'Yeah. It's just that you sound like someone I'd like to get to know.'

Amber gathered her blanket even closer, cuddling it, though she didn't need the warmth. Tom's words had flushed heat across her skin and shot flutters through her stomach. 'I suppose we could.'

'Really?'

'Only if you promise you're not a serial killer.'

'I promise, but then a serial killer would say that, so I'm not sure what sort of help that is.'

'Probably none, but you haven't sent me a dick pic yet. Maybe you are perfectly decent. Anyway, maybe I'm the black widow and you're the one who needs to be careful.'

He laughed at that. 'Maybe you are, but I'll take my chances that you're not. So ... coffee? Give me a chance to prove I'm the perfectly decent man you're hoping for?'

A coffee. She stared at the television screen. A bunch of country types were playing near a lake, girls in bikinis, blokes sucking beers, everyone laughing and having a good time. Being in love.

Longing twanged her chest. Amber closed her eyes.

The whole point of being on a dating app was to expand her horizons. What did she have to lose, except time?

'All right. How does tomorrow afternoon sound?'

'Fine by me, but isn't your footy team playing then?'

'They are. But for a decent, non–serial killing man, I'm willing to forsake my football team.' It was no sacrifice, Amber hadn't planned to watch the game anyway.

'Wow. I'm flattered. Okay, Amy with the cute avatar, how do you want to do this?'

Amber gnawed on her lip as she raced through her options. They could meet in a café, but the likelihood of someone recognising her was too high. Tom sounded charming and genuine, and his chuckles and sexy voice were melting her insides, but Ted Bundy had been a charmer too, and she wasn't ready to give up her real identity until she was sure about him.

Where was both private and safe?

Suddenly, she had the perfect place.

'Three o'clock, Civic Park. There's a bench under one of the big oak trees near the rose garden. I'll be wearing a pink jumper. Unless it's really freezing, then I'll be in a coat.'

'Cute girl,' replied Tom Jones in that husky, sexy voice, 'we have a date.'

Chapter Two

Tom alighted from his ute and straightened his clothes. He breathed in. It was stupid to be nervous, but his stomach had been full of worms all morning. He hadn't slept great either, revisiting his conversation with Amy over and over, wondering what she really looked like. She'd sounded funny and clever, with a soft, sweet voice that made him think of lazy Sunday morning sex.

Something he hadn't experienced for a long, long time.

He shut the car door and stared into the leafy surrounds of Civic Park. Shadowy trees, memorials and sculptures hid his view of the far side, where the rose garden was. At least the weather was mild. He'd woken in a sweat in the middle of the night, fretting the Bureau had got the forecast wrong and a storm would hit, but for a Levenham winter's day it was benign. A few scudding clouds, a light breeze, but dry.

He checked his watch. Ten to three. Was she here already, hiding somewhere, waiting to check him out before committing to the meeting? Maybe not. She said she'd be on the bench. Hard to hide there.

Tom glanced up and down the street, checking out the cars. There weren't many. The locals who weren't snuggled up at home were at Levenham's various sports grounds watching footy, netball, and hockey. There was a showjumping event at the showgrounds, too. His sister Eden was competing. He'd ducked around earlier to wish her luck and watched her jump the first round of one of the lesser competitions on her young horse, Admiral. She'd be riding her main mount, Ruffian, in the A-grade event at four. If things went badly with Amy, he'd be back in time to watch.

He really hoped that wouldn't happen. It wasn't that he was desperate—Tom had enough to keep himself occupied —but it was about time he started dating again. A couple of years was more than enough to get over a broken engage-ment, as Eden regularly reminded him. Not that she could talk. Eden had been in love with the same man since she was sixteen, a man who, according to her, was the master of mixed signals. The idiot. Tom's sister was the sunniest person he knew. The kind of person who made the sun come out for others, too. Humphrey Taylor-Poshpants didn't know what he was missing.

He checked his watch again. Five minutes to. He walked to the stone fence and peered into the gardens, searching for a flash of pink. Movement on a path caught his attention. Tom's excitement rose as a reddish coat moved past the trees and roses, only for his shoulders to drop when a mother pushing a pram emerged into the light.

He exhaled slowly and wiped his hands down the sides of his jeans. Time to go for it.

Tom followed the footpath to the entrance and passed beneath a wire arch that in summer would be coated in blooming climbing roses and was a popular location for wedding photos. The path wound around an ornate marble fountain overlooked by sturdy oaks, their few remaining leaves clinging like rust flakes. Fat koi in the fountain's pond flashed orange as they darted below the surface.

The rose garden was ahead. Tom's heart skipped with each step. He scanned for the bench and finally spotted it beneath a large tree. No pink brightened the scene, only greens and browns.

He reached the bench and cast a quick gaze around the rose garden. No twenty-something-year-old lurked there. He checked his watch. Right on three. Amy shouldn't be far away.

Unless she'd stood him up.

His jaw tightened. Not a thought he wanted to pursue.

Tom shoved his fists in his jeans pockets and rocked on his heels and killed time surveying the gardens. Levenham might be a smallish town of only seventeen thousand people, but it took great pride in its civic spaces, none more so than the meticulously maintained Civic Park. Besides the trees, garden beds, benches and paths, there were monuments to the town's good and great, plaques commemorating historic events, and a couple of weird modern sculptures that Tom—and many others—had never understood the meaning of, but they apparently represented the town's growth and embrace of change.

Though not its geographical centre, the manicured rose garden was the park's emotional heart, especially in the spring and summer, when it was home to posing brides, tourists, and locals in search of colour and beauty. A haven even a bloke like Tom could appreciate. Except right now Tom wasn't feeling the love. With its spiky pruned bushes, darkly cultivated soil beds and drab hues, the garden looked as bleak as Tom was beginning to feel.

He checked his watch. Seven minutes past three.

Amy wasn't coming.

He sank onto the bench and stared broodingly at the rose beds. This was shit. She'd sounded really keen, and now ...

'Tom?'

He whipped around. A pretty brunette in a pink jumper, her shoulder-length hair messy with soft curls, stood on the path, one hand to her chest as though to steady its rise and fall. Her cheeks were flushed, honey-coloured eyes wide, her lush, rose-tinted lips parting in the beginnings of a hopeful smile.

Tom leaped to his feet. 'Amy?'

'Yes.' Her smile spread, lighting her entire face.

Tom's heart ballooned. Holy hell, she wasn't just pretty, she was gorgeous. 'You're here.'

'Yes,' she said, breathlessly. 'I'm sorry I'm late. I got caught up with a—' She looked aside, more pink blooming across her cheeks. 'A last-minute thing.'

'Doesn't matter. You're here now.' Tom gestured at the bench. 'Do you want to sit, or go for coffee, or maybe just wander around?'

She chewed her bottom lip, regarding him from under her lashes in a way that made him tingle. 'Maybe wander for a bit?'

'Sure.' He waited for her to choose a direction and fell in alongside. They walked several steps, casting quick glances at one another and sharing shy smiles. He wondered what she thought of him. It couldn't be all bad. She hadn't done a runner yet.

'We've been lucky with the weather,' said Tom, and inwardly winced. The weather was the best he could do? God.

'We have.' She indicated the sun hovering low in the sky. 'We've even been blessed with some sunshine.' She glanced at him, a smile tickling the corner of her mouth. 'Could be a sign.'

'Could be.' Tom bloody well hoped so. That smile was doing strange things to his innards.

It didn't take long for them to reach the park boundary. They paused, hands in pockets, unsure what to do. Across the street was Levenham's renowned Restaurant Ten. Behind the floor to ceiling window, a waitress was setting a table for the evening service. Tom had half a mind to ask Amy if she'd like to join him for dinner there tonight.

Funny, when they'd only just met and barely spoken. But that same tingly feeling of certainty that had affected Tom last night when he heard Amy's voice was back. Back and deeper, vibrating a message right to his toes.

She was the girl.

He didn't know how he knew. He just did.

Tom slid another look at her, unsurprised to find she was sneaking one of her own his way. Eyes the colour of burnt honey. He broke into a smile and was damn near blinded when she grinned in return.

'Another lap?' he asked and had to clear his throat as the words caught. It seemed his voice had headed south along with most of his circulation.

'Why not?'

They about-faced and walked on. Amy's steps were slow, a gentle saunter as though she wanted to eke out their walk for as long as possible. Though his legs were much longer, Tom matched her stride, staying close to her side, but not too close. Despite the electricity crackling between them, he would not spoil this by rushing, even if his fingers were twitching with the need to grab her hand.

The path split at the fountain. Amy veered to the right to circle it, peering into the pond water as she ambled. The koi spotted them. Used to being tossed scraps of sandwiches and other food, they darted to the fountain wall and bobbed their noses to the surface.

'Sorry, fishies,' said Amy, twirling her forefinger lightly in the water. 'I don't have anything for you.' She looked up at Tom. 'What are your dogs' names?'

'Elf and Roxy. Both collies.'

'Cute names. I guess if they're working dogs, that means you live on a farm?'

'Yep. A property about forty k's to the north, called Glenlea. We run sheep and cattle. It's a bit soggy, but reliable.'

'We?'

'Me and Mum and Dad. My sister, Eden, still lives at home, but she works in Levenham. Town bus driver weekdays, mad horse girl on weekends. She's competing today. That's where I was before here.'

Amy refocused on the fish, her finger trailing circles, a secretive smile on her face.

'What?' he asked.

She kept her gaze on the water. 'You don't seem to have any of the qualms I do.'

'Qualms?'

'About giving out personal information.'

'No.' He ducked his head to grin at her. 'Nothing to hide with me. You get what you see.'

'And what's that?'

'The perfectly decent man of your dreams.'

She laughed and flicked a few drops of water at his chest and walked on, hands tucked into the back pockets of her jeans. Tom trailed a moment, admiring her slim legs.

She wore long brown zippered boots. He wouldn't mind taking them off.

He wouldn't mind taking everything off.

'Are you a Levenham local?' he asked, catching up alongside.

'I guess that depends on your definition of local. I'm not born and bred, if that's what you mean, but after six years I'm beginning to feel local, even though I know I'll never be considered a proper one. It's how small towns work.'

It was. There were locals and then there were local-locals. With his ancestors settling in the district in the eighteen seventies, Tom was the latter. Not that he held any pretensions about it. 'Where were you from originally?'

She hesitated over the answer, then seem to decide that it wouldn't matter. 'Gumeracha, in the Adelaide Hills. Do you know it?'

'Not really.' He shrugged. 'Hot in the summer, freezing in the winter. Bushfire prone. Expensive land.'

'That about sums it up. It's also home to the Big Rocking Horse. Whenever I hear someone mention Rocking Horse Hill, I can't help smiling. It's like my move here was fated.'

Rocking Horse Hill was the nickname Levenham locals gave to Mount Stanislaus, an imposing volcanic crater twelve kilometres to the south of town. An editor of the *Levenham Leader* had coined the name in the post-war period, when there was a movement against German names. Frustrated by the merry-go-round of squabbling, the editor had suggested they rename it Rocking Horse Hill, a name so benign it could offend no one. Despite its silliness, somehow it had stuck. So much so, Tom doubted half the younger population would have a clue about the crater's proper title.

'Lucky Levenham,' said Tom, saying a silent thanks to Fate.

Amy nodded, her expression serious but her honeyed gaze sparkling. 'I like to think so.'

Cheeky. He liked that.

'Are your family still in Gumeracha?'

'Mostly.'

Tom waited for her to elaborate, but she didn't. 'Do you miss it?'

'I used to. Not so much now. My friends have all moved on. They're all scattered about, chasing jobs and relationships, or busy with families.' She tucked some curls behind her ear. 'Adulting.'

He chuckled at the adulting reference. 'So Levenham is home now?'

'Seems like it.'

That was good news. The last thing Tom wanted was another relationship with someone like his ex, Sasha, who'd decided his world was too small for her.

The path wound through a heavily treed part of the park. Amy rubbed her arms. Though the leaves were mostly stripped, the trees' many branches masked most of the weak warmth.

'Cold?'

'A little. I'll be okay once we're back in the sun.'

'The café isn't far. We'll get coffee to warm up.'

They emerged from the shade. Amy stopped and crouched to study a garden bed filled with flowers. She threaded her fingers into the white blooms and isolated one. 'Gosh, these are pretty. I wonder what they are. Do you know?'

'No idea. Why not take a photo and do a reverse search,

or take it to Lindner's—the garden centre? Someone there will be able to tell you.'

'Good idea. Not just a handsome face, hey?'

'I'm full of wonders.'

'Yes,' she said slowly, giving him a blatant once-over. 'I bet you are.' With a wink, she tugged a phone from her pocket and lined up a bloom.

Tom blew out a long breath. Even he could recognise a come-on that obvious. The question now was, what was he going to do about it?

Amy finished her photo, then rose and continued to walk as though their flirty moment hadn't happened. 'You like football, but don't play?'

'I used to. Did my ACL a few years ago and had to have a knee reconstruction. That put an end to my playing days.'

She gave a sympathetic wince. 'Ouch.'

'It wasn't great. Rehab took forever and it's still not right. What about you? What's your sport?'

'Squash.'

'Squash?' Tom shook his head. 'I wouldn't have guessed that.'

Amy tipped her head to the side. 'What would you have guessed?'

'Netball.'

Her nose screwed up. 'I tried a few times. Not for me. I played a bit of hockey when I was younger, but running around in the freezing cold in winter turned out not to be my thing. You don't get wet with squash. Sweaty, but not wet.'

Tom forced the image of Amy hot and puffing and sweaty in tiny tight shorts and a singlet from his head. He was having enough trouble keeping calm after that wink.

He gestured towards the little café that sat between the council chambers and the library. 'Time for coffee?'

'Good idea.'

The café was packing up when they arrived, but a smiling lady accepted their orders for coffees-to-go, anyway.

Tom inspected the pastry cabinet. 'Want to share a cake?'

'Sure.' Amy stepped close and peered at the offerings. Tom's skin prickled with hyperawareness. Trying not to make it obvious, he breathed in the scent of her. Something sunny and pretty. Like her.

'We've cleaned most of the cakes out,' said the assistant as she loaded the espresso machine's filter head and expertly locked it into place. 'The lemon tarts are nice, though. So are the caramel slices.'

Tom turned to Amy for help.

'One of each?' she suggested. 'That way, there'll be no arguments.'

'I couldn't imagine ever arguing with you.'

She shot him a look. 'That's only because you don't know me well enough.'

'Working on it, cute girl,' he said, so only she could hear, and was rewarded with a blush sweeping her cheeks.

With the café packing up, they took their coffees and snacks to a park bench in a fast-fading patch of sun. Soon, the sun would be too low to offer any comfort. Tom wondered what Amy would say to a drink at one of the pubs. The back bar at the Australian Arms Hotel had an open fire and at this time of the day it'd be relatively quiet. Later, when the footy crowd rushed in for celebrations and commiserations, there'd be standing room only.

He tore open the paper bags and motioned for Amy to choose what she wanted.

Instead, she used her sugar stirrer to divide the lemon tart in half and handed him his share and took a bite out of hers. Her groan of appreciation shot a tremble from his chest straight to his groin.

Tom was sure the tart was delicious, but such was his distraction he was stuffed if he could register any flavour. Amy seemed to enjoy the caramel slice even more than the tart, sucking the last of the stickiness from each finger and making Tom a little crazy.

Amy knew it, too, the way she angled glances at him, her lips smiling around her fingers. When she finished, she folded the rubbish neatly and tucked the pile under her leg before picking up her coffee and sipping innocently.

There was nothing innocent about Amy.

To keep his mind off his groin, Tom asked about her favourite meals. From her reply, she seemed to enjoy most food, which was a relief. Sasha had always seemed to be on a diet, no matter how good she looked or how many times Tom told her he loved her the way she was.

'Can I ask what you do?' Tom asked when the conversation petered out.

Amy rotated her cup, lips slightly pursed as she watched the last of her coffee swirl. Even in contemplation, her lips were kissable. 'I work with children.'

Tom turned that over. Working with children could cover a multitude of jobs. She could be anything from a doctor to a childcare worker to a teacher or social worker. Maybe even some sort of therapist.

A caring position. He could imagine her in that.

'That's why you chose both pastries and then divided them in half.'

She laughed. 'Keeping the peace is definitely part of the job.'

Teacher, he thought. Or childcare. He'd better not mention that to his mum, or Eden. They'd get ideas. Not that Tom could talk. He had plenty of ideas, it's just that his were concentrated around the practising part of baby making.

Amy tossed down the last of her drink, tucked the rubbish inside the cup, and held her hand out for Tom's. He passed it over and trailed her to the nearest bin.

'So,' she said, dusting her hands. 'What now?'

'I don't know. What do you want to do?'

A lazy smile crept over Amy's face, plunging Tom's brain once more into visions of Sunday morning sex.

'I want to do lots of things, Mister Tom Jones. None of them wise, all of them fun. And all of them,' she placed a hand flat on his chest, 'with you.'

Chapter Three

For a long, heart-stopping moment as Tom's mouth hung open, Amber was sure she'd made a monumental mistake. This brazen behaviour wasn't her, but somehow the cover of her fake name had her acting like a harlot.

A harlot? Now she was slut-shaming herself? Amber bristled at the thought. She was a modern woman and she'd be as sexual as she liked. And Amber very much liked Tom.

A feeling that only ratcheted up when he grinned like a little boy and covered the hand she'd placed on his chest with his own.

'Wisdom isn't all it's cracked up to be,' he said.

She grinned back, then sobered. 'Just so you know, I'm not always like this.'

'Perfect, you mean?'

'I'm definitely not perfect.'

Tom shrugged. 'Right now, you're looking pretty damn perfect to me. So, these unwise things you want to do ...' He lowered his hand, dragging hers with it, and began to walk. His palm was rough, its bumps and furrows telling stories of his life on the land. She wondered what stories the rest of him would tell. Whatever they were, Amber would listen. 'Are we talking dinner, maybe?'

'They could involve dinner.'

'Hmm,' he said as they entered the shaded part of the park.

The sudden cold was solid and penetrating, like passing into another dimension. Amber wished she'd worn a coat. The pink merino wool jumper was snuggly enough, but no match for a rapidly approaching winter evening, and it was the jumper that had made her late.

When she'd proposed it as her identification, Amber had been sure it was clean and safely tucked in her dresser drawer. A frantic search that morning had found the jumper at the bottom of the washing basket. Any thought of it being wearable was scuppered the moment she'd given it a sniff. Fortunately, it was a brand that could tolerate tumble drying on a delicate setting. If she hurried, Amber had enough time to put it on express wash and shove it into the dryer. Except the dryer's delicate setting was very delicate and the drying time took her close to the meeting time.

It was a seven-minute walk from her modest limestone house to Civic Park. Praying that Tom would give her a few minutes grace, at three minutes to three she extracted the jumper, shoved it on over her long-sleeved tee and ran out the door, only to be accosted by her neighbour, Mr Giannopoulos, who was a lovely man but who wouldn't notice a social cue if it whacked him on the head.

Amber had hopped from foot to foot as she tried to get a word in edgeways, before giving up and yelling 'Got to go!' over her shoulder as she sprinted off.

Not wanting to meet Tom gasping for air, she'd forced herself to slow to a walk at the park entrance. Spotting Tom slumped on the bench nearly stole all the breath she'd recovered during her approach. The poor man must have thought he'd been had.

His expression when she called his name and turned to her, though ...

She glanced at him, wondering what was swirling around that handsome head of his. Probably the same rampantly sexy thoughts as hers.

If she weren't feeling so charged, Amber would have laughed at herself. Love at first sight was for romance novels and fairytales, yet here she was being led by a man who had turned her insides molten with want and liking from the moment she'd laid eyes on him.

Tom Jones was the whole package—good-looking, beautifully built, easygoing, intelligent and thoughtful. And it was obvious he was as attracted to her as she was to him.

Of course, the chance of him being a serial killer still existed, but right now Amber was happy to take the risk.

'I'm still a bit confused about these unwise things of yours,' said Tom. They were at the fountain, but there was no pause to look at the fish, no slow amble. He was all business.

'What about them?'

'Could they involve your place? Mine's a bit far away.'

She halted. Momentum dragged her hand free of his. Tom immediately stopped and faced her.

'Not my place.' Amber rubbed her arm and regarded the fish pond. 'It's not that I ...'

'Hey,' he said, cupping her upper arm and stroking it with his thumb. 'I understand. We don't have to ...' He puffed out his cheeks. 'I wasn't expecting ...' Tom scraped his palm over his head and let it drop. 'Shit.'

Shit indeed.

Except it was what she wanted. What he wanted. They weren't children. They were consenting adults, riding high on their attraction. This wasn't the fifties or some other straitlaced time when women had to suppress their desires. Why the hell couldn't they go off and have sex?

Unless he'd think she was ...

He wouldn't. She might hardly know him, but gut instinct told her Tom was a good man.

Amber's voice was barely a whisper. 'I was thinking we could find a hotel.'

'Right. Good. Of course.' His gaze locked with hers, the lines around his eyes crinkled with worry. 'Are you sure? We don't have to rush. We can just, I dunno, have a drink somewhere. Talk some more.'

'Tom,' Amber stepped closer. 'I know it sounds crazy, and I've never in my life felt this way, but I want to rush. I want to kiss you, I want to feel you, I want to wake up with you. I want to—' She shook her head. 'I just *want*. And I'm aware it's nuts, but it's how I feel.'

'I'm the same. I felt it the moment I saw you.' He laughed. 'I even felt it on the phone last night. It's crazy and amazing.' He cradled her face, his gaze soft and loving and wondrous. 'It's the best thing that's ever happened to me.'

'Then we should go.'

'Yeah.' His breath sounded shaky. 'Yeah.' Then he brushed his mouth against hers. A soft, fleeting, barely there touch with the force of an earthquake.

Amber's bones melted. If it weren't for the arm Tom slung around her shoulders, she was sure she would have collapsed. His hold was strong, his body against hers sturdy and warm. The purpose was back in his stride.

'Where are we going?' she asked, vaguely aware she needed to let go of him, that getting caught like this in public by a student or their parents would be an embarrassment she'd rather not experience, but was equally unwilling to ease away from his solidity.

'My car.' He looked at her. 'Unless you want to take yours?'

Amber shook her head. It would have been so easy to say she'd walked, but lingering wariness, borne from a thousand stories of women getting into trouble with stalkers or dates who refused to let go, kept her silent. The less he knew for the moment, the better. Later, when she was sure, she would tell him everything. Her real name, her phone number, where she worked, her home address. How the thought of being with him fogged her brain with lust.

'Mine then.'

His car was a blue ute with all the blokey trimmings, like chrome roll bars, a bull bar to protect the front from kangaroos or straying stock, and a long aerial.

Tom opened the door for her, his smile full of promise. He let her settle, shut the door and strode for the driver's side. Amber scanned the interior. It was clean and well maintained, with a few scrapes of dried mud on the footwell mat. A notebook and pencil sat in one of the cup holders, a tube of sunscreen in the other.

'Okay?' he asked, one hand on his seatbelt.

'Absolutely.'

'I'll need to make a short stop along the way.' He smiled crookedly. 'Condoms.'

'Oh.' How could Amber not have thought of that? 'Yes. Good idea.' She grinned. 'Make it a big box.'

He laughed and snapped his belt into place, then gripped her hand and squeezed. It was so sweet, so loving, it was like having her heart cuddled. His hold lingered for a moment longer, their gazes locked, the air crackling with their amazement at their luck. He gave another quick squeeze, let go, and started the car.

Tom pulled into the street. She watched him drive, admiring his easy competence, the way his thigh muscles moved under his jeans when he changed gear or braked.

Levenham had a couple of supermarkets, one behind the main street, another further to the west, where the main street headed towards the highway. To Amber's relief, he drove to the latter. The car park was quiet. In another hour or so it would fill as people popped in to grab food on their way home from sport and other activities.

'Won't be a moment,' he said, opening the door. Then he stopped, leaned across and kissed her. 'Don't go anywhere.'

'Not a chance.'

His smile shot a thrill straight down her spine.

Amber touched her lips, never taking her eyes off him as he hurried towards the doors. When he disappeared inside, she flopped her head back and, in a fit of pure happiness, pounded her heels on the floor and her fists on the side of her seat and giggled.

She was going to spend the night in a hotel room with a gorgeous man. Not just any gorgeous man, but one she'd stumbled across on a dating app. A man who, for some miraculous reason, hadn't been snatched up by any of the hundreds of women trawling Cupid Country. A man who, for tonight at least, belonged solely to Amber Dunn, twenty-eight-year-old primary-school teacher.

Tom was back in a short time, box in hand. He tucked it alongside the sunscreen and started the car.

'Did you have any motel in mind?' he asked as he drove for the exit.

Amber hadn't considered that far ahead. 'Not really. I've never really had a reason to think about local motels.'

'Me neither. But the Ambassador is supposed to be good.'

The Ambassador also had the added benefit of being right in town and a short walk from her home. If things soured between them, the walk—or run—home would be easy. It wouldn't come to that, though. Amber knew it in her soul.

This would be a night to remember for all the right reasons.

Tom pulled up in the driveway and headed into the Ambassador's reception, tugging his wallet from his back pocket as he walked. Amber picked up the condom box. Regular brand, regular sized. Nothing fancy or show-offy. Just reliable protection. His thoughtfulness made her breath catch.

He emerged, swinging a key and smiling. 'We're in the room up the back. She's going to bring us up some fresh milk.' He gave a sheepish shrug. 'I asked if she could bring some champagne, too.'

'Aren't you the romantic?'

'Cute girl, I haven't even got started.'

There was so much promise in that simple sentence, Amber could have swooned.

'Did you sign in as Mr and Mrs Jones?'

'Just Mr, no Mrs.'

A pity. Mr and Mrs Jones had a nice ring to it. Which made Amber want to giggle and pound her heels again. Could the man make her any sillier?

The hotel was single storey, the rooms forming a giant U around a pool and picnic area. Tom drove to the bottom of the U and parked in front of number twelve.

Tom looked at her, his hands twisting around the wheel. 'It's not too late to change your mind. I'll understand.'

'I'm not going to change my mind, Tom. This is going to happen. I want it to happen.'

'So do I.' He blew out a breath and chuckled. 'You have no idea.'

But she did. She absolutely did.

'Then we're okay. Come on.' Amber grabbed the condom box and wiggled it. 'We have a night to enjoy.'

He unlocked the room door, reached in and flicked on a light, then stepped back and waved for Amber to go first. She glanced at him, noting the smug expression, and wondered what else he had in mind.

I haven't even got started.

That there could be more wonderfulness ahead had her shuddering with delight.

For a country motel, it was a large room. Along the side wall was a king-size bed covered in a white doona with a plush grey throw folded over the end, plump pillows, and a grey velvet quilted bedhead. A television was mounted on the opposite wall. Below was a long built-in bench and desk with a grey velvet chair tucked beneath. To the rear was a kitchenette, with the usual kettle, tea and coffee supplies and bar fridge. A half-closed door led to the bathroom.

She turned to Tom. 'It's nice.'

'It's their best room.' He cleared his throat. 'I thought it'd be good to start—'

A knock sounded. Tom opened the door to a woman wearing an embroidered Ambassador jumper and thick grey beanie on her head. She held an ice bucket with a bottle inside and a mini carton of milk balanced on top.

'I've got your milk and champagne,' said the woman.

'Great. Thanks.' Tom made to take the ice bucket, but she brushed him aside.

'I'll sort it for you.' She smiled at Amber as she headed for the kitchenette. 'Everything all right?'

'Yes. Thanks. It's lovely.'

She nodded as if she had expected nothing less. Amber didn't miss her curious look at the empty luggage rack as she passed. Or the slight falter in her step as she noticed the condoms Amber had unthinkingly tossed on the bed. Amber widened her eyes at Tom, heat flushing her face.

'I'll get our bags,' he lied smoothly and, jangling his keys, headed out to the ute.

She snatched up the condoms, shoved them into the drawer of a bedside table, and pushed open the bathroom door. A two-person spa occupied the entire corner. A large shower to the right, a toilet and vanity to the left.

'If you need anything else just call reception,' said the woman. 'Extra towels, more champagne. Oh, and the restaurant does room service until nine.'

'Thanks,' said Amber, feigning deep interest in the bathroom and only half looking at her. Her face was so hot it felt sunburned.

'Enjoy your evening.'

Amber was sure she heard knowing in the woman's tone and wanted to curl on the bed and cry. Or laugh. Amber wasn't sure.

The woman closed the door behind her. A short time later, Tom knocked. Amber let him in and pressed her back to the closed door.

'She knows what we're here for.'

'So?'

Amber shook her head. 'I don't know.'

Tom stepped close and curled his finger under her chin. 'Hey, cute girl?'

'What?'

'Who cares what she thinks? All that matters is us.'

'You're right.' She smiled, her embarrassment lifting with his tender words and kind eyes. 'Of course you're right. Nice spa, by the way.'

'Nice you.'

Her voice dropped an octave. 'You really have all the moves, don't you?'

'Like I said ...' He sidled closer, gaze dipping to her mouth. 'I haven't even got started.'

Chapter Four

The moment Tom's lips closed on Amber's, she was airborne. Like an angel had swooped down, caught her in its arms and soared upwards to heaven.

Not that she'd be allowed anywhere near the pearly gates. The way Tom kissed—attentive, expert, headily—would challenge even the stoutest heart to stay pure. And Amber had no intention of staying pure with Tom. They were going to get down and dirty and sweaty and—

The thoughts disappeared in a rush of adrenaline as his hands slid to her waist and explored upward until his thumbs were stroking the undersides of her breasts. An exquisite spasm rushed up her spine and escaped from her mouth as a soft moan.

At the sound, Tom pressed closer, his erection long and swollen against her belly. She pressed back, signalling she felt him and wanted more. So much more. Ignited, their hunger caught and blazed. Breaths, skin, everything trembling and burning with need. Pants and groans, racing lips and probing tongues, the music of their kiss rose and fell, but always intensifying. Chasing a crescendo Amber had wanted from the moment she saw Tom rise from the bench and stare at her like a man who'd suddenly found his true home.

Amber tugged at his shirt and jumper until she found bare skin. He was lean and muscled and hot, and she couldn't get enough. She scrabbled at his clothes. There were too many layers. Too much distance.

She thrust back her head as Tom nibbled his way across her jaw and trailed kisses down her throat. He cupped her breasts, fingers massaging gently. His thumbs found her swollen nipples through the fabric of her jumper. Lightly, he brushed them backwards and forwards, each touch shooting electric jolts into Amber's groin, amplifying her need.

'We haven't had any champagne,' she panted. She was going to come leaning against the hotel room door if they didn't ease off.

Tom kissed his way to one of her ears. His whispered voice and breaths firing more jolts south. 'I can stop.'

They should. They really should.

'God, no.'

He sucked her earlobe, the sound loud and ridiculously erotic. 'We'll celebrate with it, after.' He drew back to look at her, wickedness flickering in his gaze. 'Or I could lick it all off you.'

Amber responded by dipping a finger inside the waistband of his jeans and slowly tracing it across to the button, smiling smugly as Tom's face and then body stilled. He looked like she felt—barely holding on.

His gaze darkened, then his mouth closed back over Amber's and the fire driving them flared even higher. Desperation replaced hunger. Tom's hands slid inside her jumper and tee, pushing them up, until her bra was exposed, while Amber fought with the button of his jeans, moaning in frustration when clumsiness didn't get it open fast enough.

'We should ...' Amber managed.

'Yeah.'

They stayed pressed against the door, too busy exploring and feeling and breathing in the essence of each other. The exhilarating sensation of heated, vibrating skin. The delicious taste of passion. The acceleration of their charged afternoon towards a furious night of discovery.

Amber groaned as Tom dipped his head to her left breast and closed his mouth over the lace. Liquid heat channelled straight between her thighs.

'Bed,' she panted. 'Now.' Before her legs ceased holding her up.

They backed their way the short distance to the bed, kisses broken with giggles and gasps as they groped and fondled and wrestled with clothing. Tom's jeans were halfway down his hips, caught on the swell of his briefs. Amber's bra was undone and shucked up under her armpits with the rest of her clothes.

Tom collapsed as he hit the end of the bed, bringing Amber down on top of him. He immediately rolled, fitting himself between her legs in the world's most marvellous join.

He eased up on an elbow and grinned at her. 'We made it.'

'We did. We're not naked, though. I need to be naked.'

His grin widened. 'I knew you were perfect.'

'I will be once I'm naked. Can we get naked now, please?'

'For you,' he said, kissing the tip of her nose, 'we can do anything you want.'

Tom had his top off and tossed across the room in seconds. Amber attempted to tackle the tangle of her own clothes, but Tom brushed her hands aside. Gently, he eased her jumper and tee over her head, then attempted to focus on her bra, only to be distracted by her exposed breasts.

'Christ,' he said, pausing in the middle of tugging her left shoulder strap down her arm to suck on a nipple.

'Naked, remember?'

'Sorry.' His mouth released the peak with a wet pop, the sudden cold making it stand to even greater attention. His gaze crossed slightly before he gave a little shudder and refocused on her bra. Tom twanged it towards the bathroom and paused to regard her body. He shook his head in wonder. 'Fantastic breasts.' He lifted his gaze and smiled. 'Fantastic you.'

Amber was so turned on she was in danger of melting to goo. Except that wouldn't move things forward. Instead, she caught her lower lip between her teeth and tilted her head. 'There's more of me.'

'Yeah.' He breathed in. 'Yeah, there is.'

There was a moment of silliness when Amber's jeans became trapped on her long boots and Tom became too distracted with curling a finger inside her knickers to solve the problem. Then another when Tom's impressive erection hooked on his briefs, and it was Amber who was thrown by the sight. Finally, they managed nakedness.

'I want to look at you,' she whispered, motioning for Tom to roll onto his back.

She sat astride him, at the top of his thighs, and drank in the mesmerising sight of healthy man. Healthy, normal, lovely man with a wide, lightly hair-smattered chest, a lean belly, and another alluring line of hair descending downward to an erection that made all those dick pics she'd been sent look like toys.

She traced her gaze back to his face. 'Aren't you looking smug?'

He tipped his head towards her. 'You'd look smug too if you had my view.'

'Mmm,' she said, and leaned forwards to kiss his belly and trail her wet tongue lower.

'Oh, Jesus.'

He didn't let her play for long. With strong arms, he flipped their positions until he was once more fitted between her legs, answering her complaint with, 'I won't last two seconds if you keep doing that.'

'So? We've all night. We can just do it again.'

'We can, but a man's got his pride. Anyway,' he said, nuzzling her neck and nibbling his way down to her breasts. 'I deserve a turn, too.'

Amber had no qualms about letting him finish what he started, although Tom took his time, mouth and hands exploring and teasing until she was almost sobbing with frustration. When release came, she clutched at any part of him she could grab as she shuddered, fingers digging in, wanting more of this. Of him.

'We need a condom,' she said as he lazily kissed and chuckled his way up her chest.

'What? You want more?'

Amber giggled and tugged on his hair. 'Funny boy.'

'Sexy girl,' Tom replied around a mouthful of nipple.

Amber waved her arm towards the bedside table and couldn't reach. 'One of us is going to have to move and it'll have to be you. I'm too jellied.'

'Jellied, huh?'

'Very jellied.'

Tom wriggled to where she pointed and retrieved the box of condoms. When he couldn't find the opening to the cellophane wrap, he used his teeth. He plucked out a condom, only for Amber to snatch it away.

'Let me.'

'If you want.'

'I want. On your back, Tom Jones.'

Tom complied and tucked his hands behind his head. Laughter filled his face. 'Have you any idea how much you saying that turns me on?'

'I don't need ideas. I can see.' She leaned forwards to kiss the tip of his cock and smiled at the strangled noise he made. Served him right for being a smart-arse, but Amber was loving every second.

The moment she finished fitting the condom, Tom raised himself up. He curled a finger under her chin and studied her face. 'Ready?'

'Are you kidding me?'

'Just doing the right thing.'

She softened. What an adorable man. 'I know.'

His gaze stayed serious. 'You, me ... I don't want to screw this up.'

Amber smiled and kissed him. 'You won't. I know you won't.'

He didn't.

Tom reached over the side of the spa and lifted the champagne bottle from the ice bucket. 'More?'

'Why not?' responded Amber, holding out her glass.

She probably shouldn't. With no food in their bellies, the first glass had gone straight to her head, but she figured she couldn't get into too much trouble sitting in a warm spa with Tom.

Because, really, what was the worst that could happen? He'd make love with her again?

The thought had her stifling a giggle.

Tom handed her the glass. 'What are you laughing at?'

'Sex.'

He raised an eyebrow. 'Sex?'

She sipped her drink and sank back into the bubbles. 'Mmm.'

Tom shoved the bottle back in the bucket, lounged back, lifted her foot onto his thigh and resumed his massage of the balls of her feet. 'Haven't you had enough of that yet?'

After two rounds of toe-curling, breath-stealing sex, and a ridiculous amount of giggly fooling around, Amber should have had enough, but Tom had opened a world of want inside her where "enough" had been expunged from her vocabulary.

It wasn't just the sex, either. Even when they faded into rest, it had been lovely, filled with cuddles and silly, sexy murmurs as they made each other laugh. Then Tom suggested they try out the spa, and that was the end of that. Although Amber had every intention of fooling around some more in the bath. Once she'd finished her champagne.

Or before.

'No. Have you?'

He grinned naughtily. Amber was beginning to love that sinful grin. She was beginning to love everything about her Mr Jones. And he *was* now hers. She was as sure of it as she was of breathing. The looks of awe and yearning he kept sliding at her weren't faked. Neither were the worshipful touches. Amber wondered if he was reading the same from her. He should. The glow of love that he'd ignited inside her felt star-shine bright.

Tom splashed her. 'What do you think?'

'I think you should come over here and kiss me.'

He set down his glass and eased onto his knees. Water threaded over his shoulders and chest, chasing muscular channels before dripping into the water.

Amber sighed. 'You have the sexiest chest.'

'Speaking of sexy chests.' He gently cupped her breasts, lifting them above the waterline and gazing from one to the other.

Amber looked down at herself, at the reverent hold of his hands, and felt a spike deep in her belly. God, she wanted him. Every inch of him. Tonight. Tomorrow. Forever. She stared back at his face. 'How did this happen? You and me, I mean.'

'I don't know.' He shifted onto his hands, so they were face-to-face. 'And I don't care. I'm just glad it did.'

'So am I.'

They continued to stare, made silent by wonder and disbelief and their expanding love. Then Tom lowered his mouth to Amber's and once more they were lost.

'Not much of a game,' said Amber.

'No.' Tom kissed her shoulder. He was sitting up with his back to the bedhead and Amber tucked between his legs, one arm around her belly, the other playing with her hair or whatever other body part snagged his attention. They'd been so busy amusing themselves with each other that they'd only caught the last quarter of the night's football game. Even then, they'd hardly watched. 'Are you hungry?'

'I am, but it's late, and the kitchen closed at nine.'

'I'll order us a pizza. Or there's that chicken place on the highway. Won't take me long to drive there and back.'

'Pizza. Pepperoni.'

'I should have known you'd be a spicy girl.'

He made the call and pulled on his jeans and jumper. They'd turned up the heating, and the room was warm and a little humid from their earlier spa. Amber stretched out across the bed and leaned on her elbow, drinking him in.

'I like perving at you,' she said with a sigh.

'More than Thor?'

She screwed her nose up. 'Do I have to answer that?'

He was beside her in a second, tickling her belly in the spot he'd discovered made her squirm and giggle uncontrollably. 'Come on, Amy, admit it. You like me better than that actor.'

Amy.

The name resonated through her giggles. Perhaps now was the time to admit her fake name, before Tom became too used to it. Except why spoil the moment when they were having so much fun? And there was the issue with his name. Tom Jones? She doubted it was all real. Tom fitted, but maybe the Jones was really Johnston or something else similar. If Tom wasn't correcting her teasing Tom Joneses, why should she correct his Amy?

By the time he'd finished tickling and then kissing her, the pizza delivery person was banging on the door and Amber had forgotten her qualms.

Tomorrow. There'd always be tomorrow.

Maybe there'd even be forever.

Chapter Five

Tom smiled to himself and rolled over. And found cold sheet. He opened his eyes and checked the bed. No soft, warm, cute girl.

Probably in the bathroom. Except the door was open, and no noise echoed from inside.

He sat up and squinted through the dark. 'Amy?'

Nothing.

He threw off the sheet and padded to the bathroom, his morning erection rapidly fading as his worry increased. He pushed gently on the door, not wanting to hit her if she was standing behind it. It swung easily open, revealing white tiles turning a hazy orange in the first blush of sunrise. The spa they'd had so much fun in. The shower in which they'd soaped each other. The toilet. No Amy.

Gut clenched, Tom flicked on the main lights and surveyed the motel room. Amy's clothes and boots were gone.

She was gone.

'Shit,' he said, sagging against the jamb and rubbing his head.

Why? Amy had mentioned a piano lesson, but surely she could have said goodbye. And she didn't have a car. She would have had to walk back in the freezing cold and dark to wherever she'd parked hers, wearing only a thin jumper with an even thinner tee underneath.

Maybe she'd just snuck out for a moment. Maybe any second Amy would knock on the door, arms loaded with something warm and delicious from a bakery. Except Tom didn't know of any bakeries open on Sunday mornings in Levenham. Coffee then. She could have gone to get coffee from the twenty-four-hour roadhouse. It wasn't far. Maybe half a kilometre's walk.

Telling himself that was the answer, Tom fetched his jeans and tugged them on, then wandered to the window to keep an eye out.

Wispy fog curled around the cars and pool enclosure. More guests had arrived during the night and three-quarters of the parking spaces were full. As the sun eased higher, rays caught the dewy surfaces, turning them glittering and jewel-like, and making him think of the playful sparkles in Amy's eyes. His dazzling one-of-a-kind girl.

Though his gut told him it was pointless, Tom kept up his vigil until the reality of passing time crushed even his optimism.

With a sigh, he faced the bed, hands on his hips. The bed in which they'd shared so much—bodies, minds, laughter. So much laughter.

So much love.

One night and he was head over heels, batshit crazy in love. And what had happened? Amy—gorgeous, funny, sexy Amy—had done a runner.

Good one, Tom. Awesome work.

For a moment he let his head bow and his shoulders sag,

then he straightened. What they'd shared was too special to let pass. He strode for his phone and stopped, a slow grin forming as he spotted the note beneath.

A snatch and he was greedily unfolding it, eyes hungry for Amy's words. For anything of her.

Her handwriting was neat and round and cute.

Sorry to leave without saying goodbye (although I did sneak a soft kiss). Don't take it to heart! My piano teacher is completely anal about punctuality, and you were sleeping like the world's darlingest baby and I didn't want to wake you.

I would love to see you again. Perhaps next weekend? Message me on Cupid Country. xxx

She'd added a drawing of a big heart with an arrow through it and Tom written in the centre.

Tom grinned, then grinned some more and gave a small whoop as relief coursed through him. She wanted more. Of him. Of them.

And Tom was going to give it to her.

He folded the piece of paper, shoved it into the back pocket of his jeans, and picked up his phone. He opened the Cupid Country app and tapped out a message. Done, he hovered his finger over the send icon as doubt played in his mind.

He reread it.

Hey cute girl of the most perfect night of my life who I'll do my best to forgive for forsaking me for a musical instrument. I want to see you again too. Next weekend feels too far away. Is tonight too soon?

Desperate? Probably, but those words had nothing on the way he felt, and better to let Amy know from the start how serious he was than risk her second-guessing. A lesson he'd learned from his sister Eden and her moans about Humphrey Taylor-Poshpant's mixed signals.

Tom tapped send and then paced, searching out his scattered clothes and dumping them on the bed as he waited for a response. When none came, he supposed Amy was busy in the shower or driving to her lesson or perhaps even already at her lesson.

After another five minutes of pacing, he sighed and headed for the bathroom, placing his phone on the vanity in anticipation of a reply. Tom was just finishing rinsing shampoo from his hair when the app pinged. He jumped out, nearly ending on his bum as he careened on the slippery tiles, and snatched up the phone, splattering the screen with shampoo foam and water drops.

Aren't you just the biggest smoothie? I've gone all smiley! I want to say yes but I have a really busy week, and I KNOW you'll cost me sleep. But I will be all yours come Friday night. Promise. xx

'Stuff it,' he muttered. Still, it was a good message. A great message. They were definitely on.

Tom couldn't resist another attempt. For a bloke as in love as he was, Friday was a lifetime away.

What if I promise you'll get your sleep? I can be good when I try.

Her answer came straight back. *I don't want you good. I want you all baaaaaaad.*

Tom laughed—at her reply and the erection she'd just coaxed out of him.

You'll have it. A proper dinner first? I need to show off my romantic moves.

Romantic moves? You sure know how to make a girl feel gooey.

His hard-on strengthened as he remembered exactly

how gooey Amy could get. He was going to play this straight, though. They'd skipped right to the sex part. Now it was time for romancing.

Sorry, sexy Tom. Gotta go, otherwise my teacher will start getting funny teeth. It's a thing.

Tom blinked. Funny teeth? Something to ask about later.

OK. Will message tonight. Play well! Lov— Tom blew out a breath. Too soon for that. He tapped the delete button three times and replaced the letters with a kiss-blowing emoji.

Then he returned to his rinsing off and planning a romantic night to remember.

Tom wandered over to where Eden was sweeping out her horse float. Admiral and Ruffian stood nearby, long noses hung over the fence, blinking big brown eyes and wearing butter-wouldn't-melt expressions, as if neither had done a naughty thing in their lives.

She looked up from her broom and gave him a once-over, then leaned on it, grinning. 'Someone didn't get much sleep last night.'

Tom scratched his neck. 'No.'

'Must have been one hot date.'

'You could say that. How did you end up yesterday?'

Eden returned to sweeping, her ponytail swinging with the rhythm. She was like him, brown-haired and chocolate-eyed, both taking after their mum, Leanne. Which was just as well, their dad, Scott, liked to joke. 'Third in the one-ten metre. Second in the one-point-four. Humphrey won the one-ten, Mandy the other.'

Tom suppressed a smile at the way Eden's voice went from adoring at the mention of Humphrey Taylor-Posh-pants to tight at the mention of rival competitor Mandy. Despite their years on the showjumping circuit, Eden and Mandy had never been close, although Eden could never figure out why. Tom suspected Poshpants had something to do with it.

'Pretty good showing.'

'Yeah, it was.' She blew a kiss towards Admiral and Ruffian. 'You're good boys, aren't you, hey? Beautiful darlings.'

The horses bobbed their heads in response. Eden laughed and swapped her broom for a pooper scooper. Using a little scraper, she collected the manure and hay and carried it to the poo pile where it'd compost with the scrapings from her stables and yards, along with kitchen and other organic scraps, until the spring, when they'd spread it on Glenlea's lawns and gardens.

Tom leaned against the float with his arms folded, enjoying the cool morning air and fresh scent of the farm. He'd stopped by his place on the way here to change into work clothes and see what his housemate, Olly Braithwaite, was up to. Nothing unusual. His oversized, scruffy-headed friend had been parked on the back step, toast and coffee at his side, and a copy of his latest poultry industry magazine on his knee. He'd let his rabidly loyal gaggle of geese loose on the back lawn, and the geese were tearing up the grass like fat white lawnmowers.

Olly had eyed Tom as he approached, then broken into laughter. 'Cool.' He'd known about the date and told Tom to go for it, citing his usual *life's too short* mantra. Not that Tom had had any intention not to.

'That obvious?'

Olly had snorted. 'Like, yeah. You're swaggering like a gunslinger.'

He felt like one. A winning one, although it was him who'd been shot through the heart.

'She's awesome, Oll. Gorgeous, funny ... Perfect.'

'Good. About time.' Olly bit into his toast and chewed. 'Can I be best man?'

'Sure. Linc can be groomsman.'

'Good. With luck, your bird will have a hot girlfriend as bridesmaid.'

Tom smiled at the memory. One night and he was already thinking forever.

'God, look at you, grinning like the Cheshire Cat,' said Eden on her return from the poo pile. 'Come on, then. Spill.'

'Not much to tell.' Other than that Amy was incredible.

'Oh yeah. What's her name?'

'Amy.'

She shouldered him out of the way and together they lifted and secured the tailgate on the float. 'Amy who?'

'Smythe.'

'Uh huh. And what does she do?'

Besides turn him on like crazy? Tom hadn't got that info out of her. 'Works with children.'

'A teacher?'

Tom shrugged. 'I'm not sure. We didn't really talk about that.'

'I bet you didn't.' Eden huffed a laugh, then sighed, her gaze turning wistful. 'Maybe I should give Cupid Country another go.'

'You don't need a dating app.' His sister had blokes lining up for her. Not that she seemed to notice. Her heart was too set on Poshpants. 'I take it Humphrey's still playing hard to get?'

'He's playing something. I just wish I was in the game.'

Tom ruffled her hair. 'He'll see the light one day.' If he didn't, he was a moron.

'Yeah.' She poked him in the belly as Tom covered a yawn. 'At least one of us is getting lucky. When are you seeing her again?'

'Friday. Not soon enough.'

Eden's eyes widened. 'Are you in love?'

'Maybe.' He cast her a sheepish look. 'Yeah. She's great, Den. Cute, funny, sexy. You'll like her. She likes dogs and football and she's learning to play the piano. That's where she is this morning, at her lesson. And she laughs all the time. Like ... I don't know. Like the world's a really good place, you know?'

'Wow. You are gone. When can I meet her?'

'Steady. We've only had one date.'

'A date that clearly ended in sex.'

Yeah, and what sex it was, too. Tom let out a sigh at the reminder. Friday was definitely too far away.

'It'll happen.' He glanced at the sky and grimaced. The day was getting away and the sooner he sorted his chores, the sooner he could get back to his romancing-Amy project. 'Better get these cattle sorted.'

Tom strode for the shed, whistling for Elf and Roxy as he went. The sun had broken through the morning fog and winter sunshine now bathed the countryside. It was still cold, thanks to a southerly breeze whipping the land, but Tom's mood was as warm as a sheepskin coat, and he felt as sunny as the day.

The paddocks, though, were still mush from the heavy rain they'd experienced the previous week. Mud splattered Tom's long leather workboots as he rode out on his quad bike, dogs on their platform behind his seat. Instead of heading for the cattle, he snuck a detour to the southern-most part of the farm, closest to the main road where the phone reception was best. Coverage across the property was more miss than hit, but the south-western pocket was gener-ally reliable.

He braked at the gate and pulled his phone from the pocket of his oilskin vest, opened the Cupid Country app and tapped out a message.

Wish you were riding with me, he wrote, then snapped a selfie of himself on the quad, grinning at the screen with both dogs peering open-mouthed from around his sides.

Tom checked the news and his email as he waited for a reply. Then sent another message identifying the dogs as Elf on the left and Roxy on the right, in case Amy was curi-ous. He followed that up a few minutes later with a funny dog playing a piano gif he'd found, then felt like an idiot for sending something so adolescent.

Tom glanced at Roxy and at Elf. 'Yeah, I know. I'm a tool.' He ruffled their heads and tucked the phone away.

He was distracted by a heifer who'd bogged herself at the edge of one of the farm's many swampy patches; freeing her required a hand from his dad and Eden on the tractor. Tom didn't finish up his day until close on five. He was muddy, cold, cranky, his knee ached, and he was so tired the walk to his ute from the shed felt like a marathon.

For the first time in ages, he experienced a moment's pang of regret that he didn't still live at home like Eden, who was no doubt soaking in a bath right now and would be fussed over by Mum afterwards. Tom, meanwhile, was going home to Olly and a dinner of dubious origin, given it was his housemate's night to cook. If the bastard had pinched all the hot water again, there'd be trouble.

It was five kilometres from the farm to Olly's property, and Tom counted every one of them. He pulled into the drive and sat for a moment, then reached into his vest pocket for his phone. If there was anyone who could cheer him up, it was Amy.

Tom frowned as his hand found only flannelette lining. He tried the other pocket. Nothing.

He unclipped his seatbelt and dug into the trousers of his work pants. Still nothing.

'No,' he said, shoving out of the car and standing to pat himself down properly. 'No, no, no.'

Tom scrambled around the ute interior, lifting mats, searching under seats. He checked the back tray even though he knew the phone couldn't be there.

He circled with his hands locked on his head and his eyes closed. This could not be happening. Not today.

But the truth remained unchanged. He'd lost his phone.

Seconds later Tom was back in the ute and tearing to the farm, his brain scrambling through all the places it could have slipped from his pocket. The possibilities were huge, ranging from where he'd last messaged Amy, to anywhere along the route he'd taken to the cattle and subsequent shift to the yards, to the shed where he'd finally parked the quad. Deep in his gut, though, was the certainty it had fallen out when they were digging out the heifer.

He banged the steering wheel. This was why he never took his phone out with him. The risk of loss was too great and there was stuff-all coverage anyway. But, oh no, he just had to take it today in case Amy messaged and he lucked it to be in a patch with coverage.

Idiot. Moron. Tool. No wonder people reckoned love made you stupid.

He breathed deep and slow, forcing himself to calm down and think. The phone had a shock and waterproof cover. A tumble wouldn't have hurt it and if it was lying in a puddle or on wet ground, it'd be okay for a while.

If the phone had been trampled into the mud, however, there was no hope.

Not an outcome he wanted to contemplate.

He called into the house, hoping to rope Eden into his search, but washed and already in her pyjamas and dressing gown, she wasn't having a bar of it. His dad regarded him over the top of his reading glasses as though Tom were ten and told him he should have more sense. His mum tried to tempt him away from his foolish quest with Sunday roast dinner and the tease of apple-and-rhubarb crumble for dessert.

Tom waved her off. He'd told Amy he'd message tonight and the thought of letting her down this early in their relationship made his stomach roil. Food would only make it worse.

He asked to borrow his dad's ute and was relieved when it was no problem. It had powerful front and roof-mounted spotlights and, with night fast closing in, Tom would need every blaze of light he could get.

'Thanks, Dad.' He snatched up the keys and headed out.

Eden followed him, huddling into her dressing gown as Tom pulled on his boots. 'She can wait one night, can't she?'

'I promised, Den.'

'I'm sure she'll understand when you explain what's happened. You won't have a hope in hell in finding it in the dark, even with the spotties, and you're already cold and wet.'

Tom shook his head and stared out at the greying landscape. How could he have been so stupid?

'Tommy,' said Eden, touching his arm. 'It'll be all right. Look, you can borrow my phone tonight if you want.'

'Yeah, well, I would, except I don't know her number.'

Eden regarded him with her nose screwed up and her head pulled back, as if she couldn't get her head around what had just come out of his mouth. 'What do you mean, you don't know her number?'

'We've only talked through Cupid Country.'

'Oh. Right.' She puffed air through pursed lips and thought for a moment. 'No worries. I've got the app. Just sign in as you.'

'Yeah, that's another problem. I don't know the password.'

She laughed and then her mouth dropped. 'Oh my God, you're serious. What, didn't you write it down?'

He breathed out hard. 'I signed up one night after I'd had a few. Anyway, it was stored in the phone.'

'Which you now don't have.' She shook her head, then brightened. 'No problem. Use the reset password function.'

Tom cleared his throat.

'What?'

'I used an old Hotmail address.'

'And?' Eden drew out the word, as though knowing something stupid was again going to come from his mouth.

'And I forgot that I'd used it for Cupid Country and deleted the account when I was clearing out obsolete stuff one day.'

Eden was silent for a long moment, then she sighed. 'Tommy, dear Tommy, you are an idiot.'

'Yeah, well done, Den. Tell me something I don't know.'

She frowned into the distance. A few meagre rays of sun hovered above the horizon. Any second they'd be gone. 'Don't stay out all night. She won't kiss you if you're dying of pneumonia.'

Tom searched until eleven, when fatigue and misery finally conquered his body. Rather than swap back to his car, he drove his dad's ute home. A quick shower to wash the mud and cold off, and he collapsed into bed, only to wake at dawn and start the search all over again.

By Tuesday he gave in to hopelessness and headed into Levenham to buy a new phone, keeping his eyes peeled for Amy on the off-chance she wasn't at work. New phone in hand, he sat in his car, downloaded Cupid Country and set up a new profile, snapping a photo of himself looking unshaven and slightly manic.

As soon as he was in, he selected Levenham and district and scrolled for Amy. Hope rising when her name appeared, then plummeting when he saw a red circle with a line through it covering her avatar.

He tried to message anyway and was instantly rejected.

Tom ground his forehead against the steering wheel. Could nothing go in his favour? Amy had set her profile to unavailable, effectively taking herself out of the dating pool and allowing only pre-approved profiles to contact her. And new Tom wasn't on the list.

With a groan, he sat back and tried to think of a way out of the disaster he'd created. Continuing the search for his old phone would be a waste of time. He'd covered as much ground as he could, and the reality was that it was probably sunk deep in mud. Even if there was mobile coverage, which Tom knew from experience would be a miracle, the waterlogged soil would likely muffle any ring. All he could do was hope she took her profile off private, or he somehow physically found her.

What did he know about Amy Smythe? She worked with children, but where? His best guess was that she was a teacher. Though she hadn't admitted to it, a few comments had Tom believing that was the most likely case. He could try the schools. Ask at the front desks, maybe check out the gates at leaving time.

He knew she played squash. He'd try the courts. Ask a few people. There was only one squash centre in town. Someone was bound to know Amy Smythe, and even if they weren't keen on giving out a contact number, they'd surely let him leave a note.

'Yeah,' he said, starting the car, suddenly set with purpose. That was the way.

For the first time since Sunday night, true hope rose again.

Tom would find her. All he had to do was ask.

Chapter Six

Amber stared at the calendar on her fridge door and clenched her fists against the urge to rip it down and stomp all over it. Venting her anger might make her feel momentarily better, but it wouldn't change the date.

It would still be Friday. Five days since she last heard from Tom. The day he was meant to show off his romantic moves. Instead, he'd ghosted her.

Ghosted. Of all the low and cowardly acts ...

She slapped her hand against the calendar and pressed her forehead against the fridge and let out a long sigh. Then she stood back, opened the door and retrieved a half-finished bottle of pinot grigio from inside.

Drinking wouldn't help either, but after the week she'd had Amber had earned it.

She took her glass into the lounge, settled on the couch and flicked through the TV guide to see what movies were on offer. A murder mystery would be good, or a thriller. Absolutely not a rom-com. She'd only end up throwing her glass at the screen.

An adaptation of Agatha Christie's *And Then There Were None* was showing at seven-thirty. She had an hour to kill.

Another hour of trying not to think of Tom and where she'd gone wrong. What she'd done to deserve this kind of treatment.

She'd replied to his messages when she returned home from her friend Niamh's. There'd been little instruction during their lesson. Niamh was too busy quizzing her about her night with Tom to remind Amber to keep her wrists and back straight and her fingers curled, and Amber was on too much of a high to pay attention to the correct playing position anyway.

Niamh had thought Tom sounded wonderful. At that point, Amber still considered him wonderful, too, and was squirmy with excitement over her luck. Then he hadn't replied to her comment about how cute Elf and Roxy looked perched behind him, or her cheeky quip about his doggy style. Or her later messages on Sunday evening, asking how he was.

She'd thought it odd and out of character. Admittedly, she'd known him only an afternoon and night, but it had been obvious from that first meeting that Tom was well-mannered, kind and considerate. Not a man to ghost anyone. The idea seemed so foreign it never crossed her mind.

When Monday passed with still no reply to her messages, Amber fretted he might have had an accident, but there was nothing on the news and no staffroom gossip. Desperation had her calling a squash-playing friend who worked at the hospital to see if Tom might have been brought in. Again, there was nothing.

Tuesday passed with still no contact. Wednesday

agonisingly the same. Amber progressed from worry to despair, tinged with annoyance at what she'd done wrong. Yes, she'd skipped out of the motel without saying goodbye, but she'd left a note, and when they'd messaged Sunday morning, Tom had been fine. He'd sounded as excited about meeting again as her. More so.

That had led Amber to fretting that putting him off until Friday night might have signalled a lack of eagerness. A ridiculous idea. Tom knew she was keen. How could he not? She'd practically promised him another sexfest with her *I want you all baaaaaaad* comment. And she'd set her profile to unavailable, indicating she was taken.

Then last night she'd seen his second profile.

The man she'd made love with, who she'd kissed and snuggled with and shared laughs and teases, who'd promised that this was only the beginning, had not only ghosted her, he'd also gone trawling for someone new.

Disgusted in Tom and the whole horrible dating game, Amber had deleted her profile from Cupid Country and declared herself done.

A symbol of her anger and hurt feelings.

Except as Amber stared at her television and cradled her glass of wine, she realised symbols weren't warm and funny and kind and generous. They were lonely.

Headlights caught her curtains. With a frown, Amber set down her wine. She wasn't expecting anyone tonight. Although, living in a dead-end street, sometimes visitors used her driveway to turn around.

The lights kept coming, then went out. A car door opened and slammed, followed by another door a few moments later.

She rose and went to the window, but her visitor had

skipped to the porch and was out of sight. It didn't matter. Amber recognised the car.

Loud knocks sounded, followed by a shouted 'Hurry up, it's freezing!'

Amber unlocked the door. 'What are you doing here?'

'I,' said Niamh, holding up two eco bags, one of which rattled loudly, 'am on a rescue mission.'

'I don't need rescuing,' said Amber, unlocking the screen door and letting her friend inside.

'Don't lie, you do.' Niamh eyed the lounge where Amber had been cuddling up with her plush blanket and glass of wine with meaning. 'I thought as much.'

'What?'

'Wallowing. We do not wallow over men, Miss Dunn. We celebrate our womandom.'

'Is womandom a word?'

'It is now. I have declared it so.'

Niamh headed for the kitchen, Amber following behind, feeling sloppy against her friend's petite glamour. Amber tried to dress well, but even at her most casual Niamh looked exquisite. Tonight, she'd matched black-heeled boots and skinny jeans with a blue silk top that tied at the waist. The jeans and boots complemented her perfectly straight, bluntly cut bob and equally precise fringe. The shirt turning her clever blue eyes even bluer and her skin even more porcelain.

Amber had never known anyone so consistently immaculately dressed. Niamh even wore sexy little navy power suits and heels to work. Rumour had it, half the staff of Levenham High, where she taught maths and physics, had a crush on her. God knows what effect she had on her teenage students.

Niamh hoisted her bags of goodies onto the bench and

began to unload. 'Pretzels,' she said, rattling the packet. 'Cracker biscuits. Dips. A mini cheese platter. Prosciutto. And ...' A colourful box appeared, condensation beading its surface. 'A six-pack of honeycomb crunch Magnums.'

Amber attempted to snatch it, but Niamh thrust the box ceilingward, stretching her tiny frame onto tiptoe to keep it out of reach. Honeycomb crunch Magnums were the best ice cream ever.

'Uh uh. These are for later.' Niamh narrowed her eyes. 'If you behave.'

Amber pouted. She could really go a Magnum right now.

'Am I not good to you?' asked Niamh as she stuffed the ice creams in the freezer.

'You are marvellous.'

'That I am. Now ...' She began digging in the clunky bag. 'We have chardonnay.' A bottle went on the bench. 'Cab sav.' Another bottle plonked alongside it. 'A-a-a-and,' Niamh extracted the next bottle with a flourish, 'Baileys for a post-dessert drink.'

'How much did you spend?'

'Not much.' Which was patently untrue. The bottle of Baileys Irish Cream liqueur alone would have cost nearly forty dollars. 'It doesn't matter. This was clearly an emergency.'

'Come here,' said Amber, waggling her hand at her friend, her eyes stinging.

Niamh obliged and Amber indulged in a long hug, punctuated by sniffles.

'What would I do without you?'

'Wallow in misery and probably reinstall that app and send that awful Tom Jones a whiny *what have I done?* message.'

'I would not.'

Niamh regarded Amber down her nose.

'I wouldn't have.' Amber waved at her. 'Stop it.'

Niamh finally relented with her schoolmarm look and reached for a cupboard. Minutes later, the food was artfully set on plates or in bowls and they were carrying them into the lounge, which Niamh promptly rearranged so they were sitting on the floor surrounded by blankets and cushions.

It was a fun night. They swapped gossip and school stories, Amber laughing over Niamh's ongoing battle to get her male students—and more than a few of the females—to take physics seriously and not spend every lesson ogling her breasts and bum. Amber was grateful her little students were too young for that. The most she had to put up with was a leg cling and the occasional toilet trauma.

'What did I do wrong, Niamh?' asked Amber, taking another sip of the Baileys on ice Niamh had prepared earlier. She was leaned against the couch, legs spread out in front and covered with a blanket, warm and full of wine, cheese, carbohydrates, and chocolate. Niamh was skilled at distraction, and they'd mostly avoided the subject of Tom, but now Amber wanted to talk.

'Nothing. You did nothing. It was him.'

'Was it?' She shook her head and stared at the television. They'd flipped it to the country music channel where Keith Urban was doing his country rock god thing. If Amber twisted her head to the side and squinted, Keith looked a little like Tom, albeit with long hair. 'He seemed so nice. So *normal*. And he was keen, Niamh. Really keen.'

Niamh straightened from where she'd been lying on her side and joined Amber against the couch. 'You need to stop this. He was the one who put up a new profile, not you.'

'I know, but what if there was another reason for it?'

'Like what?'

Amber couldn't answer. Niamh was right. The only explanation was that he was hunting for another sucker to love and leave. She sighed. 'I hate men.'

'No, you don't. You only hate one of them right now.' Niamh paused. 'And dirty Dave. Mustn't forget his cheating arse.'

Amber flopped her head to the side. 'You said arse.'

Niamh giggled. 'I know. Must be the Baileys.'

'And chardonnay.'

'And cab sav.'

Amber waggled her glass. 'Not the Baileys.'

'No, definitely not the Baileys.'

They broke into laughter.

'You'll recover,' said Niamh, patting her arm.

'Yes,' said Amber, watching Keith Urban. Although from the ache in her chest, recovery would be a long time coming.

Winter dragged on and, despite Niamh's best efforts, the hollow, aching place inside Amber refused to heal. Each time she spotted a ute like Tom's or a man of similar build or hair colour, she stumbled. Not for long, but enough to know that dismissing Tom and her one-night stand as a meaningless and stupid mistake wasn't cutting it.

It had meant something and though she'd buried the should-have-beens and could-have-beens deep, they weren't silent.

Fortunately, there were plenty of school activities to keep her mind busy and she had her Sunday morning piano lessons with Niamh, along with drinks and dinners with friends, and a few trips to Gumeracha to see her family. And she made Mr Giannopoulos's year when she asked him for advice on how to establish a modest vegetable garden.

It wasn't until winter passed into spring that Amber began to feel normal again. Her garden beds, so painstakingly prepared over the last month under Mr Giannopoulos's direction, were filled with herb and vegetable seedlings. Their eager growth made her smile. They were like little green pets reaching their limbs to the sky, hungry for sun.

Amber felt the same. Hungry for sun and fun and ready to shake off the lingering self-doubt that had clung fog-like to her through all those post-Tom weeks.

Ready to try another relationship, Amber mentioned to Niamh that she might give Cupid Country another spin. The idea garnered laughter followed by a serious and emphatic no.

'You won't be able to help yourself. You'll see Tom and next thing you'll be messaging him.'

'I wouldn't.' But Amber knew she would and so she left Cupid Country alone.

While her could-have-been and should-have-been doubts continued to whisper inside, even though an answer would never come.

Chapter Seven

Friday night. Amber breathed in the air of weekend freedom with glee and hurried to her car before yet another colleague or, worse, a parent accosted her. A quick trip to the supermarket for supplies and she'd soon be sinking into a bath with a glass of wine and soaking away the grime of another long week.

The spring weather was glorious. Levenham was still cool at night, but the days were bright and filled with promise, the air scented with bursting life and fresh growth. The world shimmered with hope, something Amber had lost for a while and was joyous to have back.

It seemed like half the town had the same idea as Amber. The supermarket car park was busy with cars backing in and out, and bustling shoppers trying to manoeuvre wonky trolleys or hurrying with shopping bags. Amber couldn't be bothered jockeying for a park close in and shot for an easy park at the rear. Besides, the extra walk would do her good.

With a cooler bag and an eco bag in her hands, Amber headed for the supermarket, digging out her list from her skirt pocket as she went. There wasn't much on it—honey-comb crunch Magnums, detergent and tissues, and some-thing easy for dinner.

Navigating the aisles took longer than she'd hoped, and she'd already been running late. That was the trouble with being a teacher. Every parent wanted a piece of you, even when you were off duty. Experience had made Amber adept at polite rebuffs, but there was always one parent who felt you owed them your time, even in the supermarket. This afternoon it was Sarina Metcalfe wanting to discuss her daughter Elyssa, who was, in Amber's opinion, well on her way to becoming a little bully but was clearly an angel in Sarina's eyes. Amber donned her best understanding smile and agreed that these were indeed serious topics that warranted proper discussion during school hours, and she should make an appointment with the principal. Besides, her ice creams were melting.

With only a few items, Amber used the self-service checkouts and headed for the exit, glad for the chore to be over so her weekend could truly begin. A glance left showed more people streaming in.

And had her locking gazes with Tom Jones.

His eyes widened and immediately he began pushing towards her. Heart pumping crazily, Amber put her head down and hurried for the doors.

She dodged around shoppers, angling for the quickest route to her car, barely looking up in case someone waylaid her.

'Amy!'

He was gaining, using those long legs to advantage.

Amber ducked in front of a slow-moving car and was jolted by an angry honk and a gesturing old man. Resisting the urge to signal her own displeasure, she rushed on, dodging trolleys, kids, harried parents and even a dog, all while cursing herself for parking so far away.

She'd known this day would happen. With them both living in the district, it was inevitable. Amber had been sure she was prepared for it. That she'd be hardened enough to face Tom with polite indifference when the time came. Except, one look into those eyes and her heart had squeezed, and all the hurt came avalanching back.

'Amy!'

He was running. Footsteps slapping the asphalt. Any second and he'd be on her.

Amber pointed her keys at the car, thumb hard on the boot button. The quicker she dumped her shopping, the quicker she could get out of here.

The footsteps behind her slowed. 'Amy, please. Talk to me.'

She laughed, the sound bitter, like she felt inside. Talk to him? As if. She strode the last few paces, plonked down the bags, and pushed the boot button to close it, still ignoring Tom.

Trying to hold on to her emotions. Trying not to spill all her festering hurt and anger.

'I'm sorry.'

Amber's control broke. She whirled, hands fisted. 'You're sorry? You ghosted me!'

'Not on purpose.' He was standing a metre away, his arms held slightly away from his sides, his palms open, and a desperate expression on his handsome face. 'I lost my phone on the farm.'

She sounded a *pfft* and cocked one hip with her arms crossed, a "pull the other one" expression on her face.

'It's the truth. That Sunday after I messaged you, I had a few chores to do. We had a bogged heifer who needed digging out.' He closed his eyes for a moment and gave a frustrated huff. 'Look, the how doesn't matter. What matters is that with my phone gone I had no way of contacting you. I didn't have your number, only the Cupid Country message set-up.'

Amber's tightly folded arms relaxed a little. 'You could have logged in from a new phone.'

'I would have.' He smiled crookedly. 'If I could have remembered my password or not deleted my recovery email.'

A car beeped, startling them both. Tom waved an apology and stepped out of the way, closer to Amber.

She couldn't help admiring him. Tall and lean in worn jeans and boots, and a faded brown work shirt that matched his eyes. His farm gear, she guessed. That she knew how delicious he was beneath his clothes only made her longing worse.

Amber didn't want to long for him. She wanted to stay angry. How could she, though, when he sounded so sincere and looked so remorseful? And that crooked smile was making her insides do somersaults.

'I thought if I created a new profile, it'd be just a matter of messaging you. Except when I got back in, I couldn't because you'd put yours on unavailable.' His mouth twisted even further. 'I kept hoping you'd see it and contact me. Instead, you disappeared.'

'I did see it.'

'But you didn't read it.'

'Why would I have? It wasn't like I was going to go there again, was it? Not when it looked like you were trawling for someone else barely days after we had sex.'

He raked a hand through his hair. 'I guess it never occurred to me you'd see it that way. That's not something

I'd ever do, but I suppose we didn't know each other very well.' He dropped his hand, his body slumping. Amber wanted to hold him. 'I wish you'd read the new profile.'

'Why?'

'I left a message on it for you. Doesn't matter now.'

But it did. It mattered a lot.

'Tell me what it said.'

He stared at her. 'Tom Jones. Age twenty-seven, likes dogs and football, lives Levenham and districts. Fell in love with a girl called Amy and desperate to get her back.'

A hot itch formed behind Amber's eyes. *Fell in love?*

His gaze stayed locked on hers. 'I looked for you everywhere. I asked at the squash courts, but no one had heard of you. You said you worked with children, so I tried at the schools and childcare centres. I even waited out the front of a couple, thinking I might see you, but people kept looking at me like I was a paedophile and I had to quit. I got Eden to ask her regular bus passengers if they knew of anyone fitting your description.' His voice roughened. 'I tried so hard, Amy. That night with you was the best of my life. When I couldn't find you ...' He blinked and looked aside, mouth grim.

Amber went to step towards him but stopped when a four-wheel drive swung into the park alongside her car. A woman alighted. Immediately, she waved. 'Amber, hi. Nice to see you.'

Amber's skin heated and prickled as Tom's stare honed on her like a laser.

She swallowed against the sudden dryness in her throat. 'Hi, Mel. How are you?'

'Oh, you know. Flat out playing taxi to the tribe.' She opened the rear door. 'Look, Jamie, it's Miss Dunn.'

Tom's stare needled harder.

Amber wanted to close her eyes and retreat to the safety of her car, but Jamie had been in her class last year and was a sweet kid. 'Hi, Jamie. How are you enjoying your new school?'

'Good.'

Mel went to speak further, then glanced at Tom and back to Amber. Fortunately, she was a parent who knew when to butt out. 'Can't chat, sorry. I promised this one fish fingers for dinner and you know what kids are like when you don't deliver. Good to see you, though, Amber. Take care.' Grabbing Jamie's hand, she smiled at Amber and Tom and walked off.

For a long moment, Tom said nothing. 'Your name isn't Amy.'

'No. It's Amber. Amber Dunn.'

He nodded. 'I had no hope of finding you, did I?'

'No.'

They stared at each other, the mistakes that had broken both their hearts throbbing between them.

'I was going to tell you,' Amber said quietly. 'That Sunday night. I thought I was protecting myself and my career. You know, being careful like they tell women to be, but then ...'

'I never messaged.'

'No. At first I was terrified you'd had an accident. I couldn't believe you'd ghost me. Not after ...' Her throat made a dry click as she swallowed, her guilt a spiky thing. 'I even asked a nurse friend at the hospital if you'd been brought in.' She rubbed at her chest as the memory of her anguish woke and stirred. 'When I still didn't hear from you, I thought I must have done something wrong. That you were angry with me for leaving the motel without saying goodbye. Or that maybe you thought me putting you off until Friday meant I wasn't keen. But how was that possible when we'd talked only that morning? When we'd made plans. God, I was practically a sure thing for Friday night. Then I saw your new profile and ...' She sucked on her lip and looked at the sky. *What a mess.*

He stepped closer. 'Amy.' He made a low, growly sound. 'Amber. We both screwed up.'

She gave a sad laugh. 'We sure did.' Amber sniffed and quickly swiped her fingertips under her eyes. 'So stupid to be crying. That was months ago.'

'That doesn't stop it hurting.'

'No.' She sighed and glanced through the rear window of her hatchback. 'There go my ice creams.'

'I'll buy you some more.'

She shook her head. 'Thanks, but it's okay.'

Another four-wheel drive pulled into the parking space on her other side, the owner barely casting them a glance as they hurried to do their shopping. More cars passed behind Tom. The five o'clock rush had arrived.

Amber rubbed her arms, gaze still on the stream of cars. 'I guess I should be getting home.' Except she didn't want to leave him just yet, and she had things she needed to know. Things she wanted him to know. Amber dropped her hands and lifted her chin. 'Did you mean it? What you wrote in your profile.'

'That I fell in love with a girl called Amy? Yes.' Tom moved closer and smiled down at her, then slowly reached for her hands and held them loosely in his. 'I never believed in love at first sight until you. But it happened. One look and I was gone, and the rest of the night only made it worse. You were perfect, Amy.' Tom huffed a laugh. 'Sorry. *Amber*.' He sobered. 'I went crazy when I lost you.'

'I went a bit crazy, too.'

'Now we've found each other again.'

And neither seemed to know what to do.

He gave her hands a little shake. 'It hasn't changed. What I feel, I mean. I'm still mad for you.'

'Would you ...' Amber licked her lips. Was she ready for this? She stared into Tom's kind eyes. Love and anticipation glowed back. She'd taken a chance on him before; she could do it again. 'Would you like to help me eat melted ice cream?'

His grin was pure joy. 'I'd love to.'

'In the bath? I don't have a spa and it's a bit small, but ...' She shrugged. 'I'm sure we can make do.'

'Yeah.' He threw his head back and laughed. 'Yeah, I'm sure we'll make do just fine.'

Chapter Eight

'I think your football team is playing tonight,' said Amber, wrestling Tom's big toe with hers. 'Isn't it the preliminary final?'

They were in the too-small bath, Amber's back against his chest, bubbles tickling their legs and waists.

'It is.' Tom nuzzled her neck and wrapped her closer. 'They'll survive without me.'

'I don't know how I did.' She rubbed her cheek against his hair, feeling like a cat. Any moment she'd start arching like one. The evening was just too delicious. 'Survive without you, I mean.'

He scooped up some water and trickled it over her breasts. 'You were running on anger.'

Amber supposed she was. And hurt. That was over now. The moment Tom had carried her bags inside and helped her save her ice cream by opening each individual packet and tipping the soggy mix into a container for freezing, she'd known it. There was no way he could have ghosted her. A man like him wasn't capable of that kind of meanness.

This was a man unafraid to tell the world of his feelings if it meant a chance to get his love back.

'Thanks,' she'd said, when she finished wiping the bench and hung the cloth over the tap to dry.

'You're welcome, Am ... ber.' Tom had grimaced. 'Sorry. I'll get used to it.'

'I hope so.'

They'd stared at each other for all of three seconds, then Amber was rushing around the island bench to crush against him. His kisses were like coming home. Loaded with joy and relief, and all the passion that had been lost to their mistakes.

They'd laughed as clothes went flinging off in all directions. None of the curtains were drawn and Amber had been vaguely aware that at any moment Mr Giannopoulos could pass one of his own windows, glance over and discover his wholesome schoolteacher neighbour acting not very wholesomely at all. Too bad. Decorum could go jump. Amber wasn't stopping for anyone.

By the time they'd reached her bedroom, Amber was topless, Tom's shirt and work trousers were undone, and they were panting like marathon runners.

He'd smelled deliciously manly and rural and Amber couldn't get enough. She'd backed him up to the edge of the bed. At her urging, Tom had sat, then fallen back. Skirt rucked up around her hips, Amber had followed on her knees until she'd straddled his groin. She'd explored his chest muscles, while his bulging hard-on pressed deliciously against the silky fabric of her underpants.

Tom had run his hands up her thighs and over her hips to her waist, progressing tantalisingly upwards until his fingers brushed her nipples. They'd teased for a heartbeat before disappearing to unhook her bra and tossing it aside.

He'd stared at her boobs with a dopey expression. 'Even better than I remember.'

'So are you,' Amber had said, leaning down to kiss him, which only resulted in her being flipped onto her back.

He'd gazed at her wickedly, the sparkle making her heart *whump-whump* and heat pool down low. He'd touched her cheek, his expression softening. 'I can't believe I found you again.'

'I'm glad you did. But can we save that bit? I'm not fully naked. I need fully naked, Tom Jones.' She'd paused and frowned. 'That is your real name, isn't it? Jones?'

'It is. Tom Winston Jones.'

'Winston?'

'Old family name.'

Amber had run it through her head. *Tom Winston Jones*. It suited him perfectly. 'I like it.'

'I like you.' He'd sucked on her earlobe.

Amber's eyes had crossed as an electric current jolted down her spine and straight into her pants. 'Naked, remember?'

Which is how they ended up in the bath, washing off their excesses and playing touchy-feely games with the soap bubbles and each other.

'I'm getting wrinkly,' said Amber, lifting her hand from the water and inspecting it.

'That's okay, I'll still love you.'

She wriggled so she could see his face better. 'You really mean it, don't you?'

'I do. Love at first sight.' He laughed at her incredulity. 'Amber, you're gorgeous. You're clever and funny and cute and you like dogs and football. You even wanted to go to a motel on our first date. I was mesmerised.' He shrugged. 'Still am.'

'I was too.' She stroked a finger down the side of his chest, delighting in its firmness. Delighting in him. She sighed, long and dreamily. If she wasn't feeling so languid from sex and the warm bath, she would have smacked herself for sounding like a lovesick teenager. 'I thought you were the loveliest man I'd ever met.'

His nose screwed up. 'Lovely? Not sexiest, most manly, best looking?'

She gave him a gentle punch. Silly, funny man. 'You were all those, too. But you were nice. Thoughtful and kind and sweet. You even ordered champagne.'

'Nah, that was just a seduction technique. My mate Linc swears by it.'

This time, her punch was harder, and he made an *oof* sound. 'Like you needed it.'

'I didn't, did I?' He used both hands to scrape her hair away from her face, his expression turning dopey again. 'How lucky am I?'

'We're both lucky.'

Their kiss could have melted an iceberg. Certainly it—and the other adventures they enjoyed—lasted until the water went cold.

Finally, Amber dragged herself out and let Tom dry her off. Thoroughly. Very thoroughly, which had them both grinning stupidly and rushing to bed.

It wasn't until much later that they ventured back into the kitchen. Amber dished up bowls of honeycomb crunch Magnum mix, which they carried into the lounge room. She turned the television on to check the football score, only to be greeted with a different scene.

Their gazes met.

'Was that on purpose?' asked Tom.

'Nope. Pure serendipity.'

Their eyes swivelled back to the television. Chris Hemsworth, glorious in his Thor outfit, was kissing Natalie Portman's hand. Amber couldn't help her soppy sigh. Although, this time, it was for a different reason. This time she'd found her own hero, and he was just as perfect. Even more so.

Her hero was real.

'Meant to be,' said Tom.

'Yes,' replied Amber. 'Definitely meant to be.'

Eager to find out if complete opposites Niamh and Olly have a chance at love? Check out the adorable *Cupid Country Challenge!*

CUPID
COUNTRY
BOOK TWO

Cupid
Country
CHALLENGE

CATHRYN HEIN

Cupid Country Challenge

Opposites attract in this charming small-town romance.

When Niamh O'Connor's best friend urges her to contact Olly Braithwaite on rural dating app Cupid Country, Niamh isn't keen. Niamh's a maths nerd perfectionist, while Olly's likely to be a hippie organic farmer who probably only bathes once a week, composts his own hair and eats too many lentils.

Except Olly turns out to be sweet, passionate about his geese and ducks, and weirdly hot. He's also far too tall and habitually late. Faults that would normally be deal breakers for punctual, petite Niamh.

Her head and heart have opposing ideas, and when Olly makes his feelings clear, Niamh can't resist. But Niamh's hang-ups are soul deep, and their differences seem insurmountable. One night of delicious passion won't change that.

Can Niamh get past her quirks and embrace love, or will she give in to her fears and forsake the sexy farmer?

Chapter One

Niamh O'Connor tried not to sigh as her friend Amber and Amber's boyfriend, Tom, made mushy eyes at each other over the pot of risotto they were taking turns at stirring.

She really didn't know why she'd agreed to come to dinner. Amber was a darling, but playing gooseberry to a completely loved-up couple was no fun for anyone. The newly reunited pair looked as though all they wanted to do was drag each other off to bed, and Niamh felt ... Jealous. Lonely. Annoyed.

Mostly jealous. But not in a mean way. It was impossible to think mean thoughts about Amber. The primary-school teacher was too nice.

Amber caught her gaze, read something there and addressed Tom. 'We should have invited Olly.'

Tom glanced at Niamh and back at Amber, a slight furrow between his brows as if chewing the idea over. He shrugged. 'Next time.'

'Olly's a sweetheart,' said Amber. 'You'll like him.'

No, Niamh was pretty sure she wouldn't like Olly.

From what she'd heard, Tom's housemate was a hippie organic poultry farmer. He probably only bathed once a week, composted his own hair and ate too many lentils.

No doubt he'd get her name wrong too, calling her 'Neem' or 'Nee-arm' instead of the correct pronunciation 'Neve'. Even thinking about it made her teeth buzz.

'He's on Cupid Country,' said Amber, clearly warming to this matchmaking idea. 'You could check him out.'

'I could.'

Tom laughed at Niamh's less-than-enthusiastic tone and pointed the spoon at her. 'But you won't. Your loss.'

Niamh doubted that very much.

Dinner was lovely. Amber and Tom managed to stop making calf's eyes and indulged in some adult conversation. They sipped good wine, ate tasty food, argued good-naturedly, laughed with gusto. Enjoyed each other the way people in love should.

Again, Niamh felt the sting of jealousy. Her romantic life had been non-existent for over a year, and it was starting to smart. Most of the time she didn't mind. Niamh certainly did not need a man to be happy. She had her teaching job at the local high school, her music, her family—though they were four hundred kilometres away—her books, her online chess games, and caring and fun friends. A good life. An *interesting* life. And she was thrilled that Amber had found Tom. The utter romanticism of their love-at-first-sight rela-tionship was not only gorgeous, it gave Niamh hope that one day she would find a good man, too.

She didn't necessarily want forever—although she wouldn't say no to finding her soulmate—but someone intel-ligent and kind to share things with? Dinner, conversation ... Sex. Oh yes, she could quite do with some sex.

Her belly full and her heart strangely hollow, Niamh

kissed Amber and Tom goodnight and headed home. Tomorrow was Monday and she had a big week ahead teaching recalcitrant teenagers physics, maths and a couple of fill-in classes on economics. A decent night's sleep was essential, but restlessness had her wandering her townhouse, looking for a distraction.

She sat at her electric piano and tinkled for a while, then stood in front of one of her many bookcases with her hands on her hips scanning the titles. Mostly non-fiction—arranged alphabetically, by author—and her small collection of high-fantasy novels on the bottom shelf. She shook her head and tried the kitchen. Except there was nothing that needed tidying. It was as pristine as it always was. Amber had once joked that Niamh must never cook. No one who did could have a kitchen that sparkling.

She wiped the bench anyway, using a paper towel to polish the stone surface until not a wipe mark or fingerprint remained. Still unsatisfied, Niamh stomped to the lounge where her phone lay on its wireless charger.

Hands on hips, she stared at it.

'No,' she said.

She stared some more. Walked away, turned on the television, turned it off. Walked back to the phone.

One look. How could that hurt?

She snatched up the phone and stabbed her finger at the Cupid Country icon, as though it was the root of her restlessness, and began to search.

It didn't take long to find Olly. Cupid Country was an app designed by a local computer entrepreneur specifically for rural people on the hunt for companionship and romance. It had been popular and successful, yet Niamh hadn't touched it in months. Not after the idiot who considered sending a photo of his mushroom-shaped penis as courtship. How Amber had found Tom among the dross was a miracle. But she *had* found him.

Maybe there was a chance for Niamh too?

She regarded Olly's profile pic and grimaced. Just as she'd expected. Shoulder-length light brown hair in need of a comb, a jaw that hadn't seen a razor for days, checked flannelette shirt with what appeared to be a knitted Afghan vest over the top, complete with hideous toggle buttons. Worse, he was holding a snowy white duck to his chest. A duck with vivid red warty things over its beak and around its eyes.

Seriously? So-called sweetheart Olly had thought it clever to pose with a diseased duck on a dating app? Was he insane?

Niamh threw the phone on the couch and slumped down next to it, her hands over her eyes. She dragged them down her face and steepled them under her chin and contemplated the blank screen of the television. What was she doing? It was after ten. She should be asleep, not playing romantic roulette.

As if magnetised, her gaze slid sideways. Olly was still on the screen, still holding his duck. Niamh felt her hand want to creep towards the phone. She ordered it to stay put, but Olly kept beaming out, daring her.

She sighed and picked up the phone and zoomed in on his face. She conceded it was a nice face. Brown eyes the colour of aged brandy, lips not too full or too thin, straight nose, smooth skin, and teeth nearly as white as his duck. A shaft of light crossed his features, as though he'd found a sunbeam and stood in its path, bringing out a sexy sparkle in his gaze.

He looked healthy. Happy. Maybe a little too fond of his duck.

She zoomed in further, this time checking the background. Though blurred, it was clearly some sort of shed. Full of more diseased ducks.

Surely ...

She opened her browser. Twenty-five minutes later Niamh emerged from her Google rabbit hole knowing far more than was necessary about white Muscovy ducks. What she had learned, to her relief, was that Olly's weren't diseased. The red caruncles around their faces were normal. Ugly, but normal.

She studied his face again. No matter how good-looking, there was no question they were incompatible. Niamh liked order, numbers, systems. *Cleanliness*. Olly farmed ducks. Ducks pooed everywhere. He probably smelt like them.

Except ...

Olly's eyes glimmered through the screen.

She checked the rest of his profile. Most of the fields had been left empty. Niamh couldn't blame him. She'd done the same when she'd set up her own profile, unwilling to reveal too much and leave herself open to scammers and catfishers. Olly was the same age as her—twenty-seven—and lived Levenham and districts, which she already knew. His *Likes ducks, loves geese* comment actually had her chuckling. At least he was honest.

He also liked music, but didn't specify what sort. Cheese toasties. Sunny days.

Under personal qualities he'd written *Chill*. That was it. Just *Chill*.

A shudder ran through her. She knew very well what chill meant, as a verb and a noun. Her students had told her often enough to chill and it set her teeth on edge.

Niamh did not do chill. Chill people were always late

and considered it funny when you got mad. Or, more irritatingly, simply grinned and told you to relax. Chill people left dishes in the sink. Overnight. Didn't make beds. Did what they wanted, without a care for how it might make them appear.

Niamh breathed in deeply. Then breathed in again. This would never work.

But Olly kept smiling that sparkly smile, and she was really warming to that duck. The quiet room reminded her how alone she was and how she might remain that way if she didn't sort herself out.

Besides, Amber and Tom had vouched for him. They wouldn't let her down.

Squaring her shoulders, Niamh started tapping.

Chapter Two

Olly Braithwaite was sprawled on his couch, ankles over one armrest, head on a cushion on the other, an open stubbie of beer on the floor near his dangling arm. On the television, Harry Potter, Hermione Granger and Ron Weasley were doing their utmost to save the hippogriff, Buckbeak, from destruction.

His phone was in his free hand, its screen lit with an article from *Australasian Poultry Magazine* about a couple who bred Light Sussex chickens and had created their own specialist, non-medicated, high-protein feed. It was designed for layers, not so much for meat producers like himself, but Olly thought it interesting all the same. Always something to learn in the poultry game.

He glanced up at the television to find Harry being attacked by Dementors. Olly always liked this bit, with Harry certain his father was going to save him, only to be forced to save himself. He snuggled down to watch and was just getting to the tense bit when his phoned pinged.

A little heart icon appeared at the top of his home screen.

'Bugger me,' he said.

Something from Cupid Country. That was a first. He'd been on the app for five months and scored exactly four messages, three of them from bots. The other was from a normal-sounding woman who, when they met at the Australian Arms Hotel, managed to prove she was anything but before she'd even finished her first drink.

Tom blamed the duck Olly was holding in his profile pic for Olly's lack of responses. That and the "likes ducks, loves geese" comment, but Olly figured he may as well be up-front about his passion. If any human bird he attracted didn't like his bird birds, then what was the point?

He opened the app. A message from someone called Niamh. Her profile picture showed a serious-faced, dark-haired girl with a severe bob and fringe. Not unattractive, but a bit scary with that blunt, perfectly aligned, sci-fi character hair. Who kept a fringe that straight?

Full disclosure: the message began, *Your housemate Tom and my friend Amber suggested I contact you. So, I have done so.*

Olly rolled until he sat upright with his bare feet on the floor. Tom and Amber, huh?

He picked up his beer and slugged a mouthful, eyes not leaving Niamh's photo. Though they shared a farmhouse on the property Olly owned with his mum, he and Tom had barely seen each other lately. Since Tom had found Amber, he'd been spending every spare minute in town with her. Not that Olly could blame him. Amber was a great girl and good fun, and she liked Olly's birds. She especially liked his small flock of Toulouse geese and that, in Olly's world, made her an excellent person.

And this Niamh was Amber's friend? That had possibilities. Maybe.

He expanded her image and wasn't reassured. The woman in front of him was too serious, too pristine, too strict looking. She may as well have *high maintenance* stamped across her picture in block letters. Not Olly's type at all. He switched to her profile, his mood sinking further as he read. Under "likes" she'd written numbers, piano, chess, squash. Punctuality. Hygiene.

A nerd then. And an anal one at that.

Not that Olly had anything against nerds. Smart people were his favourite kind, especially those with a curious bent, who were interested in discovering new things about the world. He didn't have time for hyper-focused types who didn't know how to relax and live life in the moment. Who liked things perfect. Nothing in life was perfect. Olly knew that better than anyone.

The thought had him glancing at the mantel and the photo of his dad he kept there. A brown-haired man in his forties, with deep crinkles around his eyes, grinned back. Olly's return smile was automatic. His dad always did that to him, as though even through a photo Mark Braithwaite could neutralise Olly's hurt with his easygoing goodness.

Olly returned to Niamh's message. *Full disclosure: Your housemate Tom and my friend Amber suggested I contact you. So, I have done so.* That was it.

He scratched the underside of his jaw, wondering how to respond. Wondering if he should even bother. What was the point when she of the android haircut and thing for numbers and punctuality was as far from his type as you could get? He slugged down some more beer and instead shot Tom a text.

What gives with this Niamh bird, and her name?

He set the phone down and watched the final scenes of *Harry Potter and the Prisoner of Azkaban* as he waited. Five minutes later, Tom still hadn't returned his message. Probably in bed with Amber, lucky bastard.

He couldn't leave Niamh hanging, though. That would be rude and for all Olly knew, Tom and Amber could have talked him up. The poor girl was probably at the other end all anxious, waiting for a response.

Olly considered for a moment, and began to type, only to be interrupted by a return message from Tom.

She's hot. Also mega smart. Her name's Irish. Said Neve, as in Steve.

Hot? Olly examined Niamh's photo again. Maybe she was, if you were into BDSM robots. Then again ... Her eyes were a pretty shade of blue, her mouth sweet, and Olly did like to keep an open mind.

Another message pinged in.

She's more than she looks.

What? he messaged back. *More than a robot princess?*

She's not a princess. Anyway, a princess might be just what a scruffhead like you needs.

Olly raked his fingers through said scruffhead. He raised premium quality, organic waterfowl on a farm. Most days he was knee-deep in shit, his funny, loyal geese dogging his movements. His fat ducks waddling and grubbing in their paddock. And if he wasn't in shit, he was hauling feed, tending hatchlings, loading stock for market, assessing breeders, or maintaining grazing paddocks. It was hard, dirty work and it made him happy as a pig in ... Well, as happy as his geese in their pond. Olly did not need a princess, and a princess absolutely did not need him.

Dare you! Another message quickly followed. *That was Amber, the phone thief.* Another pause, then, *I dare you, too.*

Olly laughed. They were good people, Tom and Amber, even when playing matchmakers.

But was it a challenge he needed to accept?

Whatever. If nothing else, it would fill the rest of his evening. What was left of it. The credits on *Harry Potter* were rolling down the screen. He checked the time and let out a breath. It was past Olly's bedtime and with Levenham Show starting Friday he was in for a busy week. A smart man would finish his beer and head to bed and deal with this tomorrow.

Except that would be mean and while Olly had his fair share of faults, meanness wasn't one of them. His geese would peck his butt to bits if he was.

He returned to the message he'd started composing, assessed the benign answer he'd begun and deleted it. Instead, he replied with *Do you like geese?*

That would test her.

Niamh's reply came back fast. *I don't know. I have never met one. But I did learn some interesting things about Muscovy ducks and their caruncles tonight.*

Olly half-choked. 'What the ...?'

He stared at her answer in astonishment. Caruncles? Since when did BDSM robot types know about caruncles?

What sort of things? he typed.

The message took a while to come back. *Many things! It's not necessarily just the fleshy bit over their nose. It includes their combs and wattles too. They're meant to attract females. The bigger and brighter and uglier the better. Isn't that fascinating?*

Yeah, it was. To Olly. But why the hell should it interest Niamh? Was she weird?

Yes, he returned, then slouched back, thrown.

Sorry appeared on his screen, followed quickly by, *When I saw your profile picture, I worried your duck had a disease and went googling.*

He smiled. Niamh might be odd and not his type, but she was inquisitive.

Healthy ducks have bright caruncles, he wrote. *I'm always checking mine.*

YOUR caruncles? Oh, dear. That's concerning.

Olly laughed out loud this time. The robot princess had a sense of humour. *Not mine. My flock's.*

Phew. You had me worried for a moment.

Still grinning, Olly nestled into the corner of his couch and dug his beer into the gap near his thigh to keep it from spilling. Bed would have to wait. Pointless the conversation may be, but he was enjoying this. *So ... You know I raise poultry, but what do you do?*

Teacher. High school. Maths, physics.

Which explained the "likes numbers" comment.

I like cheese toasties, too,' she added. *Especially with tomato soup. But only in winter.*

So did Olly. It was his go-to lunch on days when there was nothing else in the fridge. Warming, filling, fast to prepare and tasty. Although he was happy to indulge any time of year.

We're off to a good start then.

We are! To be honest, I'm surprised.

So am I.

We should meet.

Olly's eyebrows shot up. That was sudden.

Niamh must have read his mind because her next message was, *Too soon?*

Was it too soon? Olly glanced at his dad's photo again.

'Dead right,' he said to his dad as if in answer to a question. Life was too damn short not to take chances.

Besides, Tom and Amber figured it was a good idea, and he didn't think they'd lead him astray. And what did he have to lose? Not his heart. Niamh was attractive and funny, but they were clearly opposites. They might have some fun, though, and it'd been ages since he'd been on a date.

Sure, he typed, then, *Drink at the Arms?*

Sounds okay.

Olly gave his screen a "what the?" look. *Sounds okay?*

'Don't hold back your enthusiasm, Niamh,' he muttered.

He considered for a moment, then a slow smile curled his mouth. *Better idea,* he wrote. *The show's on this weekend. I'm exhibiting. Meet me there Saturday and I'll introduce you to a couple of my best birds.*

All the poultry judging was carried out on Friday. With a bit of luck, on Saturday he'd have at least one champion bird to puff his chest out about.

That sounds brilliant! What time?

They exchanged a few more messages to settle the details, and with every post Olly's heart began to beat a little faster.

It was stupid and getting ahead of himself, and Niamh still looked like a high-maintenance robot princess, but the hope this could be more kept fluttering.

A bird was coming to see his birds. A funny, attractive, smart bird.

Shooting his dad a thumbs up, Olly sauntered off to bed, feeling happier than he had in ages.

Chapter Three

Niamh studied the showground map, located the poultry and pigeon pavilion, and calculated the quickest route. A five-minute walk at best. It was ten to eleven now. Plenty of time, even factoring in the crowds.

From everywhere around her came the chatter of delighted children, locals catching up with old friends, show-bag and fast-food spruikers, and the occasional scream from a fairground ride. The perfect spring day had brought people out to Levenham's two-day annual show in force.

And so they should come. The show was a major regional event, enticing exhibitors from not only around the district but also from interstate, and celebrating all the agricultural and horticultural riches the land had to offer. Besides the usual sideshow alleys and rides, there were also pavilions for sheep, pigs, beef and dairy cattle, poultry and pigeons, plus multiple horses-in-action and dog arenas, and a petting zoo.

It also celebrated talent. The exhibition hall housed everything from a rabidly fought cake-decorating competition to photography, crafts, cookery, tech studies, honey production, flower arranging and other horticultural pursuits like vegetable growing and bonsai. The whole event was a showcase of skill and artistic flair.

Yet in the four years she'd lived in small-town Levenham—a service and tourist community in the far south-eastern corner of South Australia—Niamh had only visited once, and that had been a Friday school trip when she'd been too distracted by hormonal teenagers to take in the event's full glory. Levenham Show also usually fell on the same week as her mum's birthday. Never liking to miss a family milestone, Niamh preferred to spend the weekend in Adelaide. This year her parents were on a cruise, and she was free. Not that she didn't miss her family. But it was good to visit the show again, especially without school-children. The excited buzz of the crowd made her own anticipation resonate deeper.

She glanced at her watch again. Seven minutes.

Niamh adjusted her straw fedora and wove her way past the main hall to the poultry and pigeon pavilion. It wasn't long before the throng eased, and the air took on a distinctive tang.

Niamh wrinkled her nose. This wasn't the fatty smell of deep-fried chips, doughnuts, and other atrocities. This was pure animal poo, fresh and fragrant. And as she neared the pavilion, it intensified.

She paused for another time check. Three minutes to eleven. Perfect. She edged into the shade of a tree and scanned the low building in front of her. From her research, Niamh knew the poultry pavilion was long overdue for an upgrade—lacking proper ventilation, light and drainage—but funding was proving elusive. The conditions didn't seem to dissuade visitors. People streamed in and out of the dark entrance, the exiters blinking and occasionally stumbling into the bright sunshine. None appeared to be a light brown-haired, brandy-eyed man.

One minute to eleven. Niamh twisted her watch around her wrist. They'd arranged to meet at eleven a.m., and she'd checked her watch against the world clock that morning to confirm its accuracy. Surely, Olly should be outside waiting by now.

Niamh swallowed. He'd sounded keen when they'd messaged Sunday night, but even though Niamh always took care to make hers as clear and unequivocal as possible, she'd learned from experience how messages could be easily misinterpreted. And Amber had warned, when Niamh told her about their Cupid Country exchange, that Olly was a bit of a free spirit. Still. First date. A girl was entitled to some effort.

She'd certainly gone to effort for Olly. Coached by Amber to keep things casual instead of her usual tailored attire, Niamh had chosen a pair of stretchy white capris with matching white leather sneakers, and a navy silk blouse to highlight her eyes. She'd kept her accessories to a minimum—simple silver studs, a thin necklace with a diamond-studded N pendant, the silver Longines watch her parents had given her for her eighteenth birthday, a minimalist white cross-body phone handbag, and her trusty white fedora with contrasting navy band to protect her delicate, Irish-heritage skin.

Her hair was freshly washed and styled, her make-up light but carefully applied to enhance her eyes and lips and downplay her upturned nose. The result, she hoped, was attractive and approachable. A normal girl meeting up with a first date at her local agricultural show.

Or she would be if he was here.

Her watch showed fifteen seconds to eleven o'clock. It was time. Niamh kept her chin up as she crossed to the pavilion entrance. Olly could be waiting in the shade inside. Or perhaps he was having a duck emergency. Although what form that would take was beyond her. She'd spent a solid part of her week studying duck and geese breeds and their management, and while she was far from expert, she'd absorbed a great deal of information.

At precisely eleven o'clock Niamh parked herself to one side of the door, out of the flow of traffic, and tried to keep a pleasant expression as people who weren't Olly glanced her way and hurried on.

At one minute past, she dipped her head around the corner and peered inside. The concrete-floored room was dusty and gloomy and filled with rows and rows of cages. The nearer ones housed chickens. Noisy, smelly chickens. Every now and then, one would poke its head through its cage bars to take in the fuss and wobble its vivid combs and wattles before deciding the view was all too much and neatly ducking out of sight.

The noise was astonishing. Clucks and coos and the occasional cock-a-doodle-doo echoed off the floor and walls in a cacophony, worse than a schoolyard lunch break. Then there were the visitors, laughing at the range of strange and sometimes exotic breeds, and making clucking noises as if they'd suddenly learned to speak poultry.

And still no Olly in sight.

Niamh twisted her watch again and ran her tongue over her teeth. They were getting that funky feeling that always developed when someone was late, like the nerves inside were vibrating.

To soothe herself, she began to count cages. The first stand comprised two tiers, each row containing ten individual cages. It was impossible to see through the murk, but the rows seemed to go on forever. There had to be hundreds of birds inside. She rubbed her brow. Her fingers came away damp and slightly gritty.

Marvellous. Now her make-up was clogged. She'd have to apply a deep pore cleansing mask to get the grime out when she got home.

'Niamh?' said a voice.

Niamh whirled around. Behind her stood a stupidly tall, athletic man in a checked shirt, faded jeans and boots, his light brown hair knotted into a shaggy man bun, and a smile beaming across his face. In each hand he held a dagwood dog—a ridiculously phallic fairground snack of battered and deep-fried sausage—with its tip covered in tomato sauce.

'Yes?' she squeaked and hastily cleared her throat. 'Olly?'

'The one and only. I'd shake your hand, but ...' He held up the dagwood dogs. His wrists were bare. No watch. Ugh.

'You're late,' she snapped, then clamped her hand over her mouth. What was wrong with her? Niamh prided herself on her composure. Teaching teenagers demanded it. Yet she'd just snapped at her date like he was a recalcitrant thirteen-year-old instead of an adult.

Shock. It had to be shock. At no point had Amber mentioned his height and she should have. Olly had to be one hundred and ninety-five centimetres at least—six foot four in the old, imperial measure. Niamh barely reached one hundred and fifty. Forty-five centimetres, or a-foot-and-a-half difference. They'd look ridiculous together.

She'd be having words with her so-called friend and her equally culpable boyfriend when this was over.

Olly shrugged, unfazed by her rudeness. 'There was a

queue.' He thrust a dripping dagwood dog towards her like it was a bouquet of flowers instead of a heart attack on a stick. 'For you.'

Niamh shied away.

'Not your thing?' Olly gave another easy shrug and bit into the proffered snack, eyes assessing as he chewed, gaze lingering on her white shoes and trousers. She couldn't tell if his expression was appreciative or amused.

Niamh set her teeth. He'd better not be laughing at her. All her life people had mocked her petiteness. Though Niamh had learned to ignore the most patronising looks, ones coming from a potential lover were not on.

Not that sex with Olly was on her mind. Not at all. Nope. Nup. How would that even work?

Niamh forced herself to ease off the mental griping. This was not going well, but she was damned if she was going to waste a morning of primping by stomping off because her date was late, chewing a horrid snack and looking at her like she was an overpainted doll. Besides, she wanted to see his ducks.

'So,' she said as brightly as she could manage, gesturing towards the building. 'This is where you exhibit your waterfowl.'

Olly's eyebrows lifted. 'Waterfowl?' He used straight white teeth to drag the last bit of battered sausage off its stick.

Niamh's feigned cheer wobbled. Was her research wrong? She was sure that was the technical term for geese and ducks. 'That's right, isn't it? Ducks and geese are classified as waterfowl, instead of poultry?'

'Yeah, they are. I'm just surprised you knew.' He gave her another up and down and this time there was something else beyond amusement. 'You've been googling again.'

'A little.'

The tilt to his mouth revealed Olly knew it was more than a little. He held up the second dagwood dog. 'You sure you don't want this?'

'Positive.'

'Cool. Just let me finish this off and I'll take you to meet my birds.' He chomped the saucy top off the dog and relaxed his back against the pavilion wall, jaw working as he watched passers-by, saluted friends, and cast Niamh the occasional smile.

'Good day for it,' he said between bites.

'Yes.' Although what "it" meant Niamh wasn't sure. Poultry exhibiting? A date? The show? She tamped down her annoyance at his lack of clarity.

Olly continued to lounge and eat, clearly comfortable with proceedings. Didn't the man have any first-date nerves?

That's right. He was *Chill*. Ugh.

She stood alongside, unwilling to test the wall with her silk shirt and pristine capris. The dust already coating her sneakers was irritating enough. She refrained from extracting a tissue from her purse to give them a wipe-over. Instead, when Niamh thought his attention was elsewhere, she eyed Olly sideways.

Though unironed, his shirt at least looked clean and, unlike his profile photo, today he was shaven, exposing a strong, rather manly looking jaw. She leaned ever-so-slightly closer and breathed in. Olly smelled surprisingly of pine. And tomato sauce. Not a hint of poo. It was almost agreeable.

'Enjoying yourself?'

Niamh jerked back. 'Sorry,' she said, lifting a leg and scratching at her ankle as if that was the reason for her tilted body. The blush creeping up her neck belied her explanation, but she ploughed on anyway. 'I had an itch.'

Olly laughed, then scoffed the last of his dagwood dog. He pulled a napkin from his pocket, wiped his mouth and hands, and dumped his rubbish in a nearby bin. He returned and stood in front of her with his hands on his hips and a smile on face. 'Ready to meet my birds?'

'It's what I'm here for.'

'Funny, I thought we were here for each other.'

'I didn't mean—'

'Settle, petal. I know.'

Petal. *Petal?*

Niamh inflated like a bullfrog. She was no one's petal and this was clearly a waste of time. She squared her shoulders and adjusted her bag. 'Actually, I think I've changed my mind.'

Olly's smile turned upside down. Shoving his fists in his pockets, he looked at the ground, scuffed a boot then looked up. 'Yeah, you're probably right. We're not really suited, are we?'

'No. Tom and Amber had it wrong.'

He sighed and knuckled his head, loosening his man bun and causing bits of hair to stick out cutely. 'I kinda thought we still might have got on. Sunday night was funny.'

It was. But there was no avoiding the fundamentals. Olly was tall and broad, and Niamh was tiny. He was slack about time, and she was anal about punctuality. She was a born-and-bred city girl and he was as rural as they came, although after four years in Levenham her urban edges were beginning to blunt. He'd eaten two dagwood dogs without a blink and called her *petal*.

And, yet ...

Olly smelled nice and his jaw was firm and his eyes kind, and when he smiled he looked like he meant it with his heart. What had Niamh done? She'd turned that generous smile upside down with her nerves and defensiveness. She was also partly to blame for their less-than-ideal beginning, snapping at him for being late, when it was only a few minutes.

'Perhaps ...' she started, then bit her lip.

Olly's eyes lit up with hope. Niamh broke into a smile. Olly really was quite attractive when he looked at her like that, even if he did it a foot and a half above her head.

'Perhaps, seeing as we're both here, we could take a look at your birds anyway?'

Chapter Four

'We can do that.' Olly's entire face expanded into a grin at Niamh's change of heart. He had every reason to tell her to go jump, yet he seemed thrilled, and Niamh couldn't help the leap in her chest either. 'Yeah, let's do it.' He tipped his head towards the pavilion. 'Come on, you'll love them.'

Niamh wasn't sure about that, but Olly's excitement and pride were addictive.

'Have you ever been to a poultry show?' he asked as they stepped into the gloom.

Niamh had thought the smell drifting outside had been bad enough, but inside it was overwhelming. Yet none of the cages seemed dirty. In fact, they were all covered in a layer of clean pine shavings. It was warmer inside too, heated by bird and people bodies, and the late morning sun pounding on the pavilion's corrugated iron roof.

'No,' she answered, removing her hat and smoothing her hair in an effort to iron out any sweaty hat head.

'A new experience then.' Instead of leading her further inside, where she supposed the waterfowl were located, he led her towards the first cages. 'These are standard Welsum-mers. Handsome birds. Great for backyards. This one's a cock, which is why he's so big.'

Niamh eyed the self-important bird. He was indeed handsome, with glossy russet-red feathers on the chest, back and neck, and edging to brown-black with a hint of Christ-mas-beetle green at the legs and tail. A card had been tucked into the upper bars of his cage. She stood on tiptoe to read it. First prize, best male.

'What are they used for?'

'They're layers. Not bad at it either. Big brown eggs.'

They inspected the other Welsummer cocks and hens before moving on to the next breed.

'Australorps,' said Olly.

'Oh,' said Niamh bending to inspect a bird in one of the lower cages. 'They're the Australian-bred bird.' When Olly didn't reply, she straightened. 'What?'

'Nothing.' He shook his head, eyes twinkling. 'Nothing at all.' He indicated the cage in front of him. 'Not a bad multipurpose bird. Mum keeps a few as house chooks for eggs.'

He sauntered on, giving his opinion on each breed. Niamh occasionally interrupted with a question about the bird's quality and purpose, half-snorting at his disdain when they stopped at the hilarious looking Polish breeds, whose heads seemed comprised entirely of exploded feathers.

'Useless things,' was Olly's verdict, his lip curled. Which Niamh thought was mean.

'Pretty, though.'

The look he gave her had Niamh covering her mouth to hide her smile.

Niamh adored the Silkies—a chicken made to be cuddled if there ever was one—and couldn't stop giggling at the Australian Game Fowls. The cocks were like overgrown cartoon roadrunners; tall, leggy, and hugely muscular. She half expected them to go *beep beep*.

'Having fun?' Olly asked as they rounded the corner into the next row.

'I am.' She nodded, amazed to find it the truth. The birds were fascinating, and Olly's commentary was expert and interesting. 'I really am.' She cocked her head and studied him. He might have a chilled-out slacker's manner, but this was no unintelligent man. 'How do you know so much about chickens?'

He gave another of his nonchalant shrugs. 'We used to run broilers—commercial meat birds—when Dad was alive. He was a bit of a guru. I guess it rubbed off.'

'Your dad died?'

Olly nodded. 'When I was twelve.'

Niamh's heart clenched with sympathy. Twelve was such a formative age for a boy to lose his father. She wondered what the loss had done to Olly. 'I'm so sorry.'

'Thanks. He was a great dad. I miss him.' He nodded at the displays and Niamh could see he wanted to move on. 'You think I know a lot about chooks? Wait till you get me on waterfowl. I can bore for Australia.'

Niamh laughed and peered into a new cage, not so much registering the bird huddled inside but the warmth growing in her chest. The pavilion might be stuffy and noisy and smell of poultry, but it appeared their rough start was behind them.

They strolled more rows, inspecting birds, until Olly's pace suddenly picked up. He waited at the end of a stand, fingers drumming his thigh and brown eyes sparkling.

'Let me guess,' said Niamh. 'The next row is waterfowl.'

'Yep.'

The first cages held Indian runner ducks in a variety of colours. Olly had little to say about them apart from a grudging 'They're all right'. Niamh found them cute and was delighted when one poked its head through the bars and allowed her to stroke its cheek.

Campbells were next, followed by Mallards, Aylesburys and other breeds. Finally, they stopped at a series of cages housing attractive white ducks with bright caruncles and lightly tufted heads.

Niamh clapped her hands. 'Muscovies!' She scanned the cages and found one with a blue stencilled card. She stretched to read it and looked over her shoulder at Olly. Her voice was high with delight. 'You won.'

'Yeah. Best duck ...' He pointed to another cage. 'Best young drake.'

'But that's brilliant, Olly. Congratulations.' Niamh meant it, too. Based on the rows and rows of cages, competition had been fierce. She studied the ducks again. Up close, they were lovely. Bright eyed, pristine feathered, with vibrantly coloured faces and legs. Not a dirty mark to be seen. 'How do you get them so clean?'

'Wash them.'

'Seriously? You wash your ducks?'

'Yeah. It's normal showcraft. I give them a good tub with Sunlight soap and a toothbrush to get right under the leg scales, followed by a thorough rinse. Sometimes, if I think they need a bit more, I'll add a squirt of fabric brightener to the rinse.' He jutted a finger through the cage and gave his duck a caress. 'Got to be careful, don't you, darl?' He stroked a few times more and addressed Niamh. 'You can turn them blue if you get it wrong.'

Niamh's jaw dropped. 'Are you telling me you blue rinse your ducks?'

'Sometimes. Like I said, showcraft.'

She looked at the ducks and back at Olly. 'But how do you stop them from getting dirty again?'

'I put them in a cage on the back lawn and watch them like a hawk.'

Niamh was lost for words. She stared at Olly like he was an alien. Which he was, in his own, strangely appealing way.

He shoved his hands in his pockets, his voice defensive. 'It's just a poultry thing. Like rubbing olive oil or petroleum jelly on their legs and bills.'

'I had no idea.'

He shrugged. 'Not many do.'

'Can I ...' She swallowed and checked around then stepped a little closer, her voice loud enough only for Olly. 'Can I hold one?'

Olly glanced at the crowded pavilion and back at her. 'If we were at the farm I'd say yes. But if I let you cuddle one here then everyone will want a go. The ducks'll get stressed. It's enough that they're in this shitty shed with everyone poking at them.'

'Of course.' Niamh stamped on her disappointment. These were commercial breeding ducks, not pets. It stood to reason she shouldn't be allowed to hold one.

'If you come to the farm ...'

She glanced up at him. Was that an invitation? He had that hopeful glint again. Except she could hardly count "If you come to the farm" as a clear offer. Could she?

Before Niamh could think of a response, Olly was walking on.

'Come check out my geese,' he said over his shoulder. 'They're the best.'

'Likes ducks, loves geese,' she quoted from his profile.

'Yep.' He threw her one of his full-faced grins and halted in front of a large cage with a ribbon woven through the bottom of its bars. Inside, stood a magnificently haughty, long-necked, grey-and-white goose.

'Oh,' said Niamh, leaning close to admire him properly. 'He's beautiful!'

'He's a champion.' He patted the cage top. 'Aren't you, mate?'

'He won too?'

'Yep. Best gander.' Olly seemed to grow even taller. 'And overall champion waterfowl.'

'Oh, Olly, that's wonderful. Well done.' She bent to the gander again. 'And well done, you, Mr Goose.' She slanted a glance back at Olly. 'Do you name your geese?'

His reply came too slowly. 'No.'

'You do! You name your geese!' She poked him playfully in the belly. 'You big softie.'

'Yeah, well ...' Olly smiled sheepishly at his champion and then at Niamh. 'Can't help it sometimes.'

'What's this one's name?'

'Max.'

She bent again. 'Hello, Max, you beautiful boy. I bet you have lots of girlfriends at home.'

'Only one.'

'One? Really?' For some reason the idea made Niamh breathless.

'Yeah. They're amazingly loyal and can be picky buggers, but generally once they've made their choice they mate for life.'

'But that's ...' Why did she think that was romantic? They were geese, not people.

'What?'

Niamh shook her head and hoped the dull room was hiding the flush creeping up her neck. 'Nothing.'

Olly nudged her. 'And you call me a softie.'

Though they'd reached the end of the display, Olly seemed in no hurry to leave. He lounged near Max's cage smiling at his bird and the ribbon and certificate he'd won and pointing out the qualities that had made the gander a champion—the strong head, the well-set beak, long body and prominent breast, the full plumage. The list went on.

Niamh had thought she'd be bored by now, but Olly was too entertaining. In return, she asked about breeding and management, and was fascinated to hear how intelligent and full of personality the geese were. How his breeding gaggle liked to follow Olly around the farm like dogs. Niamh was so captivated, the pavilion's smell barely registered and the noise sounded natural and funny rather than cacophonous.

Finally, Olly straightened. 'I've bored you enough.'

'You haven't, actually.' She regarded Max affectionately. He was such a proud fellow, and she couldn't help thinking what a charming experience it must be to have a goose like him follow you around all day. 'It's been lovely.'

'Really?' Olly beamed at her. 'That's great. Really great.' He glanced towards the exit. 'Ready?'

Niamh took a breath. Bright sunshine and clean air awaited, yet her feet didn't want to move.

'Niamh?'

'Yes, of course.' With a blown kiss and a wave to Max and the others, she set her fedora on her head and joined the exodus.

The sunshine had her blinking despite the brim of her hat, but the light breeze was a delight against her skin. Niamh headed to the other side of the road and the tree she'd waited beneath earlier. Olly sauntered behind, his hands in his pockets.

'Well,' she said, when he was close enough. 'I guess we made up for our rocky start.'

'I guess we did.'

She dragged her front teeth over her lip. None of this changed their fundamental incompatibility though. He still towered a foot and a half over her. Was still a laid-back country boy. Still lacked a watch.

'Would you like to come for a drink? There's the cattleman's bar.' He gestured towards a farther pavilion. This time his smile was crooked. 'I could bore you some more with my waterfowl talk.'

'I think ...'

Why-oh-why was Niamh's heart telling her one thing and her head another? She rubbed her brow, wishing the confusion below would settle. Olly had proved himself the darling that Amber promised, yet surely they could only ever be a fling? Taking it further was putting off the inevitable. Neither of them needed the hurt.

She forced a smile. Niamh had always relied on her head. Hearts were fickle and rarely responded rationally.

'Thank you, Olly, but no.'

'Oh.' Again, the wonderful curl of his mouth flipped upside down. 'Right.'

Olly took a step back, his fists shoved even deeper in his pockets, radiating disappointment so badly Niamh almost blurted that she'd made a mistake. Except she hadn't. She really, truly hadn't. This was the right decision for them both. Absolutely. Yes. For sure.

For a moment he twisted lightly back and forth, as if half his body was trying to get the hell away and the other half was trying to stay. Then the beam was back, although at a lower wattage. 'Thanks for checking out my birds. That was ... cool. I guess we'll probably see each other again, because of Tom and Amber.'

'I'm sure we will.' She held out her hand. 'It was nice to meet you, Olly.'

'You too, Niamh.' He shook, his grip lasting a fraction longer than necessary and his sweet brown gaze soft. Then he released her, and with a final nod walked away.

Niamh watched him leave. She swallowed and regarded her dusty sneakers. They should have irritated her, but all she could think of was the nice time she'd had getting them dirty.

And how she'd never have that again.

Chapter Five

The cattleman's bar was a glorified shed that overlooked the main arena where much of the livestock and horses-in-action competitions took place. Olly bought a beer and carried it to one of the corrugated iron half walls that formed the bar's perimeter and rested it on the timber shelf on top.

Like the poultry and pigeon pavilion, the bar was overdue for an upgrade, but Olly liked its rustic feel and the breeze that swirled through the open sides, and this time of day it was quiet. Later, it'd be heaving with people celebrating the end of the show.

He stared despondently at the arena, lamenting his stupidity and the hours he now had left to kill until he could pack up his birds and go home.

God, he was an idiot.

He took a long slurp of beer, hoping his hunched demeanour would keep people away. Olly wasn't much of a brooder, but he sure felt in the mood for a good brood right now.

He and Niamh should be walking the grounds,

enjoying the sun and each other's company. Olly could have shown off and won her a soft toy on the clowns or at the shooting gallery. Maybe taken her hand on one of the scary rides. Shared a bucket of chips or a cloud of fairy floss together.

Or not. Given her reaction to the dagwood dogs, Niamh probably wasn't a fairground food kind of girl.

She *was* his kind of girl, though—pretty, smart, curious, good-humoured. And she'd warmed immediately to his birds. Maybe a bit anal. Even so, Olly couldn't believe his luck.

He sighed and drank some more. What a screw-up.

Olly knew exactly where he'd gone wrong. It wasn't the rocky beginning, where she'd wanted to turn tail before they'd even begun, though it probably hadn't helped. It was him. Olly and his overexcited reaction to Niamh's attention and enthusiasm.

Not once had he asked about her. Not once. It was all birds, birds, birds. And yeah, she'd seemed happy, and entertained and interested, and said she was enjoying herself, but clearly Olly's selfish stupidity had killed his chances. He'd acted like Niamh didn't matter to him. And she did. A lot.

Amazing how such a tiny person could have such a major impact in such a short time.

He dragged a palm down his face. In the showjumping arena, a dark bay horse was galloping around a shortened course, its slim rider hunched low. Olly focused closer, sure that the rider was Tom's horse-mad younger sister Eden, riding in a jump-off—the final round of a competition where the number of fences were reduced, and the fastest and cleanest combination won the day.

He mentally cheered her on. Eden was, like Tom, a

good egg. Olly had once asked Tom how he'd feel if Olly asked her out. Tom had shrugged and said Olly could try but Eden was hung up on some older bloke and it would probably be a waste of time.

Story of his life.

Though he only had a mouthful of beer left, Olly lingered to watch the rest of Eden's round. The horse cleared the final fence at an angle then horse and rider both stretched out as they tore through the finish flags.

Eden pulled up, laughing and patting her horse's neck. Then she paused by the horse and rider about to enter the ring and leaned across to speak. The male rider shook his head and rode on, but Olly could see he was smiling. At least someone was.

He sighed, downed the last of his beer, and wandered off to tour the main hall. His gran had won her section of the knitting competition and he'd yet to check it out. It'd give him something to feel cheerful about.

God knows after today's debacle he needed it.

'So,' asked Tom from the cottage entrance as he used the bootjack to tug off his boots. 'How'd it go?'

Olly eased himself upright from where he'd been stretched out on the couch, *Harry Potter and the Goblet of Fire* playing on the telly while he opened and closed the Cupid Country app on his phone and tried not to message Niamh. Hermione was dressed up for her date to the Yule Ball with Victor Krum. She looked good, too, pretty and glowing. Even as a boy, Olly'd had a thing for Hermione. Now, though they looked nothing alike, "the brightest witch of her age" reminded Olly uncomfortably of Niamh.

'Don't ask.'

Tom said nothing for a moment, then padded inside, slid his phone onto the coffee table, and slumped into the recliner next to the couch. He glanced at the telly, then at Olly, and pursed his lips.

Olly waited.

Still Tom remained silent, then he got up and headed for the kitchen, returning with two beers. He cracked both open, handed one to Olly and slumped back down again.

'Cheers,' he said, lifting the bottle and taking a long guzzle.

Olly frowned, lifted his own bottle, and drank. Not that he needed another beer. He'd already had two since he'd stomped in at eight o'clock after having settled his birds, checked on the others, and called in quickly at his mum's to see how she was and if she needed a hand with anything.

Still Tom kept quiet.

Olly caved. 'Don't you want to know?'

His housemate feigned innocence. 'You said not to ask.'

'Don't be a smart-arse. You probably already know what happened anyway.'

'Nope.'

Olly blinked. Really? He'd imagined Niamh would have given Amber an immediate debrief and Amber would have just as quickly passed on the details to Tom. It was the way girls, and relationships, worked. Or not.

'What are you doing home anyway?' It was Saturday night. Normally Tom would be with Amber.

'Amber's got some do on. Just you and me, buddy.' He held up his beer. 'You can drown your sorrows with me.'

'What sorrows have you got?'

'No Amber to play with.'

Olly rolled his eyes. 'You're pathetic.'

Which was pot calling kettle black after his performance today.

They both drank some more. On the television, Hermione was doing her nut at Ron. Fair enough, too.

'I screwed up,' said Olly, unable to keep his misery to himself. And Tom knew Niamh and might have some advice on what to do next.

Tom raised an eyebrow.

Olly sighed and knuckled his head. 'It started bad, went good for a while, then turned to shit.'

He went on to explain. The dagwood dogs, being late, telling Niamh to "settle, petal". Her decision to leave, then stay. The fun they'd had—or he thought they'd had. Olly not showing any interest in her. And finally, painfully, Niamh's refusal of a drink and subsequent farewell.

'You screwed up,' said Tom.

'Yeah, no shit, Sherlock.'

Tom eyed him as he drank. 'What are you going to do about it?'

Olly picked at his bottle label. 'Nothing. She's not interested.'

'Hmm.'

Olly looked up. 'What does that mean?'

'Not sure. She was interested, though, for a while?'

'I thought she was. Probably being polite.'

Tom snorted at that. 'Niamh wouldn't do anything she didn't want to out of politeness. She's straight down the line.'

'You think I should message her?'

Tom shrugged. 'What have you got to lose?'

Olly eyed his phone. Tom was right. He had nothing to

lose by messaging Niamh. The worst that could happen was that she didn't respond, or she told him where to go. At least he'd know exactly where he stood then.

'What should I say?'

'No idea.' Tom pushed out of his chair and started heading for the hall. '*Sorry for being a dick* might be a good start.'

Olly threw a stinky look his way, but Tom had already disappeared into the bathroom. He stared back at his phone and the Cupid Country icon, then looked up to his dad's photo.

'Yeah,' he said. Nothing was certain in this life. If a chance at happiness existed, he needed to take it and Olly's gut—more than his gut, his *heart*—was telling him Niamh was worth it.

He opened the app and began to type.

Thanks for today. You were great. I was an idiot. Olly paused and puffed out his cheeks. Should he explain? Nah. Niamh was a smart girl, she'd know.

He sent the message and took a long slug of beer. Hermione was on the screen helping Harry prepare for another Triwizard Tournament. Tom's out-of-tune singing in the shower drifted down the hall. Outside, the wind had come up, rattling the cottage's eaves.

His phone remained silent.

Olly set it face down on the couch and tried to concentrate on the television. The shower stopped, thankfully ending Tom's singing. Several minutes later he emerged wearing tracksuit pants and a T-shirt.

'Did you send it?' asked Tom as he padded to the kitchen on bare feet with his empty beer.

'Yeah. No answer yet.'

Tom grimaced and held up the beer. 'Another?'

Olly shook his head. 'Nah, I've had enough. I might go to bed.'

He left Tom to *Harry Potter* and, after brushing his teeth, settled into bed with his phone and the latest issue of the Waterfowl Association's newsletter.

He was reading a list of upcoming shows through drooping eyes when his phone pinged and the Cupid Country icon appeared at the top of his screen. Immediately, his eyes shot wide, and his heart began to thump.

Olly fumbled the app open. A message. From Niamh. He swallowed.

Why were you an idiot? she'd written.

There he was thinking she'd have figured it out. Maybe she hadn't thought he was.

I never asked anything about you. I just dribbled on about my birds the whole time. He breathed in and reminded himself again that he had nothing to lose. *And I'd like to know everything about you.*

Oh.

Olly blinked. *Oh?* That was it? Just ... *Oh?*

Another message appeared. *We're opposites.*

Opposites attract.

Maybe. But they don't last.

They can if they try.

Olly waited for a response, but nothing appeared. The screen began to fade. 'No,' he said, stabbing at it to keep it bright. He clutched it close to his face, willing her on. 'Come on, Niamh.'

Still nothing appeared. Had she gone or was she thinking?

Still there? he typed.

Yes.

Olly breathed out. He closed his eyes. How to make her see they were worth a chance? That *he* was worth a chance.

Then she messaged. *Okay. One more date.*

Olly punched the air. His fingers tumbled across the screen as he hurried to type his reply. *Awesome. When, where? Is tomorrow too soon?*

Settle, petal.

He laughed. 'Touché, Niamh,' he said aloud. 'Touché.'

Tuesday night, six-thirty pm at the squash courts.

Olly made a choked noise. She wanted to play squash? As a date?

You do play, don't you?

He avoided the question. *Squash courts, 6.30. You're on.*

Olly had never picked up a squash racket in his life. Football, cricket, basketball, yeah. Not squash. Not any racket sport.

How hard could it be, though?

Chapter Six

How hard could squash with Niamh be? Olly discovered the answer less than a minute into their first game.

Olly might be taller, with a longer reach, but Niamh's whippet body darted around him with astonishing speed. She had power, too. Smacking the little rubber squash ball with an intensity and skill he hadn't expected but came to admire once he'd recovered from the shock of her prowess and competitiveness.

She played sneaky as well. Dropping slow balls into corners while Olly was still at the back of the court trying to figure out where the damn thing had gone. Mixing up her serves so Olly was left backfooted. Keeping the ball both high and low, forcing him to stretch and half the time tripping over his own legs.

It didn't help that she was wearing a tiny, stretchy skirt with a knicker-high split up one side and a matching singlet that clung to her body like a second skin. Olly's concentration was shot from the moment she'd stripped off her zipped jacket, revealing not only a surprising set of muscled arms and shoulders but other exciting bits. Olly hadn't even struck a ball and he was panting.

The same couldn't be said for Niamh's reaction to him. Despite his best efforts, Olly had arrived five minutes late, dressed in the only gear he had suitable for squash—his old footy training kit, comprising a pair of running shorts over compression shorts and a tank top that was clean but may have seen better days—and wearing an excited grin. Other than a pointed glance at her watch and a slightly longer, and no more approving, appraisal of his legs, arms and chest, Niamh had said nothing.

Olly had done his best not to deflate. Instead, he'd offered up his most winning beam and followed it with a laconic *g'day* and *how's things?*

'Good. You?' had been Niamh's reply as she entered the building.

'Great. Really great.' How could they not be, looking at legs like hers?

'And Max and his friends? Have they settled after their ordeal in the poultry pavilion?'

'They're all happy.' Though Olly had wanted to say more, he'd learned his lesson. There was only one bird he wanted to talk about tonight and that was Niamh. 'How was your day?'

She'd cast him a bemused look over her shoulder. 'Not bad.' She'd then pointed to a court. 'This is ours. You can leave your gear out here, it'll be fine.'

Olly had dumped his gym bag on the bench she indicated and extracted a racket from it. Niamh eyed it first with a furrowed brow, then a sly smile Olly didn't understand. Then did.

Bloody Tom.

Not owning a racket himself, Olly had asked Tom if he had one he could borrow. Monday night his housemate had arrived home with a sparkly blue racket. Olly assumed Tom had collected it from his mum and dad's. Now he'd bet it was one of Amber's and Niamh knew. Which meant she'd probably also guessed he didn't have a clue how to play.

Things had gone downhill from there.

She'd started off gently in the warm-up, lobbing easy balls and revealing none of her skill. Olly had started to feel better. As he'd thought, squash was a matter of keeping his eye on the ball and giving it a whack when it came his way. Olly could belt it hard, no problem. Keeping it above the tin and below the out line was another matter. Then Niamh began to show some of her true ability and Olly knew he was in for a lesson.

It wasn't a lesson. It was a complete and utter thrashing.

'I needed that,' Niamh announced, when she'd flogged him eleven-nil yet again and was walking out of the court for her bag. They'd played five games, and Olly had only won a single point across all of them, and that had been a total fluke. Either that, or Niamh had fluffed her shot on purpose. 'Thanks.'

'You needed to flog the living daylights out of me?'

'You were late.' She wiped a towel over her forehead. Except for a few ends and a bit on her fringe that had darkened with sweat and stuck to her skin, her hair remained a neat bob. 'It made me cross.'

'It was five minutes.'

'That's five minutes I could have spent doing something productive.'

Olly regarded her like a bizarre creature—albeit a seriously sexy one, with great legs and luscious breasts—and opened his mouth to share some of his life wisdom. Then his focus dropped to a single bead of sweat about to slide between said breasts and he completely forgot what he was going to say. Something about life not being all about productivity. That happiness mattered. Whatever. That drop was going places. Nice places. Places he'd like to go too.

A towel swept over her neck and broke the moment.

Olly blinked, suddenly aware he'd been gawping like a teenager, and snatched up his bottle of water. He slid his gaze sideways to check on Niamh as he drank. She was wiping her arms, her mouth tipped in one corner and tiny crinkles around her eyes.

Amusement? Annoyance?

'Thanks again,' she said, folding the towel. When it was a perfect square, she tucked it into her bag and extracted her zippered jacket.

'Pleasure,' said Olly, meaning it. He might have had his butt whupped, but it had been worth every second. He was about to ask about going for drinks or a snack when she hoisted her bag on her shoulder.

Olly's stomach did a big slippery-slide fall. 'You're off?'

'Yes, I need a shower. I don't like being dirty and smelly.'

'You don't want to go for a bite or a drink? And you're not dirty or smelly. You're a normal healthy woman who's had a bit of a workout.'

Niamh sucked on her bottom lip. She stared at the exit, blue eyes wide with what Olly figured might be longing, then at the floor. She released her lip. It popped out swollen and sexy. Olly wanted to suck on it too. 'I don't know. I don't know what to do.' She faced him and flapped her arms. 'I *hate* not knowing what to do.'

'Come for a drink.' He smiled and shouldered his own bag. 'What's the worst that can happen?'

'I can make a mistake.'

'Mistakes are part of life. They help us grow.'

'I know.' She rubbed an eyebrow. 'I know.'

Olly waited. Other than telling her that *he* wasn't a mistake, he'd done all he could. It was up to her now.

Niamh dropped her hand. 'You sound like Amber, you know that?'

'That's not a bad thing. Amber's a good egg.'

'She is. The best.' She breathed in and slowly out. 'Okay.' Niamh nodded twice, as though she was saying yes to herself rather than Olly. 'Okay, we'll go for a drink.'

They went to the best pub in town, the Australian Arms. Niamh insisted on buying her own drink. Olly sighed and gave in. It wasn't worth arguing about.

She chose a glass of cabernet. Olly could have killed for a beer but in the spirit of compatibility, he chose cabernet too. Niamh slid him another of those bemused smiles when he stated his order. At least she noticed. He grinned back at her. Niamh rolled her eyes and shook her head, but he could tell she was laughing inside.

The thought made his stomach flutter.

They settled onto a couple of low stools in a nook near the back bar fire. It might be spring, but the night air was chilly, and both had bare legs and only thin sports jackets. Olly's knees ended up around his ears, but Niamh perched on her stool like royalty, legs together and tucked to one side. It took serious concentration to keep his gaze from her slim thighs.

It was a quiet night and, apart from Danny Burroughs

behind the bar, who Olly knew from football, only a few others nodded his way or cast curious looks. Good. The more private time he had with Niamh the better.

'How did you get to be so good at squash?' asked Olly, after they'd shared a toast.

'I practise a lot.'

Olly nodded. He had the feeling she faced any challenge the same.

'I like being good at whatever I do,' she said, eyes on the fire. 'It's a thing.' She didn't sound happy about it.

'How?'

'How is it a thing?' At Olly's nod, Niamh shrugged. 'I have a perfectionist personality. I like things to be just right.'

'What if they can't be?'

'I don't know. I get tense, I suppose.' She tucked her hair behind her ear, not meeting his gaze. 'You wouldn't understand.'

'I can try.'

She took a tiny sip of her wine.

Olly studied her profile. The small, cutely upturned nose, the tense fine jaw. Her pretty, perfectly formed shell-shaped ears. He hadn't noticed them before. Mostly her hair hung in that sleek android bob, covering them. The one facing him was so delicate Olly wanted to reach out and trace his finger around the edge.

He sipped his drink instead and mulled over what she'd said, searching for common ground. 'I'm not a perfectionist, but I'm passionate about what I do. You learned that the hard way.'

'It wasn't hard, Olly. I enjoyed meeting your waterfowl. They were sweet and Max was magnificent.'

He beamed at her. 'I'll tell him that tomorrow.'

Suddenly, Niamh laughed and shook her head. 'You and your birds.'

'I love them.'

'I know. I think it's lovely.'

'I think you're lovely.'

She stared at him. 'Olly ...' She set her glass down and cupped her hands together on her lap. 'You said yourself you don't even know me.'

'Yeah, but I like what I know so far.' He kept the smile in his voice. 'You could always tell me more. Like ...' He swirled his wine, thinking. 'Favourite colour?'

'Blue. Yours?'

'White.'

'The colour of your Muscovies.'

Nope. Olly wasn't going to touch that. No bird talk, that was the rule tonight. Or, given he'd already mentioned Max, not much of it. 'Where were you born?'

'Adelaide. I'm a born-and-bred city girl. You?'

'On the farm. I was in a such hurry I was out before Mum and Dad could make it out the back door. Mum said she couldn't hold on and went down and Dad had to deliver me. Apparently, I slithered out in the hallway and proceeded to howl like a banshee. Mum said it was awesome. Dad reckoned it was like pulling a noisy lamb.'

Niamh laughed. 'Seriously?'

'Yup.' Olly smiled, remembering all the times his parents had related his dramatic birth. The shock and joy of it. The pride they had in each other at their composure, and at the miracle they'd created. How special it had made Olly feel. 'I love that story.'

'I can imagine.'

'When did you move to Levenham?' he asked before she could get off topic.

'Four years ago. It's my second teaching post.'

'Where was the first?'

'Roxby Downs.'

'Wow.' Roxby Downs was a small town over five hundred kilometres north of Adelaide, purpose-built in the mid-eighties to support the huge Olympic Dam mine development. Some of Olly's school and football tradie mates had moved there for work and done well for themselves. It was arid and isolated and must have been a hell of a shock to a city girl. Niamh wouldn't have let it beat her though. 'How did you find it?'

'Different. Interesting. A challenge. I liked it, mostly, but I couldn't see myself staying there. There were too many things I missed.'

'Like what?'

'My family. Friends. Concerts and restaurants. All the other attractions and events larger towns have.' She smiled at him and Olly felt it like a cuddle. 'Rain. I really missed rain.'

It was Olly's turn to laugh. Levenham averaged around seven-hundred millimetres of rain a year. It was lush country. 'Plenty of it down here.'

'Sometimes too much.' Her expression turned wistful. 'When it rained at Roxby, it was spectacular. The desert would come to life and the colours ... amazing.'

Olly could only imagine. Between the farm and making sure his mum was okay, he'd never ventured too far from home.

'You like it here?' he asked.

'I do. I wish Mum and Dad were closer, but Adelaide's not that far away.'

'Brothers or sisters?'

'Yes. One brother, one sister.'

'Older or younger?'

'Both younger. My sister's in her final year of architecture. My brother's in his first year of medicine.'

Olly was impressed. 'High-achieving family. What do your parents do?'

'Dad lectures in biochemistry at Flinders University. Mum's a high-school teacher, too.'

'Let me guess,' said Olly, nudging her. 'Maths and physics.'

Niamh made her voice low and chime-y, like a game show wrong answer buzzer. '*Bung bung.*'

'Science?' At her head shake he tried again. 'Computers?'

'Nope.' Niamh grinned. 'I knew you wouldn't get it. She teaches music.'

'Ah,' said Olly, remembering the mention of piano on Niamh's Cupid Country 'likes' list and wanting to kick himself. 'Figures. You play piano.'

'And violin, and a bit of guitar. I'd like to get better at guitar, but with everything else I don't have the time. It's very annoying. I'm teaching Amber piano, did you know?'

Olly shook his head. 'Tom hasn't been around that much since he and Amber got back together. The few times I've caught up with them both they've been more interested in each other than me.'

'I know. Those two are crazy in love. It's funny and sweet, but it can get a bit much when you're the singly.'

Olly reckoned he had a fix for that, but kept his counsel and slurped his wine instead.

'Do you play an instrument?' asked Niamh.

Olly wished like hell he did, but that had never been a part of his life. There was his gran's old piano in the lounge but other than "Chopsticks" he'd never learned to play. Life on the farm had been tough after his dad died. He and his mum had managed, thanks to the help of relatives and kind people like Tom's parents, but there hadn't been a lot of time for much else. Sport was Olly's main outlet, and then only because his mum insisted that he have at least one off-farm distraction.

'No. But I'd give it a go.'

'Like squash?' Her face was pure innocence, but a knowing sparkle glinted in her eye.

'You guessed.'

'It was pretty obvious.'

Olly sighed. 'And there I was thinking I'd put on a good show.'

'You did, for a beginner.' She touched his knee briefly. 'You have excellent reach. I was impressed.'

'Really?' Olly wasn't sure if it was the compliment or her touch that gave him such a charge, but he'd take either. At her nod he beamed. 'Awesome. Maybe next time you can give me some tips, so I can give you a proper challenge.'

Niamh looked away and sipped her wine.

Olly ducked his head so he could see her face. 'Scared I'll beat you?'

That got him a reaction. 'Absolutely not!'

'There you go, then. Nothing to worry about.'

There was a drawn-out moment before she spoke again. 'I don't know if there should be a next time.'

'Why not?'

'We're so different.'

They were, but that didn't mean they couldn't find a way to get along. Or at least try.

'That doesn't mean we won't work. Look at the positives. I like you. I think maybe you like me?'

Niamh breathed in then nodded slowly.

'I think you're gorgeous.'

Her blue eyes widened, and an enchanting flush crept up her cheeks. 'Thank you.'

Olly shrugged. 'It's true.' Then he grinned. 'Great legs.'

'You have great legs, too.'

'Really?' Maybe Olly had misinterpreted that initial once-over at the squash courts. He could have sworn that was disapproval.

'You're very tall and big, though. And I'm short and tiny. We'd look weird together.' Niamh stared at the hand curling on her lap. 'I don't know how we'd ... fit.'

Olly's breath stalled. Was Niamh talking about what he thought she was? He swallowed. She'd thought about sex with him?

Whoa.

He held back another goofy grin and instead kept his tone gentle. She was nervous or scared or something. If he was to make any progress at all, Olly needed to ease her fears. Or at least make sure he sounded kind and fun and safe. 'You won't know until you try.'

She looked up, mouth tipped in one corner in that way Olly was beginning to adore. 'Is that an offer?'

'If you want.'

'I want. That's the trouble.' Niamh released a huff of breath. 'You're a really nice man, Olly, but I can't see us lasting, and I don't want to get hurt.' She held his gaze. 'I don't want either of us to get hurt.'

Olly considered a moment. He'd been right. She was scared. But she hadn't learned what he had—that life, love, could be snatched from you before it had barely begun. Better to take chances than die not having lived.

'I get that. Relationships are a risk. But don't you want to at least try? For a bit? Another date, at least. If nothing else, we might have some fun.' He leaned across to nudge her lightly. 'Fun's always good.'

She stared at him for a long time, then nodded. 'Okay.' She breathed out. 'Okay, another date.' Then she poked him half-playfully in the arm. 'This time, you'd better not be late.'

Chapter Seven

Olly was indeed late. Nearly twenty minutes late. Niamh twisted her watch around her wrist and glared at the door to Restaurant Ten, Levenham's most lauded restaurant. It was seven-seventeen on a pleasant Friday evening in spring and most of the tables were already occupied.

'Can I get you anything? Some bread, perhaps?' asked Louise, the chef's wife, who was as famous for her front of house charm as her husband, Kai, was for his cooking. She topped up Niamh's water glass. 'It's house made, as is our whipped butter.'

'No, but thanks. I'll wait.' Although how much longer Niamh would wait remained to be seen. Her vibrating teeth were driving her crazy. She threw another look at the door and twisted her watch again. It had to be seven-eighteen now. Olly wasn't coming. How humiliating.

How infuriating.

A flurry of movement outside the big street-side window caught Niamh's attention. Her heart gave a somersault as she recognised the tall frame racing towards the door. A second later Olly appeared at the entrance, head swivelling as he surveyed the room. No watch graced his wrist. Of course not. Olly was 'chill'. Even the thought of the word made her grit her teeth.

His gaze landed on Niamh. He visibly inhaled then strode to their table. Features schooled to serenity, Niamh set her hands atop her menu, fingers interlocked, the epitome of a patient date. Restaurants were not places to create scenes, no matter how much she wanted to.

'I'm sorry, I'm sorry.' He brushed a tangle of soft curls away from his face. Unlike their previous encounters, when Olly had worn his hair in a man bun, tonight it was down, falling in loose, surprisingly silky looking waves. 'Something came up on the farm and I lost track of time.'

If Niamh had hackles they would have bristled like a snarling wolf's. They were on a make-or-break date and Olly had lost track of time? Was he for real?

The thought made her want to growl. Instead, she clutched her fingers so tight her knuckles were in danger of popping.

Olly pulled out his chair and sat. He leaned forward and covered her hands with his big ones. Around them, the tinkle of cutlery on plates and the hubbub of people enjoying their food and company continued. He rubbed her knuckles with his thumb. 'You're angry.'

'Yes.' Niamh didn't see any point in lying.

'Please don't be.'

Her lips remained tight. 'You could have called.'

'I would have, only I don't have your number. We've only ever talked on Cupid Country.'

Niamh looked away. She hadn't thought of that. And

after what happened between Amber and Tom, they should have realised the danger of not sharing numbers. Still ...

'You could have called the restaurant. Or Tom or Amber. They would have passed on a message.'

'You're right. I could have and I'm sorry. But I was a bit distracted, and it didn't cross my mind. I honestly didn't think I'd be this late, either.' He squeezed her hands. Worry etched faint lines around his eyes. Olly was genuinely fearful. 'Don't let this spoil the night. Please?'

Niamh breathed in and out and finally nodded. He was here now, and Restaurant Ten served beautiful food in elegant but relaxed surroundings. And they'd been given one of the best tables in the house, next to the big window with a view over Civic Park. She should make the most of it.

Olly gave her hand a final squeeze and let go as Louise came over.

'About time you showed,' she said, but her smile indicated she was clearly delighted to see him. 'I hope you have a good excuse for keeping your date waiting.'

He stood and kissed her cheek. 'Hey, Lou. How's my favourite maître d'?'

'The usual. Overworked and underpaid.'

'You love it.'

'Fortunately, we do. It's lovely to have you here. Kai's looking forward to spoiling you both.' Louise addressed Niamh as Olly resumed his seat. 'Olly's one of our most important producers. God knows what would happen if we took his duck off the menu. Probably a mutiny. Now, what can I get you both to drink?'

Niamh ordered a sparkling wine, Olly a low-alcohol beer. Though she was softening, her nerves still thrummed. The alcohol might calm her down and allow her to enjoy the evening and it wasn't as if she was driving. Though the night was pleasant enough to walk to the restaurant, Niamh had caught a taxi.

'So, what came up on the farm?' she asked as soon as Louise departed.

Olly brushed his hair back from his face and puffed his cheeks. Now that her anger was settling, she could appreciate the effort he'd gone to with his clothes. Neat blue chinos, and a blue-and-white checked shirt with the cuffs rolled up a couple of times, but with well-ironed creases along the upper sleeves. He looked good. Normal. She wondered if the colour choice was deliberate and decided it probably was. Another show of compatibility, like his copycat wine selection in the pub.

She had to give the man full points for trying. Except for his time management. That needed serious work.

'There's a leak in one of the water pipes to the ducks' night shed.' He pushed his hair away again and Niamh recognised the concern and tiredness in the gesture. 'I had to shut off the water and fill all the waterers by hand. Normally they're automatic. This time of year, when it's still cool at night, it's not too much of a problem, but the birds still need water. I'll have to check them again when I get home.'

With his explanation, every scrap of Niamh's anger faded. 'You couldn't risk them going without.'

'No.' His smile turned crooked. 'They're not pets or children, no matter how I sometimes act. They're commercial birds that can't fend for themselves. It's up to me to keep them fed, watered and happy. And that's a responsibility I take seriously. Very seriously. It's important.'

Niamh looked down at her now open palms and sucked on her lip. 'I'm sorry I was so angry.'

'Hey,' he said, his eyes crinkling a little. 'It's okay. We're here now. Time for some fun.' He winked at her. 'You look gorgeous, by the way. No wonder blue's your favourite colour. You look amazing in it.'

Heat suffused Niamh's chest. Oh, she liked this man, with his easy compliments and passion for his waterbirds. It made her wish their differences could be overcome. Maybe, short term they could. Long term ... That would take a miracle. Yet a girl could dream and as Olly said in the pub, if nothing else at least they could have some fun. And Niamh wanted to have a lot of fun with Olly.

Except not tonight it seemed, given he had to return to his birds.

'Thank you.' Not counting the outfit selection process, which Niamh had spent two days fussing over, it had taken a full hour to get ready and she appreciated the compliment. Her blue stretch jersey wrap dress was an older one, but a favourite and very flattering. 'You've scrubbed up nicely, too.'

Olly stroked the front of his shirt. 'I call this my country farmer look. Not my thing, but Tom said I had to dress up for you.' His grin broadened. 'Which was probably an order from Amber.'

'What do you normally wear when you go out?'

He shrugged. 'Jeans. Work duds. Whatever top happens to be lying around. A shirt when I'm trying to impress.'

Niamh tried not to wince. Even as a child, her wardrobe had been colour and style coordinated. Everything matched and *nothing* was ever left lying about. Living with Olly would be a nightmare. Not that she was thinking of living with him. Not at all. Nope. Nup.

Spending time in his bedroom, though ...

'Your hair's down,' she said, dragging her mind from his bed.

'Yeah. I was in too much of a rush to tie it back. You like it?'

She did. A surprising amount. Niamh had always preferred short-back-and-sides, but Olly's locks looked clean and silky and made her fingers itch with the urge to check the texture. Maybe indulge in a little sniff. She bet it smelled nice. Maybe a bit woodsy, with a hint of pine shavings to remind her of their time in the pavilion.

She rubbed an eyebrow. Where was all this coming from? The pavilion had been hot, dusty, noisy, and smelled of bird poo.

Louise's return saved her from answering. Louise set down their drinks, then took a moment to ask Niamh if she liked seafood, which Niamh did, and relate the specials—velvet crab from off the coast of Port Andrews, a local fishing village about thirty kilometres away, mulloway from the mouth of the Glenelg River, just across the Victorian border at Nelson, and squab, also from Victoria.

When Louise had gone, Olly lifted his beer and waited for Niamh to press the rim of her glass against it. 'To special friends,' he said, gaze locked on hers and keeping it locked as they drank.

Niamh set her glass down, breaking eye contact and sucking in a breath to ease the rapid tattoo of her heart. Olly had a way of looking at her that made her skin fizz like champagne. Like he truly admired her. And desired. It was heady and wonderful and so novel she didn't know what to do with her feelings. They felt wrong, given their differences. Yet so right, too.

'Squab?' she asked when she'd calmed a little.

'Young pigeon.' Olly's voice fairly dripped with derision. 'I guess some people might like it.'

'But you don't.'

'Duck's superior.'

Niamh laughed, finally relaxing into the evening. 'Of course it is.'

Olly beamed back at her in that open, sweet way of his, lovely brandy-coloured gaze twinkling. He indicated the menu. 'Are you going to order the duck?'

Niamh hesitated. Would it be wrong to eat duck when she'd so admired Olly's Muscovies at the show? 'I don't know. I want to but ...'

Disappointment flickered across Olly's face. His chest rose and fell as though holding in a sigh. Niamh braced herself for criticism.

'I'm sure the velvet crab is good,' he said, looking down at his own menu. 'Kai's porchetta is pretty amazing, too. Mate of mine breeds the pork. Berkshires. Heritage breed. He runs them free range so they can snuffle about.'

'Like your waterfowl.'

'My birds don't snuffle.'

She smiled, trying to make up for disappointing him. 'I should hope not. Then I really would think they had an awful disease.'

She assessed the menu again. The porchetta did sound beautiful but what was the difference between eating one of Olly's friend's free-range Berkshires to trying the duck? Unlike her brother, who had declared himself vegetarian at age thirteen, Niamh had always eaten meat. It wasn't something she was usually squeamish over either and the duck was already dead. Her not ordering it wouldn't save its life.

Besides, she liked duck and Restaurant Ten's version was served with an intriguing combination of mandarin and port. And the thought of disappointing Olly was surprisingly painful.

'I think I will have the duck.'

'Niamh ...'

'What?'

'You don't have to.'

'I know. I want to, though.' It was Niamh's turn to lean towards him. 'I wouldn't order it if it wasn't what I wanted.'

'Promise?'

'Olly ... Do I look like a woman who doesn't know her own mind?'

'I guess not.'

'There you go.' She sat back, satisfied the message had got in. 'Duck it is.'

'Good,' he said, and broke into a grin. 'Great. You'll love it. Kai's a gun chef.'

She eyed her menu again. 'Are you going to have an entree?'

'Nah. I was thinking I might save myself for dessert.'

His teasing tone had her rolling her eyes, even as her heart fluttered with the idea of dessert. Sadly, the kind of dessert Olly was insinuating wouldn't be happening. She wouldn't keep him from caring for his birds. And if they were going to have sex, Niamh wanted him all night and undistracted.

They chatted a little more about their week, until Louise arrived to take their orders. When she suggested matching wines for their duck, they agreed.

'You ordered duck, too,' said Niamh. 'I thought you'd have wanted something different.'

Olly shook his head. 'We don't get to eat it much at home. We've enough trouble keeping up supply without eating the produce.'

'It must be a very good business.'

'It is. Took a while to get going, but once we gained the confidence of our customers, Duck, Duck, Goose really took off.'

'You called your business Duck, Duck, Goose? After the children's game?'

Olly fiddled with his cutlery, a blush forming on his cheeks. 'Yeah, well, I was young and dumb, and thought it was funny. And Mum—she's the other part of "we" in the business—let me have my way.'

'How old were you when you started?'

'Sixteen.'

Niamh blinked, wondering if she'd heard correctly. 'Sixteen? But that's amazing.'

He shrugged. 'Not really. We already had a poultry enterprise and Dad had been thinking about changing over. Or pivoting, as the agribiz types like to call it these days. I just took up where he left off. Ducks first, then much later geese, although that market's small and seasonal.'

'Still, that's an incredible achievement for a teenage boy.'

Olly puffed up with mock affront. 'Who're you calling a boy? I thought I was a man.'

She laughed then sobered. 'It must have been an extraordinary amount of work.'

'It was. Lots of learning, lots of mistakes. The occasional tantrum.'

'You, throwing a tantrum?' Niamh shook her head. 'I don't believe it. What happened to being chill?'

'Not easy when you're sixteen.'

And had lost your beloved dad, hung unsaid in the air.

Niamh held a hand out, open in invitation. Olly regarded it and placed one of his own against it, palm to palm, then wrapped his long fingers gently around. They stared at the connection, feeling the exchange of warmth and so much more.

'What was that for?' he asked quietly.

'I don't know. It seemed like you might need it. I thought I might need it, too.'

Olly examined her face, gaze tracing hers, roving over her cheeks and mouth and back to her eyes. His mouth tipped. 'Told you you're lovely.'

'Don't let it get out. I've my strict teacher's reputation to uphold.'

'Our secret then.'

A low cough sounded.

Louise was at the table, a plate in each hand, another loaded with toasted sourdough balanced on the crook of her elbow, and an indulgent expression on her face. 'Kai sent these out with his compliments.' She placed one plate in front of Niamh and the other in front of Olly, and the bread between them. 'Goolwa pipis with saffron butter.'

As Louise laid the bread plate down, a waitress glided up and placed a glass of white wine next to their cutlery.

'I love that man,' said Olly, eyes wide as he regarded his pipis. 'Tell Kai I'll be out for a kiss later.'

'You'd better,' said Louise. 'Or there'll be trouble. Enjoy.'

'Wow,' said Niamh, as wide-eyed as Olly. She inhaled deeply, smelling fresh sea and butter and something else she couldn't define. She picked up her glass and gave it a swirl before dropping her nose inside and inhaling. Riesling, she was sure of it. Perfect. 'You have kind friends.'

'I do. And I'm grateful every day for them.'

The pipis—a shellfish speciality from the magnificent Coorong, where the Murray River finally reached the sea after a mammoth cross-country journey—were incredible. Niamh had eaten them before. Not like this, though. Every pipi seemed to explode in her mouth with sweet buttery goodness, and the wine had been expertly chosen, its lemon-lime notes cutting through the butter and enhancing the flavour even further.

She sucked on her last shell, placed it on her plate and reached for a piece of bread to sop up the delicious juice, only to find Olly watching intently.

She waved her bread at his half-eaten plate. 'Aren't you eating? They're amazing.'

'They are.'

Niamh shot her gaze to his plate and back again. 'What's the matter, then?'

'Not a thing. I was just enjoying watching you.'

She set down her bread. 'Am I being a pig?' The thought gave her shudders. Niamh was a well brought up girl and a neat freak. She did not do piggy. Certainly not in public.

'Not even a little bit.'

'Then what?'

'Nothing, Niamh. Nothing. You looked happy, that's all. It's kind of mesmerising.'

'Oh.' Her hands slid under the table to fiddle with her watch. Suddenly her appetite for food disappeared, replaced with an appetite for something more intimate. But they were in the middle of a romantic dinner. Dragging Olly home for an early dessert would be appalling manners.

Yet she still wanted to do it.

The evening progressed almost perfectly. Their conversation ebbed and flowed. Niamh shared stories about her family and university, and holidays she'd enjoyed and places she'd like to visit. Olly told tales about his adventures with Tom and other mates, and talked about the things he loved about Levenham. He was so positive, Niamh wondered if he was selling it to her. He didn't need to. She'd been sold before the end of her first year.

'Do you like teaching?' Olly asked.

'Love it. Even if my students do call me the bondage mistress behind my back.'

Olly made a choked noise. 'Little shits.'

'My fault.'

'How?'

She sighed and took a sip of riesling. 'I wear skirt suits to work. *Fitted* skirt suits. Usually in navy, sometimes pinstriped. Always with a white silk blouse.'

'And that makes you a bondage mistress?'

She lifted a shoulder. 'I guess they find it sexy.'

Olly regarded her for a moment, a small crinkle between his brows. 'Okay, why? Why the suits?'

'Because no one takes tiny people seriously.' She shifted in her seat and cast her gaze across the room. Louise was clearing plates from a table, laughing at something one of the diners said. The other waitress was delivering drinks. People looked content. All Niamh felt was ... confused. Even worse, she felt *disordered*. It was unlike her to be so open. So vulnerable. Yet she couldn't seem to stop. 'I thought it would give me authority. But I think people sometimes laugh. The kids do.'

Olly's tone was gentle. 'Teenagers laugh at anything. It's what they do. I bet they think you're an amazing teacher. And for what it's worth, I take you seriously.'

'You're not a student or colleague.'

'No. But I wouldn't mind being someone more important.'

143

Niamh gave a huff of laughter even as her insides somersaulted at his words. 'You're incorrigible.'

'I'm hoping that's a good thing.' Olly's expression became serious. 'Life's short, Niamh. You've got to live it.'

He was right. Of course he was right. Though, when it came to fragile hearts, these things were easier said than done.

As promised, Olly's duck was beautiful. Niamh closed her eyes as she savoured the flavours and opened them to Olly watching her with that same indulgent expression. Only, this time, she didn't fret she was making a pig of herself. Her pleasure had made Olly happy and that made her happy too.

'Can I interest you in some dessert?' asked Louise when she came to clear their plates. 'We have passionfruit souffle with vanilla anglaise as a special. Mimi—that's our new apprentice—is very proud of it.'

Niamh looked at Olly. The souffle sounded gorgeous, but he had responsibilities and they'd already eaten a ridiculous amount of rich food.

'Your call,' he said.

She hesitated over which way to go. Not having dessert meant the evening would end and Niamh didn't want it to. Yet it had to end at some point. Why not on a good note, when they were both feeling happy?

'I think I'm fine. Although the souffle does sound delicious.'

'Thanks, Lou, but we might give dessert a miss.'

'You could always share. It's feather-light.'

Niamh shook her head and pressed a hand to her belly. 'I'm not sure I could fit in even that.'

'Coffee then?'

Again, Olly deferred to Niamh.

'Thanks,' she said. 'But I'll have to give that a miss too or I'll never sleep.'

'Not for me either, Lou. Fantastic meal, though. Kai outdid himself.'

'Make sure you pop into the kitchen before you leave and tell him yourself. He'll be thrilled.'

Niamh fiddled with the stem of her wineglass. There was only a sip left of the pinot noir that had been served with the duck. Olly, having to drive, had only drunk a little of his. Once she'd finished there'd be nothing to anchor them there. She pushed the glass aside.

Olly reached for her now free hand. 'Are you okay?'

'Yes.'

'You don't look it.'

'I am. Honestly. I had a nice night.'

'Good.' He squeezed her fingers. 'That was the plan.' He tipped his head, brandy eyes sparkling. 'Want to do it again?'

'Dinner?'

'It can be. I was thinking another date.'

Niamh shouldn't. She really shouldn't. The more time she spent with Olly the more she'd get attached and so would he and the harder it would be when they broke up. Except her mouth had other ideas.

'Okay. What would you like to do?'

'I'm flex. What would you like?'

Niamh scrunched her nose as she considered. There were a hundred things that appealed. An afternoon spent in bed with Olly would be one, but she wasn't about to admit that. He'd probably say yes. 'I would really like to see your farm.'

Olly beamed. 'Really?'

'What did I say about being a woman who knows her

own mind, hmm?' Which was a big fat lie, because Niamh's mind didn't know which way to leap. Actually, that wasn't true. Her mind was rational. Mostly. It was her heart being recalcitrant. She bugged her eyes at him. 'Yes. Really.'

'When?'

Niamh scraped her teeth over her bottom lip. 'What are you doing tomorrow afternoon?'

Chapter Eight

Olly had every intention of being at the house when Niamh turned up, or at least close by. Then his mum called, asking for a hand to load a portable generator into her four-wheel drive and he had to dash across the farm to help. By the time he arrived back, Niamh was backed up against the door of her car near the gate to the house, working her watch backwards and forwards as Max and the other geese huddled around her.

Her gaze as he approached was like an iced-over duck pond, dark and frigid.

'Shit,' said Olly, hands gripping the quad bike's handlebars as his stomach plunged with dread. Not a good start. Not a good start at all. He should have messaged—his unreliability was the whole reason they'd swapped numbers at the end of dinner—but it hadn't seemed worth it for a few minutes. A mistake. And today of all days, he was out to impress.

That morning he'd let his breeding pairs out to roam about like he always did, with the intention of hustling them into their run after lunch in readiness for Niamh's two o'clock arrival. Except he'd spent the morning covered in mud and muck, tackling the leaky pipe, and was in such a hurry to shower and change he forgot all about locking up the geese. Even when they'd followed Olly home, honking and cackling quietly to each other and to him, Olly hadn't remembered.

Now Niamh was paying the price.

At least the geese were only eyeing her with suspicion and hadn't gone on attack. And, to her credit, Niamh didn't seem frightened. Tight-lipped with anger, for sure, but not scared. Which was kind of impressive. Most other girls would freak.

'Bugger off, you lot,' Olly ordered the moment he alighted. The geese honked and hinked—the higher honk they used for greeting—and waddled towards him, shaking their tail feathers.

Niamh breathed out and straightened and Olly's heart gave an Olympic standard triple-jump at the full sight of her. Even arms crossed and scowling she was sexy as hell, if overdressed for a farm that had received an inch of rain overnight.

Casting an admiring eye over her now, Olly could fully appreciate why her students called her a bondage mistress. Every aspect was tight precision, from her white fedora to her polished brown knee-high leather boots. Paired with light tan skinny jeans and a long-sleeved white shirt scattered with tiny beige dots and with the cuffs folded up in precise alignment, she looked every inch the perfect equestrienne fantasy. All she needed was a riding crop to spank him with.

Not that Olly needed any more fantasies about Niamh. His recent dreams had been distracting enough.

'You okay?' he asked, hoping his broad smile would take

some of the sting out of her anger. 'Max and his mates didn't frighten you?'

'I'm fine.'

He leaned in for a kiss and got a rigid, turned cheek. Last night, when he'd farewelled her into the taxi, after she refused his offer of a lift home, she'd let him kiss the edge of her mouth. Only lightly, but still progress. 'You had no problems finding the place then?'

'No.'

Okay, so neither his smile nor his kiss had mellowed her temper. On a good note, Niamh *had* let him kiss her. Even so, Olly's hope that today would be special was sinking fast.

'Sorry I wasn't here when you arrived. Mum needed a hand. It took longer than I thought. What is the time, anyway?'

Her arms remained as crossed as her mood. 'Five past two.'

'Is that all?' Five minutes was hardly enough to stay stroppy about. Except, given the flat lines of Niamh's mouth, apparently it was. He sucked back a sigh. 'Nice boots. I don't suppose you have a pair of gumbies in the car?'

'Gumbies?'

'You know, gumboots. Rubber boots. Wellies.'

'No. I don't.'

Olly did his best to stay cheerful in the face of Niamh's frostiness, but it wasn't easy. It was only five minutes. 'I can fetch a pair of Mum's if you like. They'll be a bit big, but will at least protect your feet. The farm's muddy after last night.' He gestured at her buffed boots. 'It'd be a pity if they got wrecked.'

'They'll be fine. They're good-quality boots.'

Olly eyed them with a scrunched nose. 'You sure?' Good-quality was not the same as practical and Niamh's boots looked expensive. Probably leather soled too, which wouldn't offer a lot in the way of grip.

Niamh lifted her chin. 'What did I say about—'

'Being a woman who knows her mind. Yeah, I get it.' He shrugged. 'Your call, but the offer's there if you want to take it up.'

Her reply was a tight, 'Thank you.'

'Niamh ...'

She lifted a palm. 'I know. You're sorry for being late.'

'Yeah. I am.' He ducked his head closer to hers. 'But I'm also thrilled to bits you're here. Max is too.' He pointed to the goose. 'See?'

On cue, Max tipped his head back, puffed out his grey chest, and called out a long honky-honk.

Finally, Niamh's arms unlocked. Her mouth lost its flatness and her gaze softened as she regarded the goose. 'He's a funny thing. I thought he might peck me, but he just waddled over and fussed about, making goose noises.'

Olly beamed at Max and wished he had a treat to throw. He bloody loved that goose.

He returned his focus to Niamh. 'Look, I know you're mad and I'm sorry I wasn't here when you arrived, but Mum needed me and ...' Olly opened his hands. He didn't need to explain more. That simple sentence said it all. For him, anyway.

Niamh looked away and sucked on her lip in that adorable way she had. 'I know. I just ...' She huffed out a long breath and flapped her arms from her sides like wings. 'I get annoyed by lateness. Really annoyed.' She tapped a front tooth. 'It makes my teeth go funky.'

Teeth go funky? Olly bit back a laugh. The more weirdness she revealed, the cuter he found her. But they needed to sort this out.

'Okay. But sometimes stuff happens. The world doesn't collapse because someone's a few minutes late.'

'I know.' She let out a long sigh. 'I just don't do "chill" well. Never have, not even as a child. It's another of my *things*.'

'Like your perfectionism.'

'Yes. And I know it's irrational, but I can't help it.' She held his gaze, her blue eyes asking for his understanding. She pointed at his bare wrist. 'It might help if you wore a watch, though.'

Olly feigned a shudder. 'God, no. That'd make life far too regimented.'

Niamh huffed a laugh and Olly had to stuff his hands in his pockets to stop himself from wrapping his arms around her and kissing her silly. Quirks and all, they'd be fine as long as they kept smiling.

He turned towards the paddocks and sheds in front of them. 'Ready for a tour?'

'Yes, please.'

'Awesome. Watch your step, though. Everything's slippery.'

Olly tempered his normally long-legged stride to match Niamh's. Even with her determined walk Niamh's step length was half his. He kept a close eye on her, too. The farm's main road was gravel but still muddy and those fancy boots bothered him. He wondered if she'd let him piggyback her over the worst bits. The thought of her pressed against his back with her arms around his neck had his heart beating faster.

He waved back at the cottage. 'That's where Tom and I live. It was my grandparents', but they moved to town years ago. Bought a place two streets over from the bowling club. They're lawn bowls nuts, so they've taken to town like ducks to water. I'll show you around inside later.'

Niamh glanced over her shoulder. 'It looks nice.'

'The kitchen and bathroom need a reno but it's comfortable enough.'

'And your mum?'

'She's over there.' Olly pointed west to where a browny-green iron roof shone in the distance. The farm was looking damn fine in the afternoon sun, if a little soggy. There'd been no wind to dry it out, although it was forecast to pick up later in the day. 'She used to work part-time at the library, but when Duck, Duck, Goose took off she quit to help with the farm. I tried to talk her out of it. She loved the library but, you know parents.'

'Is she around now?'

Olly shook his head. 'She's gone to town. Dropping a portable generator into Andersons then taking Nan to the doctor.'

'Nothing serious with your nan, I hope?'

'Shingles. Poor thing.'

Niamh's hand went to her chest. 'Oh, how horrible. It's meant to be incredibly painful.'

'Yeah. Hopefully they'll give her something to help.'

They sauntered on, Olly slanting looks at Niamh as they walked. Colour was back in her cheeks. Her pink lips were open, her curious gaze travelling everywhere, arms swinging and relaxed. Olly wanted to grab her hand, as much to hold as to make sure she didn't slip. The anger and tension might be gone but he wasn't going to push his luck. Yet.

Niamh glanced over her shoulder. 'Don't look now, but I think we're being followed.'

Olly checked, unsurprised to see Max and his gaggle

waddling behind like a feathered fan club. 'They'll do that all day. They just want to know what's going on. I love it. Keeps me amused.'

'Do you talk to them?'

'Sometimes.' At Niamh's raised eyebrow he corrected himself. 'Okay, a lot. They're great company.'

'You do realise that sounds nuts.'

'Maybe, but no one's here to catch me, and the gang likes it, so who cares?'

Olly caught the lift in her mouth before she dipped her head, her fedora partly shielding her face, and smiled to himself. Things were definitely on the improve. He'd have to toss Max a treat later. Maybe some watermelon, if Tom hadn't eaten it all.

Suddenly, Niamh halted. Brow furrowed and drumming her fingers against her thigh, she cast a slow circle. The geese muddled close by, hinky-honking at the sudden stop.

'What?' he asked.

For a moment she didn't answer, then clicked her fingers. 'That's it. Dogs. That's what's missing. I expected dogs.' She waved at the geese. 'But you don't need any, do you? You have these lovelies.'

She was right in a way. Being territorial, geese made excellent guard dogs, but that wasn't why there weren't any dogs. 'Tom has a couple of collies. Elf and Roxy. Working dogs, although they're spoiled rotten.'

'But you don't?'

'I did.' Olly scuffed at a stone, head down to keep her from seeing the pain that still hollowed his chest. 'Tammy. She died a couple of months back. I miss her something stupid.'

A hand settled gently on his forearm. Olly looked up and found blue eyes pooling with sympathy.

'I'm sorry.'

He nodded, momentarily unable to speak for the gravel that had lodged in his throat. 'I'll get another one.'

'Just not yet.'

'No. But that's the price you pay for loving a dog.' Olly's voice dropped a tone. 'For loving anyone.' He swallowed, shook himself and smiled his gratitude for her sympathy, even if he did feel like a bit of a sook.

She smiled back, then gave his arm another squeeze and let go, and though the physical connection was broken, the meaning in it remained. God, he was going to kiss her silly when the chance came.

But that was for later. First, Olly had a tour to complete.

'Right,' he said, clapping his hands together. 'Duck time.'

They passed one of the overnight sheds and headed towards his bird runs—mesh-fenced paddocks where the ducks could run around in relative safety.

'Oh, look at them,' exclaimed Niamh when she spotted the first run. The Muscovies were in heaven after the rain, beaks down plucking at grass and foraging for slugs and snails and other critters the damp had brought out. 'They look so happy. And look, they have their own pond!'

'Yeah, well, you know what they say about ducks and water. There's one in every run. They're a pain in the bum, to be honest, but the ducks love them.'

'Those are roosts?' She pointed to the small iron-roofed wheeled houses scattered around the paddock, like little carriages.

'Yep. They're leftover from when we had chooks. The ducks don't really use them much, but I keep them out so they have somewhere to take shelter if they need. They're easy enough to wheel about.'

'Of course. The ducks need to be regularly moved to new pastures. I read that. It's what makes them free-range.'

'With Duck, Duck, Goose it does.'

She shot him a look. 'You mean it doesn't with others?'

He pushed down on a fence post to secure it more firmly. All the run fences were movable to allow for easier pasture maintenance and rotation but tended to loosen in the wet. 'It varies. Depending on age you can have up to five thousand birds a hectare and as long as they have *meaningful and regular*,' he pronounced meaningful and regular with distaste, 'access to the outdoors they can still be classed as free-range.'

Niamh's eyes widened in disbelief. 'But that's only two square metres per bird. That's hardly free-range.'

'Tell that to the people who make the rules. All my runs are an acre at least and I try to keep the ratio to a maximum of one bird per fifteen square metres, and sometimes I still don't feel that's enough. The worst thing is there's no requirement for ponds and there should be. Ducks need water to clean themselves, to swim and take the weight off their legs. Them not having a pond is like us not having a lounge to plonk on at the end of the day. Or a shower to bathe in.'

'Poor things.' She studied the Muscovies. 'Yours are very lucky duckies.'

'They mightn't think that if they knew their fate.'

'No, I suppose not.' Niamh's brow furrowed as she thought on that. 'But you're giving them the best life you can in the time they have.'

'I try to. Every creature should be able to live its best life. It's not only the right thing to do, it makes business sense. Happy birds make high quality meat. That's how Duck, Duck, Goose demands premium prices.' He moved to the gate, opened it, and waved for Niamh to come inside. 'Watch your step. A duck poos about every fifteen minutes on average, so it's everywhere.'

Olly let Niamh go ahead, making a grim face at her boots as she passed. Already the toes had dirty marks. He couldn't imagine Niamh being happy about that. Or about the poo stains to come.

Olly closed the gate, shutting out the geese. Max gave him a beady look before hoisting his beak in the air and wandering off. He grinned and caught up with Niamh, who'd moved further inside, her face lit with wonder at his flock, snuffling through the lush grass.

'I'll rotate them to a new run tomorrow,' he said, after he'd explained the pasture's make up, and how the land management system worked. 'New feed, new bugs to munch on. Clean pond. More soil to poo all over and fertilise.'

'How often do you move them?'

'Depends on the pasture.' Olly scratched his jaw. 'Three to five days maybe?' He shrugged. 'It changes with the seasons.'

'Can I ...' She looked longingly at a duck as a flush formed across her cheeks.

'Yeah, course you can. You might get dirty though.'

'Don't worry about that. I'll be fine.'

Olly hoped so. Like her boots, Niamh's white dotted shirt looked expensive. But it wasn't his call and if cuddling a duck would make Niamh's day, who was he to deny her?

With a swift lunge, Olly scooped up a duck, and with it balanced across his arm, cradled it to his side. 'Hey, birdie,' he said, tickling its breast. 'Want to meet a pretty lady?' He checked Niamh. 'Ready?'

'Yes.' Eager, she held out her arms.

Gently, Olly placed the bird into her hold.

She gazed at the bird in delight before glancing at Olly. 'Am I doing it right?'

'Yeah. You're doing great. Just make sure you keep its breast supported.'

'I've never held a duck before.' Wonder coloured her voice and brightened her gaze. She stroked the duck's head. 'He's ...' She looked at Olly. 'She?'

'She. You can tell by the tail and the ridge on her bill.'

'She's really soft.' Niamh bent her head and kissed the duck's crown, then laughed when the duck shook its head, as if to throw off the kiss.

Olly stared at her with his heart floating somewhere near the top of his chest. Niamh with a duck in her arms was one of the most beautiful things he'd ever seen. Yeah, she was a bit weird, definitely anal, but Niamh was lovely and clever and in this moment he wanted her in his life so badly it was like she'd become the jigsaw piece he hadn't realised he was missing.

The duck shifted, its feet waggling.

'Oh,' said Niamh. 'Has she had enough?'

'Probably.'

'I'll set her down.' Very slowly, Niamh lowered the bird to the ground and slid her arm from under its belly. The duck gave itself a good shake and waddled off. Niamh watched it with her hands clasped beneath her chin.

'Thank you,' she said, turning to him. 'That was wonderful.'

'Good.' He held out his hand. Niamh stared at it for a moment, then took it. 'Wait 'til you see the hatchlings.'

'You move the flock to a shed at night?' she asked as they headed for the gate.

'Yeah. It's safer for them. Too many foxes about to let them stay out. I know a couple of growers who use Maremma dogs as protection, but I like to bring mine in, especially in the winter when the weather's rough. Gives me a chance to feed them extra grain and give them a good once-over.'

'Foxes can attack during the day, though, can't they?'

'They can, but I'm usually about and I keep a close eye on the fences. Buggers can still get through, but not often.' He pointed at the sky. 'We get more trouble from wedge-tailed eagles. They attack from above and don't mind a bit of duck, which is also why I keep the shelters. Trouble is the ducks are usually head-down and don't often see them until it's too late. We lose a few each year, but it's something we just have to suck up. Wedgies are protected. Back in the old days, farmers used to shoot them. Reckoned they were taking too many lambs.' He tsked his disapproval. 'Bloody terrible.'

Niamh studied his face. 'You're such a softie when it comes to birds.'

'Some more than others.' Niamh was one of them.

The hatchlings in their heated, sawdust-lined pens had her in awe. Olly let her cradle one, but not for long. Duck-lings pooed even more frequently than adult ducks, and duck poo stains could be a bugger to get out. It was only dumb luck that her shirt remained as clean as it was.

'Come on, I'll show you the night shed.'

Olly slid aside the large roller door to expose the inside. Light flooded in from the rooftop skylights and the air was redolent with the smell of fresh fine pine shavings. Yellow plastic feeders were scattered around the room, along with a series of black portable drums on stands with little red cups protruding from their bases, while bright red bell waterers hung from the ceiling, giving the shed a festive air. A few cobwebs matted the higher corners, but overall, the shed was bright, clean and roomy.

Olly took a moment to explain the ventilation flaps lining the sides. 'I keep them closed when the nights are still cold, but in summer they're open to keep the air flowing and the birds cool. Unless there're storms. Once, when I was young and stupid, I forgot to lock them down. Blew off four of the damn things. Scared the living daylights out of the birds. We were lucky we didn't lose any. Never forgot again.'

'Life lessons.'

'Yeah. Some things you learn the hard way.'

Niamh poked around a bell waterer then one of the portables, gaze intense. 'This is the shed with the broken pipe?'

Olly forked fingers through his hair. He'd left it down again, because Niamh had said she liked it. 'It is. Thought I'd have it nailed this morning, but ...'

'You stopped because I was coming.'

Olly wished he'd kept his mouth shut. Now Niamh felt bad. 'It's not a problem. As long as I keep the portables filled, they'll be fine.'

She hoisted a black waterer from its cradle, gave it a shake and set it down again. 'I'll help you fill them.'

'Nah, leave it. I'll fix it later.'

Niamh cocked on one hip with her arms folded and raised both eyebrows at him.

Olly laughed and patted the air with his hand. 'Settle, petal. I get it. You're a woman who knows her own mind. Come on, then.'

Working together—Niamh using a hose and Olly a watering can—they topped up the drums in half the time it would normally take. Olly was grateful for the help. The fewer chores he had to do later, the more time he could spend with Niamh. In bed would be nice, but, the way his heart kept pounding against his ribs like a petulant child demanding more, he'd take anything.

Niamh regarded the shed with her hands on her hips. 'Do we need to do their feed as well?'

'No, there's still plenty there.'

Niamh sucked on her lip. 'You sure? I don't want them missing out because I'm here, taking up your time.'

'You're not taking up my time, and they're good.' Olly wrapped an arm around her shoulders and hugged her. 'I promise.'

They were heading to the door when Olly noticed one of the feeders had tipped. 'You head outside,' he said to Niamh. 'I won't be a minute.'

By the time he returned, Niamh was nowhere to be seen. Neither were Max and his mates. Hoping she hadn't wandered far, Olly dragged the door closed and secured the latch.

Suddenly, a cry ripped the air, followed by a burst of honking.

'Niamh!'

Olly bolted, his gut lurching. He knew exactly where she was now, and it wasn't anywhere good.

He skidded around the corner of the shed, praying what he'd thought had happened hadn't, and slid to a halt.

'Aw, Niamh-honey.'

She regarded him with a crumpled mouth and watery eyes. 'I'm sorry. I just wanted to see how the ventilations flaps worked and ...'

'Shhh. It's okay.' He crouched beside her and stroked a muddy lock of hair from her eyes. Her white hat was in the mire nearby. 'Give me your arms.'

She held them out like a child, bottom lip wobbling.

Olly braced his legs and gently lifted. For a moment he wasn't sure it was going to work. The churned-up soil from where he'd been tackling the pipe was as thick and clingy as quicksand, and Niamh had tumbled into the heart of it. Then the mud made a sucking noise, and she popped free. Hooking her to his chest, Olly snatched up her fedora and eased upright. Such was her weight it was like lifting a doll. A very muddy and stinky doll.

'I'm sorry,' she wailed. 'I wanted today to be so perfect.'

'No, no.' Olly kissed a clean patch on her forehead. 'There's no need for that. You slipped. It happens.' And those bloody boots didn't help. Olly knew they were dangerous. He should have insisted she change them and now Niamh was caked in mud and muck and bird shit. 'I'll make it better, I promise.'

He would, too, or die trying.

She sniffed and seemed to rally. 'You can put me down now.'

'Nah, I like having you in my arms.'

'I'm covered in mud, Olly.'

'Don't care. It's still nice.' He nodded at Max. 'Max approves. Look at his chest.' On cue, Max honked.

Niamh snuffled a laugh that made his heart hiccup. He could tell from her bright red cheeks and downcast gaze that she was mortified, but that didn't stop her from being brave. Or him from falling even more madly for her.

'Come on,' he said, tucking her even closer. 'Let's get you out of those clothes and into a shower.'

Chapter Nine

Niamh wanted to howl. Her farm date with Olly had been going wonderfully and she'd spoiled it by getting herself covered in mud. Stinky, pooey mud. All because she was too proud to borrow his mum's gumboots.

Talk about pride coming before a fall.

She turned her face into Olly's neck and closed her eyes. If it weren't for the sticky wetness, being in his arms would be wonderful. His hold was gentle, yet secure, and she could feel the comforting bulge of his muscles beneath his shirt. Very nice muscles.

Very nice man.

She let out a breath. The way Olly had looked at her when she'd held his duck, his expression tender and happy, like his heart had just leapt into his eyes and was waltzing around, had made her own heart dance. Then she'd ruined everything. Niamh muffled a groan. So stupid.

'You okay there?' he asked, not a break in his stride.

'Embarrassed,' she muttered.

'Hey, cut that out. No need. Shit happens.'

Niamh shifted to look up at him, mouth quirked at one corner. 'Literally.'

He huffed a laugh and kissed the same spot on her forehead he'd kissed before. Amazing how such a chaste gesture could make her insides fizz. 'Nothing that a hot shower and tomato soup and toasties can't fix.'

They were nearing the house. Niamh should insist Olly put her down. She wasn't injured and she was a woman of feminist principles, yet she couldn't bring herself to make the demand. Being held by him was too soothing.

A concrete garden bench stood against the wall of what appeared to be a laundry extension on the cottage. Olly gently settled Niamh on it and ordered her not to move, before disappearing inside. Moments later, he was back with a raggedy towel.

'For your face and hands. It's old but clean.' Then he crouched in front of her and began unzipping her boots.

Again, Niamh wanted to protest about being treated like a child, but held back. Olly wasn't being patronising, he was being kind because that was his nature. So she obeyed and tried not to imagine what a fright she must look.

When her second boot was off, he set them aside and rested his hands on her knees, his thumbs rubbing soft circles over the insides of her kneecaps. 'Okay?'

She nodded, although she wasn't. Olly's smile was causing her heart to flip-flop around her chest, and her hands twitched with the urge to cup his face and kiss him.

'Good. Let's get you clean, then.' He stood and held out a hand.

Niamh took it without hesitation, loving the way his palm wrapped fully around hers, like a cuddle.

He led her inside and up a hall to an old-fashioned bathroom, complete with pink bath and sink; the floor was covered in tiny pink, white and black tiles. They paused in the doorway and exchanged bemused smiles.

'Nice,' said Niamh. And it was, if you liked retro. More importantly, it looked clean.

'I did say it needed a reno. But the shower works and there's soap and shampoo on the shelf. I'll fetch some clean towels and head outside. If you leave your dirty clothes out in the hall, I'll come back for them once the shower's started.'

'What will I put on afterwards?'

Olly rubbed his jaw. 'I'll grab you a shirt. You can wear it as a dress.'

'Thanks.'

Casting Niamh a reassuring smile, he headed up the hall.

She stepped into the bathroom and pulled the bathmat down from where it hung over the shower door and stood hugging herself and sucking on her lip. What was she thinking, showering at Olly's, leaving herself vulnerable? A smart girl would borrow a couple of towels to drape over her car seat and drive home. Except Niamh never seemed to be able to behave smartly around Olly. He muddled her, making her want things. Making her *feel* things. Serious things.

Olly returned with two towels topped with a soft flannelette shirt and a pair of thick socks. Niamh held them carefully away from her muddy body, head down and breathing through her nose.

He tucked a finger under her chin. 'Hey? Quit that. It's okay.'

Her only response was a nod. His sweetness had made her throat thicken.

Olly backed out. 'Just yell if you need anything. Don't

forget to leave your clothes out so I can put them on to wash.'

Niamh opened her mouth then thought better of it and snapped it shut.

The look on his face indicated he knew exactly the comment she was going to make. 'Don't worry. I've been looking after Mum and myself for a long time now. I know how to wash delicates.'

He walked off. Niamh regarded the open door and the space he'd left behind. The rear screen door banged closed. As promised, Olly had headed outside to give her privacy. She tipped her head back and blinked at the ceiling. This was her last chance to leave.

'You're being dumb,' she whispered. Olly was the nicest, most trustworthy man she'd met since moving to Levenham. She was fine.

What was with the nerves and vulnerability then?

Shaking her head, Niamh set the towels on the edge of the bath, turned on the shower and closed the door. She set her watch and jewellery on the vanity and, grimacing, peeled off her smelly, sodden clothes and folded them semi neatly into a pile. Her knickers were damp but clean and would stay. Only her bra had her hesitating. Mud had seeped through her silk-blend shirt to stain the cups and back. Putting it back on was out of the question, but if she left it out for Olly, he'd know she was braless.

Excitement at the idea crept through her chest. She slammed it down. No. No. *No*. She would not be going there.

It would answer one of her questions about their compatibility, though.

Niamh gritted her jaw and ordered herself to get a grip.

With jerky movements, she unhooked her bra, dropped it on the pile and set the lot outside the door.

The shower didn't have the greatest pressure, but it was enough to get clean. She inspected Olly's—or Tom's—all-in-one shampoo and conditioner with dismay and used it anyway. Beggars couldn't be choosers and there was pooey mud in her hair. A tube of face scrub sat in the caddy alongside the shampoo. With a sigh, she squeezed a small amount onto her fingertips and hoped that it would clean the worst of her runny make-up without scouring the daylights out of her skin.

When she was done, Niamh stepped out and dried herself off. A quick check of the bathroom vanity revealed no hair dryer, but she did find a rubbery scalp-massager comb and a detangling brush that, given the long hairs caught in the spikes, had to belong to Olly. After carefully picking it clean, she ran it through her hair, marvelling at how smooth the strands felt after the all-in-one shampoo.

She pulled on her damp knickers and donned the shirt Olly had left. The flannelette was velvety from wear and smelled pleasantly of washing powder. She debated over the socks, then sat on the edge of the tub to pull them on. Olly's feet were so big the heels finished halfway up her calves.

Niamh smiled to herself. She must look a fright. Which was good. Given her overexcited thoughts, she needed a passion killer.

The hall opened to a large lounge-dining area. A proper hearth with a welcoming, newly lit fire dominated the centre of the far wall. Her cleaned boots had been placed to one side on a tea towel, out of the direct heat but close enough to warm and dry.

To the right, lit by a large window, was a rectangular

dining table with a laptop computer at one end, surrounded by papers. To the left, two cracked leather recliners and a faded chintz lounge with a stack of folded clothes perched on the back faced an oversized television. Between them sat a coffee table scattered with more papers. The effect was mismatched and hand-me-down, and a bit bachelor-y, but not untidy.

She turned around. Against the wall was an old upright piano, its top covered with photo frames. Niamh wandered closer to inspect them. Taking pride of place in the middle and in the largest frame, was a photograph of a handsome man, his eyes crinkled and mouth wide with a smile. A smaller photograph stood alongside. The same man but this time with a laughing little boy on his shoulders. She swallowed. The similarity between them was uncanny. And sad. How Olly must miss his dad.

His dog as well, given the number of photos of a silky coated golden retriever. There were other photos too—a woman who must be his mum, older couples she imagined were grandparents. Photos of Olly and Tom together, Olly and other friends she didn't recognise. Olly in a dark dinner suit holding the hand of pretty redhead in a white formal dress. Niamh's stomach knotted.

'That's me partnering my friend, Faith, at her debut.' Olly came to stand behind her, a tea towel in his fist and smelling deliciously of toast and tomato and the fresh clothes he'd changed into.

'Debut?'

'Yeah. You never had them in Adelaide?'

Niamh shook her head. Weren't debuts something that heroines in historical novels made?

'Levenham has a couple every year. For some reason, girls like to do it. No idea why. Bit dumb, if you ask me,

167

dressing up in a white frock and getting yourself presented to the mayor. But fun, all the same. We had a great time. Tom did it too, with his ex, Sasha.' He cocked out an arm as though offering it to a partner, took two steps forwards with his other hand on his waist, and twirled. 'I can dance properly because of Faith's debut. Pride of Erin, Military two-step.' He winked and Niamh's insides somersaulted. 'Hidden talents.'

Niamh bet he had plenty more of those, then mentally slapped herself for thinking of sex again.

'This is your dad?' she asked, touching the big silver frame.

'Yeah.' Olly took the frame from the piano and regarded it lovingly. 'He was a great dad.'

'I'm sorry.'

'Thanks.' He set the frame back. 'This is Mum.' He pointed to the pretty, brown-eyed woman smiling in the next frame. 'This is Nan and Pop—Mum's parents—and this cheeky pair are Dad's parents, Gran and Pa.' He indicated the dog photos. 'This gorgeous girl is Tammy. The rest are cousins and mates.'

Niamh ran a finger across the piano's key lid. It was a lovely rich dark timber and probably would have been an expensive model in its day. 'This is yours?'

'It is now. It was Gran's. She left it here when they moved to town.'

'She played?'

'A bit. I think it's a hand-me-down from somewhere further back in the family. It was just something that's always been here. Play, if you want. It's probably badly out of tune, though, and I think a few of the strings are gone.' A timer sounded from the next room. 'I'd better get back to the soup.'

Niamh opened the key lid and stroked her fingers across keys yellowed with age. She pressed middle C and was rewarded with a rich sounding note. She pressed D and was amazed to hear it, too, was in tune. E, F, and G followed. Impressed, she pulled out the stool and sat, her fingers arched over the keys.

Starting slowly, she began to play. There was some discordancy, especially in the upper octaves, and an upper G gone, but the piano's tone was warm and the grain of the ivories felt fine against her fingertips. Niamh soon became lost as she moved deeper into the music and discovered the piano's quirks. To her great chagrin, Niamh's rented town-house was too awkwardly shaped for a piano, and the adjoining neighbours too close. She was making do with a keyboard—albeit a quality, full-sized one—and headphones, and it wasn't the same. Olly's instrument was a reminder of how much she missed the feel and sound of a proper piano. One day, when she had a house of her own ...

A hand touched her shoulder. Olly.

'Don't stop. It's beautiful.'

'Chopin's *Nocturne in E-flat Major*.' She played several more bars. 'One of the most romantic pieces of music ever written. Oh,' she said, when a stretch down to the lower flat released no sound.

'Sorry. I should get it fixed but ...' Though she couldn't see him, Niamh sensed Olly's shrug.

'It's not a priority.'

'No.'

She stroked a few more keys. 'It's a lovely sounding piano, even with the missing notes.' Her breath caught as Olly's finger moved to the side of her neck and traced a line, leaving an electric current in its wake.

Suddenly, she didn't want to be sitting. She didn't want

her back to him. She wanted to be in his arms, being touched all over by those strong, gentle fingers.

She turned and locked gazes with him. Desire and more flared in Olly's eyes. His lips parted slightly. Niamh rose and pressed a finger to them. Slowly, she rested one knee on the stool, then the other, still holding his eyes with hers.

Even kneeling on the stool, Niamh was frustratingly short. Shifting one hand to his shoulder for support, she carefully propped a socked foot on the stool and heaved herself upright, until she stood, this time above Olly. His hands slid to her hips and rested lightly. Power swirled within Niamh. Not from her height advantage, but from the wonder and want in his expression. She had him, this big, adorable man. And she was going to take.

'I'm going to kiss you,' she whispered.

Olly's reply came low and a little bit hoarse. 'That'd be good.'

Niamh couldn't help her smile. The way he regarded her made her light up inside. She cupped his jaw but didn't move closer, instead savouring the anticipation buzzing between them.

His Adam's apple bobbed.

'Ready?' she asked, slowly narrowing the gap between their mouths.

'I've been ready since the day we met.'

'Really?'

'Really.'

Niamh was so close the breath of his words caressed her. She sucked on her bottom lip and was rewarded when Olly's eyes followed the movement as though hypnotised. 'You say the nicest things.'

He was almost cross-eyed from staring at her mouth. His grip on her hips firmed slightly. 'I'm a nice bloke.'

'You are. A ...' She touched her lips to the corner of his mouth and shifted away. 'Very ...' She kissed the other corner. 'Nice ...' She pressed to the centre of his mouth and spoke the final word on a breath. 'Man.'

Then she was lost, kissing him like her life depended on it. Olly groaned as Niamh flattened her body to his. The kiss deepened, desperation and desire accelerating each shift of their lips and tongues. Niamh couldn't get enough of Olly's deliciousness. His kiss, the touches that set spot fires of need burning across her skin.

He groaned again, and the pleasurable ache building between her legs throbbed in response.

This wasn't enough. She needed more. More mouth, more breath, more body. More of Olly. Desperate, Niamh pressed even closer, arms wrapping tight around his neck. She hooked one leg, then the other, until both were laced around his waist, her bum supported by Olly's strong hold, every inch of her pulsing with the primitive drive for *more*.

'God, Niamh.'

Niamh's answer was an inarticulate half-groan, half-panted *yes*. She was too busy relishing Olly's kiss for anything intelligible. Nothing in all her fantasies had come close to the utter joy and pulse-racing sexiness of Olly's kiss and touch. It was like she'd found the on switch for a depth of passion she never knew she possessed. And now it had been triggered, there was no way to stop it.

'Should we ...'

'Yes,' managed Niamh, kissing her way across his throat to suck on one ear. 'Yes, yes.'

'I have to ...' With his face and hands busy, Olly used a shoulder to shrug towards the kitchen.

'Okay.' She nibbled her way back to his mouth and for

another few minutes they lost themselves in another breath-stealing kiss.

Then Olly cupped his arm more firmly beneath her bum and began to walk. It was a bit of an adventure, involving a few wall bumps and more than a few giggles and sorries, but Olly finally managed to carry Niamh to his bedroom, after a detour to the kitchen to turn off the stove.

He lowered himself to sit on the bed, Niamh still clinging like a monkey, now wrapped around his hips. His raging erection had her cheeks flushing and liquid heat pooling in her groin.

'Down,' she ordered, and pushed him backwards but remained straddling his hips. The urge to roll herself against that lovely bulge was staggering but if Olly was as turned on as her, that probably wouldn't be a wise. Instead, Niamh dragged the shirt she was wearing over her head and threw it on the floor.

Olly's gaze locked on her breasts. His mouth pursed as air whistled between his lips, and in that moment, Niamh was very glad to have ditched her bra.

His hands slid up her belly to cup her breasts. 'Told you you're lovely.'

Lovely she may be, but Niamh was also as horny as hell. It had been a long time since she'd last had sex, and it hadn't been the best of couplings, either. If her initial experience of Olly was anything to go by, Niamh knew she'd be in for a thrill ride.

She crawled up his chest to kiss him again, hands greedily pawing his shirt from his jeans as she went. She slid it up, loving the feel of his skin against hers. It was far from enough. *More* roared again through her head, matching the thunder of her blood as it raced through her arteries and veins.

She tried to pull it over his head.

'Hey, hey ...' Olly caught her hands. 'What's the hurry?'

'Needy.'

'Yeah, I can see.' He pressed her hands between his, amusement and affection shining in his eyes. 'We can take it slow. I'm not going anywhere.' He kissed her fingertips. 'We have time.'

Niamh breathed out hard. Olly was right. They did have time. Lust had clouded her brain. *He* had clouded her brain.

'Sorry,' she said, as embarrassment at her wantonness made her cheeks prickle. Maybe Olly didn't like forward girls. 'I went a bit primitive.'

'No. Don't you ever be sorry for that. You going cave-woman is the hottest thing I've ever seen.'

'In that case,' Niamh bit her lip and regarded him coyly, 'can we get naked now?'

Olly's laugh made his beautiful chest rise. 'Whatever you want, Niamh-honey. Whatever you want.'

'Good,' she said, then leaned forwards and sucked hard on his left nipple, giggling when Olly swore and wriggled beneath her.

Oh, this was going to be fun.

Chapter Ten

Niamh roused and turned on her side. She reached out an arm, but the other side of the bed was empty. A vague memory of Olly kissing her gently on the forehead and whispering that he'd be back soon floated around her head.

Olly.

His name brought a deep sigh from Niamh's lungs. Every inch of her ached with satisfaction and an irrepressible need for more. Olly had turned her completely primitive, and she'd loved every moment.

As for her worries about how they'd fit ... They were quickly proved unfounded. She and Olly entwined so perfectly, it was as though nature had modelled them to purpose. If she hadn't experienced it firsthand, Niamh wouldn't have believed such a connection was possible. Or such sex. Rapturous, orgasmic, breath-stealing sex.

Opening her eyes, she rolled onto her back and grinned up at the ceiling, then spread out her arms and flapped them bird-like up and down, her legs opening and closing in time, making a snow angel on the sheets. Then, with a giggle, she rolled over and buried her face in Olly's pillow. She inhaled deeply and rolled back, only to grin at the ceiling before repeating her snow angel flap.

From the apricot glow outside the window, dawn was creeping across the farm. Niamh supposed she should get up and make coffee, but the thought of Olly coming back to bed kept her in place. So she lay, thinking about all the marvellous things he'd done, his unselfishness, his worship of her body, his response to her cavewoman passion. The incredible joy of being with a man who didn't hold back his adoration.

After that first, glorious, toe-curling time, the remainder of the afternoon had been a giggling, gasping sexfest, only interrupted when Olly had to tend to his flocks. Niamh had spent the time he was away in delighted exhaustion. An exhaustion she quickly recovered from when a returned Olly stripped off in front of her before heading to the shower, cheekily smacking his taut bare butt as went. Niamh had scrambled out of the bed and after him like a jackrabbit.

Afterwards, they'd eaten tomato soup and cheese toasties while facing the fire. Olly had brought in a clothes rack and hung Niamh's clothes to dry alongside.

Olly had opened a bottle of wine—one of Tom's he said; he'd apologise later for stealing it—and they'd watched a movie cuddled up on the couch, though there was more watching each other than the television. When the tension became too much, Olly had simply tilted his head and asked, 'Bed?' Niamh had done her monkey act again. Olly had laughed and carried her, clinging to his front, to his bedroom, his gaze alight with amusement and a whole lot of 'you wait, cave girl'.

The now familiar sound of the screen door banging

signalled Olly's return. Grinning stupidly, Niamh arranged herself with the sheets draped low over her hips, one arm over her brow like a fainting heroine, the other cupping a breast.

His footsteps neared, then stopped. She could feel his gaze as though it had substance. Niamh peeked an eye open. Olly was leaned against the doorjamb, his hard-on poking the loose fabric of his daggy tracksuit pants, and a lazy smile tugging his mouth as he rubbed his jaw as though contemplating what to do with her.

'Hello,' she whispered.

'Hey, you.'

Niamh circled her hand over her breast, her nipple peaking and breath quickening. Olly's smug smile dropped, and his gaze darkened.

She kept her tone innocent, though innocence was the furthest thing from her thoughts. 'Want some breakfast?'

Olly shed his top and pants so fast he tripped over his discarded clothes and fell on the bed in a tangle of overlong arms and legs. Niamh cracked up laughing, then had to swallow it back when Olly picked up one of her legs and proceeded to kiss his way from ankle to thigh.

Niamh woke to find the bed once again empty. This time though, there were clangs from the kitchen. She took a moment to stretch and savour the aftermath of Olly's attentions. Her body rang with pleasurable tiredness and something deeper. A throb in her heart that she'd never felt before. Strange and exciting and delicious.

And surely wrong.

She rubbed her palms up and down her face and dismissed the awareness creeping into her head. One night of amazing lovemaking didn't mean anything. It was just sex. Very nice sex with a very nice man, but just sex.

She rolled onto her bum with her legs dangled over the side of the bed and stared out the window. Outside, the cottage's front lawn glowed verdant in the bright sun. She smiled as Max waddled into view, his friends shuffling behind, snuffling and pecking at the lawn. The scene was gentle and bucolic, and for a moment Niamh let herself wonder what it would be like to wake up to this every day.

'Hey.' Olly was at the bedroom door.

Niamh's heart faltered at the sound of his voice. Then flip-flopped as she saw his expression, like she was the most beautiful girl in the world and he its most besotted man.

She indicated the window. 'Max is out and about.'

'Yeah. I figured he'd want to know that you were still here.'

'That's sweet.'

'You're sweeter.'

Niamh rolled her eyes, making Olly laugh, while inside her heart was ballooning so big she was in danger of floating off the bed. This man ...

'Yeah, so I'm a sap.'

'I think you're cute.' She rose to hunt for the shirt and socks he'd loaned her. The floor was chilly on her feet. The night had been another nippy one, but Olly had been so warm she hadn't noticed. 'What's the time?'

'Dunno.' He scruffed at his hair, pulling strands from the bun he'd tied it in. 'After ten.'

She stilled. 'After ten?'

'Probably. Maybe half past?'

Niamh's stomach dropped like a plunging elevator. After ten? *After ten?*

'No.' Heart racing, she swept the floor, wailing in frustration when she couldn't find Olly's shirt. 'No, no, no!'

'What?' Olly stepped into the room and held her by the shoulders. 'Niamh-honey. What's the matter?'

'I'm late!'

His face scrunched. 'For what?'

'Amber's piano lesson. Ten o'clock, every Sunday.'

'Amber? She'll be fine. She's probably still in bed with Tom.' He chuckled and tried to hug her to him, but Niamh wasn't having it.

She shoved him away. 'I am never late. *Never.* Amber knows this. She'll be waiting.'

'Niamh, come on.'

'No.' The panic was growing worse. She was late. Really late. And it was crushing her like she couldn't breathe. And her teeth were doing that funky thing, like they were about to vibrate out of her head and drop—*plop plop*—on the floor.

She shoved her way past Olly and into the lounge. Head down, she snatched up her now-dry clothes and shoved them on. Looking at Olly was hard. There were too many feelings swirling inside her, none of which she wanted to face. Worse, she knew he was thinking she was crazy, and she didn't want him to think she was crazy except in an adorable way.

A sob formed. Niamh choked it down and wrested up the zippers of her boots, not caring that they didn't reach the top. As long as they were secure enough for her to run, they'd do.

She stared around wildly, trying to pinpoint where

she'd left her watch and jewellery, then bolted for the bathroom.

'Niamh, please.'

Olly tried to catch her arm as she passed him, but she wrenched free. She snatched up her jewellery and shoved it into her pocket, catching a glimpse of herself in the mirror as she did. Sex-mussed hair at all angles from not being blow-dried, pale skin, freaky eyes, shirt buttoned out of sync. Niamh tore her gaze away.

Car keys ...

With a moan, she felt the other pocket. Nothing. The moan became a keen. She'd put them in her pocket for safekeeping when she arrived. Olly had likely put them through the wash.

'Niamh-honey, shhh.' Olly had his left hand on her shoulder and was staring at her with worry. He dragged her close and stroked her hair. 'It's okay.'

Her mouth crumpled and she blinked against the horrible prickle in her eyes. 'You don't understand.'

'I do. I do.' His hand kept stroking. 'You're late for Amber and you hate being late. And your teeth are going funky.'

She closed her eyes and shook her head. If only it were that simple.

'Then what? Talk to me.' He wrapped his arms around her and kissed the top of her head. 'Talk to me, lovely girl. Let me make it better.'

But no one could make this better.

Aware of what she was about to do, Niamh allowed herself a few more seconds of Olly's embrace before twisting free. 'Where are my keys?'

He stared at her, his Adam's apple bobbing, his gaze shiny and his voice cracked. 'Don't do this. Don't let it control you. Amber will understand. And we're ...' He breathed a few times. 'We're more important.'

Niamh had to swallow to keep the crack out of her own voice. 'I need my keys, Olly.'

For several heartbeats he did nothing but stare with pleading eyes, then he seemed to sag. He indicated the lounge. 'On the mantel.'

Niamh hurried for the lounge, her teeth wedged into her bottom lip to stop herself from howling. Seconds later she was out the door and jogging to her car, a startled Max bugling in her wake.

A last glance in the rear-vision mirror as she put the car in motion revealed a barefooted Olly in the middle of the drive with his hands locked on his head, resignation tugging at his mouth, and Max leaning against his leg, as though in sympathy.

Tears flooded Niamh's vision. She swiped them away. This wasn't her. She was tough, rational, disciplined, but Olly had a way of making her lose herself. Of making her behave out of character. Of making her forget what kept her calm and safe.

He made her feel things, intense things, that had no business interrupting her structured life.

It was too much. Worse, it was wrong. Because they were wrong. They'd been that way from the start and she knew it, but he was so sweet and sexy she hadn't been able to resist and now disaster had struck.

A quick glance at the front of her townhouse showed no sign of Amber's car. Niamh fisted her hands back and forth around the wheel. Of course, Amber hadn't waited. It was almost an hour past their lesson time. Niamh rubbed at her teeth with her forefinger, but it was out of habit. The funky feeling had gone, replaced with something far more awful.

Niamh drove to Amber's and banged on the door.

It swung open to Amber wearing an enormous smile that dropped the moment she registered Niamh's ragged appearance. 'Niamh. Oh, my God. What's happened?'

Niamh's face crumpled. She heaved a sob that seemed to drag from the depths of her toes.

'God, come in.' Gently, Amber circled an arm around Niamh and steered her inside to the kitchen.

'Holy shit,' said Tom, even more wide-eyed than Amber.

'Sit,' said Amber, placing her on a stool at the bench. She exchanged a look with Tom, who lifted his palms. Amber settled on the stool next to Niamh and took her hand. 'What happened? Was it Olly?'

Niamh nodded.

'Jesus Christ,' said Tom, fisting his hands. 'I'll kill the bastard.'

'No!' Another wave of panic gripped Niamh, this time for an entirely different reason. 'Olly's done nothing.'

Except that wasn't right at all. He done everything. All of it wonderful. This was *her*.

'Then what's going on?' asked Amber.

Niamh shook her head, unable to speak for the gravel lodged in her throat and the pain spreading across her chest.

Amber squeezed her fingers. 'When you weren't home for our lesson, I assumed you'd stayed the night with Olly.'

'I did.'

Amber glanced at Tom, before smiling uncertainly at Niamh. 'But that's a good thing.' She paused. 'Isn't it?'

'No!'

'No? But ... why?'

'Because!' Another wail was building. Niamh wanted to

squash it down, but was too overwhelmed. A choked sob emerged instead.

'Because why?'

'Because there's nothing left.'

Amber's confusion had her blinking. 'What do you mean?'

She regarded her friend with a quivering lip. 'He's broken them all.'

Amber exchanged another look with Tom. 'All what?'

'All the reasons I had for not falling in love with him and I can't. I just can't, because we're all wrong and will never last, but I have and now I don't know what to do!'

Chapter Eleven

Olly was sunk in a muddy trench when Tom turned up.

His friend hunkered at the edge and peered at the long stretch of pipe Olly had dug free. Every time Olly thought he'd found all the leaks another cropped up. He shouldn't have been surprised. The pipe had been laid for the original broiler shed and had to be forty years old. It should have been replaced when he'd had the new shed built, but money had been tight, and he'd been naïve to the dangers of false economising.

'Need a hand?' asked Tom.

Olly wiped one forearm across his brow. 'Nah.'

'Sure?'

Something in Tom's tone had Olly eyeing him. They'd been friends a long time. There was more behind Tom's question than a simple double-check. He wanted to talk about Niamh. Any other day, Olly would jump at the chance, but today wasn't like any other. He was confused and hurt and feeling more than a little bit sulky. Still, this was Tom, and Olly really could do with a hand. 'Yeah, all right. Thanks.'

'I'll get changed and come back. Want anything from the house?'

Olly shook his head and resumed his excavation. At this rate he'd have to dig out the entire pipe and replace the lot. Maybe it was worth doing. Maybe it wasn't. Right now, Olly couldn't think straight enough for those kinds of decisions.

Tom returned dressed in work clothes and heavy boots and carrying a shovel. Without a word he began to dig.

A good five minutes passed before Olly cracked. 'Did Niamh turn up at Amber's?'

'Yep.'

Olly nodded. That was good. The state she was in, she needed a friend. Clearly Olly hadn't qualified.

'She was a bit of a mess,' said Tom.

'Yeah.'

Tom leaned on his shovel and contemplated Olly. 'What happened?'

Olly wished he knew. He kind of knew, but Niamh's reaction to being late had felt over the top, even for her.

'I don't know. We were getting on great, then she asked what the time was, and when I told her she went into a flat spin about being late. I kept saying Amber wouldn't mind, but she wouldn't listen. Then she just ran off.'

'Huh,' said Tom on a grunt as he lifted a wad of thick dirt from the trench and dumped it on the pile.

Huh? Yeah, like that was a great help. Olly crouched and flicked a nail at the section of poly pipe he'd uncovered. A large crack ran its length before ending in a slight cave-in where soil had penetrated. It was a wonder any water got through at all.

He rose with a sigh. 'Leave it. The whole thing needs replacing.'

Tom did his own inspection. 'Probably the best idea. You got pipe?'

'Not enough.' Olly climbed out of the trench. Something he'd sort out on Monday.

'I'll give you a hand when the time comes.'

'Thanks.' Tom was a good egg, despite the unhelpful *huh*. Olly gathered the shovels and trudged towards the farm's machinery shed, Tom alongside. Olly glanced at him. 'What are you doing this arvo?'

'Probably head back to Amber's once the coast is clear.' The coast being Niamh, of course.

Olly looked away. Even thinking her name made him ache. He was mad for her, had been from their first date, but blind Freddy could see she didn't feel the same. If she had, she would have let him comfort her.

He brooded for several more steps. 'Did Niamh say anything, when you were there?'

'She did.'

Olly halted. Tom walked on, then turned around when he realised Olly wasn't with him.

'What did she say?'

'It was pretty garbled.'

'Yeah ... and?'

Tom's mouth twitched. Olly narrowed his eyes. This was not frigging funny. This was his future.

His mate sauntered closer and grabbed Olly's shoulder and shook it. 'She ran because she's fallen in love with you.'

Olly froze. Even his heart, which had been throbbing painfully all morning, forgot to beat. 'She said that?'

'Yep. Along with a whole bunch of other stuff about it

being totally wrong and never lasting and not knowing what to do about it.'

'Right,' said Olly. 'Right.' He shook himself. 'So, like, she ran because ...' He scrunched up his face, trying to figure it out. 'She was scared?'

'Don't ask me,' said Tom with a shrug. 'Amber hustled me out before Niamh could get to that bit. But I'm guessing yes.'

'That's ...' Nuts is what it was, but Niamh rated pretty highly on the kooky scale. It was one of the things he adored about her. She was fantastically weird, with her funky teeth and time obsession and bondage mistress outfits. She was also the cleverest, funniest, and most sexy woman he'd had the grace to know.

'Crazy? Yeah, but Niamh's like that.' Tom grabbed the shovels from an immobile Olly and sauntered on. 'You'll get used to it.'

Olly had no doubt, but would Niamh give him the chance to?

A question Olly spent the rest of the afternoon chewing over. Tom gave him a hand to shift the runs, until Amber called to say the coast was clear. Olly watched him rush off with envy. That could be him and Niamh, except she didn't want it. In her mind, they were wrong and not worth the heartache.

She didn't want to believe. Whereas Olly believed with every cell in his body.

That night, he sat in the lounge juggling his phone. To call or not to call? He glanced at his dad's photo, but for once his dad wasn't talking. Olly supposed he could send a text, or message Niamh through the Cupid Country app. What to say, though? Sorry you fell in love? Sorry for scaring you with these big feelings?

Olly wasn't sorry at all. The only thing he was sorry for was not being able to comfort her enough so they could talk.

He set down the phone and tried to watch a football panel show, but the jokey blokes did nothing for his mood. He flipped channels only to end up on one of those dating reality shows, where everyone was beautiful, and every action contrived, and reality didn't come into it anywhere. Olly quickly flicked it over then spent another five minutes channel surfing before giving up and streaming *Harry Potter and the Philosopher's Stone*.

Even that, his favourite movie of all time, failed to hook him.

Olly left it running and picked up his phone again. After a moment's thought, he began to type.

Are you okay?

For a long, torturous moment there was no answer, then the dots began to bob up and down on the screen, indicating Niamh was typing.

Sort of.

Olly didn't know what to make of that. Was she still upset? Did she blame him? He glanced at his dad and gave him a crooked smile. 'Yeah. Yeah, I know.' A faint heart never won a fair maiden, or whatever the saying was.

Do you want to talk? he wrote.

Again, there was a long pause before Niamh tapped a reply.

I don't know.

Olly's heart sank. Not the answer he was hoping for. Also, not a very Niamh answer. As she'd reminded him more than once, she was a woman who knew her own mind, and now it seemed she didn't. Olly couldn't imagine she was finding the experience pleasant. God knows, he wasn't.

He was still thinking up a response when the dots started bobbing.

Maybe soon?

The air left his lungs. He had a maybe and maybes meant chances. And a chance was all he could ask for. If space was what she wanted, then space was what he'd give her. Even if doing so would damn near kill him.

I'm here if you need me. Olly thought for a second, then added a 'x' on the end.

Thank you.

Though Olly kept hold of his phone until the end of *Harry Potter*, it never gave another ping.

It was Thursday before Niamh made contact. In the four days since their last communication, Olly's life had been a haze of half-heartedness. He got up, worked his guts out, came home, ate listlessly, went to bed, slept badly. Sensing his human friend's low spirits, Max had taken to dogging his heels, peering up anxiously as Olly meandered from chore to chore without enthusiasm.

Tom wasn't any help. Amber wasn't telling him anything, except that Olly needed to stay patient. Easy for her to say. She wasn't the one who'd lost the colour from their world.

Olly had just come in from settling his flocks into their night sheds and was pulling off his boots when a muffled *ping* sounded from his jacket pocket. Hopping on one socked foot, Olly tore off the other boot, snatched out the phone and jabbed at the screen to wake it up.

A message. From Niamh. He lowered himself to the back step to read.

Are you free to meet on Saturday afternoon?

Olly didn't even think. He punched out a *yes* and held his breath for her reply.

Is 2pm at the Civic Park fountain okay with you?

Civic Park fountain? It was a nice place, a pretty place even, but a place for a reunion of this importance? Doubt at its meaning began to creep around Olly's mind. You couldn't get more public than Civic Park. A place hard to have a row or make a scene. Not that Olly was prone to either, but maybe Niamh thought she'd need that safety when she told him they were over.

He shoved the idea away. What mattered was seeing her. Telling her how he felt, that opposites could truly attract. That they had a chance.

No problem at all.

Good. See you then.

And that was it. No "how have you been?" No "look forward to seeing you". Just a toneless *See you then.*

Olly rubbed at his jaw. He supposed the "good" was something. Not much, but something, and deserving of a something in return.

Smiling, he shot back an *xxx.* They'd had sex. Fantastic sex. *Meaningful* sex. Three messaged kisses were just the start of what he could give.

Olly checked his new Swatch watch as he closed his car door and hurried into Civic Park. With a silicone band the bright red of a Muscovy's caruncle, it wasn't the most masculine of timepieces, but it was a reliable brand and, he hoped, would be easy to locate whenever he took it off. Besides, it was for Niamh. Who cared about colour, when being on time was what mattered?

A wire arch covered with a pair of climbing roses signalled the park's entrance. Olly ducked to avoid getting caught but still managed to snarl his loose hair. Muttering a low curse, he quickly disentangled himself and strode on. Nothing would make him late today. Nothing.

He followed the path to the fountain, smiling at the few people he passed. The gorgeous spring day had brought out the strollers, and Civic Park, with its colourful blooms and gnarly old trees was a pleasant place to wander.

He hoped like hell it would prove a pleasant place for a rendezvous, too.

The fountain gurgled a welcome. Olly stood beside it with his fists in his pockets and scanned the surrounds. No Niamh yet, but he was several minutes early. He circled the fountain, trying to appear casual as he checked the paths that wound in and out of the gardens, while his stomach buzzed with nerves. Returning to the front, Olly killed a few more minutes poking his fingers into the fountain's pond, trying to attract its resident koi, only for the fish to keep shying away. Olly hoped it wasn't an omen.

Footsteps had him straightening, but it was a woman hurrying towards the council library that bordered the southern side of the park. He scanned the park again, double-checking shadows and entrance paths, hunting for a tiny figure with blunt-cut hair. Still nothing.

Olly checked his watch and frowned. Two minutes to two. Surely Niamh would be here by now?

Swallowing, he resumed his vigil. Another minute passed, then another. He shifted his weight from foot to foot. Shoved his fists in his pockets, pulled them out again. Watched a magpie pluck a bug from the lawn and trot it to her squawking offspring.

Though he knew damn well it hadn't sounded, Olly dragged out his phone anyway to check for messages, then sucked in a breath when he caught the time.

Two past two.

Niamh was late.

Niamh was never late, which could only mean one of two things. He'd been stood up or something bad had happened, and Olly refused to believe she would stand him up. If Niamh set a time, she'd stick to it. It was one of her *things*.

Olly stepped left, stepped right. Where to go? He didn't know where she lived, only that it was a townhouse not far from the park.

He punched dial on her number then groaned when it went straight to her message bank. A second try ended the same. Olly stabbed at Tom's number instead, his breath easing a little when it rang. Tom would be with Amber, and Amber would know what to do.

'You've reached Tom ...'

Her regarded the screen with horror. 'You're frigging kidding me?' Though he knew it was hopeless, he tried again, with the same result. He redialled Niamh.

Nothing.

Out of options, Olly hung up. Then he slumped on the fountain's wall and buried his face in his hands.

Chapter Twelve

Though her teeth were buzzing and her fingers opened and closed with the urge to fiddle with her watch, Niamh forced her steps slower. As uncomfortable as her version of behavioural therapy was, she had to beat this. And what was a few minutes when it came to the rest of her life?

She wiped her hands down the side of her skinny jeans and concentrated instead on the speech she'd been rehearsing.

I'm sorry for running away. I didn't know what to do. I couldn't think straight. I thought we were wrong, but then we were right and I ... I know I have issues but I'm going to make them better. For you and for me. Because I—

Niamh's breath caught. Every time she tried to articulate her feelings they turned to gobbledegook. This unhingedness was so new, so alien, she didn't have the skills or experience to cope. But she had to. *She had to.* Failure would be too heartbreaking.

Why was she finding love so impossible? People fell in and out of it every day and survived. Even thrived.

Niamh was a clever, capable woman. Surely she could, too?

Olly was the sweetest, most gorgeous and kind man she'd ever met. Every argument she'd had against the relationship had been broken down. They were still opposites—still short and tall, still city and country, still exacting and chill—and yet she'd come to realise they were also perfect together.

Except, what if Olly didn't feel the same? What if after Sunday's debacle he thought her too weird, too much hard work. Not lovely anymore.

She blinked and stared at her feet, her throat turning gravelly with the thought of losing him.

Nope. Nup. No. Not going to happen. Not without a fight.

Niamh paused at the entrance to Civic Park. Across the street, a lunchtime group of diners were spilling out of Restaurant Ten, rubbing their full bellies and laughing at their overindulgence. The same restaurant where Niamh had once believed it would take a miracle for her and Olly to overcome their differences, not realising that miracles truly could happen.

I'm sorry, Olly. She rehearsed in her head. *I was overwhelmed. I'm not used to not being in control and you make me feel out of control and I don't know how ...*

'Oh, stop it,' Niamh muttered aloud as she stepped beneath the rose arbour and into the park. Olly wasn't to blame, she was.

She rubbed at her watch, then, unable to help herself, checked the time.

Her hand shot to her chest then fluttered at the base of her throat. An instant later, her teeth bumped up their familiar vibration.

'No,' she whispered, and forced herself to a stop. She closed her eyes, pulled in a deep breath through her nose and let it out slowly through her mouth.

The world would not end if she was late. It wouldn't care. It wouldn't notice. No one would notice. Olly probably wasn't even at the fountain yet. She'd be rushing for nothing.

Niamh repeated the breathing exercise, telling herself she was fine. Her teeth were fine, secure in her mouth. There was nothing to worry about. Nothing.

Except Olly.

'Are you all right?'

She opened her eyes to see an elderly lady with a bright pink walker staring at her worriedly. 'Yes. Thank you. I'm fine. Just ... centring myself.'

The woman frowned then sniffed. 'Perhaps you could centre yourself out of the way then.'

'Ah, yes. Of course. Sorry.'

Niamh ducked off the path, her cheeks burning. The woman trundled past, eyeing Niamh sideways. Niamh forced a smile, the epitome of an everyday, perfectly normal person doing perfectly normal things. The woman only sped up.

A giggle rose. She mashed it back down. Now was not the time for nerves. Now was for action, albeit tortoise paced.

Apart from the occasional squelch, Niamh's sneakers made little sound. She'd dressed down today—the same white leather sneakers she'd worn on their first date, dark denim skinny jeans, a plain white tee. Almost girl next door, except for her hair and make-up. Letting that be anything other than immaculate was a step too far. A girl had standards.

Less than a minute later, she rounded the final bend. And stumbled to a halt.

Olly was slumped on the fountain wall, head down, knees apart, hands rubbing his face. As she watched, he gave his cheeks one last scrub, glanced at the bright red watch on his wrist, and rose. Shoulders as drooped as his mouth, Olly took a step towards the path where Niamh stood in the shade and froze.

'Niamh? Oh, shit, Niamh.'

In a few, long strides, Olly was wrapped around her, his face buried in her hair, his lips kissing the top of her head.

'You're here,' he said, his voice choked. 'I thought something terrible had happened, but you're here.' His hug turned momentarily tighter, then he let go and gave her a gentle shake. 'You're late. You're never late. You hate being late.'

'I know.' Another inappropriate bubble of laughter rose in her chest. Poor Olly looked set to faint and all she wanted to do was laugh. Perhaps it was shock. Maybe delight at his watch. Definitely relief. 'I'm trying to train myself not to be so anal.'

'You're not anal, you're precise. I nearly had a heart attack.' He massaged the left side of his chest as if still worried about his health. 'You scared me.'

'It's okay.' Niamh pressed her hand over his, hardly believing it was her comforting him. 'I'm here now.'

'Yeah,' he said, blowing air through pursed lips. 'Yeah, you are.' A furrow formed between his brows. 'Is it working? The training thing?'

She screwed up her nose and tapped her front teeth. 'My teeth are pretty funky.'

He grinned and stroked her hair. 'You're so cute.'

'Olly ...' Niamh tried to find the words she'd been practising so hard, but his smile and the tenderness in his gaze was muddling her brain. She shook her head in frustration. 'I'm sorry. I ...'

His grin dropped. He took a step back and plunged his fists into his pockets. His voice, when it came, sounded flat. 'You're going to tell me you don't think we'll work.'

'No!'

Olly blinked and jiggled his head a little as though shaking something out of his ear. 'No?'

'No.' Niamh huffed a laugh. 'God, no. Is that what you thought?'

'It's what I feared.' He indicated the fountain. 'Isn't that what girls do? Choose public places to burn blokes off?'

'Not this girl. I just thought it was a nice place. And it was close to home so if you rejected me, I wouldn't have far to run.'

'Reject you? Niamh, I'm so batshit crazy about you I can't think straight.'

'Me, too.' She laughed again. 'I'm not used to being so ...' She made circles at the side of her head. 'Crazy. I mean, I know I have my *things*, but a lack of composure wasn't ever one of them. And I've been completely discomposed by you since we first met. I still don't understand how this happened. I tried not to let it, but you've ... You've *undone* me.' She tapped a finger to her chest. 'Me, the bondage mistress.'

Slowly, almost shyly, a tentative smile crept over Olly's face. 'So this means we're on?'

'We're on, Olly. Whatever that entails.'

'It entails whatever you want it to, Niamh-honey.'

They stood a foot apart, staring. Then Olly broke into one of his trademark beams and Niamh's heart filled like a helium balloon. Unable to cope another second without his touch, she launched herself at him. Olly whooped and hauled her up his chest until her legs were wrapped around him in her familiar monkey grip. Cupping her hands around his jaw, she dragged his face in for a kiss.

A kiss that lasted a long, long time.

Loud guffaws and not-so-subtle whispers of her name had Niamh coming up for air. Disengaging her lips from Olly's, she glanced past his shoulder.

'Oh,' she said.

Olly swung them both sideways. A gaggle of teenagers stood by the fountain. Two had their phones out and pointed at Niamh.

She swallowed as a hot flush of embarrassment whooshed through her body.

'Your students?' asked Olly.

'Yes.'

'Bugger off,' growled Olly.

Which, of course, was ignored. Olly might look and sound imposing but it was hard to be taken seriously with a woman clutched to your chest like a baby koala.

'Maybe you should get a room, Miss,' said Alexander Healy, always the smart-mouth, to a round of sniggers and guffaws, and a fist bump from one of his cronies.

Niamh's grip on Olly began to loosen, but Olly wasn't letting her go. 'Little shit's just jealous,' he whispered. 'Hot teacher in the arms of a bigger, better bloke. I bet he's got a mammoth crush. I know I have.'

She glanced at Alexander. The teen was eyeing them snidely. Suddenly she was flooded with anger. So what if she'd been caught in an inappropriate embrace? This was Olly, the man she loved. They were spoiling the moment.

'Actually,' said Niamh, in clipped, cool bondage mistress tones, 'I think that sounds an excellent idea. Olly?'

'Done,' he replied, planting a kiss on her mouth.

Without so much as a mocking glance behind, he strode off through the park with Niamh still attached and the sound of shrieking, shocked teenagers fading in his wake.

'You are such a sweetheart,' said Niamh, aware that she should really get down but not wanting to. Feminism be damned, being heroically carried by Olly was fast becoming one of her favourite things.

'And you, Niamh-honey, are lovely.' He strode on a bit further. 'Where do you want to go?'

'My place?'

A grin split his face. 'Yeah?'

'Yeah. I don't know about you, but I'm feeling a bit cavewoman.'

Olly laughed and scooted around the elderly lady with the pink walker Niamh had encountered earlier, who'd stopped to inspect a rosebush. Niamh grinned at her from over Olly's shoulder and gave a little wave. 'I found my centre,' she called.

'Good to hear,' said the woman, surprising Niamh. She gave a nod. 'Enjoy yourself.'

'Thanks. I will.' She snuffled into Olly's neck, breathing him in. She absolutely would. And she'd make sure Olly did too.

Always.

Epilogue

Niamh eyed the room and smiled. With all the preparation, it had been a crazy couple of days, but worth every moment. Around her, people milled and chatted, filling the upstairs function room of the Australian Arms Hotel with happy noise. It was a disparate group, a mix of teachers, farmers, and other locals, but they all seemed to get on.

She glanced up at Olly, silhouetted with Amber and Tom at the rear of the dance floor beneath two giant linked love hearts surrounded by feathers, with "Happy Engagement" dashed across them in clumsy red cursive. It was silly and adorable and Amber loved it, because it had been made by the students at her school. Each child had also scrawled a message of congratulations and thanks, some with extra love hearts, others with kisses. A special present for a beloved teacher.

Amber and Tom had finally announced their engagement a month ago, to relief all round and mutters of "what took you so long?" The announcement had been expected at Christmas; then, when that passed, at New Year, only for that to pass without event, too. Whenever they were asked, the pair would look smug and advise patience. Finally, the deed was done on Tom's birthday in August, with Amber popping the question herself as his present. After jumping out of a cardboard cake, wearing a bikini. Apparently, the couple had laughed themselves stupid before ending up in bed. As usual.

Niamh couldn't be more thrilled for them. Or delighted, when Amber and Tom had asked Niamh and Olly to be best woman and best man. Tom was a darling and his and Amber's journey of love at first sight, only to have it thwarted before finding each other again, was ridiculously romantic.

Not as romantic as Niamh and Olly's journey, but Niamh was biased.

Olly caught her eye, muttered something to Tom and wandered over. 'You okay there?'

'I am.' Niamh was next to the man she loved, sharing a special night celebrating the engagement of two people she adored. How could she not be okay? And Amber had been right. The woolshed at Tom's parents' property, Glenlea, would have been fun, but the Arms was the better party setting for the mixed crowd. It even had a mirror ball. Niamh particularly liked the way it made her blue jumpsuit glitter. 'You?'

Olly winked at her. 'You know me. I'm pretty chill.'

Niamh rolled her eyes. Olly was always chill. So was she these days, comparatively speaking. Niamh remained as fussy as ever with her appearance, and her teeth still went funky when she was late, but she was more relaxed overall.

With his trademark sunny disposition and easygoing patience, Olly had showed her what was truly important in life, and it wasn't being on time. It was the people she loved.

As if sensing her thoughts, Olly slung an arm around her shoulders and tickled her ear. He'd discovered she had a thing about the sensitive skin behind her ear and exploited it any chance he could. Weird as they were, he loved her *things*, and she loved him even more for it.

'Dance?' asked Olly as a couple of teacher friends dragged Amber onto the dance floor, Amber hauling Tom by the hand behind. The speeches were over, the cake—an exquisitely decorated mudcake made by Tom's baking whiz aunt—cut, and the guests were loose with beer and wine and good feeling.

She and Olly joined the crowd. Niamh watched in amusement as Tom's mate and second wedding attendant, Lincoln McEvoy, sidled closer to the prettiest of Amber's friends, only to have Olly's spud-growing mate, Hamish, cut in. Dirty looks were exchanged until Amber's friend demonstrated exactly where her affections lay by sneaking off to a corner with another woman.

Several songs later, with the boys demanding a beer break, Amber hooked her arm through Niamh's and bent close.

'Rescue mission,' she said, tipping her head slightly towards the edge of the dance floor.

Niamh followed her gaze. Tom's usually cheerful sister stood alone, nursing a drink, and watching the partygoers with an expression clouded with yearning.

'Lead the way, my friend.' No one should be sad on a night like tonight. It wasn't right and as best woman, it was Niamh's job to make sure her fellow attendant was happy.

After jokes about sprained bum muscles and the antics of Tom's mates, Amber got to work finding out what was wrong with Eden. She was an attractive girl and a lot like her brother—leggy, athletic, and good-humoured. Niamh had met her several times now and liked her. She was even considering taking up Eden's offer of riding lessons, but between work, squash, Amber's piano instruction and helping Olly and his mum on the farm, Niamh had enough on her plate.

'How did it go today?' asked Amber, all of them aware what the "it" referred to. Or, rather, whom: Humphrey Taylor-Martin, Eden's long-time crush, who Tom had nick-named "Poshpants".

Eden shrugged. 'Not great. I asked him to come along tonight, and he said no.' She shook her head and looked down for a moment before addressing Amber in a weary tone. 'He did the "don't spoil our friendship" thing again.'

'Ah, that old turkey,' said Amber.

Eden snorted and stared into the depths of her drink. 'I think he meant it this time.'

Amber pressed a hand to Eden's back and rubbed. 'I'm sorry.'

'It's okay. I'm fine.'

Amber exchanged a look with Niamh, who cupped Eden's nearest shoulder. Apart from an unreciprocated— and thankfully brief—crush on a classmate when she was fifteen, and her short-term fear of losing Olly just as she realised how much she loved him, Niamh had no experience of unrequited love. She imagined it would be painful, though, to yearn so badly for someone who didn't feel the same.

'You could always try Cupid Country. It worked for us.'

'It's a thought,' said Amber, ducking to smile at Eden. 'Maybe worth a try? See what's out there?'

Eden wasn't enthusiastic about the idea, but other than joking about their own Cupid Country adventures, Niamh and Amber didn't push. Eden would work things out.

Suddenly, the dance music cut off. Fearing some sort of stuff-up, Niamh checked the DJ's booth, but he was still in his corner, fingers on buttons.

Tom began shooing guests off the dance floor. People bustled backwards, looking upwards with frowns as they tried to place the soft tune filtering through the speakers. He shaded his eyes and peered out over the crowd. 'Where are you, cute girl?'

Amber squealed and waved before racing towards her fiancé.

Oohs, sounded. Of delight and recognition as The Temptations' "My Girl" gained traction. Niamh's breath caught as Tom and Amber moved onto the dance floor, spotlit bodies held close as they smiled besottedly at one another.

'That is so romantic.'

'Yeah,' said Olly, suddenly alongside and looking down at Niamh.

His expression had her heart stuttering, and all Niamh wanted to do was throw herself at that beautiful big frame and never let him out of her hold again.

Hand out, Olly tipped his head at the dance floor. Niamh took his hand and followed him to the centre. Seconds later, Lincoln and Eden joined them, followed by Tom's and Amber's parents and extended family. A swirling, smiling, mass of happiness.

'Love you,' he whispered, bending close.

Niamh pressed her forehead against Olly's chest and gave a lovesick sigh. Oh, she adored this man and his easy, warm words. 'Love *you*,' she whispered. 'So much.'

She looked up and laughed as Tom's dad, Scott, twirled proudly past with his wife, Leanne, and shot Niamh a wink, as if to say, "This will be you next".

Would her own parents be as happy and proud? Niamh suspected they would. They'd only met Olly twice. The first time, on a visit to Levenham. Olly had been his usual laid-back self, meeting them at Niamh's townhouse for a barbecue, wandering in straight from the farm with his hair in a man bun, casual in jeans and a flannelette shirt. Niamh's dad had stared between Niamh and Olly in puzzlement.

Niamh's mum had regarded them similarly until, less than an hour later, when Olly was avidly advocating a law change to include mandatory ponds for waterfowl, understanding had spread across her face.

'He's like you,' she'd said in the kitchen, as they prepared salad. Olly was in the townhouse's tiny courtyard, manning the barbeque and drinking beer with Niamh's dad.

'Like me?'

'You're both passionate about the things you care about.'

Niamh hadn't thought of it that way, but she supposed her mum was right. Olly was mad about his birds; Niamh had her numbers and piano and curiosity. And they had each other. Plenty of passion there.

By the end of the weekend, after a visit to the farm and a tour of Duck, Duck, Goose's operations, and meeting Olly's wonderful, easygoing mum—who Niamh had come to admire and adore—her parents had been well and truly charmed and approving.

"My Girl" ended and the dancers came to a halt and applauded the happy couple. Tom and Amber held their arms wide, inviting the others to join them in a bow. The music started up again, and the room echoed with the sounds of Bruno Mars boppily singing "Marry You". Reflected light from the mirror ball danced across the floor. The party was back on.

Olly and Niamh moved to the edge of the floor. Olly's arms dropped around her from behind and his chin rested lightly on her head as they watched and smiled as the teacher contingent cut loose, Lincoln and Hamish doing their best to keep up.

'You're going to make the hottest best woman,' said Olly.

Niamh rotated in his arms and began to sway her hips. 'And you'll be the sexiest best man.'

'I could go one step further.'

Niamh stopped her sway and frowned at him. 'What do you mean?'

'You know ...' Suddenly, the amusement in Olly's face was replaced by hesitancy. He cleared his throat. 'Graduate to something bigger.'

Niamh still didn't get it. Then she did. Her eyes widened. 'Are you ...?'

'Not here. Tonight belongs to Tom and Amber. I've been thinking about it, though.'

Niamh sucked on her lip. They'd not been dating a year yet. Surely it was too soon? Except she knew it wasn't. Since Tom had moved in with Amber, Niamh was spending half the week and every weekend with Olly. She knew his quirks and habits and moods, as he knew hers. And truth was, she'd been secretly having the same thoughts since Amber and Tom made their announcement.

More importantly, they were in love. Stupidly so.

'Me, too,' she said, before quickly adding, 'I mean, not yet. But,' Niamh shrugged one shoulder, 'one day.'

'Really?'

'Yes.' She grinned up at him. 'Of course. I wouldn't say it otherwise. I'm a woman—'

'Who knows her own mind. Yeah, I know. And I bloody

love you for it. That and the fact you go all cavewoman when you're turned on. I *really* love that.' Olly leaned down and kissed her, his gaze sparkling. 'One day, huh?'

'Yes, Olly. One day.'

'Cool.' He nodded as though to himself. 'Very cool.' Then he looked at her, serious now. 'Life's short, Niamh. You need to live it every day.'

'I know. And I have every intention of living it with you.' She hooked her arm through his as Bruno faded and was replaced with Taylor Swift's "Love Story". 'Now come dance with me.' She gave him her best saucy look from beneath her lashes. 'Unless you're not up for it?'

That blew away his seriousness. 'A dance with my best bird? What do you reckon?'

'I reckon,' said Niamh, dragging him forwards and nearly skipping to the dance floor, 'we're on.'

Eager to find out if Eden and Humphrey can overcome their fears? Check out age gap and grumpy sunshine romance *Cupid Country Crush!*

CUPID
COUNTRY
BOOK THREE

Cupid Country CRUSH

CATHRYN HEIN

Cupid Country Crush

Grumpy meets sunshine in this small-town age-gap romance.

Eden Jones has loved fellow showjumper Humphrey Taylor-Martin since she was sixteen years old. Except Humphrey is convinced their age gap is a bigger problem than any romantic feelings he might be hiding and refuses to be anything more than friends.

That doesn't stop Eden from trying to change his mind. But when yet another emphatic rejection sends her reeling, Eden vows it's time to move on. She'll go on dating app Cupid Country and schedule a date a week for the whole of the showjumping season, until her Humphrey crush is cured.

Humphrey should be relieved when he learns of Eden's plan. He might crave her as much as she craves him, but bright, funny Eden deserves someone her own age, not a grizzled, grumpy old man. But as the showjumping season edges on, and Eden keeps dating, Humphrey's feelings only deepen and threaten to expose his true heart.

Can he keep his distance until the end of the season, or will one precious night change their lives forever?

Chapter One

Eden stole a look at Humphrey Taylor-Martin's delicious rear as he bent to fasten floating boots around the front legs of his horse, Tiger. For a bloke who'd just turned forty, he had a fantastic bum. Lean, yet rounded in all the right spots, and not so taut as to be unsqueezable. The sort of bum a girl would love to wrap her legs around and dig her heels into, should she get the chance.

Which was highly unlikely in Eden's case. And not for want of trying.

She returned to her own mount's boots and fastened the final velcro tab. She patted Admiral's shoulder and double-checked the belly strap of his rug, casting another surreptitious glance over Addy's back as she did. Humphrey Taylor-Martin had been her drug of choice since she was sixteen years old. Eight years on and Eden was still no closer to giving him up.

Given the way her heart lurched drunkenly at the sight of him, she never would.

Humphrey's sigh-worthy bum was still on show, except

now he was fixing Tiger's rear boots, glutes tense against his tan breeches. His breeches were the expensive, trendy sort, with a silicone seat insert for extra grip and back and front pockets with contrasting piping. Saddle stains from the day's showjumping training with their local club only made them sexier. The stretchy fabric tapered down his thighs to his ankles where, in typical Humphrey fashion, the trendiness ended thanks to a pair of red-and-white-striped socks pulled halfway up his calves, and elastic-sided leather boots.

Humphrey might come from one of the most landed and wealthy farming families in the district, but that didn't stop him being a hopeless dag. It was one of the many things Eden adored about him.

At least the socks matched the red wool beanie on his head, which was needed now the sun had dropped. It was barely spring, and the evenings still closed in fast and cold. Eden's breath was already beginning to condense in the air. Which reminded her, she needed to get a wriggle on. Tonight was her brother Tom's engagement party. Eden needed to drive home, settle Addy, feed her other horse, Ruffian, then shower, frock up and head back into Levenham, ready to party the night away in the Australian Arms Hotel's upstairs function room.

She untied Addy's lead, threw it over his neck and clicked her tongue. The horse took the cue and ambled alongside her to the rear of the float, where, without instruction, he sauntered up the ramp and settled inside.

'Good Addy-paddy,' said Eden, patting his rump. For a young horse, Admiral possessed a remarkably calm head. She secured the padded tailbar in place, raised and locked the ramp, and strode to the front to tie his lead.

Humphrey was already exiting the float door.

'Thanks,' she said, knowing he would have tied Addy off for her.

He shrugged. 'You're in a hurry.'

Eden held back a sigh. This was the trouble with Humphrey. He could spend a day hardly acknowledging Eden's existence, only to then surprise and delight her with small—and sometimes big—kindnesses. In his mind they probably meant nothing. To her, they always meant hope.

She glanced at her watch. 'And already late.'

He nodded and moved off.

'You could come,' she blurted.

Humphrey turned, staring.

Eden ground her knuckles hard into her thighs, cursing her impetuousness. But the words were out now. She may as well keep going. And why not? It wasn't as if she had anything to lose. 'As, you know, my plus one.'

Humphrey opened his mouth, closed it, then rubbed the back of his neck as he stared at a point somewhere over her right shoulder.

'There'll be dancing. Amber's even promised a mirror ball. We could disco.' Eden made jazz hands then fluttered them down in an arc before clenching her fists and swinging her arms crossways, alternating from the back of her body to the front.

The corner of Humphrey's mouth rose. He wasn't a conventionally attractive man. His ears stuck out, made worse by his severe, short-back-and-sides haircut, and his nose had a distinct kink from being broken and not reset properly. Yet his eyelashes were long and dark, and framed eyes the colour of a summer sky, while his mouth had a mesmerising sensuality that had given Eden more sexy dreams than she could count.

And when he smiled ...

Oh, the glorious fluttering joy!

'What do you call that?' he asked.

'The Floss. You know, the viral dance?' She swung some more, grinning. Surely that deliciously quirked mouth meant something. 'It's easy. Even you could do it.'

'Hmph,' said Humphrey, his signature response to anything vexing. Usually Eden.

'Or you could do the Blinding Lights Dance.' She started to run on the spot then tapped her left foot in and out, shoulders bobbing, and swung her arms up and around.

Humphrey blinked and flattened his lips. 'Blinding Lights.'

'Yeah. By The Weeknd?'

'Right. No.'

Eden froze, arms mid-swing. 'No to dancing, or no to coming tonight?'

'Both.'

'Oh.' She flopped her arms down, puffed out her cheeks and looked at the ground, eyes burning as humiliation set in. Would she never learn? Humphrey had made it clear the age gap between them made any relationship impossible, and what had she gone and done? Reminded him of their differences. Again.

Why couldn't he see that it didn't matter? Silly things like viral dances didn't mean they weren't destined to be together. What mattered was their hearts. And both of theirs were huge.

She retreated into the comfort of her usual response and feigned sunniness. 'Not to worry. It was a last-minute invite. You probably have something on.'

'I do.' He scratched at his red beanie, dislodging it so that it sat crookedly over one ear, exposing an edge of salt-and-pepper hair. 'Dinner.'

Pain stabbed Eden's chest, a mix of hurt and jealousy that momentarily collapsed her lungs. Humphrey, the man who never dated, whose entire life revolved around horses, was going out for dinner? This was terrible news.

'That'll be nice,' said Eden through a clenched-tooth smile. 'Where are you going?'

Probably Restaurant Ten, the best, most romantic restaurant in town. The Taylor-Martins never did anything by halves.

'Kulburra. It's a family thing.' He didn't sound thrilled about the idea either.

Relief almost had Eden breaking into another round of The Floss. Kulburra was the Taylor-Martin's historic homestead, twenty-seven kilometres to the west of Levenham. A massive property on some of the richest land in the state. Which meant no romantic restaurant date. Hallelujah.

'You could skip it? Come to the party instead.' She scissored her arms again. 'Dance with me under the mirror ball.'

'Eden.'

'What?'

Humphrey's voice turned quiet. 'You know what.'

Eden swallowed down the sudden thickness in her throat. 'We could work, Humphrey. If you gave us a chance.' She scraped her top teeth over her bottom lip. She'd started the conversation; she may as well keep going. 'You like me. I know you do.'

Humphrey's chest rose and fell. 'Eden ...' He shook his head and checked over his shoulder on Tiger. The horse was dozing next to Humphrey's luxurious custom-built four-horse truck with *Kulburra Equestrian* emblazoned on its side. A truck in which Eden had spent many a time talking horses over cups of pod coffee and Humphrey's mum's fruitcake. Enjoying the comforts of its kitchen and bathroom, while trying not to think about sharing its queen-size sleeping bunk with the man she adored. When he turned back, Humphrey's face and eyes were soft with sympathy. Or was it pity? 'I do like you. But we've been through this.'

'You could try.' Eden hated the croak in her voice. The vulnerability. The *fear*. There was little that scared her, but the thought of never having Humphrey, never being loved by him, rattled her deeply. They were soulmates. Humphrey just needed to recognise it, too. 'See what happens.'

'No.'

Eden hissed in a breath. Amazing how one simple word, even said kindly, could wound.

'We're friends, Eden.' Humphrey stepped forward and cupped one of her shoulders with a big, warm hand. 'Good friends. Don't spoil it.'

'I won't. *We* won't.' She knew they wouldn't. Eden *believed* in them. Had done for years. Eden and Humphrey. The grump and the happy girl, weirdly attracted and united in their love for all things equine. How could she let the dream go? How could she let what was in her heart go?

He shook his head again and gave her shoulder a last squeeze. 'Enjoy yourself tonight.'

Humphrey was several metres away before Eden sucked back her hurt and rallied. 'You're a sexy man, Humphrey Taylor-Martin. Can't blame a girl for trying!'

He didn't turn but the shake of his head told Eden she'd made him smile. Or at least caused that luscious mouth to tip. Her cheer and openness were her defences, and she needed both when it came to Humphrey.

She watched him head for his truck, chest aching in the

encroaching twilight, shoulder still hot from his touch. She'd see him again, next week at the first show of the spring season. Another chance to turn him around.

Yet as Eden journeyed home to the family farm, Humphrey's "no" kept swirling through her mind. The quiet determination behind the word, the emphasis in his direct gaze, and the tightening of his fingers on her shoulder as if, this time, he really meant it.

And with every turn of that "no", it screwed deeper into her hope.

Chapter Two

'You're late,' half-yelled Eden's brother, Tom, kissing her on the cheek while taking care not to spill his beer. Though the music hadn't yet been cranked up to dance volume, the room was loud with chatter, not to mention crowded and hot.

Eden plucked the beer from his hand and stole a sip before giving it back. God, she needed that. Her mood after leaving the Levenham showgrounds had only worsened when, less than five kilometres from home, one of the float's tyres had gone. In the gathering dark, and in a less-than-ideal spot, she'd had to unload Addy, change the tyre, reload, and make her way home, all while bemoaning yet another bill.

As if horses weren't expensive enough. Eden's job as a bus driver paid well, and she was fortunate to score free rent and agistment thanks to her parents, but there were still feed, veterinary, saddlery, and farrier costs to budget for. Then there were competition entry fees and travel expenses, and she was still paying off the four-wheel drive she'd bought the year before. Eden wasn't poor by any standards, and considered herself very lucky, but that didn't mean she didn't have to budget.

'Sorry. Float had a flat, then bloody Ruff had snuck his way into the hay shed.'

'He's a shit.'

Yes, he was, and getting sneakier in his old age, but Eden worshipped the horse. She'd had him even longer than she'd been in love with Humphrey and, unlike Humphrey, Ruff loved her back. Or at least pretended to. For that, she could forgive him anything.

Eden scanned the room for Tom's fiancée, Amber, who Eden adored and was teaching to ride. 'Where's Amber?'

Tom used his beer to indicate a spot at the edge of the dance floor where Amber was chatting with her diminutive best friend, Niamh, and a group of what Eden assumed were teacher friends. Amber was dressed in a gorgeous red wrap dress that matched the two giant linked love hearts edged with feathers hanging at the rear of the room. Niamh was almost as bright in a sexy, body-hugging blue jumpsuit.

'What the hell are those?' asked Eden, gawping at the love hearts. Tom and Amber might be sickeningly dewy-eyed over each other, but linked feathery love hearts were a bit much.

'A present from Amber's class. They've all signed it with soppy little messages like "We love you, Miss Dunn. You're the best teacher ever."' He shook his head. 'Christ.'

That brought a smile. For all his scoffing, Eden bet Tom was secretly proud, the love hearts just another sign of how universally admired his fiancée was. Eden spotted her mum and dad to Tom's right, nattering with her uncle and aunt and another couple. 'I'd better let the folks know I'm here. Tell Amber I'll catch her in a minute.'

Tom bobbed his glass at her, then downed the

remaining contents before dumping the empty on a nearby table and heading for his fiancée.

Eden spent the next hour catching up with relatives, family friends and Tom's mates, who she'd always gotten along with, especially Olly, Tom's one-time housemate and nominated best man, and now Niamh's boyfriend. Amber's teacher friends seemed to stick together, although Eden gave them full points for being fun-loving. The moment the speeches were over and the music powered up, they hit the dance floor with gusto, dragging Amber and—because they were attached at the hip—Tom, with them.

Eden chuckled to herself at the change in her brother. Pre Amber, there was no way he'd be on the dance floor. Tom's preferred position was more likely to be against the bar talking football with Olly and the rest of the boys. These days, whatever made Amber happy went. Lucky girl.

Niamh and Olly were the same. They should have looked silly, with Niamh so tiny and neat, and Olly such a tall and scraggly farm boy, yet there was something perfect about them. It was in the way they looked at one another, gazes locked, smiles broad and a little bit goofy, as though they couldn't believe their luck at finding each another.

Eden cradled her glass of wine and stared at them wistfully, yearning for some of what they had and thinking again of Humphrey's emphatic "no".

He couldn't mean it. He couldn't. Humphrey liked her. More than liked her. It wasn't wishful thinking or Eden's longing making her see things. She'd caught him—more than once, too—watching her with a rawness that made her heart stop. It happened rarely and Humphrey blinked it away the moment he realised he'd been rumbled, but she'd *seen* it. Once seen, that kind of emotion couldn't be unseen.

There were his kindnesses, too. Admittedly, Humphrey

was kind to everyone—grumpy, often taciturn, but never mean or deliberately rude—but the thoughtfulness he bestowed on Eden seemed that little more intimate. No one else had their horses tied up for them, or had water buckets carried, and she was always first to be invited to his truck for shelter and a cuppa when the weather turned bad, where Humphrey would make her coffee the way she liked it and always offer her a slice of fruitcake.

As for his wisdom, yes, Humphrey could be generous should anyone ask for his advice, but with Eden he seemed to go that extra step, offering not only his expertise but also time and patience. Precious time when he should have been schooling his own horses. His attention so intense it was as if he felt as invested in her success as she.

All that had to mean something. It had to.

Yet that "no" kept turning and worming and screwing deeper.

'God, it's hot,' puffed Amber as she came off the dance floor. She pressed her hands to her cheeks. 'I must look redder than my dress.'

'You look gorgeous,' said Eden. And she did. Her cheeks glowed prettily, and the dress contrasted beautifully with her dark hair.

'I think I've strained a bum muscle,' said Niamh, sidling up with her bluntly cut bob sleek, and not looking even remotely puffed. The lowered zipper of her jumpsuit made her look sexier than ever. No wonder her students called her the bondage mistress.

'You're quiet tonight,' remarked Amber, giving Eden a once-over. 'Not up for some booty shaking?'

'My booty's saddle sore. But I will. Later.'

Amber nudged her. 'I think Hamish might like a dance.'

Eden rolled her eyes. Hamish Thorne was a local spud

farmer and one of Tom's and Olly's mates. She'd known him too long and witnessed too much of his teenage idiocy to think of him as anything other than a friend. 'No, thanks.'

'Hmm,' said Amber, eyeing the dance floor where Hamish was attempting some sort of moonwalk while holding a beer. 'Probably a good call.'

They shared a "boys!" smile.

'How did it go today?' asked Amber.

Eden shrugged. Having confessed her situation with Humphrey in a moment of weakness during a ride around the farm together, she knew Amber wasn't referring to the training day. 'Not great. I asked him to come along tonight, and he said no.' She shook her head, body slumping with disappointment. God, she was tired. And hurt. 'He did the "don't spoil our friendship" thing again.'

'Ah, that old turkey.'

Eden snorted. It *was* an old turkey of an excuse. She studied her drink, her mouth turning down and her throat thickening. 'I think he meant it this time.'

Amber's hand went to Eden's back and rubbed. 'I'm sorry.'

Eden shook her head and blinked at the burn in her eyes. She would not cry at her brother's engagement party. It was a night for celebrating love, not bemoaning it. 'It's okay. I'm fine.'

Amber gave her a look that said she knew very well that Eden wasn't fine, but let it go.

'You know, you could always try Cupid Country,' said Niamh. She swung a finger between her and Amber. 'It worked for us.'

'It's a thought,' said Amber with an encouraging smile. 'Maybe worth a try? See what's out there?'

'I don't know ...' Eden had a Cupid Country account—

created a few years ago during another of her efforts to rid herself of her Humphrey crush—but barely used.

'Can't do any harm,' said Niamh.

'Except for the dick pics,' said Amber. 'Some of those will burn your eyeballs.' She addressed Niamh. 'Remember the mushroom?'

'Oh, God. How could I forget!'

The two friends burst into laughter.

'Yay,' muttered Eden. 'I can't wait.'

Amber sobered. 'It's not all bad. Your brother was on there.'

'So was Olly,' said Niamh, nodding.

'And neither of them are morons.'

'Or mushroom dicks.'

Amber gave a long sigh. 'Definitely not mushroom dicks.'

Eden covered her ears. She did not want to hear about her brother's or Olly's anatomy.

Niamh and Amber laughed again.

'Have a think—' Amber suddenly swivelled towards the dance floor and the small, raised dais at its end, and frowned. 'What's he doing now?'

The music had stopped. Tom was on the dais, making shooing gestures. 'Come on, you lot. Off.'

Amber folded her hands in front of her mouth and did a funny little jig. Whatever Tom was up to, it met with her approval.

The dancers shuffled towards the floor edges, exchanging puzzled looks. Tom shaded his eyes and looked out across the room. 'Where are you, cute girl?'

Amber gave a very unteacherlike squeal and waved.

Tom grinned and held out a hand. A tune began to float in the background, slowly growing louder. Eden frowned, trying to place the melody. From the slight crackle, it was an old song. Familiar.

'Oh,' said Niamh breathlessly, blinking rapidly as Amber skipped across the floor to her fiancé. 'That is so romantic.'

Then Eden heard it. The crooning first lines of "My Girl" by The Temptations.

Tom stepped down from the dais, took Amber's hand and led her to the centre of the floor where a couple of spotlights played. He cradled her close, the pair swaying slowly to the music. Though the crowd clapped and whooped and whistled around them, they continued to dance in each other's arms as if the rest of the world didn't exist.

Eden swallowed, her heart and throat thick with emotion. She glanced at Niamh but Amber's bestie only had eyes for her man, Olly. The pair shared a look and, without speaking, walked to the dance floor where they joined in the slow dance. Bride and groom, best man and best woman.

'I think you're up.'

Eden turned to find her mum nodding to where Tom's nominated groomsman, Lincoln McEvoy, stood waiting for her, mouth quirked, and one eyebrow raised.

Dancing was the last thing Eden felt like doing but she couldn't let her brother or Amber down. Shucking off her funk, she skipped across and joined Lincoln in the centre of the floor with the others. Their dance was far from elegant and nowhere near romantic, but they did their best.

As they settled, Lincoln drew her a little closer. Like Tom's other mates, Lincoln was another Eden felt as though she'd known forever. He was a nice man and recently single, with a reputation for being an expert mixologist thanks to paying his way through university with bar work, and for a moment Eden considered drawing even closer. She dismissed the idea. Playing games with the groomsman was dumb and would only create unnecessary tension.

And there was Humphrey.

Except there wasn't Humphrey, and probably never would be. There'd be no romantic dances or intimacy, no communicating with just a smile, no silly romantic gestures. Just friendship and the incredible, bone-deep ache of her unrequited love.

Eden glanced at Tom and Amber. The pair were whispering to one another, faces aglow with love, moving in perfect harmony as if bound by some magical cloth. Olly had Niamh held tight, his body hunched to accommodate her small size while she stretched up the length of him as though about to scale him like a climbing wall.

Around them, the dance floor was filling with couples, joining in the celebration with dance and more than a bit of singing. Eden's grandparents, still affectionate after all these years. Her mum and dad, so full of joy for Tom and Amber and the prospect of future grandchildren. Amber's family, just as proud and delighted. Tom's godparents, who loved a dance, spinning like the floor was a ballroom instead of a pub function room. Couples old and young and every age in between. A whirling, smiling, crooning crowd of happiness.

Eden tore her eyes away and stared at Lincoln's chest. Amber and Niamh were right. Why shouldn't this kind of happiness and love be hers, too? She was twenty-four years old. Her destiny couldn't stay hanging on a dream unlikely to ever come true.

The moment had come to face the facts: Humphrey might never come to his senses and where would that leave Eden? Alone with her big, wasted heart, that's where, while all the opportunities out there for other loves blew away like autumn leaves.

She deserved better. Much better. And this time she was damn well going to make it happen.

Eden waited until after eleven before saying her farewells. Her early departure raised a few eyebrows and inquiries if she was all right. Eden was a renowned party girl, always staying until the death, laughing and living it up. Even her parents, who would be sticking around to help pull down decorations and clear the room, offered her a lift home, saying they'd drive her back for her car in the morning if she wanted to hang around for a few more drinks.

Eden kissed their cheeks and said thanks, but she was fine. It had been a long day and she had plenty on her plate tomorrow.

At the farm, when her teeth were brushed and she was snuggled into her favourite flannelette pyjamas with the doona wrapped around, Eden leaned against her bed's headboard with her phone in her lap and opened Cupid Country.

Her profile was as it had been for a long time, inactive. She checked her likes and loves: *horses, horses, horses*. That could be either a turn-off or a turn-on. But there was no point in lying. If Mr Right didn't like horses, then he was Mr Wrong.

The little grey slider glowed at her in the dark. One swipe and it would turn green and activate, showing her as available and looking for love.

Her finger hovered. Eden stared across the room to the window. The blinds were open. Privacy wasn't an issue when she was surrounded by nearly three thousand acres of farmland. The only creatures likely to look in were either

her horses or a stray kangaroo coming to feed on the lush back lawn.

Outside, the Milky Way painted the sky with starlight, and she wondered if Humphrey was looking at the same sky. Unlikely. He was no doubt asleep, not dreaming of the girl who loved him.

Eden's hand went to her chest. She rubbed, wishing the ache away as she gnawed on her bottom lip. Cupid Country wasn't a forever thing. She could experiment. Give herself a timeframe—a beginning and an end. From now to the end of the show season should be enough.

One date per week, either locally or wherever she happened to be competing that weekend.

She would do what she'd asked Humphrey to do with her: *try*. See what happened. Dick pics probably; but maybe, just maybe, someone special would turn up. Someone so perfect he'd trump her feelings for Humphrey. Someone who truly deserved her loving, loyal heart.

Sucking in a breath, Eden slid the activate bar. Then she set her phone on her bedside table, rolled over and spent another hour staring at her room with her heart tattooing and her legs twitching, before sleep finally swept her away.

Chapter Three

'You're not getting any younger, Humphrey,' said Grandma Taylor, settling her knife and fork together on her plate and folding her hands under her chin. Her gaze held a glittery intent Humphrey knew only too well.

He drew in a breath and let it out slowly. Here they went.

'Your brother is perfectly settled,' she continued, casting a fond smile at Humphrey's older brother, Montgomery, and his partner, Damien. 'What's your issue?'

Humphrey caught his sister Clara's gaze. Not a scrap of sympathy existed there, only amusement and probably a touch of relief. When the family was picking on Humphrey, they weren't picking on Clara.

'Must we?' he asked, sounding bored, as though the subject had been done to death. Which it had, in his opinion.

'I can't see why not.'

Humphrey scanned the rest of the table. As with Clara, there was no assistance from Monty, Damien, or his parents. Humphrey was really beginning to hate family dinners. Three times a year, every four months, no excuses, except the direst of illnesses. And COVID. Even the matriarch of the family couldn't beat the lockdowns, much to her irritation. Although that hadn't stopped GT—as Grandma Taylor was fondly referred to—from scheduling dinners via a video conferencing app.

'Just haven't met the right girl.' He forked up a slice of rare roast beef. Homegrown, of course. The Taylor-Martins were one of the best beef producers in the south-east. Had been for well over a century, since an enterprising ancestor snapped up Kulburra for a song and invested a small fortune in rehabilitating the run-down, rabbit-infested land.

GT waved a hand, gold bangles jangling. 'You've been saying that for years.'

He gritted his teeth, only to jam a hunk of beef into the gap between his back left molars. He'd need floss and lots of it to get that out. 'I'm busy.'

'Are you even trying?'

All appetite gone, Humphrey set his cutlery down and lifted his linen napkin to his mouth. It had been a tough enough day as it was, without this. 'What does it matter?'

'What does it matter? Humphrey, darling ...' With more jewellery jangles, GT reached out a perfectly manicured hand as though about to take Humphrey's. No chance, given the enormity of Kulburra's solid ash, twelve-seat dining table. 'It matters because we care about you and want you to be happy.'

'I am happy.'

How could he not be? He had a wonderful—if sometimes annoying—family that he loved. Lived in a comfortable house on a property he adored, and trained and traded horses for a living, when he wasn't helping Monty. Wasn't bad at it either. That he didn't have a girlfriend didn't affect that.

His grandmother raised a finely plucked eyebrow.

Humphrey gestured at his sister. 'What about Clara?'

'What about me?' snapped Clara in her best barrister's voice.

Humphrey shook his head. He shouldn't have brought it up. There were no wins here. 'Nothing.'

Clara returned with a "just as well" glare. Shite, his sister was scary. A high achiever from birth, Clara was now a much sought after barrister at one of the most prestigious law firms in Melbourne. Humphrey had no doubt she'd end up a judge. Probably High Court, given her ability and ambition.

Though quieter, Monty was just as formidable. Monty's brain was always processing something at a million miles an hour, whether it be fecundity rates, dry matter calculations, or the business's off-farm investment returns. To be fair, Monty had mellowed since he'd met Damien, but could still bore at Olympic level when the mood took him.

While Humphrey was ... kicking along. At least he was doing what he loved.

He stared at the painting above the mahogany sideboard. An impressionist landscape from one of Australia's most prestigious artists and a leading member of the Heidelberg School art movement. In one corner stood Kulburra's historic shearing shed, a shed that in its heyday had rattled with twenty-five stands of hand shearers. Stretching out across the rest of the canvas was a lush landscape dotted with red and manna gums, fleecy sheep and fat cattle.

So much history. Such deep family roots. And so far, no new generation to carry it on. Wedded to her work, Clara showed zero sign of wanting to settle down, and Monty and

Damien were, as far as anyone could tell, uninterested in children. Which meant Humphrey was it. The end of the line.

No one had ever been so crass as to say it out loud, but the elephant was in the room and with every year that passed, its fat butt squashed the air a little tighter. It was in the comments about wanting to see Humphrey happy, the questions about his future, the occasional mention from a family member about bumping into a nice girl that Humphrey might also like to meet.

He hated it. Hated the weight of expectation, hated the intrusion, hated that he was disappointing them.

His mother Isabelle—Belle to those who knew her— patted his forearm, ever the peacemaker. 'You're fine, aren't you, love? Now, has everyone had enough?'

To Humphrey's relief, his family murmured that they had. He rose with his mum and gathered Clara's plate.

'No, love, you stay,' said Belle, attempting to take the plate from him.

Humphrey held firm. 'I'm good.' With a gentle tug he took ownership of the plate and gathered his grandmother's, who gave him a savvy, sideways smirk.

'You know she means well,' said Belle when they were in the safety of Kulburra's kitchen. The air was warm and redolent with the scents of roast meat and gravy.

'Yep,' said Humphrey, jerking open the dishwasher door. With Clara being Clara and Monty being gay, Humphrey was used to being the soft target. That didn't mean he liked it.

'Love ...'

He sighed and faced his mum. Sympathy spread soft lines around her eyes and mouth, and his heart squeezed a little.

'Sorry,' he said, feeling about ten. 'I'm just in a mood.'

'Why? Was Tiger difficult today?'

That she knew each of his horses and who he was taking where was another sign of her love.

'No, he was fine. It was ...' Humphrey shook his head. 'Just something dumb and unimportant.'

Except that was bullshit. Everything to do with Eden was important. He wished he could talk to his mum about her, but it felt wrong. Eden was sixteen years younger than him. It'd be like admitting to being a dirty old man.

He hoped she was having fun at the party. Knowing Eden, she would be. Humphrey had met the Jones family and chatted with Eden enough about them over the years to know theirs was a good one. A loving one, a lot like his own. Tom's engagement would be hugely welcomed.

For the umpteenth time since Eden asked, Humphrey wished he was there. Wished he was celebrating at her side. Wished he was part of it.

Wished he was with her.

'You sure?'

'Yeah.' He leaned across and kissed his mum's cheek. 'I'm fine. I'll be better behaved over dessert. Speaking of dessert, what is it?'

'Steamed ginger pudding.'

His second-favourite sweet thing, after fruitcake. Humphrey gave her another kiss. 'You're the best.'

Humphrey did manage to hold it together over dessert. Thankfully, the subject had moved on to politics, which, having historically produced two local state members and one federal agriculture minister, the family took a great interest in.

The evening ended at ten-thirty. Clara was catching an early flight to Melbourne in the morning, while

Humphrey's grandparents were returning to Adelaide, and the rest, including himself, had work to do. Farming didn't stop because it was Sunday.

Humphrey stepped out into the night, zipped up his jacket and strode towards the stables, his breath steaming in the frigid air. The horses would be fine, but tonight he needed their comfort.

'Hey, Tiges,' he murmured as the dozy horse shoved his nose over the stable half door and whickered softly.

He scrubbed the horse's forehead, smiling as Tiger bobbed his head as though asking for more. The horse had been good today. Confident. Moving forward through the bridle and not leaning into his hands. A nice, soft ride. The work on the flat Humphrey had put in with him was paying off.

'I thought I'd find you here.' Clara leaned against the stone frame of the stables' entrance, hands deep in the pockets of her full-length down jacket. 'Late night horse chat?'

Humphrey shrugged and swapped to scratching Tiger's jaw. Clara knew him too well. All three of them had their comfort blankets. When vexed, Monty retreated to Kulburra's library and the security of books. Clara chose the outdoors, striding miles across the paddocks as she worked off energy. Humphrey headed for the stables and the tranquilising scent of hay and horses, and their kind brown eyes.

Ever since he could remember, all Humphrey had wanted to do was work with horses. He loved them, in all their temperamental ways. Liked their company, liked their smell. They didn't judge or want anything from him except good food, access to water and the occasional scratch.

Unlike some people.

Clara eased off the wall and headed towards him. She

paused and stroked Tiger's silky neck. A placating move made for Humphrey's benefit. Though, like every Taylor-Martin, she could ride, Clara wasn't a horse fan.

'Want to talk about it?' she asked.

'Nope.'

Clara studied him and her mouth quirked. 'Eden.'

Humphrey gave Tiger a last tickle. 'I should get to bed.'

'Don't be a nong, Hump.'

Hump. It had been a long time since Clara had called him Hump. He'd never liked it, but tonight it felt okay. Almost comforting, like the stables. Clara was the only one who knew about Eden, not that Humphrey had told her. One visit to watch him ride at the Australian Showjumping Championships, where Eden was also competing, and Clara had guessed. He still didn't know what had given him away. With her big doe eyes and perpetual closeness, any fool could see how Eden felt, but Humphrey always held himself, and his feelings, tight.

That was the trouble with family. They knew too much.

'What did she do?'

'Asked me to her brother's engagement party.'

'You know Tom. You know the family. You could have gone.'

Humphrey slumped against the half door and buried his fists in his pockets. Tiger bunted his head, hunting for another scratch. Humphrey ignored him. Notwithstanding the family's longstanding dinner rules, even if he could have gone, what would have been the point?

'To what end?'

Clara shoved Tiger's nose aside as the horse attempted to scrounge attention from her. 'Don't be obtuse. What end do you think? She's mad about you. You're mad about her.

Get married, have babies. Make everyone happy, including yourself.'

That was the problem. Humphrey was forty years old. If they did get together and had a family—which would take time—Humphrey would be approaching his sixties when the children hit their mid-teens. More like their grandfather than their father. And hadn't he read somewhere that older men had a higher risk of producing offspring with mental health issues? Schizophrenia or autism and the like, the older sperm having defects or something.

Clara studied him a moment and nodded to herself, as if she'd figured it all out. 'Ah.'

'Ah, what?'

'You're worried she's another gold-digger.'

'Eden's not a gold-digger.'

'Then what's your problem?'

Humphrey flexed his jaw. He did not want to be having this conversation, but he knew his sister. She'd interrogate him for the rest of the night, until she got her answer. 'I'm too old for her.'

'What's *old*, is your excuse for not being with the girl you love.'

'I don't love her.'

Much.

Clara leaned across and patted him patronisingly on the cheek. 'You keep telling yourself that, brother. And enjoy your lonely, miserable life. I'm off to bed. See you next dinner.'

Humphrey watched her stalk out, then buried his face in Tiger's neck. 'Am I an idiot?' he asked the horse.

Tiger pulled back and with a loud sneeze, snotted on his head.

Humphrey guessed that said it all.

Chapter Four

Humphrey frowned as he watched Eden jog across the pony club grounds towards the coffee van. All morning she'd been bubbling with nervous excitement. He couldn't figure it out. Levenham Pony Club Gymkhana was a minor show, an opening warm-up for the season's bigger competitions, and Eden was a seasoned campaigner. Nerves shouldn't be a factor.

She'd ridden the first jumping competition with more aggression that usual, driving her youngster, Admiral, through the tightest and fastest route in the jump-off. She'd won, and though it was only a minor class of little conse-quence and even less prize money, Eden's grin was like a lottery winner's.

She was wearing make-up, too. Not much—a bit of mascara and some lip gloss—but enough to enhance her eyes and lips and tug at the gnawing need Humphrey kept buried deep inside. Worse, she hadn't hung around him the way she usually did, watching his every movement, gazing at him, brown eyes soft and pooled with yearning.

Something was up and the anxious clench of Humphrey's stomach told him he wasn't going to like it.

He dragged his attention back to Tiger. The horse was already glossy with good health and grooming, but he ran the body brush over the horse's coat again. Tiger shuffled, as though sensing his friend's disquiet. With a sigh, Humphrey dumped the brush into a bucket, patted the horse's rump and with his fists dug into the pockets of his fleece vest, wandered towards the junior showjumping ring. A ring that just so happened to be near the coffee van.

Eden had slowed to a brisk walk, circling along the inside rope of the warm-up arena and waving to a few young riders she knew. As she neared the van, her stride lengthened, as if she'd spotted something—or someone—exciting.

Eden was long-legged, fit and young. A leap over a loose barrier rope should have been nothing. Except she wasn't looking at the rope. Her gaze was on the sandy-haired bloke in navy twill work clothes who'd turned to watch her approach. Her back foot hooked the rope and she catapulted forwards, arms out, landing flat on her chest. Though Humphrey was too far away to hear, he could damn near feel the *whoof* of air leaving her lungs.

He was running before he could think. Only to suddenly stop when the sandy-haired bloke stretched out a hand and helped up a laughing, red-faced Eden.

Humphrey's eyes narrowed as he focused on the man. It was Cam Phillips from the agricultural machinery place in town. Good-looking. Nice bloke. Older than Eden, but younger than Humphrey.

Way younger.

'Interesting,' said a voice.

Humphrey whipped around to find Mandy Nolan watching Eden as avidly as he was.

She raised her eyebrows at him as if expecting a comment. 'Nothing to say?' she asked, when he didn't oblige.

'About what?' Humphrey feigned deep interest in the junior ring and the little girl kicking her equally little pony over the tiny jumps, while her mum jogged alongside, cheering her on.

Mandy wasn't his favourite person. They'd shared a brief relationship a long time ago, but Humphrey had ended it. She wasn't his type. Too many sharp edges and he hadn't trusted the way she'd regarded Kulburra with greedy eyes when she visited. Mandy had never forgiven him.

She also didn't like Eden, though he had no idea why. Everyone loved Eden.

'Eden, who else?'

Humphrey risked a glance towards the coffee van. Eden and Cam were standing in line, grinning shyly at each other. He looked quickly away.

'First date. How cute.'

Humphrey swung back. 'First date?'

'You haven't heard?' asked Mandy, placing a hand to her chest as though in shock. 'But of course you haven't.'

'Heard what?'

'Eden's action plan.' At Humphrey's blank look, she went on. 'She's joined Cupid Country.' When that earned an even more blank look, she huffed. 'The dating app for rurals? Surely, you've heard of it?'

'Not my thing.'

'No. It wouldn't be. Why would you need a dating app when all you need to do is snap your fingers and a dozen beautiful women come running.'

There was no missing the bitterness in her voice.

Humphrey suppressed a sigh and made to walk off. He wasn't in the mood for Mandy's sniping. What he wanted was to check out this Cupid Country app and not watch Eden. It was making his lungs feel tight and short-breathed, like pneumonia was setting in.

'Don't you want to know her plan?'

'No.'

Mandy threw him a look that said she didn't believe him for a moment. 'A date every week for the entirety of the show season, in whatever town she's in.'

Humphrey shrugged. 'Good for her.' This time, when he headed off, he didn't stop. Mandy followed. Aware of her on his heels, he stepped out harder, but she was determined to stick it to him.

'Makes you wonder what brought it on, though, hmm? Did you have a lover's tiff?'

Humphrey *hmphed* in what he hoped was a "don't be ridiculous" way, fists shoved even deeper in the pockets of his fleece.

'Come on, Humphrey, everyone knows there's a thing between you two.'

'There's no *thing* between me, Eden or anyone. Never has been. Never will be.'

'Don't bullshit, Humphrey.'

'I'm not.'

'Yes, you are.' She grabbed his arm, dragging him to a halt. Humphrey glared at her, but Mandy held on. 'We *all* know.'

Very carefully, Humphrey removed her fingers from his arm. 'Eden has a crush on me. I know that. But it's one-sided.'

Mandy shook her head and tutted. 'Humphrey, Humphrey, Humphrey, you are so full of it.'

'What's it to you, anyway?'

'Nothing,' she said with a head toss that reminded Humphrey of his old horse, Gypsy, when she was in a snit. 'Nothing at all. But for some strange reason, everyone else wants to see you happy. And *she*,' Mandy nearly spat the word, 'makes you happy, even if you can't see it yourself. Which means *you*,' that earned him a poke in the chest, 'need to put a stop to this stupid dating agenda before she falls for someone who's not you.'

Announcement made, Mandy stomped off, leaving Humphrey unsure which way to stare—at Mandy's rigid back or at Eden and her date.

Her date.

He forked his fingers through his hair. A date for every week of the show season. Surely not? The season went from now until early December, something like thirteen or fourteen weeks. That would mean thirteen or more dates.

Dates with men like Cam.

'Jesus,' said Humphrey, swallowing and rubbing at his chest where his heart seemed to be colliding against his ribcage. Unable to help himself, he glanced towards the coffee van, but Eden and Cam were gone. He scanned wider and found them near the barrel racing, watching ponies skid around the tight course. They stood alongside the barrier rope, coffees in hand, not close but not as far apart as strangers should be. It was likely Eden knew Cam already, from school or the farm or something.

She was smiling. Not shyly as before, but openly. Relaxed. Maybe even a bit flirty.

Happy.

He rubbed his neck. The cords felt wiry and taut, like

an overstrung puppet. Humphrey grunted at his capriciousness. He'd made his choice and set her free, and her happiness was a positive. It was what he wanted—for Eden to find someone closer to her own age, who she could love and grow with, get married and have kids with. Share a long life together.

Good things.

A burn flared in his chest. He knuckled his sternum, but the acid heat remained. Indigestion probably. Time to go easier on the fruitcake.

Chapter Five

Eden glanced at her watch and her stomach swooped in horror. Had she and Cam been talking for that long? It didn't feel like it.

'I'm sorry, I have to go.'

Cam shrugged. 'That's okay. You did warn me.'

Eden held up her empty coffee cup. 'Thanks for the coffee.'

'You're welcome.'

Eden grimaced and shuffled her feet. It felt rude to rush off, but she needed to walk the showjumping course before it closed to riders. It was essential she not only knew the route, but how many strides to allow between fences, any corners she could cut or would need to take wide, or sudden changes of rein that might upset Ruffian's rhythm. And Ruff needed a proper warm-up. Her beloved ageing mount was too precious to risk injury and could be fractious if he wasn't ridden in.

She pointed towards the line-up of floats and trucks. 'I'd better ...'

'Yeah.' Cam cleared his throat. 'Thanks. It was ...' He frowned as he searched for an appropriate word. 'Nice.'

Eden winced. *Nice*. Not exactly an endorsement, but she supposed it was true. They had had a nice time. Though Cam was several years older than Eden, he was friendly, easy to talk to and his younger sisters Willow and Chelsea had been teammates during Eden's short-lived netball career.

It helped that her family did business with Cam's and was aware of their reputation as honest and solid operators. Nor had he laughed at her for being a town bus driver like a lot of men did. In fact, he'd seemed impressed. Which was good. Eden loved her job. Though it varied depending on driver availability, mostly she drove the north-east loop, which included the library and the community centre. Both were popular stops and great haunts of Levenham's elderly, who were largely friendly, quick with a smile and local gossip, and showed keen interest in her riding career. There were times when she felt more like a great-niece than their council-paid bus driver.

When she'd explained, Cam had seemed to understand, and she'd liked him for that. But she had yet to feel a spark. No butterflies fluttering around her stomach, no yearning throb through her chest. No wondering what he'd be like to kiss, or more. None of the things she felt with Humphrey.

Cam gave an uncertain, crooked smile and Eden could see how another girl might find him very cute. He really was a likeable man.

'We could, you know, meet again?'

Eden bit her lip and glanced towards Humphrey's truck. He was alongside Tiger, one foot in the stirrup. With a smooth swing he mounted, gathering the reins and stroking a hand down the side of the horse's neck. Longing tugged hard. But she had to face reality: he was never going to be hers.

She owed it to herself to at least *try* to move on.

'I'd like that. We'll message?'

Cam beamed. 'Yeah. Yeah, we'll do that.'

Eden couldn't stop herself smiling back. 'Great. Now I really, *really* must go.'

'Go then,' he said, laughing and shooing her off. 'We'll talk.'

By the time Eden made it to the warm-up arena she was in an even bigger fluster than this morning, and it was transmitting straight to Ruffian. He'd shied at bunting, at a tiny Shetland pony that looked like a stuffed toy, at someone's phone ringing, at a dropped paper cup rolling across the grounds. None was enough to unseat her, but it didn't bode well for their round.

She forced herself to concentrate, urging him into a trot and then a canter, gradually pulling the horse into line. When she felt he was loose enough and she had his full attention, she popped him over one of the small practice jumps, relieved when he cleared it easily.

Humphrey was already tackling the larger fence, thighs and backside driving Tiger onwards, hands gentle on the reins as the horse made the jump in a perfect parabola. Eden brought Ruffian back to a walk so she could watch. Funny how she never tired of studying Humphrey. Other riders she'd observe but, unless they were doing something different or unusual, her attention quickly waned. Humphrey, though, was endlessly fascinating.

He took the jump again then slowed to a walk. Eden wanted to trot to his side, but his tight expression gave her second thoughts. She directed Ruff back into a canter and focused on his warm-up instead.

It wasn't until she was circling outside the competition arena, waiting for her turn, that Humphrey rode up. She eyed him, noting the mouth set more tightly than usual, the way his gaze kept sweeping the other riders, the grounds, anywhere than a direct look at Eden.

'How's Ruffian?'

'Okay. He started off a bit out of sorts but he's coming good.'

He nodded, giving Ruffian a quick once-over. 'Open course. Should suit him.'

Eden had thought the same when she walked it. Unlike Admiral, who seemed to revel in tight tracks, Ruffian liked plenty of room to line up. She pressed her palm against his silky neck. 'He's getting old, poor thing.'

Humphrey made a grumbling sound, and his jaw tightened even further.

Eden closed her eyes. *Idiot, idiot girl.*

'I heard about your date,' he said.

'Oh. Right.' It was hardly a surprise. She'd mentioned her plans to a couple of rider friends. Word was bound to get around. She inspected his face. Humphrey was staring straight ahead, expression shuttered. Eden suppressed a sigh.

'It went okay,' she said. 'He asked if we could do it again.' When Humphrey maintained his grumpy stare, she went on. 'I said sure. Cam's a nice man. Cute smile.'

'That's ...' Humphrey cleared his throat. 'Very good.'

'Is it?'

They shared a look. Humphrey was the first to turn away. 'You know it is.' He clicked his tongue and urged Tiger into a trot, tossing a "good luck" over his shoulder as he pulled ahead.

Eden poked her tongue out at his stiff back. 'Stupid man,' she muttered.

'He is. Very stupid.'

Eden released an embarrassed squeak. She hadn't realised anyone was nearby. Worse, it was Mandy Nolan, who had never liked her, despite Eden's many attempts at friendliness. She got the feeling Mandy thought she was young and silly. Which she probably was, given her Cupid Country plan.

Mandy gave her a gelid stare. 'But so are you.'

'I'm ...' Eden opened her mouth, closed it.

'Make him jealous, is that the plan?'

'Plan?' asked Eden. Shock had made her brainless. Mandy had never been nice, but she'd never been down-right rude or mean either—you couldn't afford to be in this caper; horses being horses, no one ever knew when they'd need help—yet her tone was definitely mean-girl.

Mandy lifted her eyes to the sky and huffed. 'Cupid Country? Your date-a-week campaign?'

'That's ...' None of Mandy's business. Eden gathered her reins. There were two competitors to go before she was on. She needed to get Ruffian in hand, and to slough off her irritation before it channelled into the horse.

Eden forced a smile. She would be a good sport if it killed her. 'Good luck with Mocha.'

'Eden, you just need to ...' But Eden was already riding off. 'Oh, forget it. You're both as dumb as each other.'

Which was clearly the truth; both Eden and Humphrey had terrible rounds. The course was generously spaced and well below maximum height. They should have gone clear, yet Eden had three rails down and, mortifyingly, Ruffian had run-out of the second element of the double, skittering so neatly sideways to avoid the jump, Eden was nearly unseated. Only good balance and honed thigh muscles had kept her in the saddle. Humphrey fared slightly better with two rails down.

Humphrey cantered from the ring with an expression like granite. For a moment, Eden thought he was going to ignore her, then he slowed Tiger to a walk and brought him alongside Ruffian.

'Could have been worse,' said Eden with a wry smile. 'At least you didn't have a run-out.'

'True.' He glanced at her, his tone becoming serious. 'You lost contact. Changed position too early. Ruff took the path of least resistance and dropped his shoulder. He's an old horse. Knows when he can get away with moves like that.'

'I know. I lost concentration.'

Humphrey's attention turned to the ring. Mandy and Mocha were approaching the opening fence. They cleared it easily. Mocha bounced over the next three fences with the same aplomb, Mandy cool and looking far more competent than Eden. They'd probably win, stuff it.

Eden regarded him again. 'I guess we're both out of sorts today.'

He nodded.

She sucked in her bottom lip and did her best to keep quiet, but the question burned. 'Is it because of ...'

Humphrey turned to her. 'No.'

'Oh.'

What had she expected? For Humphrey to admit jealousy? To plead for her not to go through with her Cupid Country plan?

Eden swallowed her disappointment and forced herself to do what she always did when faced with Humphrey's rejection: stay sunny. Besides, she still had afternoon events in which to redeem herself, including the major event, the Elsie Dwyer Memorial. With a bit of luck and focus, she might earn enough prizemoney to cover her entry fees.

'Well, then,' she said cheerily. 'Seeing as Ruff and I won't be competing in the jump-off, I may as well kill a bit of time by trawling for next week's date.'

Eden urged Ruffian forward, calling 'See you in the Memorial,' over her shoulder as she trotted off, while the sounds of the gymkhana echoed around her, and Humphrey, as usual, remained silent.

Chapter Six

Humprey watched Eden as she hurried from the showground's amenities block, freshly showered and dolled up for her date.

There'd been three that he knew of. Cam Phillips, followed by some weedy-looking bloke with big ears and an even bigger mouth who she'd met for coffee at the small show they'd competed at two weeks ago. Then there was last weekend's dipshit. Some bloke called Ben who'd failed to show and then shot Eden a message via Cupid Country saying that he'd turned up, but "hadn't liked the look of her" and left.

Humphrey was still in a mood about that one. Eden had laughed it off, claiming it was all part of the dating game, like suffering endless unsolicited dick pics. But Humphrey had a keen eye when it came to Eden. He recognised the artificial brightness Eden fell back on when she was covering up and putting on her brave face.

She'd chatted a while longer, then made some excuse about needing to check on something and withdrawn to the comfort of her horses. Humphrey had hovered nearby in a way that he hoped wasn't too obvious, watching her fuss over horses that didn't need any extra care, until Mandy speared him with a look that had him wandering off to calm his temper at the sheepdog trials.

He'd had a momentary thought to get on Cupid Country himself, hunt the bastard down, and give him a message about how to treat women properly. Except Eden wouldn't thank him, and he needed to stay out of this. Let her find someone who could give her the love and life she deserved.

Hmph.

Fists shoved in his pockets, Humphrey wandered over to Eden's car, where she was shoving her overnight bag onto the back seat. Ruffian and Admiral were secure in the portable yards that folded out from Eden's float, whuffling and snatching at their hay nets.

'Where are you meeting this one?'

'Pub,' said Eden, closing the back door and opening the front. She slid into the passenger seat and pulled down the visor, using its illuminated mirror to check her face. She frowned, picked at a corner of her mouth and inspected her pink-tipped finger. Whoever her date was, he warranted proper lipstick. That was a first. She eyed him. 'Why?'

Humphrey shrugged. 'No reason.'

'You don't need to worry. I told Nell where I was going.' Nell being one of the other female riders Eden was friendly with. 'She said she might come down later, too. Depends on her friend.'

'Good.'

Eden exited the car, locked it, and straightened her jacket. She'd dressed casually. Dark denim skinny jeans, a white top covered by a tan, sherpa-lined cropped jacket, and sturdy brown boots. She'd left her hair down, the stiff southerly bowling across the showgrounds snapping at it. With the rapidly encroaching sunset tracing shades of pink and peach across her fresh skin, she looked gloriously young and country-girl pretty.

Humphrey's heart pulsed with want.

'What do you think?' she asked, spinning.

'You look nice.'

Her nose scrunched up. 'I was kind of hoping for more than nice, but I guess that'll have to do.' She pulled her phone from her pocket and checked the screen. 'Gah! Gotta go!'

Without a backwards glance, she jogged off.

'Be careful,' yelled Humphrey, then wished he hadn't. He sounded like her dad. Eden waved a hand and kept going.

He watched until she crossed through the gates and disappeared in the direction of the main street. Five minutes later he was still there, staring at the empty gates, ruminating like an old bull.

He didn't like this going out on a Saturday night business. Coffee at a show, surrounded by people, was fine. Safe. He didn't care that Clara would have his balls for even thinking such patronising thoughts; it was one thing for a bloke to walk into an unfamiliar pub full of strangers to meet a girl he knew nothing about, and quite another for a young woman to do it.

Yes, Eden was more than capable of looking after herself, as she'd remind him herself if she knew his thoughts. But that didn't mean Humphrey had to like the situation.

The light was almost gone, the dark bringing even more cold. He grunted a final harrumph before checking Ruffian's and Admiral's water and straightening their rugs.

Patting Addy on the rump, he left them to their hay and headed to his truck.

Humphrey had brought three horses to this agricultural show, about three-and-a-half hours' drive east and across the border into Victoria. Tiger, his top mount, Charlie, and a youngster named Napoleon, who he had high hopes for. The show's equestrian events were scheduled for Sunday, but with distance and rings operating early, quite a few competitors were camping Saturday night.

Like Eden's, his horses were secure in their portable yards. Few shows had stabling, and the galvanised steel yards were how they made do. Which was no problem when the weather stayed fine but was less than ideal when it wasn't. Humphrey had spent plenty of competition days snug in the kitchenette of his truck, waiting for the weather to clear, while the horses stood heavily rugged outside, backsides to the wind.

Those days were some of his favourite days. Talking horses, showjumping and farming with horsey friends. Eden brightening the tiny room with her smiles and jokes. Wide-eyed adoring gaze making Humphrey feel both champion and fool.

He made himself a cup of tea, thinking he should sort some dinner. Often at these events, they'd get a group together and wander to the local pub or Asian for a meal and a few drinks. But with Eden on her date, Nell busy with a local friend, and Mandy still in a snit, nothing had been arranged. Humphrey wasn't sure he wanted company anyway.

He took his cup of tea outside. There was ham and cheese and bread for a toastie later, when he got hungry, and fruitcake for dessert. Right now, his stomach was too clenched to eat.

Humphrey sat on the cold metal step to the kitchenette and played with his phone, glancing up every now and then at the showground gates, his jaw tightening when it remained empty.

The wind picked up, dropping the temperature even further. Humphrey checked his horses and threw another rug on Napoleon, who was thin-skinned. Then he checked again on Ruffian and Admiral. The two horses were restlessly circling their small yard, pausing every now and then to stand stock-still, heads lifted and ears pricked towards the gate, before resuming their shuffle.

Humphrey knew how they felt. It was gone eight, and Eden still hadn't returned. Hardly a late evening, but there'd been the preparation and drive over and Eden was competing tomorrow. No matter how heavy duty her swag, no one could sleep properly in the back of a horse float when the wind was up.

He soothed the horses as best he could and returned to his perch, gaze once again sliding to the gates.

'You're an idiot,' he muttered, but remained where he was.

Humphrey was contemplating the second half of his toastie when a loud neigh ruptured the night. Eden's horses stood at the corner of their yard, their focus intent on the gate. A few seconds later she appeared, coming at pace.

Humphrey's stomach lurched. He dumped his plate and rose, ready to run to her, only for Eden to wave and switch direction for his truck.

'What are you doing out in the cold? It's freezing.' She

demonstrated with a shudder and a stamp of her feet, arms wrapped around herself. 'I had to jog the whole way so I didn't turn into a popsicle.'

Humphrey assessed her face in the light of the truck's open door. Other than a pair of cold-pinked cheeks, she looked fine. He'd been worried about nothing.

'Keeping an eye on the horses.' He glanced at the sky. 'Wind's making them restless.' A big fat lie, but Eden wouldn't know that.

She gave a chuckle. 'There I was thinking you were waiting up for me.'

Or maybe she did.

He bent for his toastie and took a bite. The congealed cheese was like rubber in his mouth, but he forced himself to chew.

'How did it go?'

She shrugged and regarded Ruffian and Admiral, who were still staring at her like a pair of lovesick puppies. She blew them a kiss. 'Not great.'

Which had Humphrey's stomach lurching again. He threw the toastie down and narrowed his gaze towards the main streetlights.

Eden bumped his shoulder with her own. 'Nothing like that. I don't think so, anyway, but it's hard to tell.' She lowered her head and toed something in the dirt. 'He was pretty bitter about his ex.'

Humphrey grunted. He'd known men like that. Men who blamed everyone but themselves for whatever went wrong in a relationship.

'For a dud date you were out a while.'

Eden looked up. 'Oh, yeah. Nell and her friend turned up, so I used them as an excuse to escape and joined them for a drink and a dance. There was a band playing. Pretty good one too. I would have stayed for a bit only ...' She indicated Ruffian and Admiral, but Humphrey could hear a note of despondency in her voice. It took all his willpower not to fold his arms around her.

Just for comfort—a friend there for a friend—but Eden would likely misinterpret it.

Humphrey offered her the next best thing, jerking his thumb at the kitchenette. 'Got some of Mum's fruitcake if you're interested.'

'No,' she said, shaking her head and surprising him. Eden usually jumped at the chance of a cuppa and fruitcake in the truck. 'But thanks. I need to give my boys a cuddle and get some sleep.'

'Right,' said Humphrey, thinking he wouldn't mind a goodnight cuddle too. 'Night, then.'

She smiled, a genuine one. 'Good night to you, Humphrey.' Then she winked. A pure sunny Eden that made the blustery evening suddenly warm. 'Thanks for staying up.'

Humphrey watched her go, rubbing at his chest where a weird feeling had lodged. He busied himself with his horses, glancing her way now and then to see if she'd change her mind. Only when she headed to the amenities block, toothbrush and toothpaste in hand, did he wearily climb the steps into the kitchenette.

He opened the fruitcake container, stared at the contents, then closed the lid.

What was the point of fruitcake if he didn't have someone to share it with?

Chapter Seven

Six weeks, seven dates—including two further no-shows—and a whole lot of frustration later, Eden was no closer to her goal of exorcising Humphrey from her heart. In fact, impossible as it seemed, her feelings for him were deepening.

Every date simply demonstrated how much better he was as a man, as a friend, as a potential lover.

Even when he was behaving weirdly, as he had been this past month.

The only exception was Cam. They'd met one Thursday night, two weeks after their coffee date, for drinks in the back bar of Levenham's Australian Arms Hotel. As usual, the front bar was lively, with people trying their hands at the football club meat raffle and celebrating payday and the upcoming weekend. The back bar was quieter, had squishy chairs and an open fire, and was redolent with the scent of pub food from the busy adjacent bistro.

Though it was mid-spring, in this part of South Australia—low down towards the coast and the Great

Southern Ocean—the nights were still cool. Eden and Cam found a table facing the fire and settled alongside each other with drinks that Eden insisted on buying, despite Cam's protests. It was her turn and, though she didn't think Cam was that kind of bloke, some men liked to keep IOUs. With payment not necessarily in drinks.

They talked about their weeks, the weather, Cam's twin sisters, and local news until conversation finally petered out. The quiet wasn't awkward, more contemplative. As though they were both figuring their next moves.

Like their first date, it was all very ... nice. Nice company, nice conversation.

Perfectly nice and perfectly depressing.

Cam seemed a decent man. A man from a good family with a stable job and no black marks against him with women that Eden could discover from the local grapevine. Attractive, too.

Surely, she should feel something?

There was warmth and friendliness—no denying that—but that flutter of anticipation, that teetering sensation of being on the cliff edge of something truly exciting, truly wild and burning and *needy*? Non-existent.

It was just all too ... nice.

The thought had Eden accidentally letting out a sigh.

'Sorry,' said Cam. 'I'm boring you.'

'No. *No*! Please don't think that. It's been a busy week and I'm just tired.'

He gave her a look that showed he knew she was lying, then it was his turn to sigh. 'You know I like you? You're sweet and funny ...'

'But?'

His mouth twisted, cheeks reddening as he focused on the fire.

Eden touched his knee and finished for him. 'No spark.' She dropped her voice as weariness and disappointment flattened her. 'I really wanted it to work.'

'Me, too.'

'Crap,' she said, staring gloomily at her beer.

'Yeah. Crap.'

They looked at one another and laughed, and suddenly Eden was launched out of her funk. No point being morose. Cam was still here, being nice, and she still had plenty of dates ahead.

'Friends?' asked Eden.

'Definitely.'

They sat in companionable silence for a while, enjoying the fire and the last of their beers.

'Will you keep going with your plan?'

For a moment Eden didn't know what Cam was referring to. Her mind had trotted off to Humphrey, thinking how they had friendship, too, but it was friendship with an electric current running through it.

'Plan?'

'With Cupid Country.'

Oh, yes. That plan. When they'd spoken after their first date, Eden had thought it only fair that she disclose her dating scheme. Cam had been nice about that, too.

'I think so. It's only been a few weeks. You?'

'Yeah, I'll give it another go. There's bound to be someone for me out there.'

Except, as the weeks went on and the dates went by, and

Humphrey kept acting increasingly oddly, Eden wasn't so sure.

She had another date tonight. Drinks again, although this time at a wine bar. Fancier than her usual pub adventures, but she doubted it would turn out any better. Stewart was older—about five years younger than Humphrey—and Eden's gut was telling her that this meant he was likely looking for wife number two.

Not that she had anything against divorced men. People got divorced for all sorts of reasons, and not necessarily reprehensible ones, but it made her wary.

At least it was a gorgeous day. Beautiful blue sky the colour of Humphrey's eyes, and a zephyr of breeze to keep the horses cool. They were at one of the bigger regional shows, across the border in Victoria, not far from Geelong, and there was good prize money on offer. Which also meant serious competition. She and her boys would need to be right on form to feature in the winner's circle.

Eden was walking the course for her first event when Humphrey came alongside, long-limbed and muscled in his fawn-coloured breeches and tall leather riding boots. She hunted for something in his expression to tell her why he'd joined her, but his focus was on the jump in front.

It was bizarre. Everywhere Eden went, she'd catch a glimpse of Humphrey. Not close, but in her periphery. Like he was keeping tabs.

If Eden went to warm-up, Humphrey would arrive soon after either on foot or on one of his mounts. When Eden went to fill a water bucket, he'd be there, offering to carry it back. Last week, at a small show only an hour and a half from Levenham, Eden had bumped into her brother Tom's soon-to-be best man, Olly, who had been exhibiting his prize waterfowl and, knowing Eden was likely to be competing, had decided to kill time by dropping by to say hello.

Olly had hugged her, lifting Eden off the ground with his six-foot-four frame, and causing her to squeal. They'd spent half an hour or so chatting and watching the junior ring, Olly making her laugh with his stories about his girl-friend, Niamh, and her precision plagued approach to life.

A perfectly innocent catch up with a friend she'd known most of her life. But throughout their chat, the back of her neck kept goosebumping, as though Humphrey's glower from across the ring was a physical thing. Each time Eden had glanced over, he'd been intent on a rider, but she hadn't imagined his attention. He'd been watching her. Unhappily.

What it all meant she didn't know.

It was probably protectiveness. Humphrey had always looked out for her, been kind. This was no different.

She wished it were more. She wished it was jealousy. But wishes and hopes had only ever brought her pain.

'Hmph,' grunted Humphrey as he finished stepping out the distance between the double, a simple vertical followed by an oxer—essentially two vertical fences set a distance apart to create a single wide jump.

Eden followed suit, counting her steps and using the total to estimate the number and length of strides needed to make the second fence in the combination.

She paused at the oxer, frowning, then looked across to Humphrey. 'It's very long.'

'It is.' He rubbed at his jaw. 'Ruff will be okay. Addy won't like it.'

'No. It'll be long for Tiger, too.'

Humphrey shrugged. 'I'll just have to use my bum.'

'And what a bum it is,' said Eden wistfully, then, realising she'd said that out loud, she hastily stepped out the jump again.

The expected exasperated *Eden* didn't come. She reached the upright and turned back. Humphrey was staring at her with one of those looks. The raw one, where his heart leapt into his eyes and made her believe that he felt the same as her.

Eden's stomach did a mad flip. The look should have been a there-and-gone flash, like all the other times, so quick she'd wonder if she imagined it. Yet there it was, lingering. A burning, blistering thing.

Her heart thudded. Humphrey wanted her. Really wanted her.

'Long, isn't it?' asked a female voice.

Eden glanced left. Nell was eyeing the distance between the vertical and the oxer. Mandy stood alongside, arms folded and a smug smile on her face. When she looked back at Humphrey he was walking to the next fence.

'Yes,' she said, her voice tremulous.

Eden was still shaken when she mounted Ruffian and headed to the warm-up arena. She'd caught Humphrey looking at her that way before, but today ... just thinking about it made her breath short. Today had been pure fire.

It had left her feeling uncertain and fractious, asking herself over and over what it meant. And more importantly, what she should do about it.

Nothing right now. She had a round to prepare for.

Eden broke Ruff into a trot, then canter, and circled him around the outside of the arena, concentrating on getting him in hand and listening. There were two practice fences —a simple upright and a spread, both lower and narrower than competition fences, and easy to jump. When she was satisfied the horse was ready, she faced him at the upright.

Ruff knocked the rail down.

Eden frowned and went to dismount to set the rail back in place, but the marshal waved and indicated he'd take care of it.

Her second and third attempts produced the same result. Instead of tucking his forelegs up neatly, Ruff was hanging them over the jump. A few riders threw her dirty looks at the delays while the jump was rebuilt. The marshal pursed his lips.

Experience told Eden it was a rider problem, but she couldn't figure out how. She didn't feel like she was riding differently to normal, yet ...

She circled Ruff again, her brows furrowing deeper as she puzzled over the issue.

She faced the jump, only to steer away when she spotted Humphrey standing alongside. He'd shed his jacket, exposing his chest-hugging white competition shirt. Combined with his form-fitting breeches, he was beautiful, even with the stained and battered felt hat he'd plonked on his head.

'Come at it again,' he called.

Needing to catch her breath, Eden cantered a full lap of the ring before riding at the jump. The rail fell again.

'Again,' instructed Humphrey as he hoisted the rail back into its cups.

Eden obeyed, growling at the rap of Ruff's hooves as they hit the rail. She brought him back to a walk and stroked his neck. It wasn't his fault. It was hers.

'It's your shoulders,' said, Humphrey striding over. 'You're rolling them forwards. It's putting pressure on his front.'

'Oh.'

He reached up and pressed one hand to her lower spine,

the other on her shoulder and pushed gently back. His touch felt like a brand. 'You're out of line.'

'I hadn't realised.'

He shrugged. 'Happens to us all sometimes.'

She doubted that. Humphrey was an incredible rider.

'Thank you,' she said quietly, wishing she could find the courage to ask him about the course walk, what that look had meant.

'Happy to help.' He paused, his voice as quiet as hers. 'Always.'

Their gazes collided, and though his sky-blue gaze lacked the heat of earlier, there was still something there. Something simmering. It took every ounce of Eden's control not to tumble from the saddle into his arms.

Humphrey broke contact. He cleared his throat. 'Try him again.'

Eden did as she was told, concentrating on her position. The rail stayed up, Ruffian clearing it with his usual ease. She did three more jumps, Humphrey watching each time, before easing back to a walk. Humphrey accompanied her to the exit, his hand on Ruff's neck. Eden wished it were on her thigh. On her anywhere.

A woman smiled as she sent who Eden guessed was her daughter into the warm-up ring. 'You're so lucky to have your dad to help. Alicia's father wouldn't know a horse from a hound.'

Her dad? This woman thought Humphrey was *her dad?*

No. *No, no, no.*

Eden went to protest but the damage was done. Humphrey's expression had turned to stone. His jaw was clenched, as were his fists. Without a glance or farewell, he turned on his heel and stomped away.

Eden urged Ruffian to follow, only for a steward to call her number. Her round was up.

For a second she considered withdrawing, but what would it achieve? She was here to compete and pulling out would probably only made Humphrey angrier. There'd be time to talk later.

Casting him a final longing look, Eden turned Ruffian to the ring.

Chapter Eight

Humphrey had known he was being stupid. But he hadn't realised quite how stupid until that woman mistook him for Eden's father.

The pain had been swift and powerful, like a horse kick to the chest.

One moment he'd been thinking of joining Cupid Country and contacting Eden to ask if she'd like a date, and the next he was thrown back to reality with the reminder of the age difference between them.

Her father. *Jesus wept.*

Somehow, Humphrey made it through the day. He focused all his energy on riding the best he could and avoiding people. Not easy, when Eden was dogging him, as determined to get him alone as he was to stay away from her.

Several times, he caught her looking worriedly in his direction and every time he turned his back. Those simple but true words had hollowed him out, left him a desiccated shell of a man. The growing fantasy of being able to love

Eden was gone. For his own wellbeing, as well as hers, he needed to keep his distance.

It was over. Which was ironic, when he'd never allowed it to begin.

It was a relief when the day's competition was done and the horses settled, and he could retreat to his truck and shut the door on the world. At least in here the only person who had to put up with Humphrey's shitty company was him.

Except Eden had a date. And whenever Eden had a date, Humphrey's stupid heart overrode his sensibility.

He made a coffee and sat on his step, phone propped on his knee as though he was reading, and doing his utmost to radiate a don't-come-near vibe.

Eden trotted across the camping area to her car, wearing jeans, long boots and a silky looking red top. Her hair was pinned up in some sort of knot and she'd threaded dangly gold earrings through her ears.

Humphrey's heart twisted as she sat in the front of her car and applied make-up. He hated that she wore make-up for these dates. He hated that she thought she needed it. She was already pretty. Beautiful, in fact.

Young and beautiful and deserving of someone better than him. Someone who wouldn't be mistaken for *her father*.

His teeth gritted. Even thinking of that comment had him wanting to chew those words to mush and spit them out and grind them under the heel of his boot.

Eden applied some lip gloss, exited the car, and slid on her coat. She tucked her phone in a pocket and hit the car fob, locking it. With a martial stride and an even more martial expression, she made a straight line to Humphrey.

He half rose, then sat again. What was the point? She'd

only corner him later and at least no one else was around right now.

She halted in front of him, hands buried in her pockets. The pink on her cheeks wasn't all blusher. She was irked. 'You've been avoiding me all day.'

Humphrey shrugged.

'That woman was either a fool or had forgotten her glasses. If she'd looked at you properly, she would have realised how young you were.'

'I'm not young. I have grey in my hair.'

'That means nothing.' She sucked on her bottom lip. 'Not to me.'

'It should.'

'No, it shouldn't.'

Humphrey made a dismissive gesture. This conversation served no purpose. He shouldn't even be having it. He cursed himself for not escaping inside when he had the chance.

'Right.' Her eyes sparked. She plonked a hand on her hip. 'So that moment this morning at the double was nothing then?'

Humphrey stared at his phone. That moment had been everything. He'd looked at her and *wanted* so badly it had drained the air from his lungs. All he could think was that one step would be all it took. One step to what Clara and Mandy kept insisting would be his happiness. *Both* their happinesses.

Now it never would be. A few throwaway words from a stranger had hammered reality home, like a nail in his coffin.

He eased up from the step, feeling every inch an old man, aching to his hollow core. 'Enjoy your date.'

'That's all you've got to say?'

'Yep.'

Eden flapped her arms. 'Oh, for God's sake!'

Humphrey opened the door, then hesitated. He looked back at her, so frustrated and lovely and pointlessly mad for him, a man who could never be what she needed. His throat turned thick. Loss, heartache, and desperate, desperate want blocking it.

He cleared his throat, but his voice still sounded gravelly. 'Be careful.'

She gave him a long pitying look and shook her head and for a horrible moment Humphrey thought he caught a glimmer of tears. Then her shoulders went back, and she tossed her head.

'Fine. Be like that. But it's your loss, Humphrey Taylor-Martin,' she said, poking a finger in his direction before striding off and throwing another 'Your loss' over her shoulder as she went.

Yes, and didn't he know it.

Though the early evening was cooling rapidly, and the last thing he wanted was anyone thinking he was inviting company, Humphrey kept the door to his truck open, watching for Eden's return.

He tried to read a book, but he had zero concentration. There was stuff-all on the television—a game show whose host bounced about like a kangaroo on steroids flashing impossibly white teeth, some besuited political talking heads, a rerun of an old *Midsomer Murders*, and a documentary about a dead rock star he'd never heard of.

Bored and churning with turmoil, Humphrey paced the kitchenette, pulling out drawers and sliding them shut again, looking for he didn't know what. He found an old pack of cards and sat down to play patience, only to discover he didn't have any, because all the cards made him think of was Eden, playing snap with him as they sheltered from a squall. The way she'd once kept her hand on his, when he'd called "snap" and claimed the cards and she'd come in too late.

He checked his horses, then Eden's, then Mandy's, although carefully, so she didn't notice. Until, finally, Humphrey flirted with danger and messaged his sister with a simple, *How's lawyerland?*

Clara knew him too well. *A rare message from my brother. Hmm. There must be trouble.*

No trouble. Just saying hello.

Don't make me laugh. Let me guess. Eden.

Humphrey *hmphed.* Served him right. *Some woman called me her father today.*

Ouch.

Yeah, ouch. His chest still felt bruised from the kick of those words.

The little dots danced up and down as Clara kept typing.

I guess now you're using that as an excuse to dither, even though it's rubbish.

It's not rubbish. I AM too old for her.

Three words: Lonely, miserable life.

Humphrey sighed. Clara was never one for sympathy. *Thanks for that. Very helpful.*

You're an idiot also fits.

Again, helpful.

It's what sisters are for. Anyway, what do you want from me? I've told you what to do. Marry Eden. Have babies. Make everyone, especially yourself, happy.

Clara's suggestion sounded so simple. Except, after today, Humphrey couldn't bring himself to believe it possible. For a while he'd fantasised it might be. That what mattered was how they felt about each other, and Humphrey was in no doubt about his feelings. It was as though all the emotion he'd squashed down deep inside him was leaching forth, permeating every capillary and nerve ending, filling him to the brim with love.

His jealousy of her dates was insane. Every time he watched her skip off to meet one of them, a knife twisted in his guts. Worse, he couldn't stop thinking about her. On the farm, in the training arena, driving the truck. In the shower. Jesus, in the shower was the worst. That was when his fantasies really went nuts.

Love had given him hope. Made him wonder if he was being as dumb as Clara said. That their age difference wasn't the impediment he thought. And it had grown, that hope, like a tumour pressing against his vital organs, in need of urgent attention. To the point where he'd decided to act. To do what Eden kept entreating and try.

Humphrey buried his head in his hands. What a fucking day.

His phone beeped. Clara again.

Love you, brother, even though you're an idiot.

That gave him a short laugh. *Love you, sister, even though your sympathy was excised at birth.*

Chapter Nine

The next three shows were all small and only day trips. Shows not worth the expense, really. Except Eden loved the show season, especially the little events put on year after year by the district's agricultural and horticultural show societies, community groups and service clubs, and their tireless volunteers.

She loved showjumping and the camaraderie and the competition. She loved the old exhibition halls and stands and rings. The celebration of country life and work and craft and produce.

Being frustrated to the eyeballs by a scowling, taciturn Humphrey wasn't going to change those loves. He could grump all he liked. Deny *them* all he liked. Eden was nothing if not resilient. She would rise above, foil him by dialling her sunniness up as high as it could go and skipping off to her dates as though they meant the world.

Which was far, far from the case. Last week's date would have been funny, if it weren't so irritating. The man she'd thought was a young mechanic in his twenties turned out to be a truck driver in his fifties who'd pinched a random photo off the internet for his profile. Then had the nerve to get stroppy when Eden told him *thanks, but no thanks*.

The week before's date had been covered in tattoos, which was fine, but when he'd shucked up his sleeve to show a busty naked woman riding what looked to be a snake, Eden had known there wasn't much hope. The proud admission of a bolt through his penis had sealed it.

Today she was meeting her date at lunchtime at the front entrance to the hall, but the overrun of her showjumping class meant Eden was fifteen minutes late. Hurrying from a hastily untacked and watered Addy, she found him pacing anxiously up and down the side of the hall, phone in his hand.

'Darren?' she asked.

'Eden?' An enormous, relieved smile lit his face. 'Thank goodness. I thought you weren't coming.'

'I know. Sorry.' She waved back towards the horses-in-action rings. 'My class got held up. Would you like to get a coffee, or something? Or just walk about? I don't have a lot of time, sorry.'

'A drink would be good. It's a bit hot here. But I'll just text Mum first.'

'Your mum?'

'Yeah, she's waiting in the parking area.'

He brought his mum on his date?

'Oh.' Eden glanced to the adjoining paddock, which had been roped off for parking, but couldn't spot anyone mum-like. 'Sure. Go ahead.'

She eyed Darren sideways as he typed, a churn in her stomach. He was pleasant looking—sandy-coloured hair, a few freckles, kind of cute—and a fraction taller than her. Not as tall as Humphrey and a bit leaner, but the rolled-up sleeves of his perfectly pressed checked shirt showed muscled forearms. And no naked lady tattoo.

His mum probably wouldn't allow it.

Eden chided herself for the mean thought. She shouldn't be so judgemental. It was entirely possible his mum was ill and couldn't be left on her own.

'Done,' he said, pocketing his phone in his equally well-pressed chinos. 'She'll come over later on. You can meet her. Now, where to?'

Eden was too polite to cancel the date immediately, but it quickly became clear that Darren was a dedicated mummy's boy. Worse, he didn't seem to think there was anything wrong with a twenty-six-year-old being that dependent.

Only when he suggested that it was time for Eden to meet said mother did Eden make her excuses and bolt, taking a long and windy route to her car and horse float in case Darren decided to follow.

She buried her face in Ruffian's neck and groaned. This date plan was really beginning to get her down. Stopping, though, would only do herself a disservice. Unless she wanted a future tortured by her unrequited love for Humphrey, she had to keep trying.

'Eden?'

Humphrey. Of course it was.

Eden shifted her head just enough to check his expression. Worry had replaced the scowl he'd been sporting for weeks. Tension strained his body, his fingers flexing as though he was stopping them from reaching out.

Frustration rose in a hot tide. Why must the rotten man be so kind? Didn't he realise it only made things worse?

When she made no response, he stepped closer. 'Are you okay?'

'Fine.' She puffed out a breath, plastered on a wide smile and gave Ruff's silky neck a pat of thanks. 'Perfectly fine, if you don't count having to endure a date who brought his mum along.'

'Jesus.' Humphrey's face screwed up as he rubbed his head. 'What was he, twelve?'

'Probably about that in maturity.' Eden began to peel off Ruff's lightweight rug. Their next event was scheduled for one-thirty, and she needed to prepare. 'He was nice enough, otherwise.'

Humphrey's grunt revealed what he thought about that statement.

Eden surveyed him. 'Did you want something?'

'No. I saw you with Ruff and just thought ...' He shook his head. 'Nothing. Better go. Good luck.'

Eden proved how much she hadn't risen above his behaviour by poking her tongue out at his back.

'Poking your tongue out at him won't help.'

Eden squawked. She turned to find Mandy leaning against the end of the horse float. Just the person she didn't need.

She folded Ruff's rug and hung it over the chest rail inside the horse float, then used a body brush to give him a quick groom before strapping on his open front tendon boots. Lightweight but thickly lined and with a hard outer coating, the boots protected the foreleg tendons from knocks caused by overreaching hind legs, while the open front kept the horse careful.

Mandy didn't get the hint. 'Jealousy won't work.'

'I'm not trying to make him jealous. I'm trying to give myself a life.'

'And how's that working out for you?'

Eden ground her teeth and moved on to securing Ruff's fetlock boots to his hind legs.

Sliding her hand around Ruff's rump, Mandy moved closer until she stood at his tail to regard Eden down her nose. 'I heard about the other day.'

'What other day?'

'The "mistaken for your dad" day.'

Oh. That day. The day when Humphrey's gaze had shone with raw want. The day when she'd glimpsed hope. And the same day when a casual comment from a stranger had Humphrey snapping his heart closed again like a startled clam.

She didn't want to remember that day. That day had made her realise he would never change. Except, for her own sanity, for her future, she had to. How else was she to move on?

Eden moved round to Ruff's off hind leg. Mandy swivelled to follow, her gaze intent. 'You need to talk to him, Eden. Talk properly. Lay out all his fears and debunk them.' Mandy leaned closer. 'Then seduce the bejesus out of him.'

Eden choked. Oh yeah, great plan. Like Eden hadn't thought of that a gazillion times. It might work, except Humphrey would never let her get that close. A lesson she'd learned from experience.

Besides, Eden's goal was to move on, not to worsen her heartache.

And how's that working out for you?

Eden set her jaw. 'Don't you need to get Mocha ready?'

Mandy stared, then rolled her eyes and gave an "I give up" huff. 'You can lead a horse to water ...'

Yes, thought Eden sadly as Mandy stomped off. *You can. But you can't make him love you.*

Chapter Ten

Eden leaned closer to her car's passenger-side vanity mirror as she applied a last brush of mascara. She tipped her head one way then the other, checking the blusher she'd applied. Not bad. She was getting better at this.

She blew herself a kiss and laughed at her silliness, but it was hard not to feel high. Today was day one of the last of the big shows, running over the whole weekend, and it had gotten off to a cracking start. She'd had two wins, both on Addy, beating Humphrey and Tiger in one jump-off and Mandy and Mocha in another. And tonight, Eden had another date.

From his profile and the brief messages they'd exchanged, Jack seemed perfect. A local farmer close to her own age who worked on his family's irrigated property, growing certified clover and lucerne seed.

They were meeting at a Thai restaurant. Eden's first dinner date. Surely a positive sign?

Humphrey was sitting on his truck step when Eden alighted, fiddling with his phone and faking not paying attention to her, despite the closeness of their camps. His messy, hat-flattened hair was flopped over his forehead. He was still in his breeches, a pair of brown socks pulled up over his calves and a pair of old workboots on his feet.

The Humphrey she adored—unaffected, horsey, masculine, and possessing that indefinable something that had captured her heart as a teen and never let go.

A familiar fist squeezed Eden's insides. She breathed hard against the longing tightening her chest. It would fade. All it would take was the right man. Cam could have been it, if not for the lack of spark, and while none of the others from Cupid Country had been right, perhaps tonight, with Jack, it would be different.

And how's that working out for you?

Rotten, rotten Mandy. She'd uttered those words two weeks ago and still they echoed. The horrible woman had got into Eden's head and wouldn't leave.

But what was Eden meant to do? Attempt to seduce Humphrey like Mandy suggested? Eden knew from experience it would only end in humiliation and Humphrey distancing himself further.

Then again, perhaps that could be a positive.

Eden shunted the idea away. Humphrey was her friend. She didn't want to lose that.

The man in question looked up. His blue gaze scoured her, head to toe, taking in every aspect of her outfit, before returning to her face where it lingered, his expression unreadable.

For a moment, Eden stared back, her heart stretching as though reaching for him, then she pulled herself together.

'Looking like a babe?' she asked, lifting her arms and pirouetting, ballerina-like, and almost tripping over her own feet as she came to a stop.

The corner of Humphrey's mouth lifted. 'I'm sure you'll do.'

'Wow, Humphrey. Don't overextend yourself with the encouragement or anything.'

Humphrey opened his mouth, then closed it. He shook his head and looked away. 'Where are you off to?'

'That Thai restaurant next to the town hall.'

'Dinner?'

'Yes.' She gave a smug shimmy. 'Clearly my date, Jack, is a classy man.'

Humphrey gave one of his trademark *hmphs* and regarded his phone. He hesitated then used his index finger to tap out something on the screen. A dismissal, but hope kept Eden anchored, yearning for something, anything from him.

The evening was full of colour and noise—laugher and chatter, teens screaming as a show ride whooshed them skyward, birds screeching and squawking as they settled into the showground's surrounding trees for the night.

Still Humphrey remained silent.

Eden could hope all she liked. There would never be an acknowledgement of what existed between them. Never a change of heart. Never a "please don't go".

Humphrey's heart was as closed as his mouth.

'I'll see you later, then,' she said, unable to keep the snap from her voice. Why was unrequited love so persistent? She was young, pretty when she put in an effort, a nice person. She deserved better than this horrible, frustrating hurt.

Shoving her hands in her pockets, she headed off.

'Be careful.'

Hurt suddenly flared into fury.

'Like you care, Humphrey.'

Eden regretted the words as soon as they were out, but

she didn't stop to apologise. She yanked open her car door and fired the engine, blinking rapidly as she put the car into gear, wishing the world was different. Wishing she was.

When she glanced across, Humphrey was standing, shoulders slumped, arms by his side, palms open.

The vulnerability on his face had her swallowing. Her foot moved to the brake and hovered there. Despite this mess of emotions, they were still friends. And friends didn't deliberately hurt one another.

Except she'd been hurting for years, and his dismissal and false care had ignited the fury she'd kept buried. She wanted him to feel it. To feel a little of what it was like to be her.

Her mouth a thin line, Eden moved her foot back to the accelerator and pressed down. No more. This had to stop. She let out a half-laugh, half-sob.

And how's that working out for you?

She sniffed and forced herself to concentrate on the short drive into the centre of town. All the parking spots along the street were taken. Eden circled the block, finding a space next to the town's ANZAC memorial. She alighted and spared a few seconds to study the statue, a heart-rending figure of a soldier on a thick stone column, leaning on his upturned rifle, head bowed over his hands. The sides of the column were covered in names. Men lost too soon.

She shook herself and walked on. Tonight was not the night for despondency. It was a night for sunniness and optimism and a date with a decent man.

Cheerful light poured from the restaurant's big glass windows and front door. There were busy tables every-where, little red candle votives flickering on each, along with containers of napkins and brass spoons and forks. A waitress hustled past bearing multiple plates of steaming food. Even through the glass, Eden could hear guests' chatter competing with the restaurant's piped Asian music.

Eden entered and paused to surreptitiously wipe her hands down the side of her jeans as she cast around the tables for her date. Only one table held a single person. A dark-haired man in intense conversation with a twenty-something waiter.

'Be with you in a minute,' said the waitress as she hurried towards the back of the restaurant.

Catching a dirty look from the table closest to the entrance, Eden closed the door with an accidental bang. At the sound, the single man glanced up. He quickly rose, a shy smile curling his mouth.

Jack.

He waved her over. The waiter glanced at Eden then back at Jack and drifted off.

Eden's stomach gave a little flip. She'd known Jack was attractive from his profile photo, but reality was very different. Jack wasn't just handsome, he was country boy gorgeous. Completely out of her league.

She looked over her shoulder to double-check there wasn't some mistake, and he was gesturing to someone coming in behind her, but the street was empty.

This was her date. *Holy hell.*

Eden took a deep breath and headed for the table. She could do this. She absolutely could.

'You must be Eden,' he said, blushing cutely and holding out his hand. 'I'm Jack.'

She took his hand. His grip was firm, if slightly clammy. Nerves, she guessed. That made two of them. 'Good to meet you, Jack.'

'Please,' he said, indicating the spare seat.

Eden drew off her coat and hung it over the back of the

chair and sat, trying not to gawp at her ridiculously attractive date.

His hair was cut short at the sides but tousled at the top, the spikes held up with some sort of product. Sculpted eyebrows rose above striking hazel eyes surrounded by a thick fringe of dark lashes that put Eden's mascaraed ones to shame. For an outdoor bloke, his skin was flawless, except for a tiny red nick on his chin. A shaving cut, perhaps.

And that full, luscious mouth. That was a mouth to dream about kissing.

He caught her staring and gave another crooked smile. Eden flushed an even deeper pink than Jack. She adjusted her bamboo placemat, desperate for a conversation starter, but her mind had gone blank. It was hard to believe this man was real. Real, and about to have dinner with her.

The waiter came back and handed them menus. 'Can I get you any drinks?'

'Just tap water, thanks,' said Eden. Having driven, Eden was only allowing herself one glass of wine and it could come later.

'I'll have a Singha,' said Jack.

'Of course.'

Jack smiled his thanks before concentrating back on Eden. 'Do you like Thai?'

'I do.'

'Great. They do good curries here.'

Eden opened her menu and read the opening dishes. Curry puffs, spring rolls, fishcakes. All the usual suspects. 'You're a regular?'

Jack's gaze slid sideways to where the waiter had paused at another table. 'I've been a few times. I don't get into town that much.'

'How far out are you?'

'About thirty-five k's.'

Eden set down her menu. 'We're about forty, so similar.'

'What do you run?'

They settled into a conversation about their family properties until the waiter returned with a carafe of water, glasses and Jack's beer.

'Ready to order?'

Jack checked with Eden who shook her head. 'Sorry. Not yet.'

The waiter's mouth thinned. 'I'll come back in five.'

Jack watched him leave with a frown, then seemed to give himself a small shake before clearing his throat and pouring Eden's water. He pushed the glass towards her and lifted his beer.

Eden pressed her glass against it, their fingers touching lightly.

'To new friends?' said Jack.

'New friends.'

They drank. Jack placed down his beer and began picking at the label. He was about to tear off a strip when he stopped and grinned sheepishly. 'Sorry. Nervous.'

'Me, too.'

The admission had them sharing smiles.

'So, you're riding at the show?'

'Yes. Showjumping.'

He nodded. 'My cousin Lucy is competing too. Perhaps you know her? Lucy Rusciano?'

Eden shook her head. After years on the circuit, she knew most of the showjumpers, but the name wasn't familiar.

Jack screwed his nose up. He even did that cutely. 'I think she's doing dressage or something.' He spread his hands. 'I don't really follow it.'

'She's probably competing in the hacking competitions. Prettiest horse and rider wins.'

'Sounds like Lucy.' He tipped his head to the side. 'You prefer danger?'

'More like action. It's fun. What about you? What do you do for fun?' Eden slapped her hand over her mouth. 'Oh, God. That sounded like a come-on, didn't it?'

He laughed. 'A bit, but I knew what you meant. I don't know. I'm usually so busy on the farm I don't have a lot of time for sport.'

'No football, cricket?'

'No,' he said, an edge to his voice. 'Much to my dad's disappointment.'

'Sorry.'

'Don't be. You can't always please your parents.'

'No.'

Silence reigned, then their gazes met, and again they both smiled. Eden's heart gave a tumble. Jack was not only handsome, he was nice.

The waiter passed their table, carrying a laden wine bucket. He glanced down at their menus and shot Jack a pointed look.

'Oops,' said Eden, making a face. 'Better choose before we get into trouble.'

Agreeing to share meals, Eden opted for a chilli-and-basil stir-fry and Jack the Penang curry, with steamed rice.

'So, did you ride today?'

'Yes.' Eden's chest puffed a little at his interest. 'I had four events.'

'And?'

She regarded him from under lowered lashes, aware she was being flirtatious, but unable to help herself. 'Won two.'

'But that's great. You must be very talented.'

'Mostly it's my horses. They're good boys.'

Jack leaned forward and rested his chin on his curled hands. 'Tell me about them.'

Eden did just that, delighted when Jack chuckled at her anecdotes about Ruffian's naughtiness, and life on the circuit. Encouraged, she told him about her bus route and the people she picked up, thrilled when he sounded impressed at her skill and humour.

When their meals arrived, Eden ordered a glass of chardonnay and Jack another beer. Conversation continued to flow as they tucked into their dinner and, with it, Eden's optimism that Jack could be exactly what she hankered for grew.

Jack couldn't have been sweeter. He asked questions about her family, urged her to share his food, picking out bits of capsicum and carrot for her when she admitted how much she craved vegetables after a day of junk food.

He had sisters, too. Three of them. All older, all married, two of them with children.

'I know not to leave the loo seat up,' he said, laughing.

'What made you go on Cupid Country?' asked Eden, pushing her plate to the side. 'I mean, look at you.' She waved her hand, indicating his face. 'You're gorgeous. Surely you should be beating them off with a stick.'

For a second, his face clouded, before that cute, crooked smile appeared. 'Thanks.' He lifted his beer and drained it, then carefully set it back down and began picking at the label again. 'Truthfully?'

Eden nodded.

'I got nagged into it. Sisters, you know?'

Eden could guess. Three sisters with a little brother, stuck out on a farm, handsome and single. They probably wanted him to have what they did—love, a family. Happiness.

'Have you been on many dates?' she asked.

'You're the first.'

'Wow. I'm ...' Honoured? Flattered? Whatever Eden's confused feelings, she liked being first. It made her feel special.

'What about you?'

'A few.'

'And?'

'It's been a mixed bag.' She twirled the stem of her wineglass. 'Some good, some pretty diabolical.'

He leaned closer, one perfect eyebrow raised and a sparkle in his lovely eyes. 'This one?'

'This one is definitely one of the good ones.'

Their gazes locked, and once again Eden had the sense she was teetering on the edge of something wonderful. All she had to do was step forward.

Jack pointed behind him, to where a toilet sign hung high on the wall. 'Excuse me for a minute?'

'Sure.'

She watched him make his way to the back of the room, admiring his lean body. Not quite in Humphrey's league when it came to great bums, but nothing to complain about.

Eden chuckled softly to herself. Complain about Jack? As if.

'Finished?' asked the waiter, already leaning across to pick up dishes.

'Yes. Thanks.'

He cleared and stacked plates, casting her glances as he did. 'You're on a date.' It wasn't a question.

Eden's brow furrowed, wondering what business it was of his, then she supposed he was just being friendly. 'Yes.'

He nodded and glanced towards the toilets and back at Eden. 'He's not what you think.'

'What?'

'Jack. Your date. He's ...' He breathed in deeply. 'You're wasting your time.'

Eden's hackles rose, her voice rising with them. 'I beg your pardon.'

'Shh.' His head jerked rapidly from side to side, checking the adjacent tables. 'Look, he's gay, all right? Always has been. Always will be.' His voice grew sad. 'Even if he won't admit it to himself.'

'Right,' said Eden, crossing her arms. 'And you would know this how?'

'I just *know*, okay?' His eyes widened meaningfully, and Eden realised that his knowledge wasn't derived from gossip, it had come firsthand.

Shock, cold and shaky, rushed through her. Jack. Gay.

Dishonest.

She slumped back, all the hope and happiness that had been building inside her leaching to the floor.

Unshed tears burned her eyes. She forced them away. She would not cry in the middle of a restaurant. She would not cry in front of Jack and she sure as hell wouldn't cry in front of that arsehole waiter.

Except, if what he said was true—and her gut was screaming it was—then he wasn't being an arsehole, he was stopping her from doing something foolish.

Jack returned to the room, his smile wide as he threaded through tables, only for it to falter and fade when he caught Eden's expression.

He slid into his chair and reached for Eden's hand. She snatched it out of reach. 'Eden, what's wrong?'

She swallowed as her eyes began to prickle. 'I think I should go.'

'Eden, please. What's the matter?'

'Nothing. I have to get back to my horses. Evening feed.' Which was a lie. They'd already been fed.

She rose and pulled her jacket off the back of her chair and hurried for the front counter. She needed out. Right now. Now, before she cracked.

Jack tried to catch her arm, but Eden was too quick. She stood at the counter, credit card tapping a rapid tattoo on the Laminex top.

'Eden ...'

She shook her head. Jack finally got the message and let it go. He stood beside her, confusion creasing his handsome features.

Finally, the waitress bustled over. 'Enjoy your meal?' she asked, as she pushed the bill across.

'Yes, thanks,' said Eden. 'Can you split this in half?'

'I'll get it.'

She turned, her face set, her tone stony. 'We'll split it.'

Jack shot up his palms. 'Okay, okay.'

The waitress gave them both a look before processing Eden's payment, then Jack's. Eden was already out the door by the time he'd finished.

The urge to run to her car was huge, but ingrained manners kept her in place. She moved out of the light, to the darkness of the shop next door, and wrenched on her coat, preparing for escape.

Jack said nothing as he approached. He stood looking at his feet, fists deep in the pockets of his jeans. 'I'm sorry. For whatever it was I did wrong. I thought ...' He trailed off, a crack in his voice.

And in that moment, Eden's heart went out to him.

'Jack ...' He deserved an explanation, except how the hell was she meant to broach this? 'The waiter ...'

His head jerked up. 'Daniel?' He stared furiously back at the restaurant, then his eyes scrunched closed. 'He had no right.'

'Is it true?' Even now, Eden desperately wished it wasn't.

'Yes. No.' He ground the heel of his hand into his forehead. 'It's complicated. My parents ...' He regarded Eden, a plea in his gaze. 'They're really religious. My whole family is.' His fist thumped his chest. 'I am.'

'And being gay isn't acceptable.'

'I'm not gay.' His eyes scrunched closed again, that beautiful mouth crumpling. Eden braced herself. Nothing undid her more than a man crying. 'I'm trying not to be.'

'Oh, Jack.' Eden couldn't help herself. This lovely man, despite his deceit, was in terrible pain. She wrapped her arms around him. 'You need to be yourself.'

He held her back tightly, his body tense with denial. 'I can't do that to them.'

Eden sucked back a sigh. This wasn't her area. Jack needed professional help to work through his conflicts. She let him hold her a little longer then wriggled free and stepped back.

'I have to go.'

'Yeah.' He scuffed a boot along the concrete. 'For what it's worth, I had a good time. I think you're great. I think, maybe, you and I could've—'

'No. We couldn't.'

He blew out air through pursed lips. 'I'm sorry.'

'Me, too.' She patted his arm and took a few steps. Then she wheeled around. 'Do something for me?'

'What?'

'Talk to someone. Someone impartial. A professional. Someone who won't judge. Please?'

He nodded, but Eden had the feeling it wouldn't happen. A sobering thought. Everyone deserved love and happiness.

'Perhaps we could swap numbers?' She extracted her phone and opened her contacts. 'That way I can call and see how you get on. Plug yours in and I'll text you back, so you'll have mine.'

Jack stared at the proffered phone like it was toxic. Swapping numbers meant he had to hold his word, and Jack was scared. Eden gave the phone an encouraging waggle.

'Sure,' he said, after another moment. He tapped in a series of numbers, hesitating over the last, then drew in a breath, entered the final digit and passed the phone back.

'Thanks.' She smiled, then, on impulse, gave him another quick hug. 'Take care, Jack.' Tucking her fists into her coat, she walked away.

'Eden?'

Eden frowned at him.

'Good luck. With everything.' A crooked smile lifted his face. 'You're a special girl. I hope you find someone who deserves you.'

So did she.

But given her experiences, that wasn't looking promising.

Chapter Eleven

Humphrey was heading back to his truck after checking on his and Eden's horses when he caught her hurrying, head down and shoulders hunched, towards the stables.

His gut flipped, then clenched when her mouth formed a horrified "O" at the sight of him.

What the ...?

She tried to skirt around him, but Humphrey wasn't having that. With a nifty move honed from years of catching sheep, calves and horses, he stepped into her path.

'Hey, hey.' He caught her upper arms, forcing her to a stop. 'What's wrong?'

'Nothing. I just want my boys.'

She tried to wrench out of his grip, but Humphrey held firm. Eden was upset. Really upset. Her mouth was pinched, her gaze darting everywhere but at him. 'What happened? Did that bastard hurt you?'

'No.' She shook her head, still refusing to make eye contact. 'I'm fine.'

'You're not fine.' He curled a finger and used it to tip up

her chin. Her eyes shimmered in the moonlight. Humphrey's heart felt like it was clawing up his chest. 'Jesus, Eden, what happened?'

'I don't want to talk about it. I just want to check on my boys and go to bed.'

'They're fine.' He relaxed his hold. 'I've just been in there.'

Taking advantage of his loosened hand, Eden dodged around him, clearly still intent on visiting Admiral and Ruffian.

'Eden, leave them to sleep. They've had a big day and have another tomorrow. They need rest. Come to the truck.'

That gave her pause. She stood staring at the stables' entrance, hands opening and closing.

Though he felt sick with fear at what had rattled her so badly, Humphrey put a tease in his voice. 'I've an open bottle of red. And there's Mum's fruitcake.'

Still, she hesitated.

'It's warm inside.'

She closed her eyes, hands still fisting and unfisting.

Humphrey cupped her shoulder, thumb rubbing what he hoped were calming circles. 'Come to the truck.'

Her mouth crumpled and she made a small, pained sound that tore at his insides. But Eden let herself be led. The tightness in his chest eased a little.

As promised, the truck was warm and smelled of Humphrey's earlier ham and cheese toastie. He ushered Eden onto one of the kitchenette's bench seats and pulled a pair of wineglasses from an overhead cupboard. He poured a good measure of red wine in one and slid it towards her, then cut a slice of fruitcake and placed it on a plate.

She stared at both, then looked up at him and smiled

wanly. 'That's the trouble with you, Humphrey. You're always kind.'

Why kindness was trouble, Humphrey wasn't sure, but he wasn't about to ask. Not after Eden's pre-date outburst and not now, when she was so downcast. All he wanted was to fix whatever was wrong and, for that, he needed her to talk.

He shrugged and settled opposite her. He poured himself a glass but didn't sip. The book he'd been attempting to read lay open where he'd left it. He flipped the cover closed.

Eden regarded it with a frown. 'A biography of Bart Cummings?'

'It's interesting.' And it was, when he could concentrate, which he'd managed for a grand total of five minutes since Eden left for her date. The late Cummings was one of Australia's most successful racehorse trainers, fondly known as the Cups King for the number of Melbourne Cup winners he'd trained.

'He's a racehorse trainer.'

'Still a legend.'

'Hmm,' she said, staring off into space.

'Eat your cake, Eden. It'll make you feel better.'

She sighed and picked at a corner. 'I'm sorry I snapped at you earlier. You know, before I left.'

'It's okay.'

'This whole thing is ...' Her eyes scrunched closed. Humphrey wanted to hug her. Make whatever pain she was suffering disappear. Instead, he said nothing, waiting for Eden to finish whatever it was she was about to admit. She blinked rapidly, gave a little shudder, picked up her wine-glass and sipped.

'What happened?'

Again, that wan smile. 'Nothing. We had dinner. Talked. Figured out we weren't right for each other.'

'He didn't ...' Humphrey swallowed. The thought of someone hurting Eden made heat crawl over his body like nettle rash.

'No. Nothing like that. It was fine. He was just ...' A wince, a look away. 'Not right for me.'

It was more than that, but if Eden didn't want to talk then Humphrey couldn't make her.

She indicated the book. 'So that's what you've been doing tonight? Reading?'

'Mandy dropped by for a while.' To tell him how stupid he was being. Mandy had caught the tail end of Eden's pique and decided to offer her unsolicited advice. If you could call "pull your head out of your arse, you're making both of you miserable" advice, that is. 'Nell called in to ask if I had anything for a headache.' He shrugged. A normal show night. People popping in and out.

Eden pushed her plate away. 'Sorry. I don't feel like eating. I think I'll just go to bed.'

'You could stay.' Humphrey cleared his throat. Where the hell had that come from? 'I mean,' he made another raspy noise, 'you can have the bed. I'll camp here.' He patted the bench seats.

He'd be fine. Not as comfortable as the queen bed nook, with its proper mattress and doona, television and privacy curtain, but Eden needed the rest more that he did, and there was plenty of space. The truck could sleep six when configured properly. The benches converted into a service- able double bed and somewhere in the truck's storage drawers were spare sheets, doonas and pillows.

Eden stared at him, her eyes giant pools of surprise. Humphrey squirmed. Only in the worst weather had

Humphrey invited Eden to stay, and then it was in her swag, and usually accompanied by at least one other competitor needing shelter.

But he wasn't about to take the invitation back. Clara's lonely, miserable life prediction still stung, and Mandy's rebuke about Humphrey making them both unhappy had been blundering around his mind like a cranky elephant. That he might be to blame for Eden's dispiritedness didn't sit well.

Whatever she believed, he did care. Too much.

She sucked on her lip and stared at her wineglass. 'I don't think that would be a good idea.'

'Why not?' She'd be in the bunk, he'd be on the folded-out bench seats. There'd be a good metre and a bit between them. Nothing untoward. 'If I snore you can throw a pillow at me.'

Eden's head remained down. He hated her being like this. Eden was bright, funny and optimistic. This Eden made his heart ache.

'I'll make you breakfast.'

Finally, she looked at him, a furrow between her brows as though he'd turned into a weird man-puzzle. 'Are you pleading with me?'

Yeah, he was.

'No. I just think you'd be better off here tonight.'

With him. Where he could keep an eye on her. Make sure she didn't cry in the night or have bad dreams about dickheads called Jack, who'd obviously done something to distress her.

She considered for a while longer. 'If you're sure?'

'I'm sure.' Humphrey stood, feeling relieved and stupidly pleased. 'Why don't you go grab your stuff and I'll start setting up?'

As soon as the truck door closed behind her, Humphrey raided the bunk bed, hunting for old jocks and socks, or anything else he might have left behind and wouldn't want her to find. When he was sure it was safe, he straightened the pillows and doona. Then he gobbled down Eden's piece of fruitcake. No way he was wasting that.

He eyed the two glasses of wine. What the hell. They might even help him sleep. He gulped down those as well and set the glasses in the dishwasher.

After a bit of rummaging, he found a fitted sheet, doona and pillow—a bit stale smelling but serviceable—and left them on top of the kitchenette bench while he folded out his bed.

Bed made, he brushed his teeth, used the loo, changed into a pair of tracksuit pants and an old singlet, and waited for Eden.

And waited.

Finally, there was a soft knock and the truck door opened. Eden stood in the cold, nose slightly red and a carry bag in her hand.

'I thought you'd changed your mind,' he said.

'I wanted to say goodnight to the boys.'

Of course. He should have realised that.

'Come in. The bed's all set. Did you want a shower? There's plenty of hot water.'

'I had one before I went out, but I'll need to scrub my face and brush my teeth.'

Yeah. The make-up she'd applied for dickhead Jack.

'I'll get you a towel.'

Humphrey lay on his back, doona draped over his thighs, hands behind his head, listening to Eden going about her business. Wondering what had happened that night.

Not just the date. Before, when she'd snapped at him

with that "like you care" comment. As far as Humphrey could tell, he hadn't done anything different that could have set her off. And they were friends, had been for years. She knew he cared. Didn't she?

'Just yell, if you need anything,' he said, when she emerged and placed her clothes and bag in a corner. 'Master switch for the light's above the bed.'

'Thanks.' She stood next to the steps up to the bunk, wringing her hands. Like him, she'd swapped her jeans and top for fleecy tracksuit bottoms and a loose T-shirt. The fabric was thin enough to reveal she wasn't wearing a bra. He had a feeling she probably wasn't wearing knickers either.

Humphrey muttered a mental "shit" and looked away, but couldn't erase what he'd seen. Round breasts. Little pebbled nipples. The smooth skin of her neck, the sharp edge of her collarbone.

He should have drunk more wine. He was never going to get to sleep.

The doona rustled as Eden settled in. She lay quietly for a while, then more rustling as she rolled over.

Humphrey stared at the ceiling. It was a clear night, and soft moonlight from the skylight saturated the cabin. Apart from some muted music—probably from Mandy's truck, parked the next row over—the showgrounds had grown quiet. The rides had shut down, the food stalls closed until tomorrow.

He listened to the song, catching snatches here and there, and trying to work out what it was. Then he rolled his eyes. "Iris", by nineties band the Goo Goo Dolls. A song about impossible love.

Jesus.

He closed his eyes and wished the song away. Wished

his feelings away. No matter what Mandy and Clara said, Eden was too young for him. She deserved better.

The song ended. Humphrey breathed out a sigh of relief, only to almost groan when he recognised the opening riff to The Rolling Stones' "Satisfaction".

He'd bet his gonads Mandy was doing this on purpose.

More rustling. He tried not to think about Eden in that thin T-shirt but, of course, that's exactly what his Neanderthal brain locked on, and where his brain went, other parts followed. Within seconds he was hard.

'Humphrey?' came a whisper.

'Yes?'

More shifting about.

'Eden?'

The soft pad of feet touching down on the floor. Then movement. Humphrey's nerves began to hum.

He turned his head. Eden stood beside his bed, light coating her angel white.

He sat up. 'What's wrong?'

'Everything.'

'What can I do?'

'Hold me?'

Humphrey swallowed, except whatever had lodged in his throat wouldn't budge. He opened his mouth, but the words wouldn't form. A husky groan emerged instead.

She leant her knees against the bed, her gaze intent on his, and shuffled closer, bunching the doona as she went. Cloaked in light, she was young and beautiful and vulnerable. A stronger man would gently push her away, make his position clear. Put an end to this right now.

Except, when it came to Eden, especially an Eden in need of comfort, Humphrey would always be weak.

She lifted the side of his doona. Her gaze swept over his

chest and further down. One corner of her lips rose. She'd seen.

War broke out inside him. Stupid Humphrey was high-fiving himself, ecstatic she'd seen his desire, knowing this was only going to progress one way. Sensible Humphrey was jiggling his legs, preparing to bolt out the door.

'It's not what you think,' he said.

'Yes, it is.'

She was so close. On hands and knees, the loose T-shirt gaping. He tensed his jaw, ordering himself not to look down it.

He looked.

'Eden.'

She leaned closer, her breath feathering his cheek. Then she lowered herself until her lips found the edge of his jaw.

Humphrey's heartbeat went ballistic. Everything tightened. Sensible Humphrey was yelling himself hoarse, but stupid Humphrey wasn't going to budge an inch. He closed his eyes.

'We shouldn't. It's not right. You're upset. You don't know what you're doing.'

Even he could hear the lack of conviction.

'I know exactly what I'm doing.' She moved her mouth up and down his jawline, kissing, nibbling with her soft lips. Slowly, teasingly, she kissed her way to his mouth.

Humphrey tried his damnedest not to respond. If she thought he wasn't into it, maybe she'd stop. A good strategy.

Or, it was, until she leaned back on her haunches, reached for the hem of her T-shirt and pulled it over her head.

Pale skin in the moonlight. Pert, pink-nippled breasts. Slim waist. Beautiful, beautiful Eden.

Humphrey had no defence. Not against this.

He rallied. A last try at being a decent bloke. 'We can't.'

'We can.' She kissed his mouth and pushed him down. She stretched alongside him, body half covering his, one leg draped over his groin, his hard-on pressing into her inner thigh. Her left hand began to trace down his chest. 'One night, Humphrey. That's all I'm asking. One night.'

One night. He should refuse. He should stop this now. Apologise for ... whatever it was he should be apologising for. Throw on some boots and bolt out into the night until the fire inside him cooled. Until he could think straight, instead of being overwhelmed by all this *Eden*.

But the feel of her against him. The hardness of her muscled riding body. The softness of those breasts against his chest. The rub of her firm nipples against his skin. Her wandering, luscious mouth, so hungry for him.

He wanted this one night as much as she did.

Sensible Humphrey gave a last small bleat before a sandstorm of pure need crashed over and smothered him forever.

Humphrey rolled Eden onto her back. He hovered over her, regarding her face, loving the way her body softened, as though already preparing for him.

'One night,' he said, thinking of the condoms in the drawer above the bunk bed. They'd have to move. Good. Eden deserved to be made love to in a proper bed.

She traced a finger down his cheek, smiling. 'One night.'

'Are you sure?'

'I've always been sure. Now kiss me. We only have one night. Make it count.'

Chapter Twelve

Humphrey rolled over to drag Eden against his belly. His hand patted around. No Eden.

He jerked up and banged his head against the nook's roof. Fortunately, the roof had padding, but the shock still caused him to blink. Swearing under his breath, he dragged himself to the edge of the bed and peered out.

Eden was pulling on her jeans.

'Good morning,' he said, admiring her legs. Legs that had been wrapped around him last night, heels digging into his butt. The thought had his hard-on stiffening further.

'Hey,' she said, looking up with a perfunctory smile before concentrating on her fly and button. Picking up her boots, she sat on the edge of the bunk bed and pulled them on.

'How are you feeling?' As amazing as him, he hoped. Last night ...

Humphrey was lost. So very, very lost. He gazed at her, feeling like a lovesick teenager. Eden. His beautiful angel, Eden.

'You want coffee?' he asked, edging his legs over the side

of the bunk and putting himself on show. He made his voice jokey. 'Or maybe something else?'

She didn't even glance his way. 'No, thanks.'

'Oh. Right.' He cleared his throat and scrubbed at his hair, then ran his palm over his stubbly jaw. A shave wouldn't go astray.

He inspected Eden. Yep, definitely signs of stubble rash on her cheeks. Next time he'd make sure he was clean-shaven.

He gave an internal mushy sigh. Last night had destroyed any protest he'd had against their relationship. He was still too old for her, but he'd do whatever it took to make up for that. What they'd shared ... He'd never experienced anything like it. It was as if every suppressed emotion he'd ever felt for her had suddenly unleashed and was now bursting forth in a fountain of feeling.

No way was he letting her go now. No. Way.

She gathered up her bag. 'I'd better get going. Big day.'

'Yeah.' Humphrey slid off the bed and sauntered towards her. He hoped his breath didn't stink because he wanted to kiss her stupid. Then maybe undress her and go back to bed. The horses would survive.

He never got close. At his approach, Eden released a squeak and scurried for the truck door.

'Eden?'

'Like I said, big day. Must go.' She wrenched the door open, blasting the space with chilly morning air. Humphrey's hard-on shrivelled, and it wasn't because of the cold. She cleared her throat. 'Horses.'

'The horses will be fine. Stay a bit. Have coffee.'

Have me.

She shook her head. 'No. I need to go. Thanks for ...' Her gaze darted to the bed. Then she gave him one last wide-eyed look, a look that seemed to scream "what have I done?", and plunged down the steps, the door slamming behind her.

Humphrey yanked it open. 'Eden!'

But she'd broken into a jog.

He went to yell again, only to realise Mandy was watching him, arms folded, one eyebrow raised, and a "you dickhead" look on her face. She tipped her head, indicating downwards.

Humphrey frowned and glanced down, then stepped back and slammed the door shut. Eden's forgotten coat swung from a hook on its back like a mocking metronome. He stared at it, fingers drumming against his bare thighs. What the hell just happened?

Five minutes later, he was still trying to figure it out. Only when it sank in that he was freezing his butt off did he move.

Humphrey showered in record time, hating that he was washing away the scent of Eden on his skin, threw on jeans and a jumper and his boots, and raced for the stables.

Ruffian and Admiral had had their overnight rugs removed and were enjoying their morning feed, but Eden was nowhere to be seen. Humphrey hurriedly checked over and fed his own horses before dashing back outside.

Mild panic had him clutching at his damp hair when he found Eden's car and float empty. At least they were still here. But of course they were. Her horses were here, unlike Humphrey's brain, which seemed to have gone on holiday.

He surveyed the showground, scanning the other trucks and floats for someone she might visit, but it was the usual activity of riders readying horses. No Eden chatting happily, brightening someone else's day.

He looked further afield. The sideshow was quiet. Only

the other animal areas had movement, and then it was few people. Where had she run to?

And more importantly, why had she run?

'If you're looking for Eden,' said Mandy from behind, 'she's gone with Nell to get coffee.'

The band that had wrapped around Humphrey's ribs loosened. 'Right. Good.'

Mandy folded her arms. 'You finally did it.'

Yeah, he had. Not that he was about to tell Mandy about it.

'Not very well, if Eden's bolt from your truck is any indication.'

Humphrey opened his mouth, closed it. Is that why she left? He'd given a dud performance?

Surely not?

But what if that was it?

No, no, no.

He thought back over the night. Eden kneeling on the edge of the bed. Dragging her T-shirt off. Skin luminous in the moonlight. Angel Eden.

Her kisses. Her opening for him. Her gasps. The way she flushed from her chest up to her neck. The way she'd said his name. The way her body shuddered as she came.

Heaven had nothing on last night.

For him.

Alarm washed through Humphrey. What if it hadn't been the same for her?

'I need coffee,' he said.

'Pod machine broken?' asked Mandy in a tone that indicated she knew it wasn't.

'What?'

Mandy waved him off. 'Oh, forget it. Go find Eden and apologise for whatever it was you screwed up.'

Humphrey didn't need telling twice. He crossed the grounds with hungry strides, mentally rehearsing his words.

Eden, last night was amazing. Eden, give me another chance.

Eden, I love you. And I'm sorry it's taken me so long to admit it, but last night made me see it was true, and now I never want to let you go.

He had no idea where the coffee stand might be, but it was early. There couldn't be many places open and there'd be more than one person needing their morning fix.

In the end, he didn't have to search. Humphrey rounded a bend and there was Eden, walking and chatting with Nell, lidded cup in her hand.

Humphrey's heart soared. Eden. His Eden.

God, she was perfect.

She caught his approach. He waited for a trademark Eden smile, that broad, sunny expression that lit her from the inside and made the world feel bright and warm.

It didn't come. What he got was a bland mouth twitch. The meaningless smile you'd bestow on someone you didn't like out of politeness, and as far from a lover's smile as you could get.

'Morning, Humphrey,' said Nell.

'Yeah, g'day.' He cleared his throat. Where to start? And what was with that weird look?

'Come for your morning fix, too? Hang on, don't you have a coffee machine?'

'Not working.' Which was technically true. The coffee machine only worked when turned on, and it wasn't.

He couldn't take his eyes off Eden. But she kept vacantly sipping her coffee, seemingly uninterested in making eye contact.

'Actually, I wanted to talk to Eden.'

Nell glanced curiously from Eden to Humphrey and back again. Then her lips curled into a knowing grin. 'Of course you do.' She patted Eden's shoulder. 'I'll catch you later.'

'What? Oh. Um. I was just ...' Eden's gaze darted left then right, then it caught on something behind Humphrey and her expression buoyed. She gestured across the grounds. 'I was just off to the loo. So, um, gotta go. Sorry. Nature calling.'

Before Humphrey could protest, Eden dashed off towards the amenities.

'Wow,' said Nell, looking after her and then at Humphrey. 'You must really suck in bed. She can't even face you.'

'How did—'

Nell rolled her eyes. 'Everyone knows.'

'Right. Brilliant. Good.'

Except it clearly wasn't.

Though she was out of sight, he stared after Eden. What the hell had he done wrong?

Chapter Thirteen

Avoiding Humphrey was exhausting. Everywhere Eden turned, he seemed to be near and closing in, demeanour turning more and more grumpy as the day wore on.

Eden made sure to hang in groups—with fellow competitors, the occasional band of spectators, even some hacking competition riders—or to be on horseback where escape was easy. Anything to prevent a conversation she didn't want to have.

She wouldn't be able to bear his kindness. His *Humphrey-ness*. The sympathy and regret when he told her how great she was, but how nothing had changed. He was too old for her. And he was sorry, deeply sorry, but they would never be a couple.

She knew that already. Last night was a one-off. Eden had made the promise when she'd pulled her T-shirt over her head and lain down beside him, and she was going to stick to it.

And covet that precious memory until time eroded its bittersweet edges enough to let her move on.

'Easy-peasy,' she muttered to Admiral as she led him to the rear of the float.

It was just after three in the afternoon and though she'd registered for a final competition, Eden had withdrawn. She was in no state to perform and refused to risk her boys with her distraction. Fatigue weighed her body. Every action took energy she didn't have. Her steps were plods. Even her bones felt hard to lift.

Too little sleep. Too much joy and delight and passion, and now, in the brightness of day and with her dream over, too much anguish.

She pointed Addy at the float ramp and patted him on the rump. The horse walked calmly up the slope to join his friend, who was already secure. After locking the tailbar and raising the tailgate, Eden trudged to the front to secure Admiral's lead.

Humphrey was leaning against the side of the float, the coat she'd left in his truck folded over one arm, expression not so much grumpy as wary.

He lifted the coat. 'You left this behind.'

'Oh,' said Eden, her stupid, ever-hopeful heart dropping. That's why he wanted her. To hand back the coat. 'Yes. Thanks.'

She took it, wanting to cuddle it to her chest like a stuffed toy.

'You're leaving.'

Eden rubbed her brow. 'I'm really tired. I just want to go home.' Go home, settle her boys and tend to her sore, miserable heart.

He reached out and stroked her cheek, sympathy softening his striking blue eyes. Eyes that had devoured her body last night. So hungry, so adoring, and all for her.

For a moment Eden wanted to lean into him like a cat

being petted, then she stepped hurriedly back. 'Please don't do that.'

'Do what? Care for you?'

'Be kind, like you always are.'

'What's so bad about being kind?'

Everything. It was his kindness she loved. Gruff on the outside, molten on the inside.

She shook her head, unable to answer, blinking at the hot prickles forming at the back of her eyes.

He refolded his arms and regarded his boots for a moment. 'We're going to have to talk about last night at some point.'

Lovely, gorgeous, Humphrey. Her friend. Her one-time lover. Wanting to make sure she was all right, because that's the man he was. A good man.

'There's nothing to talk about.'

'There's plenty.'

'No. There's not. We had sex. It was wonderful. Now we can move on.' Ruffian gave an impatient stamp. Addy responded with a soft whicker. Eden glanced inside the float. Her boys stared expectantly back. 'I need to go.'

Humphrey pinched the bridge of his nose, brow furrowed as if he had the world's worst migraine.

'I don't understand.'

'There's nothing to understand.' She smiled at him, summoning brightness out of her misery. 'We're still friends, though. Aren't we?'

'Of course we are.' He dropped his arms. 'Why would ... Jesus, Eden. I don't get what the matter is. Last night was—'

'A one-off. It won't happen again. You have nothing to worry about, and I really have to go.' She grabbed one of his hands and squeezed it. 'Thank you.'

'I don't want your thanks, Eden. Last night wasn't some

favour.' His Adam's apple bobbed as he swallowed. 'It was special.'

'I know it was, and I won't forget it.' She gave his hand another squeeze and let go. 'Maybe you should skip the last round and head home, too. Get some sleep. It's been a big couple of days.'

He stared off for a long moment. 'When will I see you?'

'I don't know. Next show, I guess.'

'Okay.' He breathed out. 'Okay. Good. We'll talk then.'

Except Eden knew they wouldn't. Next week was only a minor show, easily missed, and it was her mum's birthday. They were having a party at the farm. Nothing special, just a family barbeque, an event Tom and her dad could easily prepare for. Except it offered a perfect excuse for Eden to stay home.

One she planned to use.

It was cowardly, but the less she saw of Humphrey for a while the better.

Eden was helping Tom wipe down and arrange dusty folding chairs around the fire pit in her parents' backyard when her phone pinged with a message.

Humphrey. For a heady second her stomach fluttered, then she caught what he'd written.

Where are you?

'Oh,' she said.

'What's up?' asked Tom.

Eden slid the phone back into her pocket. 'Nothing important.'

'Oh, yeah?'

'Just Humphrey.'

'Poshpants? What did he want?' Aware for years of Eden's unrequited yearning, Tom wasn't Humphrey's greatest fan, believing Humphrey's continued friendship only made Eden's crush worse. He and Olly had come up with the nickname "Poshpants" one day and it had stuck.

'He wanted to know where I was.'

'Aren't you going to answer him?'

'Maybe later.'

Tom studied her. 'You all right, Den?'

'Fine.'

'Seriously, are you?' Tom sat another chair near the fire pit, plucked an old wool rug from the pile under the verandah, and draped it over the chair's arm. The pit was already loaded with kindling and logs, ready for the evening. It was a magnificent spring day, but a frost was forecast for overnight, and a fire and lap rugs would be needed once the sun sank below the horizon. 'You've been quiet all day.'

It was only lunchtime. Hardly all day. There'd been that moment first thing, when she'd let Addy and Ruff out into their big paddock, and the two had indulged in a silly game of tag, nipping at one another before running off. Their high spirits and the vivid orange and peach of the rising sun had made her smile. Eden might have been a coward for avoiding Humphrey, but she'd been right to give her boys a weekend off.

Eden wiped the last leg of her chair and carried it over. 'I'm okay.'

'Sure?'

'I'm fine, Tom. Honest.' But as she said the words, her phone pinged and the ache in her chest that had been there all week throbbed again. If Tom hadn't been eyeing her so intently, she would have ignored it, but Tom knew Eden's feelings for Humphrey. Ignoring a message from him would require an explanation, and that she didn't want to give. No matter how much she loved her brother.

She suppressed a sigh and read the text.

Are you ok? The horses? You're not here. Why?

Eden grimaced. She'd better reply. As she went to start tapping, another message appeared.

I'm worried.

She swallowed. Why did he have to do that? She gnawed on her bottom lip, mentally composing a bland reply. One that said she was perfectly unaffected by what had happened between them. That she wasn't weighted with heartache and still desperately wishing he loved her.

All good. Skipped show for Mum's birthday bbq.

She waited, expecting an immediate response but none came. Not even the bouncing dots to indicate Humphrey was typing. With a sigh, she repocketed the phone, grabbed a rug and set it over the chair. Tom had nabbed the last seat and was dusting its arms and back.

Eden put her hands on her hips and searched for something else to do. Anything to stay busy. Except for last-minute preparations, there was little left to organise. Hardly a surprise when she'd been at it since after breakfast. Mowing and weeding the yard, sweeping pavers, setting the fire pit, trimming the jasmine that splayed over the timber pergola, cleaning the barbeque. Even cobwebbing around the house. Finding chores. Waving off her mum when she scolded Eden for doing too much.

Guests would start arriving midafternoon. Her grandparents first, Nan bustling in with homemade sausage rolls, mini quiches and other nibbles. Her grandfather hauling an esky full of ice, beer and wine. Then aunts and uncles and cousins and friends. The whole rowdy, loving clan.

Heaviness settled on Eden. A ton of loneliness and loss, and the knowledge she had a whole afternoon and evening ahead of acting normal, when she felt anything but.

'I suppose I'd better go shower,' she said.

Tom checked his watch. 'Yeah. I'd better get home and showered myself.' He set the last chair in place. 'Amber will be here soon. You know, if you need someone to talk to.'

Eden smiled. Sometimes her brother could be an annoying turd. Other times, he was just like Humphrey: kind. 'Thanks. I'll see how I go.'

She stood in her room, assessing the party clothes she'd arranged on the bed. A pair of dark jeans, a dark pink, fine wool jumper, long leather boots, and the same coat she'd worn on her fateful date with Jack. The coat she'd accidentally left in Humphrey's truck after the best night of her life.

As though summoned, Eden's phone pinged with another message from the man himself.

We miss you.

She closed her eyes. We. Not I. We.

Which about summed it up.

Eden tossed her phone on her bedside table, stripped off, donned a robe and hurried for the bathroom, where she could wash her tears away under the shower.

Later that night in bed, more than a little bit drunk on red wine and with a stomach lined only with a single sausage roll and a slice of chocolate birthday cake because she hadn't felt like eating, Eden opened Cupid Country.

She wasn't really interested or in the mood, but there had to be a man out there for her. Someone decent and nice. Someone who liked horses and a laugh.

Someone like Humphrey, but not Humprey.

Her inbox held two messages. She tapped on the first,

not expecting much, and was rewarded with another dick pic.

'Really?' she said, rolling her eyes and stabbing the "block" button.

She skipped to the next message. Some bloke from western Victoria called Sam Smith. His profile showed a broad-shouldered figure wearing a flannelette shirt and a wide grin, the brim of his battered felt hat set low and shading his eyes.

She skipped to the message.

I love horses too. Usually minced and in a juicy burger. He'd followed the sentence with a feral looking emoji.

Eden squeezed her eyes shut. Why was she doing this to herself? The world was full of dickheads.

Except it wasn't. There was Humphrey, Olly, Lincoln. Her own brother. Her dad. Good men. Decent men with big hearts.

Which meant ... Maybe it was her.

'No,' she said. Eden might have her faults, but she was a nice person, and she didn't deserve any of this torment. She deserved a man who loved her.

Mr Right would out there, somewhere. Just not on Cupid Country.

She regarded the screen. Then she pressed her finger on the green slider and dragged it left, setting her profile inactive.

There. Her experiment was over. Tomorrow would be another day, another start. One day in the future, probably when she least expected, she'd bump into someone who shot a tingle down her spine. Who liked the same things she did. Who was kind and good-humoured and treated her properly. Who'd relegate Humphrey to the shadows, an old crush, forgotten in the handsome face of new hope.

And she'd find love.

Chapter Fourteen

The sun had barely begun its ascent when Humphrey left Kulburra in his truck. Though he itched to press the pedal to the floor, he took it slow. This time of day, and particularly on this stretch of country road, there were too many kangaroos to take chances, and he knew from experience the kind of damage even a medium-size grey kangaroo could do. Besides, the higher classes Eden would be competing in weren't scheduled until later.

Assuming she'd decided to come.

He rolled his hands around the truck's steering wheel. The nerves that had been twanging his insides all week were worse now Saturday had arrived.

If only Humphrey had some insight into where Eden's mind was at. He'd thought the *We miss you* message might have earned a response but there'd been no reply. He'd spent the rest of the day and night composing messages in his head but had sent none. Nothing felt right. And he needed to grow some balls and explain himself in person.

That didn't stop him setting up a Cupid Country

account, using the name Hump Grump and a camel as his avatar, in the hope that he'd discover something helpful from her profile. Except when he located it, an ugly red stamp of a circle with a line through it covered Eden's sunny face. She'd gone inactive.

Which could only mean one of two things: she'd given up on her scheme or she'd found someone.

Thought of the latter shot a wash of cold through Humphrey so frigid he had to crank up the heating, and still he shivered.

He reached the main highway and with the forests and pine plantations behind him, he could put his foot down. Today's show was only sixty kilometres away. Another small one, with limited classes. He'd loaded his youngster, Napoleon, leaving the others at home for a rest.

That was his excuse, anyway. What he really wanted was minimal distractions, and taking a full contingent of mounts would mean less time for important matters.

Eden matters.

The horse float would have been more appropriate, but Humphrey wanted the option of privacy should he manage to get Eden alone and talking. Neither of which was a given. He didn't even know if she'd show. When he'd messaged her yesterday asking, she said she would, but that's what she'd promised the previous week.

He gusted out a breath. This had to work. It had to. He'd go insane without her. In his worst moments, Humphrey thought he might even be already there.

Hump Grump. Jesus wept. How embarrassing. Even worse were the scarily sexual messages about humping his profile seemed to encourage. Some things you couldn't unsee.

But Eden was worth it. Eden was worth anything.

He pulled into the showgrounds. As he guessed, it was still quiet, but the gate was manned, with a cheerful volunteer on hand to take entrance fees from early arrivals. Humphrey pressed his phone against the card reader and waved his thanks at the woman's call of good luck.

He unloaded Napoleon and settled him in with water and a hay net and readied his tack. When there was nothing left to do, Humphrey retreated to the kitchenette for coffee and a slice of fruitcake, leaving the door open and an eye out for Eden.

Ninety minutes and three cups of coffee later, Humphrey was about to tear his hair out, which would have been a challenge, given his mum had run the clippers over his head and left him with a short back and sides the day before.

Humphrey shoved aside his barely read Bart Cummings biography, used the loo, then changed into his competition breeches and clambered down the steps to saddle up Napoleon. There was at least another hour, probably an hour and a half, before his event, but the youngster could do with the warm-up, and Humphrey was only getting more anxious sitting inside.

Murphy's Law had Mandy lying in wait when Humphrey emerged.

He girded himself for whatever stone she was about to throw and nodded her way. 'Mandy.'

'Humphrey.' Folding her arms, she lounged against the wall of his truck and watched him remove Napoleon's rug. 'Beautiful day.'

Humphrey grunted.

Yeah, the sky was an endless crystalline blue. The air a pleasant spring warm that was perfect riding weather. Not too hot, not too cool, and blessed with an occasional cut-grass-scented zephyr. The kind of day that made people hopeful and happy, and excited for the approaching summer.

How could he feel any of that without Eden?

'Eden shouldn't be far away.'

Humphrey said nothing. He carried a saddle and saddlecloth from the truck's tack room and set them on Napoleon's back, checked both were properly positioned, then flipped the girth over and reached beneath the horse's belly to gather and buckle it in place. All the time he could feel Mandy's sharp gaze shooting darts into his back.

'I guess that means you two haven't sorted things out.'

With the saddle secure, Humphrey crouched to fix jumping boots to Napoleon's fore and hind legs.

Mandy sighed. 'Look, Humphrey, I'm not here to be a bitch.'

He glanced at her. Not a bitch? That'd be a first. Although, that was unfair. She'd been telling him all season that he was going to lose Eden if he didn't make a move, and now look where he was.

In limbo. Confused. And so, so scared.

Mandy tipped her head as though she'd read his mind. Then she patted the back of his shoulder. 'I just wanted to wish you luck and hope that you'll finally get your shit together. If only to put the rest of us out of our misery. You probably haven't noticed, but it's been hell watching you two. Frustrating as all crap. Ah. Speak of the devil ...' Mandy smiled and nodded past the horse's rump. 'She's here.'

Humphrey nearly fell backwards on his butt such was his hurry to see around Napoleon's hind legs.

Sure enough, Eden's blue ute was pulling up in a bay two rows over.

He stood, wiping his hands on his breeches, not caring that he'd dirtied the pristine white. His heart was going nuts, banging against his ribs like a boxer. He glanced at Mandy.

'Go on,' she said, nodding towards Eden.

Humphrey looked back. The float door was open. Eden must be inside untying her boys. He blew out a breath and straightened his shoulders, then remembered he had a saddled horse.

'Just go. I'll watch Napoleon.'

He stared at Mandy for a moment, then quickly kissed her cheek.

Mandy blinked several times. 'What was that?'

'A thank you. For, I don't know ... Pushing us together.'

She shrugged. 'I told you all along, everyone just wants to see you happy. *I* want to see you happy. Eden does that. End of story.' She gave him a shove. 'Now go sort it out.'

Humphrey didn't need any extra encouragement. He broke into a jog. Eden was at the back of the float, unlocking the ramp.

Humphrey grabbed the other side. 'Hey,' he said, then swallowed at the look she shot at him. A perfectly polite nothing look, as if he were just another man and not the man she'd made love with two weeks before.

'Hey, yourself.'

'You came.'

She laughed. 'Of course I came.'

They lowered the ramp. Humphrey climbed up to unlock the left-hand tailbar, Eden the right. She was so close that with one step he could be cupping her face, telling her all the things he'd been saving.

Except her expression remained neutral, her voice even

but not warm, and Humphrey's gut was telling him he had to take it carefully.

Why, he didn't know.

He stood aside as first Addy then Ruff backed out from the float. When Addy was far enough down, he caught the horse's lead and tied him to the side of the float, while Eden did the same with Ruff.

With the horses secure, Eden reached into the back of her ute for water buckets.

'I'll do that,' said Humphrey grabbing them from her.

'No need. I'm fine.'

'I want to. I'll get the water. You sort the rest out.'

She frowned at him again, then shrugged and focused on peeling off Addy's rug.

'Thanks,' she said on his return and Humphrey damn near sighed in relief at the softening in her tone.

'No problem.' He leaned against the back of her ute, folded his arms and studied her. 'Are you okay?'

'Me? Yeah. I'm fine. A bit tired. It was a busy week.'

She looked it, too. Her cheeks were pale, her eyes slightly red rimmed. Humphrey felt sick. This was his fault.

He rubbed at his cleanly shaven jaw, then went for it. 'I went on Cupid Country.'

For a moment Eden froze, then her shoulders slumped, and her mouth tucked as though holding in a sound. Her back rose and fell, before rising once more. She placed a hand on Addy's neck, breathed another breath and straightened. 'That's nice. I hope you have better luck than me. And watch out for the dick pics.' She paused, frowning. 'Do guys get dick pics? Or is it just women?'

'I suspect everyone gets them. Look, Eden, I didn't go on there to score. I went on there to find you.'

'Me? Why would you do that?'

He shrugged, as if his next words meant nothing when they meant the world. 'I thought I might ask you on a date.'

'A date?'

'Yeah. A date. For your plan.'

'Oh, right. Too late. I've given up on it.' She fluttered a hand. 'It was a dumb idea anyway. I'll just do things the old-fashioned way. Meet someone when I'm out.'

'Right.' Humphrey regarded his boots. God, this was hard. 'Is it because of—'

'No. No, it's not. I just decided I've had enough.'

'Okay.' He breathed in, breathed out. This was not going how he'd hoped. She didn't want to date him. She didn't want to date anyone.

Eden gave him an up and down. 'Shouldn't you be warming up?'

Humphrey glanced across at Napoleon. Mandy was perched on the step to the kitchenette, watching them. She lifted her hands in a "What the?" sign. Humphrey looked away.

'Look, Eden, about that night ...'

'Please don't.' Her voice sounded reedy, as though she was on the edge of tears. 'There's nothing to talk about. I'm fine. I really am fine. You don't have anything to worry about, or to feel guilty for.' She made another dismissive gesture. 'Go date whoever you want. I'm fine.'

'No, you're not.' He stepped closer and touched her pale cheek with the back of his curled finger.

She closed her eyes, her lip trembling. 'Why can't you ever be mean? It'd be so much easier if you were mean.'

'I don't ever want to be mean to you.'

Her head dropped.

'Eden. Look at me.' When she looked up, he put every ounce of love into his expression he could summon. He stepped towards her, close enough so his hand could caress her neck. 'What are you doing tonight?'

'What?'

'Tonight. What are you doing?'

She blinked at him, brow furrowed, voice wary. 'Amber and Niamh invited me to a barbeque at Amber's place. I don't think I'll go, though.'

'What if I came along, too? As your plus one?' He scrunched his nose. 'Can you bring a plus one?'

'Plus one?'

'Yeah. Me. With you.'

Eden opened her mouth then closed it. She gave him another of those confused frowny looks.

'Or we could go out for dinner.'

'Dinner?' She shook herself. 'Humphrey, what are you doing?'

'I'm asking you out on a date.'

'A date. Like ... a proper date?'

'Yeah.' A smile began to tug at his mouth. Eden's wide-eyed astonishment gave Humphrey hope his clumsy proposal might actually work. 'A proper date. You, me. Whatever you want to do.'

'But ...' Her bewilderment was so cute all he wanted was to kiss her. 'You're too old for me. That's what you keep saying. What you've *always* said. You're too old for me.'

'I *am* too old for you. And I've tried and tried to stop feeling the way I do, but I can't. The other night made me realise I don't want to stop. Ever.' He stepped even closer and drew his other hand to her face, cradling it, his gaze locked on hers. 'Eden, I can't change our age difference, but I promise I will do all I can to make it not matter.'

'Are you saying you want us to be an ... us?'

'That's exactly what I'm saying.' He smiled crookedly. 'If you'll have me.'

An uncertain smile broke across her face, then turned into a beam. Eden, his Eden, was back. Humphrey wanted to whoop, except she still hadn't answered.

'Will you?' He cleared his throat. 'Have me?'

'God, Humphrey, of course I will. I've loved you since I was sixteen years old. You think I'm going to say no?'

'I don't know. I've been a bit of an idiot.'

'True.' She plucked at the front of his shirt. 'You gave me a horrible fright when you said you'd gone on Cupid Country.'

Poor Eden. He winced, realising now how that must have sounded. As if what they'd shared hadn't mattered. As if *she* hadn't mattered, when the truth was, she meant the world.

'I'm sorry. Like I said, I've been an idiot.'

She smiled and patted his chest. 'Not just you. I've been one too. Avoiding you. Making it so we never had a chance to talk.' She shook her head. 'I was so sure there was no us. That the only reason you were desperate to talk was to give another of your gentle thanks-but-no-thanks apologies. Tell me again there was no hope.' She looked up, her eyes glistening. 'I didn't want to hear it. I didn't want you being kind again. Everything hurt as it was, and I needed you to think I was okay. That I was fine, and you didn't have to worry or feel guilty. That I'd stick to my promise, and you'd be free.'

'I could never be free of you, Eden. You're my world.'

'And you are so, so mine.'

Humphrey stared at her face, at her happy, loving gaze, before shifting focus to her mouth. The lush, yielding lips that had tortured his dreams. His days.

Eden chuckled softly and curled her fists into his shirt. 'Are you thinking what I'm thinking?'

'Yeah.' He glanced around. Mandy had been joined by Nell and three other riders and every one of them was focused on him and Eden. Catching his eye, Mandy gave a thumbs up. 'Don't look now, but we've got an audience.'

Eden looked and laughed, then smiled up at Humphrey. 'Should we give them a show?'

His gaze dropped straight to her mouth. 'What did you have in mind?'

'Oh, I don't know.' Her teeth caught one corner of her bottom lip, and she eyed him from beneath lowered lashes in a way that made Humphrey's groin twitch. Not good when wearing breeches. 'A dance? I could teach you the Blinding Lights dance. That would entertain them.'

'You could. Or I could kiss you. Right now, in public.'

'Okay.'

Humphrey grinned, then, very slowly, lowered his mouth to Eden's.

Applause, cheers and a wolf-whistle sounded, but Humphrey didn't care, and from the intensity Eden was putting into their kiss, neither did she.

They'd both found home.

Epilogue

I t was the last Saturday of May, and the air was redolent with the scents of fertile countryside. The autumn break had been delayed this year, with little rain of consequence until a week-long drenching late the previous month. Now, green blanketed the land around Kulburra and the property's stock were all head down, grazing on the sweet fresh pasture.

Eden's boys were out there, too, enjoying one of the two hundred hectares of paddocks that Humphrey leased from Kulburra to run his horse-training business. Eden's parents' property, Glenlea, was a fine one and had served her boys well, but Kulburra was an equine luxury resort in comparison. The pastures were seeded with tailored mixes of species suited to horses. Troughs and feeders were rounded heavy-duty plastic designed to minimise the risk of injury, while the fences were either timber rails or coated wire, with not a strand of barbed wire in sight.

Eden loved it. Kulburra was not only beautiful, it had every facility any horse-mad girl could want.

Most of all it had Humphrey.

She slid him a sideways glance. One corner of his mouth was tucked in, his blue gaze bright in the late afternoon sun. He was leading the young ex-racehorse colt he'd bought over the summer to the stables after a schooling session in Kulburra's stabilised sand arena. Eden had helped with rearranging poles and constructing small practice fences, relishing watching him work, admiring his gentleness and patience. A master.

Except today Humphrey had been in a funny mood. Nothing she could pinpoint, exactly, but he definitely wasn't himself. Normally he was the epitome of quiet and calm. Today he was still calm, still not prone to a lot of talking, but he had an air about him. An air Eden could only describe as buzzy. As if, inside, Humphrey was thrumming.

Eden had kept staring around, expecting a surprise visit or delivery. Nothing of the sort happened. Saturday had progressed as normal. They got up, they checked and fed horses, led those being turned out to their paddocks, mucked out stables and yards, then saddled mounts and rode.

The only unusual event planned was the cocktail party they were attending tonight at Amber and Tom's to celebrate the newlyweds' return from their honeymoon. Hardly something Humphrey would get excited about.

Sensing her gaze, he turned and smiled properly. 'Okay?'

'Perfect.'

'Good.'

And it was good, despite Humphrey's odd mood. More than good.

They'd been a couple for almost four months when he asked if she'd like to move in with him at Kulburra. Given Eden was practically living there anyway, it made sense and would save her commuting from her job to her parents' farm to care for Admiral and Ruffian, and back to Kulburra whenever she wanted to enjoy a night with Humphrey, which was every night.

The offer had filled Eden with delight, but also a touch of disappointment. They'd known each other for years, been in love for as long—even though *someone* had refused to admit that fact—and were ridiculously, stupidly happy. Why couldn't they just get married? Eden wanted it and she was certain Humphrey did, too. As for the Taylor-Martins, they tried their best to be subtle, but their hope rang through the air like overstretched wire. Meanwhile Humphrey was now so accepted into the Jones family, Tom had stopped calling him Poshpants.

Whenever the subject of an engagement came up, Humphrey would simply smile and respond with a 'No hurry.'

Which, for a man who'd spent years denying his feelings because he considered himself too old, was more than a touch bemusing, and left Eden wondering what was going on inside her boyfriend's gorgeous head.

It didn't matter. They didn't need to be married to be content. Their life, their love, was perfect as it stood.

Eden smiled as Ruffian spotted them from his paddock and released a loud neigh. He trotted to the fence, Addy close behind, then veered suddenly away, kicking up his heels and tossing his mane, showing off. Or maybe simply as high on life as his mistress.

The pair went racing away, fit, glossy coated, full of spirit.

They washed down the colt and settled him in a yard to dry off while Eden brought her boys in for the night. When all the horses were fed and settled, they hopped into

Humphrey's four-wheel drive and headed home. The sun was lowering quickly, gilding the paddocks, trees and live-stock in metallic shimmers.

Humphrey drove one-handed, the other stretched across the seat to clasp Eden's, keeping them connected. It had become his custom and one Eden thought she would never tire of.

Humphrey's house was a simple stone cottage, about a kilometre from the homestead, and sheltered by a stand of old cypress trees, drooping with age, that Humphrey kept threatening to cut to the ground. Though they probably needed it, Eden wasn't sure he ever would. The trees shielded the cottage from prying eyes and Humphrey loved being private with Eden.

Something that wouldn't be happening until later tonight thanks to their party invitation.

Half an hour later, Eden and Humphrey were show-ered and dressed and heading for Humphrey's ute, Eden carrying an enormous bouquet of wildflowers that Humphrey's mum, Belle, had picked up in Levenham for them that morning. Humphrey was toting a shopping bag of chips, nuts and pretzels.

'I just need to call in to the main house,' said Humphrey, turning up the track to the homestead instead of the road into Levenham. 'Won't be long.'

'Is everything all right?'

'Yeah, fine.'

With a shrug, Eden went back to watching the horses as they passed the yards. Her boys were stabled in the original, although modernised, stable block, but the young ones were kept in yards with a shelter at one end so they could comfort each other with over-the-rail nuzzles and mane scratches and other horsey solace.

'I'll come in,' said Eden, reaching for the doorhandle when they pulled up. 'I need to thank Belle for the flowers.'

'I'll thank her. You stay here.'

Eden went to protest but Humphrey was already out the door and jogging to the house. As promised, he was back in the car in minutes, another of those half-smiles on his face.

'What's got you so smug?'

'Me? Smug?'

'Yeah, you.'

He started the engine and took her hand. 'Why shouldn't I look smug. I have you.'

'This is true,' she said solemnly, then grinned and leaned across to kiss his cheek. 'And I have you.'

Forever.

Eden didn't bother knocking on Amber and Tom's front door. The door was already wide open, with only the screen closed, and music and laughter filtered down the hall. The party had started without them.

'It's me!' she yelled, pulling open the screen door with one arm while the other tried to balance the flowers.

'About bloody time!' came a yell from the kitchen. Tom.

Amber appeared. She grinned widely then jammed her hands on her hips as she took in her guests. 'What did I say about not bringing anything? Hi, Humphrey.'

'Amber. Looking good. Honeymooning suits you.'

'I think honeymooning suits everyone.' Amber winked at him. 'You should try it one day.'

Humphrey laughed and reached behind him to shut the door against the rapidly encroaching cold.

Eden said nothing. Instead, she kissed Amber's cheek and stepped aside so Humphrey could do the same.

Humphrey was right. Honeymooning did suit her new

sister-in-law. While Amber wasn't quite as radiant as on her wedding day, she was still pink cheeked and pretty, glowing with happiness. But Eden supposed a three-week loved-up trip around France and Italy would do that to a girl.

It had been a delightful autumn wedding. Amber had wanted a simple ceremony, while Tom hadn't cared, as long as it happened. Their civil service in Civic Park, the place they'd first met, with its leafy trees and autumn floral displays, thrilled family and friends. The weather had been glorious, the bride stunning in a diamante-studded strapless dress with a tulle skirt that frothed like fairy floss around her legs and made her appear as though she floated instead of walked. The groom and groomsmen were handsome in their suits, and the best woman triumphant that the entire day went off on time and without a hitch.

Amber had chosen sapphire blue for Niamh's and Eden's attendants' dresses, in a convertible contemporary design with soft twistable fabric that could be formed into dozens of styles and draped beautifully against Eden's skin.

After what felt like a hundred trials, Niamh had settled on a one shoulder configuration, with a flowing skirt that made her look like a tiny Grecian goddess. Olly had feasted his gaze on her so intensely during the ceremony he almost forgot the rings.

Eden fashioned her dress into a halter-neck to show off her straight, muscled shoulders. She'd walked with Niamh ahead of Amber down a strip of carpet laid over the lawn, beaming at the guests and feeling like a princess until she locked gazes with Humphrey. And in that moment, all she'd been aware of was his adoration. Powerful, magnificent and all hers.

She'd swept on, back even straighter, heart even fuller. No longer a princess, but a queen. His queen.

It had been the best of days.

When Humphrey had finished his greeting, Eden held out her bouquet. 'Welcome home.'

'Thank you. They're beautiful.' Amber tipped her head towards the kitchen. 'Come on through. The others are already into it.'

Tom, Olly, Niamh and Lincoln crammed Amber's small kitchen. Tom at the end of the bench, beer in hand. Olly with his arm draped over Niamh, idly tickling the skin below her ear as they watched Lincoln work his mixologist magic.

Handshakes, hugs and hellos were exchanged. The wedding party together again.

'What are you making?' asked Eden, inspecting Lincoln's collection of bottles, shakers, strainers, juicers, knives, bowls and toothpicks.

'Espresso martinis to start with,' replied Lincoln. 'A pick-me-up.'

Humphrey eyed the collection with worry. 'This could get dangerous.'

'Only if you've got to drive home,' said Olly. Who clearly wouldn't be, and from the wideness of his grin and eyebrow waggle he was planning to make a night of it.

The discussion settled on Amber and Tom's honeymoon adventures, while Lincoln measured and poured before making everyone laugh with his hammy cocktail shaker routine. He pushed six martinis across the bench with even more panache. Three for the girls and three for him, Olly and Tom. Humphrey was sticking to light beer.

Cheers were said and the drinks sampled. Eden's eyes widened as the cocktail washed over her tongue, the others doing the same as they tasted.

'God,' said Amber, looking into her glass, then at Lincoln. 'That's delicious.'

Lincoln sampled his own and gave a nod of approval. 'Not bad.'

'It's fantastic,' said Eden, already wanting another one, but knowing she shouldn't. She and Humphrey had a training day at the showgrounds tomorrow and were taking a full contingent of mounts.

'You'd make someone an excellent husband,' said Niamh, before taking another slurp. 'Don't you shake your head. You would.'

'You would, you know.' Amber held up her glass and admired the contents. 'This is worth marrying you for.'

'Hey,' said Tom.

Amber blew him a kiss. 'I'm talking about for single ladies, sexy boy. Not me.'

'Just as well,' said Tom, narrowing his gaze with feigned menace.

'You should get on Cupid—'

'No.'

Niamh wasn't letting the subject go that easily. 'It worked for us.'

'Not for me,' piped up Eden. 'I had a horrible time.'

'See?' said Lincoln. 'Horrible.'

'But it still worked,' said Amber. 'If you hadn't gone on all those dates, Humphrey mightn't have come to his senses.'

'Yeah, I would have.'

All three girls regarded Humphrey with their eyebrows raised, then laughed when he gave a very Humphrey *hmph* and took a slug of his beer.

Though it hadn't been there at the beginning, as the evening carried on, Eden became aware of a weird undercurrent. A tension that, like Humphrey's mood throughout the day, she couldn't quite identify.

Amber kept making eye contact and grinning. Niamh began obsessively checking both her and Olly's watches. Tom kept drifting off in quiet conversation with Humphrey. Only Lincoln seemed unaffected, busy with his drinks and garnishes.

At precisely seven, Niamh started laying out plates of salads and cold roast chicken that Amber had picked up from a local takeaway. At ten past seven, she ordered everyone to sit and eat.

Eden exchanged a smile with Humphrey. Niamh's cognitive therapy still needed work.

Thank you speeches from Tom and Amber followed, then, refusing help, Amber and Niamh cleared away the food and wiped down the benches.

Amber's microwave clock had just blinked to eight when Niamh clapped her hands together. 'Movie time!'

'Oh,' said Eden, looking around. She hadn't expected that. Amber's lounge was small, furnished with only a two-seater couch, a coffee table, and a couple of armchairs. They'd have to drag some of the dining chairs in and Eden couldn't imagine they'd make for a comfortable viewing experience.

'What's the film?' asked Eden.

'*Harry Potter and the Philosopher's Stone*,' said Olly, sounding thrilled about the fact.

Harry Potter. Right. So much for partying.

She glanced at Humphrey. 'Maybe we should—'

'Go?' said Amber. 'Probably a good idea. You've a busy night.' She coughed. 'I mean, day tomorrow.'

'Oh,' said Eden again. She swallowed, her eyes beginning to sting. Her new sister-in-law, a woman she adored and considered a good friend, was kicking her out of her house.

A warm hand folded around hers. Humphrey. Kind-eyed, gorgeous Humphrey. 'Amber's right. Busy day tomorrow.'

'Yes. Sure.' She forced a smile, then squeezed Humphrey's fingers and let go. She hugged Amber, surprised by the intensity of Amber's response. As soon as they parted, Niamh took over, her hug almost as fierce. Olly then Lincoln, then Tom. All seemed extra affectionate. All wore huge grins.

'What's going on?' she whispered to Humphrey as they made their way to the door.

'Nothing.'

'They're all following us.'

'I guess they want to say goodbye.'

'Yeah, but it's not like we won't see them again.'

Humphrey shrugged. Eden checked behind. Yep, there they all were, smiling madly.

Despite the cold, despite it being past Niamh's announced movie time, the smiling stalk-a-thon continued outside and to the car.

'Why are they acting so weird?' Eden asked, once they were safely inside. Humphrey, having been on light beers all night, in the driver's seat. Niamh and Amber stood in front of the three boys, everyone waving like it was Eden and Humphrey who were the newlyweds.

'Too many cocktails.'

Which was probably right. Still ... Eden peered around him. No one looked like they were about to move inside yet.

'They look like a crazy cult.'

Humphrey laughed. 'They do a bit. Maybe it's a Harry Potter thing.'

'Maybe.'

Eden studied the side mirror as Humphrey headed down the street. The girls were bouncing on their toes. Olly and Tom were slapping each other's backs. Then, as Humphrey indicated and turned, they all skipped back into the house like a bunch of spring bunnies.

Very, very weird.

The scene kept Eden quiet and contemplative for most of the trip home. Only talking when Humphrey squeezed her fingers and asked if she was okay.

It was a relief to finally turn down Kulburra's long drive. Home. Home and Humphrey and hopefully no more weirdness.

'Bugger,' said Eden as they approached Humphrey's cottage. 'I must have left the lights on.' Except she was sure she hadn't.

And it wasn't just in the house. Lights also lit the path. Little orbs that flickered orange and yellow, like candle flames. The front door was wide open, too, and more golden light twinkled inside.

She turned to Humphrey. 'What's going on?'

Humphrey's half-smile deepened. 'You'll see.'

Eden's stomach flipped. She regarded the path again, the glowing house. Lustrous white flakes littered the stones leading to the entrance. Eden swallowed.

'Are they ...'

Oh, God. They were petals. Someone had strewn the path with petals.

Shock had her voice emerging like a croak. 'Humphrey?'

He shut down the engine. 'Come inside.'

He waited for her at the start of the path, one hand out for her to grab. Eden took it and together they made their way to the door, white petals soft underfoot. Each step brought the faint scent of roses. Eden wanted to say something, but she had no words in the face of such wonder.

Humphrey led her inside. Apart from the hallway and its aisle of faux candles, the rest of the house was in darkness.

As they passed the kitchen, Humphrey snatched something off the bench and slid it into his pocket. Then they were through the rear door, to their favourite part of the house.

Eden stopped and stared, eyes and mouth wide, fingers splayed over her chest and her rapidly thudding heart.

More candles surrounded the rear deck, arcing out and around the extension that housed Humphrey's precious hot tub. Steam rose from the tub's surface. Alongside, stood a white tablecloth-draped stand with an ornate silver champagne bucket on top, from which two bottle necks poked, one already open. Two heavy crystal flutes sat beside it, more rose petals strewn around their bases.

Hovering behind, like a giant bauble in the velvety sky shining over Kulburra, was a bright, bright moon

'Oh, my God, Humphrey.' She grinned at him, then raced to the tub and dunked her fingers. The water felt like warm silk. She turned back. 'I can't wait to—'

Humphrey was crouched on one knee.

'Oh. *Oh!*'

Eden blinked then blinked again, but her eyes continued to mist.

'Eden.' Humphrey cleared his throat. 'Eden, you know I love you.' He gave a crooked grin. 'At least, I hope you do.'

She took two steps closer, her entire being incandescent with love for this beautiful, wonderful man. 'Of course I do. I love you, too. So much. So very, very much.'

'Then would you do me the incredible honour of being my wife?'

'Yes.' Eden nodded. Then nodded some more.

Next she was yelling 'yes, yes, yes!' and lunging at Humphrey. The force tipped him backwards. He landed on his back with a grunt, Eden sprawled on top, laughing and crying as she kissed him between yeses.

It was some moments before she came up for air. Humphrey was too delicious and now he was going to be her husband. The dream she'd had since she was sixteen had come true.

Finally, she propped on his chest and eyed him.

'What?'

'What took you so long?'

Humphrey reached out and tucked a stray lock of Eden's hair behind her ear. 'I wanted you to be sure. I wanted you to experience me, here. To be certain this is what you wanted. That you'd be happy.'

'Silly man.' She kissed him again. 'I've always been sure.'

'Yes,' he said, cupping her face and smiling at her with wonder. 'You have.'

Eden took in Humphrey, the candles, the moon and sighed deeply. 'Who knew you were so romantic?'

'I wanted it to be special.'

'It is.' She made a face. 'Everyone was in on it, weren't they? That's why they were all so weird and why Amber kicked me out. Why you called in to see your mum before we left.' She bent and kissed the tip of his nose. 'Why you've been funny all day.'

'Pretty much.'

'I guess your mum arranged this.' She swept a hand to encompass the staged deck.

'And Clara.'

'Clara's here?'

He nodded. 'And the others.'

'Why?'

'I don't know. Something to celebrate?'

Eden laughed. 'I guess there is.' Her expression dropped. 'We have showjumping club tomorrow.'

'Nope. I cancelled us.'

She twisted around to look at the hot tub then back again. 'In that case.' Grinning, Eden shed her jacket and threw it towards the back door. Her long-sleeved tee came next. Humphrey's eyes hooded at her bra clad body, his hands sliding to her waist. 'Should I do the rest?'

A rumble sounded deep in Humphrey's chest.

'I take it that's a yes.'

'No.'

Eden froze, one bra strap halfway down her arm. 'Pardon?'

'Don't you want to see the ring?'

'Ring? You have a ring?'

He scowled slightly. 'Well, yeah. It's usually what happens when you get engaged. Proposal. Ring.' The smile returned. 'Mad hot tub sex.'

He reached beneath himself, where his jacket had tucked, and dug around with a grunt before extracting a box and balancing it on his chest.

Eden eyed the blue velvet box and tugged her teeth across her bottom lip, her heart doing its crazy thud thing again.

Slowly, watching her the entire time, Humphrey lifted the lid.

Eden's hands flew to her mouth. 'Oh my God. Oh my God, Humphrey.'

'It's a family heirloom.'

She stared at the rock. Or rocks, if you counted the diamonds either side of the enormous central sapphire. Eden didn't know anything about gems, but even she could see the stones were exquisite quality. They sparkled like the stars.

'It's beautiful.' She stared a little longer. 'But if it's an heirloom, shouldn't it be Clara's?'

'She wants you to have it.'

'Me?' Eden was finding her breath hard to come by. 'Why?'

'Because you make me happy. Because you love me. As long as you promise to pass it down to the next generation, then it's yours.'

The next generation. The thought filled Eden with warmth. Humphrey knew she wanted a family one day. She'd mentioned more than once the gorgeous children he'd produce, and it had been a sensitive subject for a while. But they'd talked, and though it had embarrassed him painfully, Humphrey had booked himself into the family doctor to discuss the matter. And, he admitted somewhat smugly later, after the glowing report had come back, get a semen analysis. Anything for Eden, for their future together. Her heart had almost burst with love for him.

'I do love you. So much.' She leaned forwards to kiss him, causing the box to slide off Humphrey's chest.

He caught it before it landed. 'Maybe you should put it on.'

'Oh, yes. Good idea.' Eden widened her eyes. She was half naked, about to put on a ring worth God knows how many thousands of dollars. Not to mention a Taylor-Martin heirloom. 'Should I get dressed? Is it bad to put it on

wearing just a bra.' She looked down at herself. 'Half wearing. This is a bit momentous.'

'I don't mind.'

'No, you never do.'

Though he had to be getting cold, lying flat on his back
on the timber deck in the damp night air, Humphrey made
no move to sit up. He removed the ring from its box, took
Eden's left hand and carefully slid the glittering jewel onto
her finger.

They both stared at it, then at each other.

Humphrey stroked Eden's face, his voice barely a whisper. 'Hey, fiancée.'

'Hey, fiancé.'

'Time to celebrate?'

Eden glanced at the steaming tub, at the ice-cold champagne, and the glowing, glorious moon.

'Yeah,' she said with a beam to rival the moon above.
'Time to celebrate *forever*.'

And they did.

Thanks so much for reading the first three Cupid Country
books! Keep informed about new releases in the series by
joining my newsletter team at cathrynhein.com. You'll also
gain exclusive and free access to a bunch of heartwarming
and romantic short stories, many set in Levenham.

In the meantime, if you're after more of the same, check
out *Rocking Horse Hill*, book one in the Levenham Love
Story series. Same location, more wonderful characters!

About the Author

Cathryn Hein is a popular author of rural romance and romantic adventure novels, a Romance Writers of Australia Romantic Book of the Year finalist with *Santa and the Saddler*, and a regular Australian Romance Reader Awards finalist.

A South Australian country girl by birth, Cathryn loves nothing more than a rugged rural hero who's as good with his heart as he is with his hands, which is probably why she writes them! Her aim is to make you smile, sigh, and perhaps sniffle a little, but most of all feel wonderful.

Cathryn lives in Newcastle, Australia with her partner of many years, Jim. When she's not writing, she plays golf (ineptly), cooks (well), and in football season barracks (rowdily) for her beloved Sydney Swans AFL team.

Join Cathryn's newsletter team for exclusive access to her collection of free stories, plus all the news on upcoming book releases, bonus content, and more.